Books by Alison Lurie

*Love and Friendship*
*The Nowhere City*
*Imaginary Friends*
*Real People*
*The War Between the Tates*

# The War Between the Tates

# The War Between the Tates

## ALISON LURIE

Random House • New York

Library of Congress Cataloging in Publication Data
Lurie, Alison.
The War Between the Tates.

I. Title.
PZ4.L965 War 3   [PS3562.U7]   813′.5′4   73-20437
ISBN 0-394-46201-7

Manufactured in the United States of America

2 4 6 8 9 7 5 3

*For*

DINO READ

NELL MOORE

PEGGY ASHFORD

Deep in the mirror we will perceive a very faint line and the color of this line will be like no other color. Later on, other shapes will begin to stir. Little by little they will differ from us; little by little they will not imitate us. They will break through the barriers of glass or metal and this time will not be defeated. . . .

Others believe that in advance of the invasion we will hear from the depths of mirrors the clatter of weapons.

JORGE LUIS BORGES

*The Book of Imaginary Beings*

# The War Between the Tates

**1**

March 20. A cold spring morning. It rained last night, perforating the crusted snow of the Tates' front lawn, and everything is wet and glitters: the fine gravel of the drive, the ice in the ditch beside it, the bare elm twigs outside the bathroom window. The sun shines sideways at the house, brilliantly, impartially. Seeing it through the kitchen window when she comes down to make breakfast, Erica Tate feels her emotional temperature, which has been unnaturally low of late, rise several degrees.

"Tomorrow's the beginning of spring," she says to Jeffrey Tate, aged fifteen, as he stumbles into the room fastening his shirt.

"What's for breakfast?"

"Eggs, toast, jam—"

"Any sausages?"

"No, not today." Erica tries to keep her voice cheerful.

"There's never anything to eat in this house," Jeffrey complains, falling heavily into his chair.

Suppressing several possible answers to this remark, Erica sets a plate before her son and turns toward the stairs. "Matilda! It's twenty minutes to eight."

"All right! I heard you the first time."

"Look at that sun," Erica says to her daughter a few minutes later. "Tomorrow's the first day of spring."

No reply. Erica sets a plate in front of Matilda, who will be thirteen next month.

"I can't eat this stuff. It's fattening."

"It's not fattening, it's just an ordinary breakfast, eggs, toast . . . Anyhow, you're not fat."

"Everything has gobs of butter on it. It's all soaked in grease."

"Aw, shut up, Muffy, you'll make me barf."

Again Erica suppresses several rejoinders. "Would you like me to make you a piece of toast without butter?" she asks rather thinly.

"Okay. If you can do it fast."

The sun continues to shine into the kitchen. Standing by the toaster, Erica contemplates her children, whom she once thought the most beautiful beings on earth. Jeffrey's streaked blond hair hangs tangled and unwashed over his eyes in front and his collar in back; he hunches awkwardly above the table, cramming fried egg into his mouth and chewing noisily. Matilda, who is wearing a peevish expression and an orange tie-dyed jersey which looks as if it had been spat on, is stripping the crusts off her toast with her fingers. Chomp, crunch, scratch.

The noises sound loud in Erica's head; louder still, as if amplified: CHOMP, CRUNCH, SCRATCH— No. That is coming from outside. She goes to the window. In the field beyond the orchard, something yellow is moving.

"Hey, the bulldozer's back," Jeffrey exclaims.

"I guess they're going to put up another ranch house," his sister says.

The tone of both these remarks is neutral, even conversational; yet they strike Erica as more coarse and cold than anything that has yet been said this morning. "You don't care what's happening to our road!" she cries. "How can you be so selfish, so unfeeling? You don't really mind at all, either of you!"

Her children go on eating. It is evident that they do not.

Chomp; smash. The hands of the clock over the sink move

4

toward eight. Jeffrey and Matilda rise, grumbling, grab their coats and books, and leave to catch the bus for junior high. Alone in the kitchen, Erica clears the table. She pours herself a cup of coffee, puts the buttered toast Matilda refused on a clean plate, and sits down. She starts to reach for the sugar bowl, and stops. Then she puts her head down on the table beside a splash of milk and some blobs of cherry jam, and weeps painfully. Tears run sideways across her small, slightly worn, delicate features, and into her crisp dark hair.

There is no one to hear her. Her friend and husband, Brian Tate, is away lecturing on foreign policy at Dartmouth. If he were there, she thinks, he would understand why she had screamed at the children, and not blame her (as he sometimes does lately) for being unable to handle them. He would listen to her, share her feelings, and console her afterward—possibly back in bed. Lately the Tates have taken to making both love and conversation on weekday mornings before Brian leaves for the university. In the evening there is always the suspicion that the children might be listening—at first from the sitting room for the unguarded exclamation, the raised voice; later, overhead, for the thump and squeak of bedroom furniture.

Once, Erica had liked the acoustical permeability of this old house, because it meant that she could always hear Muffy or Jeffo if they should wake crying with an upset tummy or a bad dream. Now, at night, she and Brian dare not either laugh or cry. In the dark, in their pajamas, they may begin to speak or move: "They were so rude today," Erica will sigh. "That ass McGruder, my grader, you know what he's done—" Brian will begin. Then upstairs the floor will creak, and he will fall silent; or will remove his hand from her breast. "We live in the same house and we sleep in the same bed and we never see each other any more," Erica had whispered once recently.

But now it is eight-fifteen. Brian is in Hanover, New Hampshire, and she is sitting with her head on the kitchen table, weeping, trying to understand her situation. How has it all come about? She is—or at least she was—a gentle, rational, even-tempered woman, not given to violent feelings. In her whole life she cannot remember disliking anyone as much as she now sometimes dislikes Jeffrey and Matilda. In second grade she had briefly hated a bulky girl named Rita who ate rolls of pastel candy wafers and bullied her; in college freshman year a boy with a snuffle and yellowed nylon shirts who followed her around everywhere asking her to go out with him. She had, in the abstract, hated Hitler, Joseph McCarthy, Lee Harvey Oswald, etc., but never anyone she had to live with and should have loved—had for years and years warmly loved.

They were a happy family once, she thinks. Jeffrey and Matilda were beautiful, healthy babies; charming toddlers; intelligent, lively, affectionate children. There are photograph albums and folders of drawings and stories and report cards to prove it. Then last year, when Jeffrey turned fourteen and Matilda twelve, they had begun to change; to grow rude, coarse, selfish, insolent, nasty, brutish, and tall. It was as if she were keeping a boarding house in a bad dream, and the children she had loved were turning into awful lodgers—lodgers who paid no rent, whose leases could not be terminated. They were awful at home and abroad; in company and alone; in the morning, the afternoon and the evening.

But the worst moments for Erica were at night, when they were asleep. She would go into a bedroom to close the window against wind and rain, or make sure they were covered. In the filtered light from the hall, the childish features she remembered so well could be recognized again beneath the coarsening acned masks. Her dear Muffy and Jeffo were still there, somewhere inside the monstrous lodgers who had taken over their minds and bodies, as in one of Jeffrey's science-fiction magazines.

One windy evening not long ago, after this had happened, Erica got back into bed and asked Brian if he had ever thought that they might try to have another child before they were too old. But Brian replied that they were already too old. If they conceived a baby now, for example, he would be past retirement when it finished college. Besides, they had to remember the population problem. He forbore to mention what the babies they already had, had turned into, which was just as well, for Erica would probably have cried out, "Yes, but before that happens we would have at least twelve good years."

Though equally awful, the children are awful in somewhat different ways. Jeffrey is sullen, restless and intermittently violent. Matilda is sulky, lazy and intermittently dishonest. Jeffrey is obsessed with inventions and space; Matilda with clothes and pop music. Matilda is extravagant and wasteful; Jeffrey miserly and ungenerous. Jeffrey is still doing all right in school, while his sister's grades are hopeless; on the other hand, Matilda is generally much cleaner than Jeffrey.

Erica knows and remembers that Jeffrey and Matilda had once loved her. They had loved Brian. Now they quite evidently do not like either of their parents. They also do not like each other: they fight constantly, and pick on each other for their respective failings.

The worst part of it all is that the children are her fault. All the authorities and writers say so. In their innocent past Erica and Brian had blamed their own shortcomings on their parents while retaining credit for their own achievements. They had passed judgment on the character of acquaintances whose young children were not as nice as Muffy and Jeffo— But everyone did that. To have had disagreeable parents excused one's faults; to have disagreeable children underlined them. The parents might not look especially guilty; they might seem outwardly to be intelligent, kind and charming people—but inside were Mr. and Mrs. Hyde.

It was agreed everywhere, also, that Mrs. Hyde was the worse; or at least the more responsible. A father might possibly avoid blame for the awfulness of his children—a mother never. After all, they were in her "area of operations," to use Brian's term. An admirer of George Kennan's early writings, he had long subscribed to the doctrine of separate spheres of influence, both in national and domestic matters; he attributed the success of their marriage partly to this doctrine. He might advise Erica on important policy decisions, but ordinarily he would not question her management of the home, nor would she ever try to intervene in his professional life. If he lost his job (which had never been very likely and was now impossible, since he had tenure), it was his fault. If the children became uncontrollable, it was hers.

The fact that they had been quite all right until last year was no excuse. Erica has read widely on the subject and knows that there are several unpleasant explanations of this. Only last week she came across an article which spoke of the tendency of women who marry older men to remain, and wish to remain, children. (Brian is now forty-six, seven years older than she.) It was pointed out that such women tended to identify closely, "even symbiotically" with their children. The author of this article would probably say that Jeffrey and Matilda are now struggling to break out of a symbiotic neurosis. Other experts might maintain that Erica has bewitched them out of spite and envy of their youth, energy and "developing sexuality," while still others would assert that the children have been assigned to work out her and Brian's repressed antisocial drives. And any or all of these experts might be right. Erica is not aware of these motives in herself, but that does not prove anything; naturally, they would not be conscious.

It is all academic by now, because now she consciously dislikes her children, and this alone would be enough to poison them spiritually, morally and emotionally. She dislikes them for being what they now are, and for having turned her into a hateful, neurotic, guilty person. For if the truth were known, that would and must be her reputation in the world.

Outside, the bulldozer continues to operate. Crack; crunch; smash. Blackberry and sumac bushes are uprooted; wide muddy wounds are scraped in the long pale winter grass. What is happening to Jones Creek Road seems to Erica all of a piece with what is happening to Jeffrey and Matilda: natural beauty and innocence are being swallowed up in ugly artificial growth, while she watches helplessly.

Eight years ago, when the Tates first moved to Corinth, they found on this back road a big deserted, sagging gray farmhouse smothered in broken dark pines. It had been for sale for over a year, but they were the first to see its possibilities. The trees were thinned, the house remodeled and painted yellow; suddenly they owned a beautiful, even a rather grand place, only a few miles from campus.

Not far enough, as it turned out. Three years ago Jones Creek Road was widened and resurfaced, and the first ranch homes began crawling toward them over the hill to the west, blocking their sunset. Brian and Erica, realizing what was happening, tried to buy more land around their half-acre. But it was too late; the developer was not interested. Each subsequent year the bulldozers have moved nearer; soon they will be surrounded.

The Tates have talked about moving farther out, of course; but to be safe now they would have to go ten or fifteen miles, beyond the school district. Besides, Erica cannot bear to abandon her house: the chestnut woodwork she has scraped and scrubbed and refinished; the double daffodils and white narcissus she has planted under the old trees; the asparagus and strawberry beds—hours, years of loving labor.

It is not only the ruin of the landscape which is so painful, but also the redefinition of this part of town, now renamed "Glenview Heights"—what it means now to live there. Not that their new neighbors are poor white trash—indeed, most of them are richer than the Tates. The Glenview Home to their left, a "Charleston" model with false white pillars and wrought-iron balconies glued to the façade, costs twice as much as their house; the "Paul Revere" next to it not much less. The Homes are full of expensive built-in appliances; their carports bulge with motorboats and skimobiles. The children who live there watch 25-inch color TV every evening, their eyes reflecting the artificial circus lights. Jeffrey and Matilda watch with them when they are allowed. "You're not against television on principle; you just don't want to spend the money. You want us to freeload off the Gobrights and the Kaisers," Jeffrey had accused recently, voicing an opinion which Erica suspects is shared by her neighbors. She knows that the Glenview Home-owners, who are mostly not university people, regard her as unfriendly and a little odd, though she has tried to maintain cordial relations, and has never mentioned aloud that she believes them partly responsible for the awful change in her children. And even if they are, she is not exonerated, because it means that the heredity and environment provided by the Tates were faulty or ineffective. Anyhow, why mention it? It is already too late, and it will go on being even later.

Jeffrey will be living at home for nearly four more years. Matilda will be with them for nearly six more years. As Erica is contemplating these facts, with her head on the damp table, the telephone rings.

She sits up, rubs her eyes dry, and answers.

"Hello, this is Helen in the Political Science office, how are you today? . . . Oh, I'm very well too . . . There's a letter here for Brian, it's marked 'Urgent—Personal,' and I wondered . . . Well, if he's going to call you tonight, that's fine . . . That's a good idea. I'll phone Mrs. Zimmern in the French department now and ask her to pick it up . . . You're welcome."

This conversation, though banal, raises Erica's morale. It reminds her that she is successfully married, whereas Helen is a widow, and her best friend Danielle Zimmern a divorcée; that Brian is an important professor who receives urgent business letters; and that he calls home every evening when he is out of town.

She is encouraged to stand up, to clear the table and do the dishes and start her day's work. She picks up the house, skipping the children's rooms; washes out two sweaters; draws for an hour and a half; and makes herself a chicken sandwich. After lunch she goes shopping and to the bank, driving cautiously, for the sky has darkened again and an icy drizzle is falling from it. Her morale has fallen also, and a parody of Auden, composed by her friend Danielle some years ago, keeps running tediously in her head:

*Cleopatra's lips are kissed*
*while an unimportant wife*
*writes "I do not like my life"*
*underneath her shopping list.*

She drives home, puts away the groceries, makes a raspberry mousse, and is mixing some lemon cookies when Danielle's VW pulls into the driveway.

"What a hell of a day, huh? Spring, it says on the calendar . . . Oh, here's that letter for Brian, before I forget," Danielle says, stepping out of her slushy boots on the back porch and coming into the kitchen in purple tights.

"Thank you. How is everything?" Erica puts the letter on a shelf in front of her cookbooks without looking at it. "Would you like some coffee?"

"Love it. The kids won't be home till four, thank God." Danielle pulls off her coat with the careless, angry energy that has lately marked all her actions, and flings it toward a chair. Twenty years ago, when Erica first met her, she had a similar energy—only then it was not angry, but joyful.

Erica and Danielle had known each other at college, though not intimately—Danielle being a year ahead, and in a different set. After graduation they lost touch; in the autumn of 1964, when Danielle's husband joined the English department and the family moved to Corinth, Erica was not aware of it; nor did Danielle realize that Erica already lived there. But a few weeks after their accidental meeting at Atwater's Supermarket, each accompanied by a nine-year-old daughter, it was as if they had remained friends uninterruptedly.

Danielle, like Erica, has been described by her admirers as tall, dark-haired and beautiful. But where Erica is narrow, in the shoulders and hips, Danielle is broad; she is deep-bosomed, and stands on sturdy baroque legs. Her hair is long, heavy and straight, with a russet overtone; her skin has a russet glow even in the northern winter, when Erica bleaches to the color of cream. People who do not much like Erica admit that she is pretty, while those (a larger number) who do not much like Danielle admit that she is good-looking.

In college they had avoided each other slightly, as women who are attractive in conflicting styles often do—for the same motive that prevents Atwater's Supermarket from placing cases of ice cream and sherbet next to cartons of beer. But now that they had both been purchased and brought home, this ceased to matter.

That first day Erica accompanied Danielle back to her house and stayed there, drinking coffee and talking, for two hours. Soon they met or telephoned almost daily. Erica recommended to Danielle her pediatrician, her garage, her cleaning woman, and those of her acquaintances she thought worthy of the privilege. They lent each other books, and went with their children to fairs and matinées and rummage sales. Muffy Tate and Ruth Zimmern (known as Roo) also became inseparable.

Equally agreeable, and more surprising, was the friendship that developed between Brian and Leonard Zimmern. For years, both Erica and Danielle had had the problem that their husbands did not get on very well with any of their friends' husbands. Now they realized, with relief, that this was not due to prejudice or character defects. It was merely that men of their age (Leonard was then forty-three, Brian forty-one) could not be expected to become intimate with the fledgling editors, lawyers, artists, teachers, etc., whom their wives' friends had married.

Since they were in different divisions of the university Leonard and Brian could not share the concerns of colleagues; but this very fact prevented competitive jockeying and the tendency to talk shop on social occasions, so tiresome to wives. Neither could hinder or further the other's career; so they were able to risk disagreement, to speak their minds freely. The differences of temperament and background which had made Erica and Danielle fear they would quarrel actually endeared the men to each other—and to themselves. Leonard congratulated himself on a range of interests and sympathies that allowed him to get on with a WASP political scientist, while Brian felt the same in reverse. Moreover, the existence of the friendship proved to both men that any revulsion they might feel from some of the pushy New York Jews or fat-ass goyim bastards they ran up against professionally was *ad hominem* and not *ad genere.*

Even the fact that Danielle did not really care for Brian; and that Erica, though she liked Leonard, found him physically unattractive (too thin, and with too much wiry black hair all over his body) helped to stabilize the relationship. The sort of complications which often occur when two couples spend much time together were avoided almost unconsciously, by mutual consent.

"I see they're at it again." Danielle gestures with her head at the field next door. The bulldozer has now made what looks like an incurable muddy wound there, with the white roots of small trees sticking up from it like broken bones. "I thought maybe they wouldn't come back this year, the way building costs are rising."

"That's what I hoped, too."

"What you should do, you should plant some evergreens; then you won't have to look at it."

"I'd still know it was there." Erica smiles sadly.

"Or you could put up a redwood fence," continues Danielle, who has learned since Leonard's departure to take a practical view of things and cut her losses. "That'd be faster. And if you did it now, before the people moved in, they couldn't take it personally."

"Mm," Erica says noncommittally, pouring her friend a cup of coffee. Redwood fences, in her view, are almost as bad as ranch houses.

"Thanks." Danielle sits down, spreading her full purple tweed skirt. "You've been drawing," she remarks, glancing into the pantry, where Erica's pad lies open on the shelf. "Let's see."

"Just sketching. I was trying to work out something for the Ballet Group; Debby asked me to do a program for their spring show. Freezy, of course."

"That's slick." When alone, Danielle and Erica use the language of their college years; the once enthusiastic phrases have become a sort of ironic shorthand.

"Virginia Carey is doing the poster, but she told them she hadn't time for the program."

"Yeah, man." Among the old slang, Danielle, since she started teaching, mixes that of the present generation.

"I don't mind really. I'm better on a small scale. I know that."

"There's one thing about posters: they get thrown away," Danielle says encouragingly. "People save their programs for years." Erica does not reply or smile. "Maybe you should do another book."

"I don't know." Erica sighs, stirs her coffee. In the past she had written and illustrated three books dealing with the adventures of an ostrich named Sanford who takes up residence with an American suburban family. These books had been published and had enjoyed a mild success. ("Gentle and perceptive fun for the 4–6 age group"; "The drawings are lively, delicate, and colorful.") But the last of the series had appeared over two years ago. Erica does not want to write any more about Sanford. For one thing, she cannot think of anything else for him to do. And she does not want to write any more about Mark and Spencer, the children with whom Sanford lives. She knows that they would have grown up by now, and what they would be like.

A silence, broken only by the regular humming of the new refrigerator. Aware that she is being dull, even unfriendly, Erica rouses herself. "How's your class going?" she asks.

"Oh, okay. Hell, you know I really love teaching; the only thing that gets me down is De Gaulle." This refers to the head of the French department, whose name is not De Gaulle. "He asked me again today how my thesis was getting along, in this smiling threatening way. You know I can't do any work on it until I have some time off, and I can't afford time off. But he has no conception of what my life is like. I ought to be at the grocery right now, there's nothing to eat at home."

"Would you like to have supper with us? You could bring Roo and Silly. Brian's not coming back till Friday."

"Well . . . yes, why not? Or you could all come to my house. I've got to shop anyhow."

"No, let's eat here. I ought to be home when Brian calls."

"All right."

For a few moments both women are silent, thinking the same thing: that Danielle now has to come to dinner behind Brian's back, and how uncomfortable that is. Danielle, however, blames the discomfort wholly on Brian, while Erica blames it partly on Danielle and partly on her ex-husband.

It is nearly two years now since the trouble between Danielle and Leonard Zimmern started. At first, as often happens, their disagreements brought them closer to their best friends. Danielle confided in Erica, and Leonard in Brian; the Tates spent hours discussing the rights and wrongs of the case, and more hours conveying their decisions to the Zimmerns. It was their often-expressed conviction that Danielle and Leonard were both intelligent, serious, decent people who had deep affection for each other, and that they would, with help, be able to work out their difficulties.

As time dragged on, however, it became more and more clear that the difficulties were not being worked out. This was very depressing and annoying to Erica and Brian, who had put so much thought and effort into the case, and whose opinions and advice had been neglected. Finally they declared to Leonard and Danielle that there was no point in talking about the problem any more; they just had to wait and hope. The result of this prohibition was to make relations between the couples strained and artificial. Whenever they met, it was as if they were actively supporting rival parties, Marriage and Divorce, but had agreed not to discuss politics. The agreement, however, did not preclude wearing campaign buttons and carrying signs. Brian and Erica, without intending it, found themselves silently demonstrating their support of Marriage in a rather theatrical way: smiling fondly more often than necessary, deferring to each other's opinion, holding hands at the movies, etc.; while Leonard and Danielle, more noisily, demonstrated the opposite.

After Leonard left home, early last year, things got even worse. The superior political qualifications of Divorce was the last matter the Zimmerns agreed upon. Bitter quarrels over money and objects began; recrimination and self-justification; deception and self-deception. Friends and acquaintances of the couple began to choose up sides, declaring that Leonard (or Danielle) had after all behaved pretty unforgivably, and that it would therefore really be wrong to forgive him (or her).

The Tates, however, refused to choose sides. They announced that they still loved and respected both the Zimmerns and intended to remain friends with both of them. This high-minded and generous impartiality naturally irritated everyone. Each party suspected that the Tates were really on the other side, and were only pretending sympathy for theirs. Possibly they were even conscious spies. At the very least, Leonard finally admitted, he was hurt and surprised that Brian and Erica could still feel the same toward Danielle after what she had done to him and the children. Danielle thought the same in reverse; and she said so whenever they met, which was beginning to be rather less often.

The attachment between Erica's and Danielle's husbands, which had once helped to cement their friendship, now threatened to drive them apart. The continual recital by Danielle of Leonard's many faults and crimes did not move Brian. Leonard was his friend, he finally told her outright, and he refused to judge Leonard's character and behavior—or, presently, even to discuss it.

There were also social difficulties. If the Tates had Danielle to a party, they could not have Leonard, and vice versa. Moreover, if it was a dinner party, there was the problem of finding an extra man whom Danielle would not resent being paired with, or suspect of having been asked "for" her, or both. Danielle despised the idea of her friends' matchmaking: she could take care of that problem herself, she declared. It became easier to have her alone, or with her children, to family suppers where such suspicions could not arise.

If Leonard was invited to dinner, on the other hand, he usually asked if he might bring along some girl, always a different and hateful one. Most of these girls were not intrinsically hateful; but the way they sat in Danielle's place at the table all evening, their eyes fixed proudly upon Leonard as he spoke about politics and the arts—just as Danielle's once had been—was horrible to Erica. She ceased having Leonard to dinner at all, and only asked him to large parties where she would not have to notice his girl friends.

But when Danielle heard of these large parties from mutual acquaintances she became upset, and since it was not her nature to conceal her feelings, the next time she came to supper she mentioned them. She also asked what Leonard's current girl friend was like, which was not quite fair. On one occasion she remarked bitterly that she understood quite well why the Tates had asked Leonard to their last such party instead of her: it was because he was an important professor and literary critic, while she was just a deserted housewife and underpaid French instructor.

That night after Danielle had left, Brian announced that he was tired of seeing her. Erica replied that she was tired of seeing Leonard and his girl friends. After considerable discussion, it became apparent that it might be better to let both relationships cool off for a while.

In effect, this turned out to mean that Brian went on seeing Leonard and Erica went on seeing Danielle, but both avoided mentioning it. A fog of silent discomfort settled over that area, and was not much dissipated last fall when Leonard went back to New York alone.

Erica and Danielle are still best friends, but their friendship now is full of Swiss-cheese holes in which sit things which cannot be discussed, which have to be edged around. Brian is in one of these holes, a rather large one. He has moved onto Leonard's side: he resents Danielle because her obstinate and promiscuous behavior has driven his friend out of Corinth. Erica, on the other hand, sympathizes with Danielle's view, which is that Leonard had taken her and the children to a distant provincial town and abandoned them there, probably on purpose, to live on macaroni and cheese, while he has returned to New York and eats every night in gourmet restaurants.

Danielle breaks the silence. "Is there more coffee?"

"What?"

She repeats the question.

"Yes, of course. I'm sorry." Erica stands up. In slow motion, she tests the white Pyrex pot with her slim pale hand, lifts it, and pours, off-center. An umber lukewarm stream runs across the blue-sprigged oilcloth. "Oh, how clumsy. I'm sorry." She reaches for a sponge and slowly wipes the table, wrings the sponge out into the sink, and sits down again.

Danielle looks at Erica, registering her appearance, which is dim today, even washed-out. Characteristically, she meets the problem head-on. "Hey. Are you feeling low about something?"

"Not especially. Sort of betwixt-between. I think it's the weather, and . . ." Erica pauses. The local climate, the encroachment of Glenview Homes, the fact that she has been asked to do elaborate artwork without remuneration, are too familiar to explain her mood. "And Brian's being away, that—" She swallows the rest of the phrase, recalling that Leonard is now always away; that from Danielle's point of view she has little to complain about. "And the children."

"Oh?"

"They were rather tiresome this morning. So loud. And rude too, really. It used to be fun getting up and having breakfast with them, but now— Whatever I cook, they don't like it; they want something else. They're so awful to each other; and they don't like me much either. And I don't always like them. Sometimes I think I hate them." Erica laughs to take the weight off this declaration, which she had not intended to make. The fact that she hates her own children is her darkest, most carefully guarded secret. Even to Danielle she has never fully revealed it. In public she speaks of them as everyone else does, with proud concern or humorous mock despair. Her acquaintances protest that on the contrary they have always found Jeffrey and Matilda most polite (as apparently they can sometimes pretend to be). Then, in a light, humorous tone, they complain amusingly of John's room or Jerry's attitude toward homework, which makes Erica wonder if they too might be harboring monstrous lodgers. When Susan says, smiling, that her children are "quite dreadful," does she mean in reality that she dreads them? When Jane exclaims that her daughter is "hopeless," has she indeed lost hope?

"Adolescents ought not to be allowed to live at home. There ought to be a law against it," she says, hopping back into the convention.

"You're telling me. I thought last night, when we were arguing about what to do with those mud turtles, how I'd love to give Roo to Reed Park along with them, and the hamsters and the chameleon and Pogo. They could all live in a cage there together and kind people could feed them through the bars."

Danielle, unlike Erica, can afford to be frank about how awful her children are. It is self-evident, at least to Danielle's self, whose fault it is: that of their father, who has deserted them and given them neuroses, so that now Roo prefers animals to people, including her former best friend Matilda Tate, and Celia, age eight, has become shy and withdrawn.

Erica laughs. "I'd like to send mine there too sometimes. Both of them." She looks around guiltily at the kitchen clock, but it is only three: Jeffrey and Matilda won't be home for half an hour. "It's not really that I don't like them any more," she lies. "It's just that I don't know how to cope with them. And I know it's my fault if they're difficult."

"Your fault? Why shouldn't it be Brian's fault?"

"Well, because I'm their mother. I must be doing something

*19*

wrong— Oh, I know I am. This morning, for instance. They were late for school and they started shouting at me, and I shouted back at them."

"Hell, everyone loses his temper sometimes. You can't always be right."

"Mm," Erica replies, not expressing agreement. Her greatest ambition is to be right: seriously and permanently in the right. Until recently, that was where she usually felt she was. "It's the same with the house. Lately it's as if everything I do goes wrong." She laughs consciously.

"But you're the best housekeeper I know."

"Not any more. I keep forgetting to buy detergent and I leave the parking lights on in the car and I lose the library books. Brian keeps asking what's wrong with me."

"There's nothing wrong with you," Danielle pronounces. "Everyone forgets things like that sometimes. Brian's just making you feel guilty."

"Oh, I don't think so. Certainly not consciously."

"It doesn't have to be conscious," Danielle says impatiently. "Men can make you feel guilty, and stupid and incompetent, without even trying. Because that's how they really believe women are."

"Uh." Erica makes a deprecating noise. She wishes she had never mentioned Brian. But it is too late: Danielle is already off again on her new hobby-horse, the awfulness of men. Erica sees this horse as a large gray-white wooden nag mounted on red rockers, unattractively and aggressively female.

"It's the truth. And what's worse is, we accept that judgment. They get us to believe at one and the same time that we can't do anything right and that everything is our fault because we don't."

"You make it sound like an international conspiracy." Erica smiles.

Danielle shakes her head. "There doesn't have to be any conspiracy. It's all been going on so many hundreds of years that it's automatic with them." She leans forward; Erica imagines her

*2 0*

urging the old gray mare on, its coarse white hair and tail, and her own dark mane, flowing roughly in the wind. "You know that conference I had Monday with Celia's teacher? Well, at first, like I told you, I felt Mrs. Schmidt was being overanxious. Celia didn't mind her nickname, I thought. She knew we meant it fondly, that nobody thought she was really silly, any more than they thought her sister was a kangaroo. But yesterday I was talking to Joanne—you know, the woman I met at that last WHEN meeting . . ."

"Mm." Recently Danielle has been going to a campus discussion group called Women for Human Equality Now; Brian refers to them as the Hens.

"Well, Joanne said that if Celia were a boy, nobody would dream of calling her Silly. Men don't have nicknames like that. Even in college they aren't called things like Bubsey and Ducky and Sliver, the way our friends were."

"No," Erica agrees.

"But you know, our names, yours and mine—they're just as bad. They're not real names, only the feminine diminutives of men's. Little Eric and Little Daniel."

"I never thought of it that way," Erica says.

"No, neither did I. But once I had, it really bothered me. I don't like the idea of being called Little Daniel all my life." She laughs. "I was thinking, maybe I should change my name."

"What would you change it to?"

"I suppose to Sarah. My middle name."

"I don't know if I could get used to that. I have a conviction that your name is Danielle."

"I don't know either . . . Oh damn. I've got to go, Silly'll be coming home. I mean Celia. You're right: it's not going to be easy. Well, we'll be over later."


As she stands by the kitchen window, watching her friend drive off into the wet, chilly afternoon, Erica thinks of Leonard Zimmern with irritation. It is one more thing to hold against him that he has turned Danielle against men in general—since women judge men in general by the behavior of their husbands.

But, after all, Danielle's open dislike of men is better than what Erica had grown up with: the lies and subterfuges with which her own mother tried to cope with the same situation, the desperate playacting, the feinting and flattery— Erica frowns, staring out into the empty yard. She does not think of her mother very often any more; Lena Parker has been dead for seven years. Even when she was alive Erica thought of her as seldom as possible. She thinks of her now: a tall, slim, bony woman with a distinguished face and slightly protruding eyes; always well-dressed and carefully made up; unconventional, intelligent but ill-read, impulsively and effusively affectionate. Since adolescence Erica had not cared for her very much. Perhaps that was unfair: Lena Parker certainly had her troubles; perhaps Erica's old dislike is now being dreadfully revenged through Jeffrey and Matilda.

It had not always been like that, of course. For the first ten years of Erica's life everything was peaceful and ordinary. Like Dick and Jane in the reader, she lived with her Daddy and Mommy and her baby sister and her dog Brownie in a nice house on a nice street in Larchmont. Things began to change in 1940 when Daddy, motivated perhaps as much by restlessness as by political sympathy, enlisted in the Canadian Army. He revisited Larchmont in the following years, but less and less often. Presently he did not revisit it at all. He had not been killed in the war, reported missing, or even injured—although Lena Parker later sometimes allowed these things to be supposed. Actually he had married a Canadian lady and gone to live with her in Ontario, though it was some time before Lena admitted this even to her own daughters. She never admitted to anyone, possibly including herself, that she had been unilaterally deserted, but took equal or greater responsibility for the separation ("Harold agreed with me that it would be best . . ."). Even now Erica is not absolutely sure that it had not been Lena's idea, or at least her secret intention.

In any case, her adjustment was rapid. Within a month of her divorce she had a job at Manon's, a local dress shop; in two years she was assistant manager, in five manager. She developed a special effusive manner—half ingratiating, half domineering—which was successful in flattering or bullying well-to-do women into buying clothes. She learned to suggest that the imported blouses and scarves and "frocks" in which Manon's specialized were at once more fashionable and more timeless, more delicate and more durable than American-made goods. She learned to believe this, and also all that, in the largest sense, it implied.

As time passed, Lena Parker's preference for the foreign increased and spread, like an exotic imported plant which at first merely survives, then flourishes, crowds out the native flowers, and at length jumps the garden wall to become a pestilential weed. As they wore out, Lena replaced first her own and her children's clothes, then her books and furnishings, and finally her friends with those of alien origin. She began to sprinkle her professional conversation with French phrases (*"Magnifique!" "Mais non!"*) and ended by speaking English, even at home, with a foreign intonation.

To Erica, entering junior high school in a mood of "Ballad-for-Americans" patriotism and in the wrong sort of clothes, it was all false, disgusting and hateful. Her mother made Erica wear shopworn rejects, but she hoarded sugar and canned goods in a cupboard in the basement. She collected extra gas coupons; she cheated her customers in small ways, cutting off labels and passing part rayon as pure silk—Erica had heard her boast of it. Worst of all, she justified herself for doing all these things. If she only hadn't justified herself, it wouldn't have been so bad.

Erica did not excuse Lena because of her financial difficulties. She would rather have had one plain ordinary American sweater and skirt than all her elaborate dowdy hand-hemmed and silk-lined foreign dresses, and she said so. But Lena could not bear to waste money on "shoddy factory stuff"—besides, it was against her principles. Determined to go on living in her nice house on the nice street, but on half the income, she had made the discovery that foreign things do not so easily proclaim their price. The Mexican equivalent of wicker chairs and dime-store china, the Indian equivalent of badly printed bedspreads and thin frayed rugs, can be seen as bohemian and chic rather than cheap. A French name and some squares of dry toast will disguise vegetable soup as a meal, and costs even less than hot dogs.

Visitors praised Lena to her daughters for the marvelous way she managed, and called her a remarkable woman—meaning among other things one about whom remarks are made. Erica hated these remarks, and the men who made them. They were mostly foreign too, often from obscure stamp-album countries like Guatemala and Estonia, refugees from what her mother called The Fascist Persecution. They ate the vegetable soup and sat on the wicker furniture. Some borrowed the clothes Erica's father had left behind and did not bring them back, and one from Albania who smelled of onions tried to hug her in the corner behind the piano.

Erica was also embarrassed by the fact that her father had left home and her mother worked in a store. The hours after school which she and her sister Marian spent in the cluttered back room at Manon's, because Lena did not trust them alone at home and could not afford a sitter, were among the worst she had ever passed. She hated everything about it: the backside of the beige velvet curtains, like the belly of a scruffy old cat; the stained and scratched plywood of the cutting table, on one end of which she did her homework; the racks of dresses which crowded against her like pushy women (it was the sort of shop where most of the clothes are kept hidden, to be brought out a few at a time with dramas of appreciation).

Marian, being some years younger and of a more docile temperament, did not mind Manon's. She played on the floor among the cartons of painted wooden hangers, the piles of bags printed with beige and pink roses, and the stacks of cardboard glazed beige and pink on one side, ready to be folded into dress boxes; she dressed her dolls in the scraps left from alterations. Marian did not mind going into the showroom to be displayed like a dress to some favorite customer, being introduced to them as "Marianne." But for Erica it was shameful, hideous, to have her name called out in Lena's penetrating phony-foreign voice; to try to pretend not to hear; finally to be dragged, or pushed from behind by Lena's assistant, through the scruffy cat-fur curtains—lanky, awkward, silent, in her traditional junior-high saddle shoes and knee socks and one of those wrong, awful, tucked and scalloped dresses. "*Voyez,* this great overgrown child, *si jolie,* but I can do nothing with her!" Lena would cry—mock despairing, false—while Erica glanced rapidly around the room to see if the worst thing of all had occurred and some girl she knew was there watching the scene.

During those hours in the back room Erica resolved to become as much unlike her mother as possible. Whatever happened to her in life, she would be honest and straightforward about it. She would avoid and suspect everything and everyone foreign.

This prejudice persisted for years, and had far-reaching effects. It was partly responsible for her initial coolness to Danielle, who was legitimately half-French. And it was certainly not the least of Brian's original attractions that his family had been in this country for generations and that he was studying American government. Moreover, he had not (like so many of Erica's other friends) been charmed by Lena or found her remarkable. It was even in his favor that Lena was not charmed by him. She pretended to be, of course: she smiled and flattered and posed and deferred to his opinion, as she did with all men; and after Erica announced her engagement she did so even more. But Erica knew that her mother disliked in Brian exactly the qualities she liked: she thought him humorless, solemn, unsympathetic, overcritical.

Her true opinion came out the morning of the wedding day. It suddenly started to pour, so that they could not have the ceremony under a striped awning in the garden, but would all have to crowd inside among the shabby wicker furniture and burlap curtains. Erica, standing in her long white satin slip looking out the window into the heavy rain, just as she is doing now, began to weep with nerves and vexation. And Lena, who was already dressed for the occasion (apricot pleated silk and real lace), put her hand on her daughter's bare shoulder and said, "Don't cry. Suppose it doesn't work out, you can always get a divorce."

Well, there is no use being angry about that now: Lena has been dead for seven years. Erica takes the cookie dough out of the refrigerator, arranges it on a baking sheet, and puts it into the oven. She is going into the other room to start the ironing when her glance falls on Brian's letter from the university. Probably what she should do is open it now and see what they want so that when he calls tonight she won't have to waste any time.

Inside the long official-looking envelope, marked URGENT— PERSONAL in mercurochrome red, are several awkwardly folded sheets of typing paper covered edge to edge with large round manuscript, written with the same vermilion marking pen.

Saturday

Dear Mr. Professor Tate!

I came round to see you this a.m. before I left town but no answer too bad. I mean bad. I left yr. J. S. Mill with Mr. Cushing next door, sorry not to return it sooner.

I keep thinking of you, how are you doing up there? I am not doing that well here; this scene is really bringing me down. It was juicy the first couple days with me and Ma, the Good Relationship, but neither of us could keep it up. Friday night Linda & Ralph came by with a couple of friends and kind of took over the place. Ma went upstairs which I thought showed real understanding but next morning we had the whole generation drama again. Of course she wouldn't admit she was pissed at being turned out of Her Own Living Room, and how grungy we left the kitchen, we had to talk about Larger Issues. You know Wendee Ma says to me smiling anxiously I am worried about the kind of boys you are seeing so much of these days, and Linda too, I wonder what her parents think of them. Their long hair no I don't mind that she says smiling tolerantly as long as they keep it washed.

It is the rudeness the loudness the total lack of consideration for Others and well their unkempt dirty appearance that too. I sometimes try to imagine how it must be for your professors having to face a class full of students looking like that, I really feel sorry for them she says smiling pityingly.

By now Erica has determined that the red letter is neither official nor urgent—merely the chatter of some eager, confiding student, such as Brian frequently receives. She reads on only out of inertia, plus mild curiosity and some sympathy with Ma.

I guess you would like it better if I was seeing a professor, I said. Well maybe Ma said smiling ruefully. I am a mother after all and naturally I want to feel that my child is safe and well taken care of. You may laugh now but you just wait until you are a mother and you will see. Okay, I said, I can wait. Mother! I thought, what if I told her. Don't worry Ma I have already taken your advice and I am seeing a professor. Oh good Wendee are you seeing a lot of him. Oh yeh I am Ma I am seeing his face and his hands and his arms and his legs and his ass and his cock. But not right now, which is a big drag. Dear Brian, I just hope it is for you too. I want to lie down on your floor again. I need very bad to be with you and talk and argue with you and think and learn and grow and fuck.

yours yours yours yours you

Erica returns to page one and reads this letter over again. She begins to feel hot and cold as she reads, as if she were running a fever; she holds the contagious paper farther from her, by its extreme edges, not touching the writing. The last blood-red word has been written over the margin so that part of it is missing. Erica supplies the rest: rs yours yours yours . . . an endless train of this word, steaming off the page into her kitchen and out the window across space and time; over the wet snow-crusted front lawn, the ice-pocked road, the cold fields and hills beyond.

Slowly, methodically, she refolds the letter and replaces it in its envelope. There is a peculiar burning odor in the room, like explosives. For a moment Erica thinks she is having a hallucination. Then she opens the oven door: at once the kitchen fills with smoke and the hot, sweet, ashy smell of scorched cookies. The war has begun.

## 2

May 11. Brian is sitting in his office at the university waiting for Wendy Gahaghan to come in so he can tell her that their affair is over. The script for this scene has been worked out in advance in his mind, the significant speeches written and rewritten. Twice already he has spoken the opening lines—but without success. Wendy had not responded as she should have responded; she is in another play, or film.

For instance, the statement "My wife has found out" did not, to Wendy, constitute a sufficient reason for ending the affair. That was a heavy scene, she admitted, but it was not her scene. And his suggestion that the relationship was bad for her education had been met with eager denials. Her interest in learning and her grades had both risen, she insisted, since they started making it together—didn't he know that? And in fact, Brian did know it.

And yet the thing has to be done. He realizes now that letting Wendy into his office had been like trying marijuana (not that he has ever tried marijuana). From the mild, pleasant stimulant of her conversation he had gone on to stronger drugs: her admiration and finally her passion. Before he becomes addicted, he has to give her up. Just thinking and worrying about it has begun to exhaust his energy to the point where he is functioning only in second gear as a teacher and is completely stalled on his current project, a study of American foreign policy in the Cold War period.

Moreover, Erica believes the thing has been done. Indeed, without actually lying, Brian has implied that the affair was almost over when she read that unfortunate letter. Actually lying, he has said that it was as brief and unimportant as such an affair could be.

He would much prefer to wait until the end of the term, but the danger that Erica may make another such discovery is too great. He might lecture Wendy for hours on discretion, she might fervently promise to be careful; but she is impulsive, given to sudden romantic gestures. Only last week, seeing him unexpectedly in the hall, she ran toward him and embraced him. Since it was late afternoon, the hall was empty; but the door to one of the other offices was open, and a colleague of Brian's was sitting in this office, observing them. "I just raised the grade on her exam," Brian had lied afterward to this man, with a phony grin. And this was a double lie: Brian has never raised the grade on a student's exam—he is against that sort of thing on principle.

How has he, Brian Tate, got into this tangle of phony grins and lies? How has he, who for years was a just, honorable, and responsible person, become involved with someone like Wendy Gahaghan?

Or let's look at it from the other end for a change. Why hasn't he become involved with some girl like Wendy long before this? Not through lack of opportunity: he can remember many occasions over the last twenty years when students—some of them much more his type than she is, a few almost as attractive as his wife Erica—had made it apparent that they would welcome a more personal relationship with him. Among his colleagues he knows many who have admittedly, or by repute, taken advantage of such welcomes. But for sixteen years he had privately scorned these colleagues. He had even rather looked down on his friend Leonard Zimmern, who had the excuse of an angry, impossible, unfaithful wife. He, Brian Tate, had no time for such hole-and-corner games. He loved Erica, and he had serious work to do.

But during the last year or two this work has changed. The wrong way of putting it: his work has not changed, and he has recognized that it never will. He is forty-six, and according to local criteria a success. His students think him interesting and well informed. His colleagues think him competent and fortunate; many of them envy him. He holds an endowed chair in the department and is the author of two scholarly studies in his field and a widely used and profitable text; he has a beautiful intelligent wife, two attractive and intelligent children, and a desirable house in Glenview Heights. They are not aware that internally, secretly, he is a dissatisfied and disappointed man. He bears the signs openly: a sharp W-shaped frown between his neat dark eyebrows, a pinched look around the mouth. But those who see these signs assume Brian is disappointed not by his own condition, but by the condition of the world.

Whenever he speaks in public, as he often does, on American foreign policy; or when an article by him appears in some journal, his students and colleagues are reminded of his success. Brian is reminded of his failure. Why, he asks himself sourly, is he speaking on foreign policy instead of helping to make it? Why does he still discuss other men's theories instead of his own?

He cannot blame his failure on ill fortune. He had been born with all the advantages: the son of a well-known professor, nephew of authors and lawmakers, grandson and great-grandson of ministers and judges; healthy, handsome, intellectually precocious, well-loved, well-educated. But after all these gifts had been bestowed, some evil fairy had flown in through the delivery-room window and whispered over his crib, "He should be a great man." All his life, that imperative has haunted him. His colleagues, born into cultural or economic slums, the ugly, clumsy sons of provincial neurotics or illiterate immigrants, might be proud of having become Corinth professors—not he.

As if symbolically, when he reached adolescence Brian did not grow as fast as his peers at Andover, nor in the end as far. When he entered Harvard (at sixteen) he was still small for his age. He would catch up, his relatives said, and he believed them; but he did not catch up. He remained, though not a very short man, considerably below the average in height: five feet five, if he stood up straight and held his neck in a certain way. Erica was nearly three inches taller. When she married him, she gave away to a Congregational church rummage sale all the high-heeled shoes which showed her spectacular long legs to such advantage, and accepted a lifetime of flat soles, because he was going to be a great man.

All these years, Erica (unlike his relatives) has never either overtly or covertly accused him of disappointing her. Only once years ago, after a New York party at which several famous persons were present, had she even admitted, laughing as she spoke and pulling a yellow flowered silk petticoat over her dark curls, that she would like Brian to be famous too. Previous to that evening, and subsequently, she had denied any such wish; but Brian was not convinced.

Erica had also insisted that same evening that she didn't hold it against him that he had not yet become famous. It was bad luck, that was all, like Muffy's allergy to house dust, and would similarly be outgrown. After all, she had added, still laughing softly, leaning on his shoulder to steady herself as she took off her white silk sandals—he was already a famous professor: hadn't he just been given the Sayle Chair of American Diplomacy at Corinth? Brian had replied that this meant very little—only that Clinton had retired and he was now the senior man in the field. But (as perhaps he had intended) she took this protest for modesty.

Erica still expected him to become a great man that evening—next year, or the year after. But Brian suspected even then, and knows now, that he will not. It is too late, for one thing: he is nearly as old as Lindsay, and five years older than Bobby Kennedy would have been. Erica knows it too, and affects not to mind; or possibly does not mind. She has said that she is glad of it, because she values their privacy and dislikes official social life of the sort she had to be involved in during the two years when Brian was head of his department. If he were to become any more prominent she would see less of him, she has explained, and more of people she doesn't care for.

Brian has done his best to become a great man. He has written many long and serious political articles; he has served without pay on committees and commissions; he has offered himself at various times and more or less subtly to the Democratic, Independent Republican and Liberal parties as an adviser on foreign policy. But his theories have attracted no real interest; his opinions have been voted down, and his offers declined.

He regretted this not only for personal reasons but because he sincerely believed, even knew, that he had much to contribute. He was one of the few people he knew, for example, who realized that political expediency and idealism are not incompatible. Yet for years he had been misunderstood, just as the public figure he admired most, George Kennan, had been misunderstood; he had been considered either a fuzzy-minded theorist or a small-minded politician.

Even within the university he has been disappointed in his ambitions. He did not want the Sayle Chair, which carried with it no reduction in teaching load or significant increase in salary; what he wanted was the chair, and the desk, in the office of the Dean of Humanities, or some similar large office. Everyone agreed he had done well during his turn as department chairman, and several of his colleagues appeared to think he would make a fine dean; but when the opportunity came none of them nominated him for the post.

Brian's most inward belief is that all these defeats and his size are connected: that his appearance is the objective correlative of a lack of real stature. Years ago, some invisible force had set a heavy hand on his head to keep him from growing any taller, as a sign to the world. And this sign had been heeded. The opinions and candidacy of a man barely five feet five, weighing a mere one hundred and thirty-five pounds, were seldom taken seriously. It was felt everywhere that he was in every sense a small man, not suited to authority over anything beyond a small department. Had he been even a few inches taller, he might have fulfilled his promise and the expectations of his relatives—obeyed the imperative spoken over his crib. Conversely, once he had fulfilled this promise, his size would not have mattered. He never spoke of this to anyone, but he thought about it—not every day, but frequently.

Throughout his adult life Brian had behaved so as to compensate for, even confute, the sign set on him by fate. He had decided in college that he could not afford to make jokes or mistakes as a larger man might, lest he be thought lightweight. For a quarter-century, therefore, he had done and said nothing which would have seemed frivolous, injudicious or immoral in a university president or a candidate for Congress.

Was it the realization that all this solemn self-regulation had been for nothing—a foolish mistake, a long joke on himself—that had made him susceptible to Wendy Gahaghan? Brian does not know. He is aware of no decision to cast off his self-discipline; certainly of no decision to cast it off for Wendy.

Even as a political scientist he finds it impossible to determine when and how the affair had begun. Possibly it dated from the day two and a half years ago when he became aware that Miss Gahaghan, a small hippie-type blonde in his graduate seminar on American Institutions, was prominent among those students who remained after class to speak to him more often than necessary, and made excuses to consult him during his office hours. This might have been viewed variously: as apple-polishing, infantile dependency or simple academic anxiety. Which, Brian did not trouble to determine, since it would presumably end with the course.

American Institutions ended, but Miss Gahaghan, who had received a grade of B-plus from Brian, continued. She audited his undergraduate lectures; she waylaid him in the department office. Apparently she had formed some sort of attachment to him. This had happened before with students, and Brian had handled it, always successfully, as he tried to handle it now. That is, he began, slowly but steadily, to turn down the thermostat of his manner from faintly warm to neutrally cool. In the past he had never had to go below about 55 degrees to chill affections sufficiently; but Miss Gahaghan was not discouraged even by lower temperatures. She continued to come to his office; and he let her continue. He did not, in fact, turn the temperature down to freezing. Why not?

Principally, he thinks, because Wendy was not a graduate student in his department, but in Social Psychology. She had taken his course more or less by accident, and discovered an enthusiasm for American history which he believed to be largely real, even if it was confused in her mind with enthusiasm for him. One of her ambitions was to go into the wilderness and live in a commune based on mutual cooperation and mystical philosophy. Her department treated such groups as examples of social pathology. From Brian she learned that they were in the mainstream of the American utopian tradition.

"All those dumb old uptight behaviorists, they think anybody who believes in love and community is a deviant," Wendy exclaimed when these facts fully dawned upon her. Brian had smiled noncommittally; though he did not admit it, he shared her descending opinion of the graduate school of Social Psychology. He believed most of the men in Wendy's department to be self-seeking fools, and their courses to be composed in equal parts of common sense and nonsense—that is, of the already obvious and the probably false.

He was pleased, but not surprised, that Wendy should consult him rather than her adviser (a cynical, nervous young man called Roger Zimmern who was a cousin of Leonard's). He liked to answer questions, to explain things. What made explaining things to Wendy especially gratifying was that she wanted nothing from him but knowledge—or so he thought in the beginning. Her reactions were naïve sometimes, overemotional often, but never bored or contrived. There was no academic reason for her to listen to what he said, or read the books he suggested. He was not responsible for her examinations, her financial support, or her M.A. thesis; he would not have to recommend her for jobs or fellowships. He never saw in her eyes as he spoke the dull-red stare of academic duty and boredom; or the hard glaze of self-concealment as a prelude to self-advancement—the yellow signal "Caution" which glowed so often in the eyes of his own graduate students. Her gaze was pure green light.

Wendy's conversation also had a certain interest. She was outspoken about her professors and courses as no student in Political Science would have been, and it amused Brian to learn about another department from the underside in this way; the more so perhaps because she did not always know how much she was revealing. He encouraged her, as he would not have done had he expected to see more of her. But he assumed that the coming summer would mean the end of the acquaintance. Wendy would have her degree; she was planning to hike around Europe and then teach high school and live in a commune she had heard of in Massachusetts.

But in September of the following year she was back in graduate school and back in Brian's office. Europe was a great trip, but you couldn't stay there long without bread; the commune was a good scene until there got to be too many freeloaders, runaway kids and old acidheads; the Green River school system was a bad, ugly trip and scene. Brian was not sorry to see Wendy again: her letters from Holland, Yugoslavia and Green River had been amusing; he had missed her reports on the psychology department, and was glad to have them resume.

What was even more important, or soon became so, was the news Wendy brought of the "youth scene." Brian had known for some time that he and his colleagues were not living in the America they had grown up in; it was only recently though that he had realized they were also not living in present-day America, but in another country or city-state with somewhat different characteristics. The important fact about this state, which can for convenience' sake be called "University," is that the great majority of its population is aged eighteen to twenty-two. Naturally the physical appearance, interests, activities, preferences and prejudices of this majority are the norm in University. Cultural and political life is geared to their standards, and any deviation from them is a social handicap.

Brian had started life as a member of the dominant class in America, and for years had taken this position for granted. Now, in University, he finally has the experience of being among a depressed minority. Like a Chinaman in New York, he looks different; he speaks differently, using the native tongue more formally, the local slang infrequently and as if in quotation marks; he likes different foods and wears different clothes and has different recreations. Naturally he is regarded with suspicion by the natives.

Of course Brian does not have to spend all his time in University. In the evenings, on weekends and during most of the summer he can return to the real world, where other standards are in effect. The trouble is, he can see quite well that the "real world" is growing to resemble University more every year, as the youth culture becomes more dominant; and he is aware that all he has to look forward to is the prospect of joining the most depressed minority group of all, the Old.

Brian had never attempted to pass as a native of University, although he realized there were certain rewards for doing so. He did not want to become assimilated, and rather despised those of his colleagues who did. He felt no impulse at all to take drugs, curse policemen, wear beads or study Oriental religions. At the same time, as a political scientist, he felt increasingly that it was his job to know something about these developments.

Unlike his other students, Wendy Gahaghan did not conceal the nonacademic side of her life from Brian. In simple, confiding tones, she related how she and her friends smoked hash, deceived draft boards, "lifted" goods from store counters, and made casual, violent love. When something politically or culturally controversial happened in University, Wendy came and told Brian what the students thought about it, concealing nothing, as if unaware that he was the enemy. In return he tried not to be the enemy: he made an effort never to show shock or disapproval, merely a steady interest.

*37*

Gradually Brian began to look forward to Wendy's appearance, especially at times of crisis—to think of her as his Native Informant. He began to be aware that because of her visits he was pulling ahead of his colleagues in knowledge of student motives and reactions—even sometimes ahead of those who attempted to ape these reactions. They were disguised as natives, but he understood the indigenous customs and language better than they; often he could tell them what SDS or the Society to Legalize Marijuana was going to do next. Scrupulously, he declined to reveal his sources. Indeed, he often concealed the fact that he had a source, preferring for several reasons to suggest that he had many student informants; or that he was only brilliantly guessing, theorizing as a political scientist, about what might happen.

The final reason Brian had not discouraged Wendy's visits, he thinks—indeed, had begun to encourage them—was that he didn't believe she could ever constitute any threat to his emotional or physical equanimity. He would have been on his guard if she had been anything like his wife at that age. But Erica had been exceptional: an honor student, elegantly dressed, extraordinarily pretty; she was president of the Arts Club, an editor of the literary magazine, and one of the most popular girls in her class—always surrounded by admirers and friends.

Wendy, by contrast, was an ordinary female graduate student. She was not plain, indeed quite attractive by conventional standards, but she was completely undistinguished—a well-rounded baby-faced ash-blonde, with pink cheeks and lank silky hair. She dressed usually in Indian style, but—like his children when they were small—confusing the Eastern and Western varieties. She wore, indiscriminately, paisley-bedspread shifts, embroidered velvet slippers, fringed cowhide vests and moccasins, strings of temple bells, saris, shell beads, sandals, and leather pants very loose in the ankle and tight in the ass. In spite of all this paraphernalia, she never looked like either sort of Indian. Rather, with her round pink freckled face and limp yellow hair, she resembled a solemn schoolchild got up for a Thanksgiving or United Nations Day pageant. Even when not in costume, she often tied a beaded or embroidered strip of cloth tightly across her brow in the shape of a headache.

"Don't you mind that thing around your head?" he had once asked her. "It looks uncomfortable. Doesn't it hurt?"

"Uh uh," Wendy replied, smiling eagerly—for at this point Brian almost never made any comment on her appearance. "It feels good. It's like— It kind of, you know, keeps my brains together."

"I see." Brian could not help smiling back, for it was true that Wendy tended to be, not so much scatter-brained (which suggests a restless movement of ideas) as mentally diffuse. Simple facts she knew very well—like the names of books she had studied and courses she had taken—became hidden in fog from time to time, causing her to stamp her foot and exclaim that she was "too stupid." Sometimes whole areas of information seemed to drift toward the misty periphery of her consciousness and fall off the edge.

Publicly Brian held this to be the result of too much marijuana and not enough sleep, and scolded her for it; but privately he suspected it was also due to lack of interest in graduate study. Wendy was intelligent enough, but her mind was not scholarly. Until very recently, girls like her, whatever their SAT scores, didn't usually go to graduate school. But nowadays, if they hadn't found someone to marry as undergraduates, they continued their education and their search, often in fields like psychology or sociology which seemed relevant to the situation.

With the slightest encouragement, Wendy would have transferred into Political Science, but Brian had no intention of giving this encouragement. He had already disregarded several hints, so he was ready when she mentioned the matter openly, on November 11—but he was not prepared for what followed.

When Brian told her that no, he definitely did not think she should enter his department and do a thesis on utopian communities under his direction, Wendy's pale-blue eyes watered; she blinked her flaxen eyelashes. "You think I couldn't do the work," she asked or stated, her pink-smudged lower lip wobbling with the effort not to cry. "You think I'm not smart enough."

No, that wasn't it at all, Brian replied. It just seemed to him that at this stage in her graduate career . . . He went on repeating his arguments while Wendy, in a trembling voice, repeated hers. As he spoke it occurred to Brian that if Wendy wanted to, she could probably transfer into the department without his help. She was a hard-working, conscientious girl; her record in general was good. He was not on the graduate admissions committee this year; to stop her, he would have to make a written statement casting doubts upon either her sanity or her honesty. That he should even think of doing so cast doubts upon his own.

But, glancing at her again as she spoke, at her lank lemonade-blond hair parted in the middle Indian style and descending smoothly over her cheeks like the flaps of a wigwam, he realized that Wendy, like the squaw or Hindu maiden she affected to be, would never do anything he did not advise—because his approval was more important to her than her education. And at that moment, as if she had read his thoughts, Wendy said hesitantly, looking first up at him and then down at the notebooks in her lap,

"It's not so much that I can't stand my psych seminars— It's just that I want to do something you really respect— It's because, you know, I'm emotionally fixated on you, I guess you dig that." She raised her round blue eyes, but not her face, to his.

Reviewing history now, Brian realizes it was at this moment that he should have been frank. He should have met Wendy's offensive head-on; made it clear at once that he wasn't the sort of professor who encouraged, or even allowed, the emotional fixations of students. He should have recommended that Wendy either unfix her feelings or stop coming to see him. Instead he chose to pretend that nothing had happened, to treat what she had said as unimportant. He assured Wendy in a light, humorous tone that it would pass; that she was confusing appreciation of his ideas with something else. He waffled—the word was accurate, suggesting something cooked up, full of little square holes.

In effect, on November 11 of last year he had given Wendy Gahaghan permission to be in love with him, and to add this to the list of problems she came to discuss with him, two or three times a week now. The convention was maintained, on his part at least, that the attachment was a sort of mild delusion from which she would eventually recover, and which was therefore to be treated with humorous tolerance. Wendy accepted this convention to some extent. She refused to admit that she was deluded in loving Brian, or that a cure was likely; but she preserved a certain detachment from her infatuation. In his presence, at least, she took the sort of ironic, stoical attitude toward it that he had known older people to maintain toward a chronic disease.

In the weeks that followed it came to be assumed that when Brian asked, quite routinely, how she was, he was inquiring about the state of her disease, her hopeless passion for him. "Well, I thought I was a little better, until I heard you talk at the Department Colloquium last night. What you said about Cordell Hull was so beautiful, I couldn't *stand* it," she would report. Or, "I've really been trying to get over it. I was rapping with Mike Saturday night; he said what I needed was a good fuck, that was all. So we tried it . . . Uh-uh. It didn't work. I mean, it was okay: Mike's a nice guy, and he's very physical— But this morning it was like it never happened, sort of." Wendy would have gone on; but Brian, with a sense of moral scrupulousness, always changed the subject—whereas the truth was that he should never have allowed it to come up at all.

This state of things continued for about three weeks. Then two events of little apparent importance, but far-reaching effect, occurred. First, on December 3, Wendy contracted the Asian flu. For over a week she did not come to Brian's office. His first reaction was slight relief, followed in a day or so by concern. He thought back to their last meeting, and remembered her complaint that every single time she saw him she adored him more. "Well," he had replied jokingly, "in that case, perhaps you'd better see less of me." Unaware that Wendy was in the infirmary with a fever of 103 degrees, he told himself that she must have taken his advice; that this would be hard for her, but that it was probably the right decision. In the days that followed, he found these thoughts repeating themselves in his head with irritatingly increasing frequency.

The second event of slight apparent importance involved the Sayle Chair of American Diplomacy—not in the symbolic, but in the physical sense. Six years ago, when Brian inherited the Sayle Chair, he had also inherited an actual piece of furniture: an ancient, battered Windsor armchair with a high round back and a cracked leg, which had been presented to the first incumbent by some waggish students about 1928, and bore a worn label in imitation nineteenth-century penmanship: "Wm. M. Sayle Chair of American Diplomacy." This object now occupied a corner of Brian's office, which was already too small in his opinion, without serving any useful purpose. Nobody could sit on it safely; you could not even put many books on it.

Gradually, Brian had begun to feel that the Sayle Chair did not like him; doubtless it thought he was not of the stature of its previous occupants. For a while he tried hanging his raincoat over it, but this only made it even more obtrusive. It looked like someone tall and thin and round-shouldered, probably Wm. M. Sayle, crouching in the corner with his head down. Brian would have liked to throw the chair out, but that was not feasible, for it had become a Tradition in a university which valued Tradition.

On the morning of December 12, there was a knock at Brian's door.

"Yes?"

"Hi." Wendy Gahaghan, in her fringed leather costume, entered the office.

"Well hello, stranger!" Brian forgot that Wendy had been avoiding him for her own good—his voice expressed only pleasure, and slightly injured surprise.

"I had the Asian flu," Wendy panted, out of breath from

running up two flights of stairs. "I was in the infirmary, I couldn't even call you."

"I'm sorry to hear that." Under her long, untidy, damp-streaked hair (there was a cold rain outside) Wendy was paler than usual. "You look tired."

"Yeah, I just got out this morning." She smiled weakly.

"Well, sit down then, rest yourself— No, not there!" he cried, as Wendy sank into the Sayle Chair. Too late: there was a sharp crack; the seat split, the left front leg collapsed, and Wendy collapsed with it. Her legs sprawled out, her books skidded across the gray vinyl floor.

"Ow, ooh!" she shrieked as she landed hard on her back and the chair fell forward on top of her.

"God damn." In what seemed to him slow motion, Brian got around his desk and crossed the room. He lifted the chair. "Are you all right?"

"I guess so." Wendy flexed her arms and legs. Her fringed cowhide miniskirt had been pushed up to the waist, below which she was now covered only in a transparent pale nylon membrane, faintly shiny, like the sections of an orange or pink grapefruit. "Yeh, I'm okay. Hey." She smiled weakly, but made no move to adjust her skirt or get up. "I broke your chair."

"It was cracked already," Brian said. "I told you before not to sit there." He set the chair down; it sagged lamely against the bookcase.

"Oh, wow." Wendy began to laugh. From where he stood above her, the effect was strange. Her transparent eyes rolled back; her mouth opened, showing wet pink depths; her full hips shook inside the nylon membrane. Brian felt a strong mixed emotion which he chose to interpret as impatience.

"Here, get up," he said firmly, almost angrily, holding out his hand.

Responsive to his mood, Wendy stopped laughing at once. She scrambled up off the floor, looking frightened; her hand in his felt

*43*

cold and small. Brian removed the *Times* and some books from another chair and pushed it forward. Wendy sat down.

"Hey, listen, why I was laughing. I'm sorry, I didn't mean— See, I didn't know your chair was broken. I thought you just didn't want me to sit in it all this time because I wasn't worthy of it." She grinned timidly. "I thought you were saving it for, like, important people."

"That's ridiculous."

"I know it. Oh, I'm always so stupid, stupid, stupid." She hit her freckled face with her small freckled fists, half humorously, half melodramatically. "You probably must hate me now," she added.

"Of course not."

"But I ruined your famous chair."

Both Brian and Wendy looked at the Sayle Chair, which was down on one knee in the corner; its right arm hung broken at its side. It could be thrown out now, he realized. It would be thrown out.

"Looks like it," he agreed, smiling.

"I guess you'll never forgive me."

"I'll forgive you," Brian said generously. "As long as you don't break anything else."

No reference was made that day to Wendy's infatuation; nevertheless the situation had changed, in some way Brian did not understand. In the days that followed, instead of being aware of her desire only for brief moments while she was in the office, he felt it continually. The waves of her passion reached him like the vibrations of a distant bombardment, out of sight and almost inaudible, but still shaking the stale academic air. Also he could not forget the sight of her lying on his floor. The image kept returning, photographically sharp: the lank yellow silk hair loose on the marbled vinyl, the matching curlier hair visible through the glossy nylon membrane. There was a hole in the hose just inside the left knee; a slightly convex circle of pink flesh appeared in the hole,

*44*

and a long run, or ladder, pointed up to heaven— Trite, ridiculous, vulgar.

Alternating with this image in Brian's mind was a sense of his own self-denial. A pretty young student was passionately in love with him, but he refused to take advantage of her infatuation, which few men in his position would have. He had tried to do the right thing, to cure her of her attachment. He had rationed her visits to twice a week, and limited them to a half-hour; he had encouraged her to see and screw other people; he had refused to discuss her feelings at any length. That these methods did not work, that she was still in love with him, was not his fault.

Christmas vacation arrived. Brian had resolved that during this period he would cease to think about Wendy. It proved difficult. Continually, and often at inconvenient times, he saw her face; he heard, inside his head, her small, almost childish voice. "I guess you'll never forgive me," the voice said. "I want to give myself to you completely," it said. And Brian would look across the table—or across the bed—at his wife, who had never given herself completely to anyone; who merely lent herself. Graciously and sometimes even enthusiastically, yes. But like an expensive library book, Erica had to be used with care and returned on time in perfect condition.

Perhaps illogically, Brian had felt that he deserved an unusually merry Christmas; that Erica and the children ought somehow to reward him for his self-denial, his loyalty, by giving him at least a little of the sort of unquestioning love he was refusing for their sakes. Instead, Jeffrey and Matilda were uncooperative, dissatisfied with their presents, and sulky because there wasn't enough snow on the ground for their new skis. And Erica, as if perversely, seemed to become less understanding and affectionate every day. She complained a great deal of how difficult the children were, blaming herself compulsively, without trying to do anything about it. She seemed not to realize that he had the same problem, only geometrically multiplied. She had to cope with two adolescents; he

*4 5*

had to deal with several dozen—equally ill-mannered, uncooperative and dissatisfied.

For Brian's students are by no means all as appreciative as Wendy; many are indifferent to what he has to teach them, or even hostile. Wendy understood this, and sympathized. Erica did not: when he complained she thought he was exaggerating, remembering her own more tranquil and earnest college days. The reassurance she offers seems thin and shallow. When she tells Brian not to worry, that he is a brilliant professor, this statement is not based on knowledge, but merely on the wish to reassure, even to shut him up. She is not really interested in his problems, or concerned with his welfare or pleasure. Often she argues with him, and is unwilling to make love when or as he likes.

The truth is that sexual novelty has never been Erica's forte. Though passionate, she is a traditionalist. The suggestion that she wear her new lace bra or her patent-leather boots to bed, or assume some unusual position, is apt to provoke suspicion and unease. If he even mentions it, Erica will suspect that Brian is tired of her as she really is; she will feel hurt. She will suspect that he is trying to make fun of her, to exploit her, even to humiliate her.

Sometimes, if he waits until Erica is warmed up, he can introduce desirable novelties without her objecting, or even noticing. But on New Year's Eve, after a boring party at which Brian had drunk more than he wanted without feeling any better, he went too fast.

"Wait, what are you doing?" Erica exclaimed as he lifted her off the bed onto the floor. "Ow, too cold!"

"Come on. Let's lie down here."

"Well; at least get the quilt," Erica said, her pelvis and voice tensing. "Put it under me . . . Wait . . . No, on the rug, that way. All right, go ahead."

What followed, for both of them, was not more satisfactory than usual, but less so. It was further marred for Brian by the persistent image of Wendy Gahaghan lying on his office linoleum —exposed, silent, willing. He knew from hints she had dropped, anecdotes she had told, that she was not similarly wary of innovation. He knew that he could without a word have fallen on her there on the floor and possessed her in any way he liked, and earned only her passionate gratitude.

In that moment, early in the morning of New Year's Day, the tide of Brian's resolve had changed. Slowly at first, it began to flow in toward the shore, covering the stern moral rocks with foamy waves of self-justification. He did not, however, give up the idea of himself as a serious and responsible person, concerned to obey the categorical imperative and seek humanistic goals.

What he did was to turn the problem inside out. Wendy was suffering (he told himself), and had been suffering for perhaps a year, from unconsummated love. It was the worse for her because, in her world, such feeling was so rare as to be almost unknown. Among her friends even the most transitory physical attraction was consummated as a matter of course, and at once. But romantic passion, as De Rougemont has pointed out, is a plant which thrives best in stony soil. Like the geraniums in Erica's kitchen, the less it was watered, the better it flowered. That was why Wendy loved him; while for the boys she casually slept with she felt little.

Therefore, Brian argued with himself as the soapy waves of false logic sloshed toward the shore, what he really ought to do was to sleep with Wendy himself, as soon as possible. She would see then that he was only a man like other men; her disease would be cured. He owed it to her to provide this cure, even at the cost of deflating his value in her eyes and ruining his moral record. He didn't *want* to commit adultery, he told himself, but it was his duty. It was a choice between his vanity, his selfish wish for moral consistency, and Wendy's release from a painful obsession.

Looking back now, Brian finds it hard to understand how he had entertained such self-righteous nonsense; how he, a serious political scientist, had been able to fool himself with the old means-end argument. For he had applied this argument to himself as well as to Wendy; he had hoped to cure his obsession as well as her passion by sating it. He had been intermittently aware, he recalls now, that outsiders might not appreciate the extent of his altruism in screwing Wendy Gahaghan, if they heard of it—but he had counted that almost one more thorn in his martyr's crown.

He did not realize then that he was already becoming addicted to Wendy, and that he was planning to increase the dose partly because he needed to quiet the anxiety that he was in every sense, including the most private, a small man. In a shady part of his mind which he did not usually visit he wished to learn her opinion on this matter. Erica could not judge it, any more than she could judge his professional competence, since, having known no other men, she had no means of comparison. It was true that earlier in his life several women had assured Brian that he was of average size. But what if they had been politely lying? Or what if he had shrunk, in fifteen years? Brian recognized the childish, neurotic stupidity of these ideas, but he could not suppress them entirely. "Just once; just one shot, that's all, to cure you both," his addiction whispered; and at last he promised it what it wanted.

When Wendy appeared in Brian's office after Christmas vacation he was momentarily embarrassed. He had denied her for so long that changing direction was awkward. Fortunately, almost miraculously, she provided him with an opening.

"How are you?" he asked, falling into the traditional starting gambit.

"Just the same." Wendy grinned. "Or worse, maybe."

"I'm sorry." Uncharacteristically, Brian had risen when she knocked, ostensibly to shelve some books, but in fact to get out from behind his desk—that old defensive fortification which had now become a military impediment.

"Nothing helps any more. Being away from you hurts. And being here hurts worse, some ways."

"I don't like to see you unhappy." Having replaced his books, Brian was now standing next to Wendy. He thought that he hadn't realized before how small she was, how childlike. He towered over her not only intellectually and chronologically, but physically. A pleasant sensation.

"I know." She gave a little apologetic smile and shrug. "If you would kiss me, just once, I'd feel better."

"You know, I've been thinking about that," Brian said, smiling down. "I think just possibly you might be right." He had imagined that he would explain his analysis of Wendy's problem and outline the solution he proposed, before putting it into practice. But events moved too fast for him. It was not until the next day that he was able to present his theory—which, by then, was already being proved incorrect.

Waiting in his office now, Brian vows to himself that the end of his affair will be better governed than the beginning. His two previous attempts to break it off had not worked because they were based on a faulty political analysis of the situation—possibly due to unconscious resistance on his part. Wendy does not care if his wife knows of the affair; among her friends such matters immediately become public anyhow. She knows also that her work has not fallen off since January; and even if it had fallen off, she wouldn't have cared.

But there is one thing which will convince her that the affair must end; one sentence Brian can speak which will make her almost as eager to end it as she had been to begin. When she comes in today, Brian can tell her that his own work is suffering; that he has been unable to write his new book, a project she regards with awe.

"Too much of my energy is going into our relationship," he will say, in a few minutes now. "There's not enough left for my work."

And what is more, this will be the literal truth. It is not only that his affair with Wendy consumes certain hours; more profoundly, it consumes the emotional and physical energy which at other times has been sublimated into the writing of political history. As his roommate had put it once back at Harvard, when Brian made a similar choice before an important exam: "Brian thinks it all comes out of the same faucet."

*49*

"I know it does," he had replied.

"You're nuts," said his roommate cheerfully. "The way I look at it, the more I screw the better I work." But time proved him wrong: he received a grade of only B-plus on the important exam, while Brian was rewarded for his abstinence with a straight A.

# 3

July Fourth. It is summer now, the time of year Erica Tate once liked best. The climbing roses are in bloom over the screen porch; the students have gone home; the town is green, sunny, silent. Her husband's affair with that girl is over. Erica wants to forget it, and she is trying to forget it. She knows this is the only way. It is not enough for her to forgive Brian; what she must do is get the whole thing out of her mind entirely. Then, and only then, can life go back to normal.

And if not now, when? It is a warm, soft evening, unusually quiet. Jeffrey and Matilda are not playing the phonograph or the radio or quarreling or talking on the telephone; they are away, at the fireworks show in the stadium. The sun has just set, and the sky beyond the porch, behind the apple trees, is layered with white and rose chiffon clouds, like a nightgown Erica had when she got married. She sighs.

"What?" Brian says, looking up from his coffee and the *Village Voice*.

"I was thinking about the children," says Erica, who is not aware of having sighed aloud. "I'm not sure we should have let them go alone." She uses the word "we" with an effort, for it is Brian who gave permission for the excursion.

"They're not alone," he says impatiently. "They're with three thousand other people."

"That's what bothers me. Among three thousand people there's sure to be some bad characters."

"Don't worry about it. Most of them are kids. Or students."

"What difference does that make?"

No reply. Erica opens her workbox and selects a spool of thread. Lately she has been much troubled by fantasies of awful things that might happen to Jeffrey and Matilda, fantasies which she fears from her reading may also be wishes. But adolescence is a precarious time, and crowds at night are dangerous. Somewhere in the huge, dark stadium there are teenage hoods looking for boys like Jeffrey to rob and bully; there are depraved older men looking for silly, reckless young girls like Matilda. But it is no use saying this to Brian. He doesn't care what happens to the children— No, worse than that; he himself is one of the bad characters. He has already seduced a girl half his age.

Erica looks up at her husband, an important professor aged forty-six, well dressed, small and compact in build, with a handsome, steady face, reading the paper. What had happened between him and Wendee was three months past. He just didn't think about it any more, he had told her last week, with such casual impatience that she at last believed him. He doesn't think of Wendee; he doesn't think of her, Erica; he doesn't think of the children. What does he think of, for heaven's sake? No doubt, of recent American political history; of the Cold War, about which he is writing a book.

It seems to Erica horribly unfair that she should continue to find herself brooding, almost obsessively, about a girl she has never seen, while Brian, who has lain naked on top of this girl and partly inside her on his office floor, is able to forget.

But why his office floor? Well, because there was a blizzard outside, Brian had explained stiffly, and they didn't want to walk to Wendee's apartment in Collegetown and back again; there wasn't time. It was details like that which caused trouble. If Erica had known either more or less it would have been better, she thought. Instead she had just enough information to be able to visualize the scene. She involved herself emotionally by the imaginative effort of completion. As if she were watching television on a defective set, she created a whole reality out of speckled hints and blurry shadows. She created the naked arms and legs on Brian's floor, which was of vinyl mottled greeny-gray and glossy with institutional wax, slightly chilly and dusty to the touch; the hissing of the radiator, like a coiled iron serpent; the sleet and snow beating and melting down the office window.

This vision and others like it come to Erica against her will and desire at the worst possible moments, blotting out will and desire. When Brian touches her, even casually, she stiffens. When they lie together she cannot free herself of the thought that every gesture he makes, every caress, has been sketched on Wendee's body; that every whispered word has already been breathed into Wendee's ears; every sigh of passion—

"What's the matter?" Brian asks.

"I didn't say anything."

"You made a noise. You were groaning."

"I didn't mean to."

—That Brian should have forgotten only made it worse. If he had loved the girl passionately, seriously, that would have been more tolerable. Had they been carried away, snowed under by a blizzard of real feeling, they would have had some excuse. Instead Brian tried to excuse himself by assuring Erica that the affair had been minor, casual. "It just wasn't that important," he had said several times, as if unaware how much this devalues both of them.

Erica sighs again and rotates the skirt she is hemming. Of course some professors became involved with their students; she knew that. Girls got crushes on them—it was a recognized occupational hazard, which had existed when she was in college. It had never happened to Erica, but several of her friends had at one time or another thought themselves in love with some professor. Conventional morality being different then, they did not undress in offices as readily, but tended more to tears, declarations and gifts of homemade fudge and homemade verse.

But there is a new sort of student now: less romantic, much more matter-of-fact about sex—and Wendee apparently is one of them. Suppose you are a middle-aged professor, and such a girl comes into your office and boldly declares that she wants to sleep with you—no strings attached, no emotional commitment. It is, after all, the stock situation of most men's fantasies. Erica could see how many might jump at the chance.

But she would never have expected it of Brian. She had always thought of him—he had thought of himself, and apparently still does—as a serious, responsible person. He saw a reason and purpose to life; he disliked frivolous and meaningless pleasures. He therefore had little time for things like watching television and going to large parties. Occasionally, for instance when alone at large parties where TV programs were being discussed, Erica had regretted this. But simultaneously she had admired Brian for his position; valued his influence. Without it, she sometimes thought, who knew how shallow her life might have been, how much time she might have wasted? The world would be a superior place if most people in it were like Brian Tate, she often thought.

And all this virtue had been false. Brian had sat opposite her night after night, as he is sitting now, and delivered his moral opinions, blaming his friends who got involved with students, listening to her accuse herself of being a bad mother, while all the time—

"Amusing letter here on those women's rights protesters," he says, lowering the *Voice* and looking at her over the top margin. "Did you read it?"

"What?" Erica turns her head, pushing aside her hair, which needs to be cut, washed and set.

Brian repeats himself; ending with a little chuckle which invites her to join in.

"Oh. Yes." Erica does not laugh; she smiles briefly. "I saw it."

She does not say she read it, which would not be true. She hates the *Village Voice*, and it also bores her. Their subscription is about six months old—it dates, that is, from the beginning of Brian's involvement with Wendee, and might well, Erica considers, have ended with it. Instead the paper keeps on coming, full of dull, obscene political articles and advertisements for light shows and used Army coats. That Brian still reads it means to her that he has secretly abandoned the adult side and gone over to the adolescent enemy, represented by Jeffrey, Matilda, Wendee and all their invisible friends.

"This about their list of grievances," Brian says, chuckling encouragingly.

"Mm, yes," replies Erica, who has no idea what he is referring to. It is not enough; Brian returns to his paper, disappointed.

All right, so he is disappointed. But how can he expect her to laugh with him now at women, at their grievances; above all at a letter? How can he not be reminded of another letter, a really amusing letter?

As a matter of fact, one of Erica's first ideas after reading that letter had been that it was intended to amuse—that it was some sort of esoteric joke. A colleague had sent it—Leonard Zimmern, perhaps; there was no Wendee. Another possibility was that Wendee existed but was mentally deranged; and her husband no more responsible than she, Erica, had been for the men who used to call up and breathe at her over the phone when they lived in Cambridge. If you have a certain appearance, these things happen to you.

When Brian called that night she said nothing. She waited until he was home again and then brought out the letter, explaining in what sounded to her like an unnaturally flat, bleak tone how she had come to read it. Giving it to him felt strange: she had so often in the last eighteen years handed over other letters and watched Brian read them, waiting for his comments, his judgment—often for his solution. It was as if she now hoped that he would explain

Wendee's letter away. He would tell her calmly, convincingly, that it was all a joke; a preposterous fantasy that had nothing to do with them.

Because it was unlikely, wasn't it, that such a letter should have anything serious to do with people like Erica and Brian?

But Brian had admitted that it did, merely offering, over and over, the wrong excuse: It was nothing, it had meant nothing, it was not important, and anyhow it was finished. He was only sorry she had ever had to hear of it. (Were there, then, other things of which she had not had to hear? Brian declared there were not, but how could she trust him now?) He expressed regret, pain at having troubled her—but all as if he were apologizing for having come home with dirty clothes. He had walked into a bog by mistake, and got mud on his shoes and socks, even on his pants—a nuisance, but they could be sent to the cleaners; Brian himself was not muddy, in his opinion. He did not realize that he had betrayed not only Erica, but himself; that he had become permanently smaller and more ordinary.

And he had made her smaller. The wife who is betrayed for a grand passion retains some of her dignity. Pale-faced and silent, or even storming and wailing as in classical drama, she has a tragic authority. She too has been the victim of a natural disaster, an act of the gods. But if she was set aside merely for some trivial, carnal impulse, her value also must be trivial.

What is so awful, so unfair, is that identity is at the mercy of circumstances, of other people's actions. Brian, by committing casual adultery, had turned Erica into the typical wife of a casually unfaithful husband: jealous and shrewish and unforgiving—and also, since she had been so easily deceived, dumb and insensitive. Her children, by becoming ill-mannered adolescents, had turned her into an incompetent and unsympathetic mother. And the bulldozers grinding toward them over the hill, surrounding them, had turned Jones Creek Road into Glenview Heights, without her lifting a finger.

It was like being on stage. The lights change from amber to

blue; the scenery alters behind the actors: the drop curtain showing cottages and gardens is raised. The villagers have not moved, but now they appear awkward, small and overdressed against the new backdrop of mountains and ruins. And nothing can be done about it. That is the worst thing about being a middle-aged woman. You have already made your choices, taken the significant moral actions of your life long ago when you were inexperienced. Now you have more knowledge of yourself and the world; you are equipped to make choices, but there are none left to make.

What Danielle said is true, Erica thinks: it is better for men. Brian has an important job, he makes decisions, he uses his knowledge, he gives lectures and writes books and votes at meetings for or against and lies on his floor on top of graduate students and gets up again. But for her there are no decisions, only routines. All she can do is endure.

It is darker out now. The sky still holds some light, but its color is leaching away; the layered clouds have become gray and mauve. Brian folds his paper. "I'm going to put those stones on the trash cans," he announces.

"What? Oh, good," Erica says dully.

Often recently the Tates' garbage has been disturbed at night by dogs or some wild animal. In the morning they find the cans overturned and bones, crusts, vegetable peelings, and shreds and chunks of wet newspaper scattered about.

Brian crosses the yard. In the shadows by the trash bins he feels around for the three large rocks he has brought down earlier from the old stone wall behind the vegetable garden. He finds two, and lifts them heavily into place on top of the garbage cans. But he cannot locate the third rock—his hands, groping, meet only thready long grass and the slightly greasy rounded flanks of the plastic cans.

As he starts around the house to get another rock, swearing quietly to himself, Brian passes the screen porch, which appears to him as a cube of artificially lit yellow space blurred by wire screening. It contains porch furniture, two lamps, and a beautiful woman who is sitting in a white wicker armchair, intermittently sewing. Though she does not know he is looking at her, she wears an expression he has seen often lately—one of melancholy and injured feelings.

How long is she going to keep this up, for God's sake? What more does she want from him? He had been unfaithful, which was not a good thing. All right. He has apologized; he has done his best to minimize the duration and importance of his affair. He has made considerable efforts to behave just as before or better: to go places with the children and inquire about their activities with a show of interest; to converse with and make love to Erica with a show of enthusiasm. He is careful never to make any remark which might even remotely recall Wendy. Officially, he has forgotten her.

It would be reasonable, certainly, for Erica to forget her also, Brian thinks, crossing the loose uneven earth of the garden in the thickening dusk, since she knows that Wendy has left for Southern California, and for ever. He had told her about this as soon as Wendy announced her plans, assuming that she would be as relieved as he was, and that she might as well be relieved a fortnight sooner.

And he was relieved. Wendy's reaction to the end of the affair—her animal wails, her stunned silences—had frightened him. He had tried to tell himself that it was a healthy abreaction: that she was just getting rid of all her feelings at once. When she was across the continent she would forget him, probably long before he had forgotten her.

None of what he had predicted and hoped for happened. Wendy's departure did little for his wife's morale—and nothing for his own, since it never actually took place. At this very moment Wendy is still in Corinth, hanging about the campus and suffering.

Brian had foolishly hoped and imagined that they would remain friendly: that Wendy would continue to come to his office, though perhaps less often, and talk to him. This had proved impossible. As soon as she got inside the door she began weeping;

sometimes quietly, sometimes so loudly that he feared Steve Cushing next door would hear. Presently he had to ask her not to come any more, for her own good. The sentence of banishment was difficult to enforce. At first she continued to appear anyhow, though apologetically and always with an excuse—some academic question only he could answer, the promise of being perfectly good and just bothering him for a second. But almost at once she would begin to gasp for breath, to sob. Brian had to give up his habit of calling "Come in." When he recognized Wendy's knock, or thought he did, he had to get up from his desk and go to open the door, not too far. "I'm sorry, but I can't see you," he would have to say in a forced calm tone, if it was she, or, "You know we agreed you wouldn't come here this week," and shut the door again.

Even then Wendy did not always go away. She would wait for him to come out, shuffling up and down the far end of the corridor, or sitting in the chair outside Dorothy McCall's office across the way, like the pile of unclaimed student papers that sometimes occupied it. Brian removed this chair, hiding it in the men's washroom. Wendy was not discouraged, but sat on the floor, her small plump feet, in tan fringed moccasins—or, as the weather grew hotter, bare and gray-soled with dust—sticking out in front of her so that people had to step over them. If he objected to this ("What will it look like to, for example, Mr. Cushing, Mrs. McCall, Mr. Lewis, your sitting here all afternoon?") she would wait farther off: on the stairs, or below in the hall—sometimes pretending to read a book, sometimes staring at the notices of past concerts and lectures and roommates wanted on the bulletin board. She did not care who saw her there or what they would think. And this lack of social shame, like her lack of emotional and physical shame, gave her a tremendous advantage in the wars of love. She knew what she wanted, and wanted it wholly. She was not divided against herself as Brian was; one voice crying Halt, another Forward, a third railing about responsibility.

For Brian too was in pain. It had been hard for him from the start, and soon became horrible to have to act the part of a cruel, heartless person; to see Wendy look every day more like a child who is beaten every day; to sit in his office and know that this child is waiting outside his door or somewhere else in the building.

And not in vain: because when Brian did leave the office and found Wendy still there he could hardly refuse to speak to her. Struggling to contain emotion, she would present her excuse, ask her question, and Brian would answer it. Then, "How is your book coming?" she would ask breathlessly, looking up at him, reminding him that she believed its completion would mark the end of her banishment. He would make some noncommittal reply. To say that the book was going well would have implied that reprieve was at hand; to admit that it was going badly would have implied that her self-sacrifice (and his own) had been useless. For two or three days thereafter Wendy would not appear.

This last time five days had passed. Wendy did not knock on his door; she was not waiting for him when he came in to work, or on the stairs when he went to lunch. Brian began to wonder why the siege had been lifted; what had happened to her. He began to feel worried; guilty; finally even frightened.

Then yesterday, the sixth day, as he was leaving the office he happened to glance outside and saw her standing in the quadrangle below, a yellow spot off-center on a triangle of green grass, looking up at his window. He felt relief, or something like it.

As he left the building, she approached.

"I have to see you."

"Yes?" Brian stopped walking and stood holding his briefcase, looking at Wendy. She had apparently spent time outdoors since their last meeting: her bare round arms, her round face, were reddened and freckled. Large pale ovals around her eyes, where sunglasses must have been, gave her a pathetic, lemurlike appearance.

"I have something to tell you. Good news." Wendy smiled wistfully. "Could we like sit down somewhere?"

Feeling both generous and curious, Brian suggested the

student-union cafeteria. At this time of the afternoon and year, no one he knew was likely to be there.

"I won't be coming around to hassle you any more," Wendy announced, sitting down opposite him with her plastic glass of 7-Up.

"No?" Brian set down his plastic glass of iced tea, anticipating the news that Wendy was finally about to leave town. He felt relief and regret.

"You know I've been going down to the Krishna Bookshop." Wendy leaned forward; her jumbled silver beads and spiral silver wires swung out over the table.

"Yes, you told me." Brian ceased smiling. In any university town there are many forces operating against education: forces social, political and moral (to be more accurate, immoral). Brian, like other professors, has had for years to contend for his students' time and interest against beer parties, political meetings, film series, theater rehearsals, poetry readings, athletic practice and games, good swimming or skiing weather, and sex. He is tolerant of all these activities in moderation, recognizing that they are part of a liberal education. Recently, however, a new counterforce has sprung up, one which he cannot tolerate, since it refuses to present itself as an addition to, or relaxation from, the business of getting a college degree, but sets itself up instead as a rival.

The appearance in town earlier this year of the Krishna Bookshop—an outlet for texts on Eastern religion, a center for lectures on astrology and yoga—was at first a matter for academic curiosity and amusement. The thing could hardly be expected to last long, to survive financially, even in its obscure downtown location. But it did survive; it prospered. It expanded its shelves to include works on organic gardening and primitive music; it gave courses on a variety of dubious subjects from astral projection to Zen Buddhism—assigning homework and papers in competition with the university. Too many students began spending too much time there: sitting about for hours drinking herbal tea and wasting their limited funds on intellectual trash; encouraging each other in escapism and fuzzy thinking; absorbing bogus ideas and bringing them back to clutter up Brian's and other professors' seminars. By now, the Krishna Bookshop has become a matter for serious annoyance.

"I know you don't groove very much on it," Wendy added.

"Mrm." Brian dislikes the idea of Wendy's hanging around the bookshop, and had often said so. But it was summer, and most of her friends were away. Having denied her his companionship, he had no right to deny her that of others. He therefore made a neutral noise, the auditory equivalent of a shrug.

"I went to a lecture there last night, on meditation. Did you ever try meditation?"

"Not in the sense you mean," Brian said.

"I don't dig the theory much; maybe it's just over my head. But the exercises are really fine. Especially if you're hung up on some intellectual problem, or obsessive emotion—well, like I am." Wendy grinned ruefully, and leaned her face on her hand, pushing aside her long limp hair. "For instance there's this one exercise. You sit on the floor, cross your legs—yoga position if you can, only I can't manage that yet—and put your hands on your knees so you're in perfect physical balance. Then you close your eyes and visualize a white circle against a dark background. You don't think of anything else, just concentrate on that one spot." Wendy had shut her eyes in demonstration; now she opened them and looked at Brian. "Yeah, well, I was skeptical too. But it really works. I forgot everything that was ripping me: I forgot you, and me, and where I was— I felt very calm, very together . . . You know, I figure if I do it regularly, I might get over wanting you."

Brian hesitated. He was acutely aware that all his efforts over the past two months had failed to cure Wendy of her attachment; they had only caused pain. If she could cure herself by sitting cross-legged and visualizing a white spot, or indeed by standing on her head and visualizing white elephants, he ought to be delighted.

"Ye-s," he said judiciously. "I think you might get over it anyhow, in time."

Wendy shook her head. "That's not how I am," she said. "I never get over anything. I had this cat when I was a kid, maybe I told you, a big white tom named Crisco. He used to sleep on my bed. But when we moved into the apartment in Queens my folks had to give him away to the SPCA. I cried for that cat at night for years. Sometimes I cry for him even now." Her pale-blue eyes brimmed with shiny tears—for Brian, for Crisco, or possibly both.

Hastily, he changed the subject. "Are there many people there, at those lectures on meditation?"

"Not too many now, in the summer. Maybe ten, twelve. I've only been this once. And I've been talking to Zed some more. You know, he's amazing. He's read like everything. Philosophy, psychology, history, poetry, metaphysics—"

"Is that so." Brian had never seen the proprietor of the Krishna Bookshop, who (according to Wendy) chose to be known only by this syllable. He apparently declined to reveal his actual name, origins, education or history; he had renounced them all for religious reasons, along with his former job, friends, family if any, home and possessions. He lived in his bookstore, sleeping on a cot in the back room and cooking his vegetarian meals on a hot plate.

"He's really a beautiful person," Wendy said, leaning forward even further. "You ought to meet him, honestly."

"Mrm." Brian leaned back. According to reports, Zed was not in either sense a beautiful person. Students, even admiring students, described him as tall, skinny and sort of funny-looking. His clothes, acquired at charity sales, seldom fit well, they said, and he was going bald. His age was uncertain. ("Man, he could be anything; he could be maybe thirty, or he could be really old, like even sixty.") Whatever the truth, Zed was obviously old enough to have known better, and Brian had no desire to meet him.

"He acts sort of vague sometimes," Wendy admitted. (Brian translated this as "He's stoned out of his mind sometimes.") "If he doesn't feel like speaking, he just doesn't answer you. Or maybe he'll hand you a book and go into the back room. That's how he was with me at first." Giving up the attempt to speak confidentially across the table, Wendy now began a flanking movement, shifting her chair around toward Brian. "But this week he talked to me. It was weird. I didn't tell him what was on my mind, he just seemed to *know*."

"He knew, eh? What did he know?"

"Well, that I was hopelessly and desperately in love. I didn't tell him who with," Wendy added, responding to the expression which had appeared on Brian's face. "Zed doesn't want to know things like that; he says, 'All names are lies.' "

" 'All names are lies'?" Brian repeated, refraining with difficulty from adding that the name "Zed" certainly was a lie.

"Uh-huh." Wendy shifted her chair again. "You know, I think he's the first person who's said anything about it that wasn't just bullshit, or laying their own trip on me." She leaned toward Brian; the fan behind them blew shreds of her lank pale hair out sideways. "Like I've been trying all this time to distract myself, to do different things and make it with other people to take my mind off you, you know?"

"Yes." This was in fact the advice Brian had given her, now presumably redefined, with the help of the Krishna Bookshop, as bullshit.

"Well, what Zed said convinced me I was going at it all wrong. I've been trying to replace one selfish personal desire with another just like it. Even if I could do that, I wouldn't be getting anywhere; I'd still be caught in the whirlwind. What I've got to do is reach the end of desire." Wendy edged her chair around further.

> *"Teach me to care and not to care.*
> *Teach me to sit still"*

Brian quoted ironically, looking at Wendy's chair, which she had now shifted so far around the table that it was touching his. Her plump, sun-reddened left thigh, bare to the hip below the brief yellow dress, was half an inch from his own.

"Yeh. That's it." Wendy's leg moved or sagged, as if of its own weight, against his leg.

"And Zed is going to teach you this." Brian tried to keep the sarcasm out of his voice; but the knowledge that she had confided in that occultist crank, fraud and drug addict irritated him profoundly. The idea that she planned to follow his idiotic advice made him furious. He moved his leg away.

"He can't teach me. He said so. Nobody can teach the Way; you have to find it yourself, through prayer and meditation."

"You mean you've really fallen for that mystical crap? I thought you were too intelligent for that."

"It's not crap. You don't understand." Wendy's voice started to quaver. "It's the same thing you're doing yourself already, with your book—putting your energy into something outside yourself that's greater than you." Wendy gulped down a sob. "I told Zed about it, and he agreed with me. He's very interested in you. He wants to know what hour of the day you were born."

"What the hell does he want to know that for?"

"So he can cast your horoscope. I already gave him the day and year."

"I don't know what hour I was born," Brian said with great disagreeableness. "And if I did, I wouldn't tell him." Wendy began sobbing aloud. "Oh hell. Please don't do that. People are watching us." Brian glanced quickly around the coffee shop to see which people these were. Fortunately, at that hour the place was nearly empty; he recognized no one.

*Blam!*

Standing in the dark at the far end of the vegetable garden, Brian starts, and looks up. The fireworks have begun. He can see them quite well from here—though, since the stadium is nearly two miles away, there is a considerable lag between light and sound. The rockets appear to burst silently, and it is only as the shower of sparks extinguishes itself in the trees that he can hear the detonation and the accompanying muffled *Ahh!* of the watching crowd. His children's voices are part of this roar; and Wendy's. She really grooves on fireworks, she told him yesterday, especially when she is high; she was planning to attend in that condition tonight, along with some of the Bookshop people.

The show, designed by professionals, is artistically varied in a primitive way, Brian notices. First a single rocket will sketch on the sky a huge imaginary umbrella; next two or three will open together, each a different primary color. There are comets that climb in crazy spurts, hissing comically and spitting random bursts of light; then what look like handfuls of giant flashbulbs begin to pop and smoke, brightest and noisiest of all.

On many earlier July Fourths, Brian has been there in the stadium with his children; he knows how the crowd looks at such a moment, photographed in stark black and white. He can see the smoke drifting up and smell the gunpowder. And he can see Wendy there, sitting on one of the worn slat benches, the pale circle of her face raised among three thousand raised faces. Suddenly he wants badly to be there too, sitting next to her in the smoky gloom, feeling the weight of her head against his shoulder as she tilts it back and gazes up open-mouthed, the warmth of her bare leg against his leg. He thinks of getting into his car, now—telling Erica he intends to look for the children— Stupid, of course: there will be no place to park within half a mile of the stadium; no way of finding her in the monstrous noisy crowd.

Wendy enjoys crowds, and likes the feeling of being part of one. Though intelligent, she is not of independent mind. She is a born follower, a true believer; and if he, Brian, forbids her to follow and believe in him, she will find other and less scrupulous teachers, other and false gods.

Some of the fireworks explode quickly above the trees; others seem to last a long time. Brian watches the spark of a Roman candle shoot upward, diving into black gravity as if into water and meeting a similar resistance. From it, as it finally unfolds high in the air, long trails of white stars fall almost lazily. After each burst of light comes the appropriate explosion, which varies from a single rifle crack to a complex grumbling roar. Occasionally there is a set piece on the ground; then he sees nothing, and can hear only a distant prolonged crackling volley. At intervals there is silence, accompanied by the sound of crickets and of leaves blowing.

At the finale every kind and color of rocket is sent up together, a long barrage of stars and scrawls and dotted lines. It is like watching a lesson being written on a huge blackboard in some unknown script which disappears as Brian tries to read it, followed and overlapped by explosions of sound in some thunderous unknown language. The sky and hills echo, and the air is heavily streaked with smoke and spotted with after-images in strange hues of purple and green. Lower down a dusky red glow shows through the trees, as if the stadium were burning.

In the smoky gunpowder light Brian can see written clearly what is going to happen next if he continues to reject Wendy. Lonely and sore, she will spend more and more time at the Krishna Bookshop. She will forget the truths she has learned from Brian and remember instead lies and nonsense pronounced in an impressive false manner by Zed. Eventually, without desire, out of gratitude and admiration, she will offer herself to him. And there is no doubt in Brian's mind that the offer will be accepted. Zed is supposed to have given up sex along with other kinds of flesh, but a dish like Wendy obviously doesn't come his way very often. Brian imagines how the drugged eyes of the proprietor of the bookstore will light up with carnal greed; how he will reach out his thin, dirty hands . . . No. It does not bear thinking about.

Groping in the dark along the line of fallen stones which was once a pasture wall, Brian selects a suitably large, flat rock. He lifts it and starts back downhill toward the house as the light in the sky fades. He avoids the row of beanpoles, but steps heavily on a tomato plant which has not yet been staked.

At the end of the garden he stops for a moment among some lettuce which has gone to seed, steadying his rock, catching his breath. He contemplates the woman exhibited on the back porch as in a lighted display case, and compares her to a Radcliffe student he had met one evening some years ago after a public lecture at Harvard. A beautiful, fresh young girl—slim and delicate, with small, perfectly finished features and curly dark hair cut short behind and falling into her dark-lashed eyes in front—from which she would, with a graceful, impatient gesture, toss it back as she spoke. Her manner was gay, almost childlike, yet at the same time serious and even dignified. "A young princess," Brian had thought.

He began to take her out, and was extremely pleased when he realized she preferred him to her many other admirers, though not extremely surprised. He was, after all, several years older than most of them, and people in the Government Department agreed that he had an important future ahead of him. But Brian was astounded, presently, to discover that Erica was still a virgin at twenty. He felt awe and gratitude to Fate for having, as it were, signaled his importance by saving this special treat for him.

Since she was an intelligent modern girl, and in love, Erica slept with Brian before their marriage—but not very often, nor with very great success. He had experience enough to know that in spite of her sighs of pleasure she did not really enjoy the sexual act. He had not been too concerned about this, thinking that she would learn after the wedding. But instead she unlearned—or rather, gradually ceased to pretend.

For nearly three years all his natural skill and invention, all the warm-up techniques he had heard or read of, were unsuccessful. Or, more accurately, they were too successful: Erica much preferred them to that for which they were intended to prepare the way. She loved it when Brian blew into her ear, gently bit the base of her thumb, or stroked her breasts in circles. She sighed and smiled and stretched like a cat when he licked a slow line down the length of her spine, and further. "Oh love, love," she murmured. "Oh bliss." If only he had been satisfied to stop there, he could feel her thinking. But no, he always had to bring out, or up, what she called "that thing." "Don't put that thing in yet please, darling; I'm not ready."

"My cock, my prick, my penis for God's sake," he had shouted at her once. "Can't you call it by its right name?" No, she couldn't. She didn't like any of those words; she never thought them in her mind and she couldn't say them. She knew words for the other difficult parts of the body: "behind" for ass and "stomach" for belly, but there was no word for That Thing. Or occasionally, when Erica was really hurt or annoyed with him, Your Thing. Ordinarily, out of good manners, she overlooked the fact of his connection with the Thing, and when possible its very existence. She avoided looking at it directly, and never touched it unless she was specifically requested to do so. It was as if Brian were a neighbor who owned a particularly ugly dog. "*The* dog is scratching at the door," you might say to him politely, not wishing to underline their relationship—but, in anger, "Your dog bit me."

Two years passed in this way. Then Erica became pregnant. Her obstetrician, a cautious, prissy man, advised that she "avoid intercourse" from the sixth month on, and for two months after the birth—in effect, a five-month abstinence. Abstinence, that is, from the sort of lovemaking Brian liked; the sort Erica liked was allowed to continue. Brian began to look at girls on the street; though a sense of his own moral dignity, and fear of social exposure, kept him from approaching any of them.

But the woman who was restored to him when Jeffo was eight weeks old was worth waiting for. Whether the cause was physiological or psychological, Erica had matured sexually. She retained her verbal modesty, but now she spoke of Brian's organ gently and affectionately as "it," and in moments of enthusiasm as "he." For fifteen years (with five more months off for Matilda) they had made each other happy.

Now it is as if the bad, half-forgotten early period of their marriage had returned. In bed Erica is compliant; but He is called Thing again, and under the soft rhythm of her pleasure Brian thinks he can hear a counterbeat: the heavy creaking and thumping of a deadly struggle between his will to enter and her will to delay the invasion as long as possible so that the occupation might be as short as possible. His main weapons in this battle are force and persuasion; Erica's fuss and delay. She can't get into bed at night now until she is sure, absolutely sure, that the doors are locked, the gas turned off, the thermostat down, the cat shut in the pantry with a full box of Kitty-Litter, and the children sleeping soundly and warmly covered. Then it takes her up to five minutes to find and insert her diaphragm (she refuses to go on the pill because of blood clots), and longer to get out of her nightgown than it takes Wendy to undress completely. And these are only the preliminary maneuvers.

A real victory for Erica took place on the few occasions when she was able to hold back the invading troops for so long that, fatigued and impatient, they discharged all their artillery at the frontier. But real victory for either side is rare. Usually, rather than face Erica's wounded body the next day ("I'm still a little sore down there," she would say, placing a cushion on her kitchen chair), he held back for a while. And she, rather than face his wounded spirit, finally gave way; but she gave way condescendingly, with a characteristic *noblesse oblige*. For as she became a woman, his young princess had developed a less impulsive, more gracious and queenly manner: a gentle, charming air of always being in the right. This was something Brian had not minded in the past; had even liked. Erica's views had generally agreed with his, and reinforced them. For years they were moral and social allies; together they observed and judged the world. Now she judges him. They judge each other, and each finds the other guilty.

Yes, perhaps, Brian thinks, standing among the lettuces. But he has committed no overt act of aggression against Erica, deprived her of nothing. He had held to the Kennanite principle of containment, of separate spheres of action. Within the family, the marital sphere, he had been faithful. The idea of sleeping with

Wendy in the marital bedroom, even if it could have been done with absolute safety, revolted him.

And even if he is guilty, he is guilty of adultery, a form of love. Erica is guilty of unforgiveness, a form of hate. Besides, his crime is over; hers continues. Three months have passed; but still in every look, every gesture, Erica shows that she has not forgotten, has not pardoned him.

It is as if he has incurred a debt which his wife will never let him repay, yet which she does not wish to forgive. She likes to see me in the wrong, Brian thinks, looking across the dark lawn at Erica; she intends to keep me there, possibly for the rest of my life.

Very well. If he is to be imprisoned for life in the wrong, why should it be a solitary confinement? Let him have some company there, the company of a warm and willing fellow criminal. Or, to change the metaphor, if he is to be hanged for his crime, he might as well be hanged for a ram as a lamb.

Brian sets his rock atop the third garbage can and returns to the house. He passes through the rooms and enters the display case.

"I was watching the fireworks," he explains.

"I hope the children will get home all right. I'm worried about their trying to hitchhike back in the dark," Erica says in a thin voice. "You never know who might pick them up."

"You worry too much," Brian remarks, sitting down and taking up the *Village Voice* where he left off. Erica does not reply. Silence.

It is night out now. Brian turns a page; its shadow flaps slowly across the table. Hearing another sigh, he looks up at his wife. She is staring into the middle distance out of eyes circled in muted blue.

Now Erica turns her head. For a moment their eyes meet; then both look down. Erica knows that Brian knows what she is thinking about, and he knows she knows he knows. This mutual knowledge is like a series of infinitely disappearing, darkening ugly reflections in two opposite mirrors. But if he asks her what she is thinking, she will not admit it. She knows that he does not want to ask her anyhow; he does not want to bring up the subject again. And she knows she must not bring it up.

So they say nothing. There is nothing to say.

# 4

A hazy, hot Saturday afternoon in September. Erica is at Danielle Zimmern's, where she has gone in response to an agitated phone call. The Zimmerns' dog, Pogo, has been hurt in a dogfight and rushed to the vet. Danielle and Roo are still anxiously waiting with her there, and someone ought to be in the house when Celia comes back from the children's film show. So, leaving her own children with Brian, who was not pleased, Erica has driven over.

Now, sitting but not rocking in a Victorian plush rocker, she looks around the living room. It is the first time she has been alone there since the days when she and Danielle used to exchange baby-sitting. The furniture is still in the same places; the squashy old sofa and chairs upholstered in green plush; the geometric-patterned Oriental rug bought at a house sale by Leonard—its worn spots cleverly recolored by Danielle, Erica, Muffy and Roo with felt markers one winter afternoon years ago.

The rug still glows red and gold where faint oblongs of sun lie on it; the window is still laced green with climbing and trailing plants. But the room seems both more disordered and barer. Much more wall shows through the shelves beside the fireplace; half the records have gone with Leonard, and more than half the books. An early painting by Roo of a blue-striped cat browsing among giant tulips has been fixed with masking tape over the mantel in place of Leonard's Piranesi, and the mantelpiece itself is littered with letters and plants and sewing as it would never have been when he lived there.

But though Danielle's house has changed externally with the departure of her husband, it remains in other ways more comfortable and familiar than Erica's own, which is physically unaltered. It is not occupied territory: Danielle's children have not yet become unfriendly aliens. Celia, of course, is only eight—a sensible, serious child, not old enough to become an alien. And Roo, though now thirteen, still scorns adolescent culture and is interested only in her animals. Erica, who likes most children, gets on with them as well as ever; that is, exceptionally well. She feels a deep affection especially for Celia, whom she has known since the age of three.

Now that Leonard is gone, Danielle and her daughters live together in moderate harmony broken by brief rebellious skirmishes. Once or twice a week there is a conflict of interests: an outbreak of shouting and/or tears; then the loser retires from the field. Celia withdraws to her room; Roo barricades herself in the basement with her hamsters, her turtles, her fighting fish, Pogo, and any other livestock currently in residence. If Danielle loses, which happens more rarely, she retreats to her campus office.

"Hell, they're no better than your kids, they can be really impossible," Danielle had said inaccurately but kindly two weeks ago. "But when I can't take it, I just go up to school." She set down her coffee mug and looked across the kitchen table at Erica. "That's what you need, to get out of your house sometimes," she pronounced. "You need a job."

And after additional discussion, Erica had agreed that Danielle might be right. Very possibly she would enjoy working part-time; she would make more money than she did doing occasional artwork. But above all it would be a distraction, and she needed distraction. She spent too much time brooding about the children, and about what Brian had done last spring. She knew she

*74*

ought to make some effort to distract herself from this henlike brooding: to, as it were, get up off the nest and stop incubating her grudge, her despair.

"If you were working, you wouldn't have so much time to worry about Jeffrey and Matilda," Danielle said; she did not mention the other egg, since Erica had never told her about it. She had not done so because she knew too well what Danielle would say when she heard of Brian's infidelity: how warmly she would welcome Erica to the shabby fellowship of mistreated wives; how coldly she would speak of Brian, whom she had never liked much in spite of his friendship with Leonard, and now liked less because of it.

At Danielle's suggestion, Erica went to the university employment office, and was offered employment doing library research three days a week for a professor of psychology named J. D. Barclay. She assumed Brian would approve, for at various times in the past he had suggested she might look for a job. But this time his reaction was negative.

"No, I don't like the idea, not at all," he almost shouted. "I'm amazed that you should commit yourself to something like this without discussing it with me." Calming down, Brian explained to Erica exactly how inconvenient it would be to the whole family if she were to start working now. The house and children would suffer from the diversion of her time and energy, he pointed out, and Erica herself would suffer. Being both delicate and conscientious, she would wear herself out, possibly even become ill.

Besides, Brian said, this job was beneath her—routine academic drudgery. And she did not really need the money; she would be taking work away from some graduate student who did. Moreover, he finally admitted, smiling, he disliked the idea of her working for John Barclay. Not that he was jealous, Brian said— and they both laughed, for J. D. Barclay was a fat, fussy elderly man with very little hair. But he was convinced that Barclay had offered Erica the job because she was his wife. It would amuse someone like Barclay, who was definitely not a friend of Brian's, to have Brian's attractive wife working for him, and be able to order her around.

The intensity of Brian's reaction, the number of his arguments, surprised Erica; it also pleased her. For the first time in many weeks her husband was really looking at her and talking to her about something which was not household business or a current event. He was smiling at her, laughing with her, telling her that she was dedicated, attractive and superior to drudgery. She had better things to do with her time, he said, than check Barclay's references; and presently he led her upstairs and proved it, with a considerate attention he had not shown in months.

Afterward, as they lay in bed, Erica told Brian that he was probably right. Upon reflection, next morning, the idea that she was not after all going to work for Mr. Barclay did not trouble her; but she felt regret that the discussion with her husband was over. She would have liked it to continue longer; she began to wonder if it might somehow be resumed.

The following day Erica reported to Danielle that she was not going to take the job. She had been impressed not only by the logic of Brian's arguments, she said, but by the evident strength of his feeling. It was obvious that he wanted her not to work much more than she wanted to work.

Danielle's response was immediate and indignant. If Erica wanted to work at all, she announced, she had a right to; wasn't it her life? It was not her obligation to consider the unconscious motives of J. D. Barclay or the financial needs of hypothetical graduate students. As for the domestic problem, if Erica was making $2.50 an hour she could hire someone else to clean the house and do the laundry, couldn't she?

Yes, Erica said; she could. And armed with these counterarguments she returned home, anticipating another long, stimulating discussion. In order to enjoy it fully, she waited until late that evening, when the children had finished doing their homework to rock music and gone to bed.

"I was thinking some more about that research job," she said. "I ought to let Mr. Barclay know by Monday if I'm going to take it; it's only right."

"I thought we'd decided you wouldn't," said Brian, glancing at his wife briefly and frowning with impatience. "I thought we decided that two days ago."

"Mm, but you know, I was thinking about it again." Erica smiled charmingly.

"Oh, really." Brian looked up; his frown and her smile collided in midair; both exploded.

"Yes." Erica kept her voice even and clear. "It occurred to me that I could easily manage it if I got someone to come in two or three afternoons a week. Someone who could be here when Matilda and Jeffrey get home; and maybe she could do some of the cleaning and laundry too. A sort of housekeeper. Do you think that's a good idea?"

"No, not very," Brian replied. This was the wrong answer. He should have said, as he often did, that of course she could have help if she wanted it; whereupon she would have said, as she always did, that she wasn't sure she wanted to have any other woman taking care of her house and family.

"You know I don't like to have strangers in the house," Brian added.

"I know." Erica frowned; now he was saying her lines.

"Anyhow, we can't afford it."

This too was her line. Erica began to feel that she had decided against the job for Brian's reasons and not her own. After all, her first impulse had been toward it. If she were to back out now she would have wasted a lot of time and effort for nothing, except possibly to prove her own cowardice. Privately, she had thought of the job as a test: in a week she would be forty, and she had never earned money for anything except writing stories for children and drawing pictures and baby-sitting. She had a fine college record, but that was nearly twenty years ago, and she occasionally doubted that her intelligence had survived its long hibernation. "If I were working we could afford it," she said.

"I don't want strangers taking care of The Children," Brian announced, his tone capitalizing the noun like a honorific or divine title—which it was. Though they considered themselves agnostics, during the course of their marriage the Tates had worshiped several gods, of whom the most prominent were The Children. Like most divinities, they were served only intermittently. At certain moments, to express disrespect for The Children would have been blasphemy. At other times they were treated as ordinary beings called Muffy and Jeffo—and sometimes even (under the names Mouse and Pooch) as household pets.

Mouse, Pooch, Muffy and Jeffo had long ago left the house on Jones Creek Road, to be replaced by two disagreeable adolescents; but The Children remained. Public observance of the faith continued, though they were worshiped less frequently and more formally—mainly at religious holidays such as birthdays and Christmas, and during visits to and from relatives. That Brian should call upon them now seemed to Erica unfair. Still, if he could summon the old gods, so could she.

"Darling, strangers take care of The Children all day," she said in a clear soft reasonable voice. "Their teachers at school are strangers, as far as you're concerned," she added, alluding to the fact that Brian had declined to go to any PTA evenings for the past year.

"If one of their teachers wants to resign and come to work for us, that'll be fine," Brian said. "But you know the kind of person you'd be able to get."

"No."

"Some woman who can't find any other sort of job. Illiterate, undependable—very possibly sick in some way."

"Oh, I don't think— There must be women who—" Erica gasped, stopped, rallied her forces. "If we were worried about that, she could have a checkup. Of course we don't want Jeffrey or Matilda catching anything. She could go to Dr. Bunch."

"I didn't mean physically sick; though that's possible too I suppose. I meant in the head. The sort of person you're likely to find is going to, at the best, neglect The Children." Brian's voice was beginning to get tight, as if a heavy rubber band of the sort which propels toy fighter planes were being wound up in his throat. Erica knew that if the topic of conversation didn't change soon, he would take off. But she could not bring herself to change it.

"I don't see why—"

"I've explained to you why." Another twist of the rubber band. "I don't want you to take on an exhausting job, and I don't want you to hire anybody. I wouldn't be comfortable if I knew we were both away from home, and there was someone here who might hurt Matilda or Jeffrey, or burn down the house." Brian's voice was dangerously tight now, knotted.

"No, of course not. Neither would I." Erica beat off the implications of her husband's remark. "I think you're being a little ridiculous," she added, laughing. "I imagine I could manage not to hire a psychotic housekeeper."

"I'd rather be ridiculous than have to worry about The Children," Brian hissed. The plane had taken off; he was, in effect, whirring about the room now, his face pale and hard, his eyes glaring.

Erica cowered and flung up her arms. "Of course, if you feel that strongly about it," she bleated.

"I feel extremely strongly about it." The plane buzzed overhead once more, then cut its engines and returned to base. "You know that." Brian grinned at Erica—the conspiratorial, condescending grin of a moral victor.

"Yes." She smiled weakly and falsely back.

All the rest of that evening, and ever since, Erica has felt guilty. She has been exposed as selfish, greedy and thoughtless of her family's welfare: the sort of woman one cannot trust to do the right thing. Even though she has not taken a job, or hired a psychotic housekeeper, she has wanted to do so. Therefore she is, and will continue to be, in the wrong. Whatever she says or does, Brian's attitude implies, she will remain there.

Light steps on the front porch; a harmonic screech as the screen door is pulled back.

"Celia?"

"Hi." A wispily pretty little girl, with Danielle's brown complexion and Leonard's dark, sad, acute gaze, comes into the room. "Where's Mommy?"

"She and Roo had to take Pogo to the doctor. They'll be back soon."

"Is Pogo sick?" Celia asks, curiously rather than anxiously.

"No, she was in a fight with another dog."

"Oh. Can I have a chocolate milkshake?"

"I guess so." Erica gets up, follows Celia into the kitchen, and opens the refrigerator.

"You don't have to help me. I can do it myself," Celia says coolly, moving the milk and ice cream away from Erica along the counter.

"All right."

Erica had held Celia, then called Silly, on her lap when she had the mumps, feeding her orange sherbet by teaspoonfuls; she had taken her to her first county fair, her first puppet show. She had kissed and bandaged her cuts, scolded her for calling Roo a "fat hippotamiss," read aloud to her, bathed her, and shampooed her stubborn, wiry hair, so unlike Muffy's and Jeffo's. But since Leonard left, Celia has declined to be held by anyone; she reads to herself and bathes herself.

While Erica looks on, Celia measures milk, ice cream and cocoa mix carefully into the blender. She stands on tiptoe to do this, on thin legs like Leonard's, and lifts the heavy milk carton with thin brown arms. Celia lacks the animal solidity and strength of her mother and sister; Erica has worried sometimes that they would wear her out without noticing. In previous years she had

*8 0*

been glad that Leonard, whose energy was also mostly nervous, was around to prevent this.

Celia turns on the blender, counts aloud precisely to ten and turns it off as the contents foam up to the brim.

"You can have some too, if you want," she remarks.

"Oh, no thank you." Erica meets Celia's gaze; it has a wide, strained quality. "Well, all right—if you have enough."

"I made extra." With some difficulty, Celia pours the milkshake into two glasses, and then back and forth between them until the level is exactly even. She sets the glasses on the kitchen table and climbs onto a stool opposite Erica.

"Is it good?" she asked presently.

"Very good," Erica replies. Across the table, they look at each other awkwardly, like polite estranged lovers meeting after a long separation.

"Is Muffy coming over?"

"Not today," Erica apologizes. In the years when Muffy and Roo were best friends they had made rather a pet of Celia. She always had the baby's part when they played house, the favorite serving-maid's part when they played kings and queens. But Matilda no longer "plays" with anyone, and Roo has other pets. "She's at home listening to her records," Erica adds. "That's about all she does lately." She laughs to suggest that they both understand how ridiculous this is.

Celia sucks out the last of her milkshake with a small noise and sets the glass down. "Lennie likes records," she says in a high, childish version of Leonard's voice. "When he comes home he always plays them."

"I know." During the final and most disagreeable months of the Zimmerns' marriage, Leonard had taken to putting on one of his records at top volume almost as soon as he entered the house, drowning out whatever Danielle and the children might want to say to him. It was among those of his actions which Erica privately most disliked. Another was his recent request that Celia and Roo should call him "Lennie" instead of "Dad."

Celia tilts her head and rests her cheek on her fist—one of Danielle's gestures. "Lennie was here," she remarks.

"I heard that," Erica says, consciously refraining from adding that it was nice.

"He brought me a model of the Transparent Man, but I couldn't put it together. It was too hard."

"That's a shame." This time Erica speaks with feeling, recalling accusations Danielle has made against her former husband: that his mind is cold, analytic and destructively critical; that he is only interested in finding out how people work, not in knowing or loving them—that he wants to see everyone, in fact, as a Transparent Man. Also, that he was disappointed Silly hadn't been a boy, and is trying to turn her into one; that he wants her to become as cold, analytic and critical as himself. "What happened to it?"

"Lennie came over, and he put it together."

"That's nice," Erica lies. She looks at Celia—at her wide full mouth, so like Danielle's, but contradicted by Leonard's suspicious, heavy-lashed eyes—and thinks how unfair it is that people who have grown to thoroughly dislike each other, and have separated by mutual consent, nevertheless remain united in their innocent children, in whom the warring elements are fused forever.

"Do you want to see it?" Celia slides off the stool and moves nearer. "It's up in my room."

"No thank you. I don't like models of the insides of things much." I don't like Leonard much, Erica hears herself say. Celia hears it too, very likely; she takes a step away. I used to like him, Erica thinks as they look at each other. You remember that, and you want me to like him now because nobody else in this house does; but I can't. I can't like what he has done to you, and to Roo and Danielle. I can't forget that he has deserted you.

Yes, Erica thinks; but that's not all. Since Leonard left, Celia has also been deserted by Danielle, who now works full time. She has been deserted by Roo and Matilda, who no longer play with her or each other. And because they don't play together, Danielle and I meet when they are in school. Therefore I, who once saw Silly nearly every day, have in effect also deserted her.

It hadn't been conscious, deliberate—but meeting Silly's eyes now, Erica feels terrible and guilty. She wants to apologize for the past year; to hug her; to cry even. But she is afraid to touch Celia; afraid to embarrass them both. Besides, what apology can she reasonably make?

"There's Mommy and Roo." Celia turns her head, then runs out of the room. Erica, more slowly, follows.

"Hello! How's Pogo?" she asks the sturdy girl in torn jeans and an old T-shirt who has just come into the house. She is carrying in her arms a large brown and white dog of indeterminate breed somewhere between spaniel and beagle, with drooping ears and one leg heavily bandaged.

"She's going to be all right." Roo bends over the sofa and tenderly lowers Pogo onto it, adjusting pillows around her. "She was very, very brave."

"Whew." Danielle lets the screen bang shut behind her. "What an afternoon! Hi, Erica. It was great of you to come over . . . Hello, ducky. How was the cartoon show? . . . That's good . . . Roo, I don't want Pogo on the sofa . . . Come on, now; you know the rule."

"But she's wounded. This is an emergency." Roo shifts from beside Pogo to a defensive position between the dog and her mother, spreading her arms protectively.

"The emergency is over." Danielle moves toward the sofa.

"Pogo has a sprained leg and eight stitches, and you don't even care," Roo says, pushing her heavy red-brown braid back over her shoulder, and setting her jaw. "You hate Pogo. I bet even if she was dead you wouldn't let her lie on your stupid sofa."

"I wouldn't let any dead dog lie on my sofa," Danielle replies. "Come on, Roo. Why don't you take Pogo up to your room? She probably wants to sleep now, after all that. She looks kind of groggy to me, and we'll just keep her awake . . . That's right . . . God. What I need now is some sherry. Erica?"

"We were lucky," Danielle says presently, as she sits where Pogo has just lain, holding a glass of her favorite golden California sherry—which Leonard, a wine snob, had always refused to have in the house. "I was scared to drive Pogo out to the kennel, she was bleeding so much, so we rushed her up to the vet school. You can't imagine what a mess she was. Not only the blood, but she was so dirty; and panting and whining, obviously in bad pain. As soon as they saw her they sent us into an examining room, and this really nice vet came in, a big bald red-faced man. Roo was howling too, she thought Pogo was going to bleed to death and she didn't want to leave, so he let us both stay and help . . . He joked with us, kidding Roo, and telling me about how he'd just fixed up a prize Pekinese who'd got into bad company. Her owner was frantic that she'd have unpedigreed pups. Apparently abortions are already legal for dogs, did you know that?"

"They get better medical care now than people do, Brian says."

"Could be. That vet reminded me of what doctors were like when I was a kid; he had that same great calm, slow, patient manner. Now of course they're all computers, ticking out a diagnosis as fast as possible and on to the next case."

"Like Dr. Bunch."

"Exactly like Bunch. But this guy, the minute he took hold of Pogo she stopped whining; she knew it was going to be all right. 'You poor bitch,' he said to her. 'You got the worst of it in that fight, eh?' He went on talking to her all the time he was cleaning her cuts and stitching them up, explaining what he was doing and what a brave girl she was. I thought, it's really funny—he's treating Pogo like a person, and when I go to Bunch he treats me like an animal."

"Dr. Bunch never tells anyone anything. He doesn't talk to you at all if he can help it."

"That's right. But what's worse is that he never listens to you. I don't know why everybody goes to him. I only wish we had a GP in town like that vet, whatever his name was."

"Dr. Bernard M. Kotelchuk," says Roo, who has just come downstairs.

Erica laughs. "Really?"

"That's his name. I saw it on a sign in the office. He's going to come next week and see my turtles." Roo falls solidly into a chair.

"I wouldn't count on it," her mother suggests.

"Why not? I asked him, and he said he'd like to come. He's very interested in turtles." She sits forward belligerently. "Don't you think Dr. Kotelchuk is a person of integrity?"

"I'm sure he's a person of integrity. But he might be too busy to come." Danielle sets down her glass and looks at her daughter. "Roo, your shirt! You look as if you'd been in a fight yourself. You'd better go and take everything off. Put the jeans and shirt in cold water in the bathroom sink, to soak out those bloodstains. How is Pogo?"

"She's asleep on my bed." Roo stands up.

"And you might as well take a bath too."

"I don't need one. I had a shower last night, and a bath the night before, and the night before that."

"Okay . . . what a relief Lennie's going back to New York," she adds after Roo has clumped upstairs. "I should be over it by now, but every time he comes I get uptight about having the house picked up and the kids clean. 'Civilized people bathe themselves every day,' he says." Danielle imitates her husband's precise, cool diction.

"Mm," Erica assents, not adding that she shares this view. Danielle too, in her opinion, could have used a bath and clean clothes. Her red Mexican cotton dress is badly wrinkled; her brown feet stained with dirt.

Danielle's slovenliness is a recent development. Like her house, she has altered since Leonard left, and in some of the same ways. There is less of her—nearly ten pounds less—and what remains is more untidy. The elaborate, almost European elegance she had gone in for during her marriage—the silk blouses and lace-patterned stockings, the smoothly shining constructions of hair, as carefully braided and rolled as French pastry—is gone. Danielle still looks European, but no longer in the style of the aristocracy. Now she wears bright, heavy, embroidered peasant dresses; her legs are bare and often unshaven; her hair is roughly held back by a leather thong. It is as if, lacking a man's love, her sense of her own value has decreased. But this is an uncomfortable thought; Erica puts it aside and tries to attend to what her best friend is saying.

"—in his new place on West Fourth Street he's got a built-in kitchen and everything organized. His ideal environment." Danielle laughs briefly and pours herself more sherry.

"Brian says there's only one room, not much larger than this," Erica reminds her comfortingly. "And no view. Just a brick wall."

"Yeh, he complains about that. He always looks on the down side, especially around here of course; he doesn't want me to get envious. I'm supposed to feel sorry for him and think how hard his life is." She laughs again harshly. "But he's pretty well suited. He never could take being responsible for a whole house. And you know the yard drove him nuts. As soon as he got it in order something would start growing and fuck it up again."

"I remember how cross he was about Matildy and Roo playing with the gravel, getting it into the grass."

"Yeh. He never liked living with children. I think that's the real reason he left."

"Mm." Over the past fifteen months Danielle has put forward many possible real reasons for Leonard's departure. When she does so her voice becomes rough, her language coarsens; but her eyes—wide, brown, damp—give her away. In spite of everything she is still, as Jeffrey or Matilda would put it, hung up on him. Erica imagines Leonard as a free-standing metal coatrack of the type placed by Corinth University in the corners of offices. She visualizes Danielle, hung up on one of the raised metal arms by the back of the neck of her red dress, the yoke of which is embroidered with yellow birds and flowers; Danielle has hung there, swearing and sweating, kicking and struggling to get down, for a year and a half. Erica feels thankful that she has never been in that position.

"—and of course he loves living in Manhattan, but he complains all the time how expensive it is and how much better off we are here. He'd like to cut down on what he's sending us. Or stop it entirely."

"He wouldn't do that," Erica says.

"Don't kid yourself." Danielle leans forward, putting her empty glass down on Leonard's teak coffee table, now marked with overlapping rings. "Men will do anything they can get away with. And in this society they can get away with a hell of a lot. Look at my husband." Though their divorce is over a year old, Danielle still speaks of Leonard as her husband. "Nobody thinks the worse of him for taking his family to the middle of nowhere and then deserting them. If I'd left the girls and Lennie here in Corinth and gone back to New York by myself, everyone would say I was very irresponsible, immature and selfish—if not sick." Danielle laughs. "Oh, well." She leans back into the soft, dusty pillows of the sofa, resting her head on one raised brown arm and putting her dirty brown feet up on the coffee table. "So how's everything at your house?"

"All right, I guess," Erica lies.

"Did you go back to see about the job yet?"

"No. I called and told them I couldn't take it. Brian's so set against the idea, it didn't seem worth arguing about it any more. And it's not as if I were absolutely dying to do library research."

"No." Danielle frowns. "But you did want a job. After all, it's the principle of the thing."

"Oh, don't say that." Erica giggles sadly. "That's what Brian says. He thinks it was very underhanded and thoughtless of me to go looking for work without consulting him first. It makes him feel he can't trust me."

"It makes *him* feel he can't trust *you*," Danielle mutters with emotion. "That's really—" She swallows and is silent.

Since she has never told Danielle of Brian's untrustworthiness, Erica looks at her friend with surprise. Apparently, news of Brian's behavior last spring has somehow reached her. She hesitates, doubting whether she should admit it now. After all, the affair with Wendee is in the past; she is trying to forget it, and has partly forgotten it. Danielle too says nothing; she folds her arms and looks out the window, visibly setting her jaw. Presumably she thinks Erica is ignorant of what Brian has done; that she remains a pitiable dupe. But Erica has no wish to support this character in addition to that of betrayed wife.

"I didn't know you knew about all that," she therefore says finally.

"I didn't know you knew. Oh, shit. I'm sorry."

"That's all right." Erica smiles weakly.

"Here, have another drink." Danielle slops sherry into Erica's glass. "I only just heard this week," she apologizes. "I thought about calling you, but then I thought, Well, hell, how do I know it's true, I didn't see it." Her usually strong voice wavers.

"Of course, I understand," Erica says, touched—and rather proud to realize that her friend is more upset now than she.

"How did you hear about it?" Danielle asks.

"I found a letter the girl wrote to him."

"Then it is true."

"Yes." Erica smiles again, conscious of doing so bravely. "He admitted it."

"You know I really didn't believe it." Danielle sighs. "I mean, it just didn't sound like the sort of thing Brian would do. He's always been so moral, so righteous."

"I know." Erica sees that she has been wrong. Danielle is too loyal to blame her or think less of her for Brian's unfaithfulness. She could have told her story sooner.

"And I didn't figure he would ever take up with a girl like that, either. Do you know her?"

"No." Erica shakes her head. "I never saw her." She does not add that she had looked for Wendee all last spring whenever she was on campus—or rather, that she had looked for a beautiful young blonde. Several times she thought she had located the right person, and managed to ask her name; but she had always been wrong. (Actually Erica had seen Wendy often on campus, and once sat at the next table to hers in the coffee shop, without noticing her, for she was not anywhere near pretty enough to be the Wendee she imagined. And Wendy, who did not expect to see Erica on campus and was not looking for her, had not noticed Erica.) Since June, when Brian told her that Wendy had left town, she had ceased to look.

"She's nothing special. One of those moon-faced girls with sad blue eyes and stringy bleached hair. Honestly, I was surprised."

"It is surprising," Erica says, frowning so hard her head begins to hurt. Obviously something is wrong, either with Danielle's information or with Brian's description of Wendee. Love is supposed to be myopic, but not that myopic; and anyhow Brian has always denied being in love. This means, what?

"When I saw her having coffee Thursday I thought, What a dumb-looking girl."

"You saw her Thursday," Erica says, choosing the words as if out of a barrel of live wet crabs which her best friend had just proffered to her.

"Yeh. In the Blue Cow."

Erica's head begins to hurt more, especially toward the back; to vibrate like the electronic music on Jeffrey's records. Among the vibrations is one which announces to her that Brian has begun another scummy affair, this time with an ugly girl. It is the new affair of which Danielle has heard.

"Who told you about it?" she asks through the electronic static.

"Oh, it was one of our TAs; Gail Farber her name is. She's kind of a chatterer. We were having coffee, and this girl came in. Gail waved to her—she knows her from the Krishna Bookshop— and then she told us who she was." Danielle's voice is apologetic, warm with sympathy.

"What else did she say?"

"Nothing else. Of course she didn't know I'm a friend of yours."

"Did she tell you the girl's name?"

"I don't think so. She said she was a graduate student in psychology. Hey!" Danielle bounces forward. "You know what I think? I think the actual reason Brian doesn't want you to work for Barclay is that he's in the psych department. He's afraid you'll meet this girl, or hear something about her. Hell, I'm positive that's it." The temperature of her voice has risen to a rolling boil.

"I never thought of that," Erica says falteringly, staring around the living room. "But I guess you might be right."

"What a lousy trick. Hey, I'm really sorry." Danielle puts her hand on Erica's arm, a comforting gesture.

"That's all right." Erica shifts nervously, causing her friend's hand to fall off; she dislikes being touched, and hates to be pitied, which always implies to her that she is pitiable. "I suppose everybody in that department knows by now," she says. "I suppose even Barclay knows."

"Oh, I don't think so, he—"

"Probably he knew when he interviewed me." In contrast to Danielle's, her tone is cool, even cold. The words seem to fall onto the Oriental rug like invisible lumps of ice.

"I'm sure he didn't. He's not the type to hear gossip. He's never been friendly with students, as far as I know."

"Mm." Erica does not want to enter into a discussion of Mr. Barclay's social contacts. Her vehement wish is to get out of Danielle's living room and be alone to think. "Listen," she says. "What time is it? . . . I'd better get home, B—" (she suppresses the name, unvoiced) "—the children will be wondering what's happened to me."

And what has happened to me? Erica thinks as she walks with her headache along the uneven sidewalk in the direction of her car, a block away. Danielle's street is near the university, and dominated by two large fraternity houses; there is always a parking problem. The curb is lined with dented metal and stained plastic cans, overflowing with the week's offal. There are also paper bags full of bottles and beer cans, and bundles of rain-sodden newspapers tied with string. In front of one fraternity a maroon overstuffed chair, badly spotted, lies on its side vomiting kapok— apparently a casualty of last night's brawl. Garbage, Erica thinks. Litter, pollution, filth.

Walking through the muggy afternoon, she thinks that she had believed the filth was gone, that she had begun to forget it; and now it has appeared again, and worse; much worse. She had thought that by casually and lovelessly screwing a pretty girl Brian had polluted and dishonored their marriage as much as he possibly could. But she was wrong. Now he has gone further in dishonor— he is screwing an ugly girl. He has become unclean, revolting—like that can there, tipped over and spewing out beer bottles and old bones.

Litter and lies. Danielle was right: Brian has concealed his real reasons for not wanting Erica to work in the psychology department. He has invented false arguments and spoken of The Children, pretending a false concern for their welfare, blaming her for lacking concern. And even that evening last week, when she agreed not to take the job, and he put his arms gently around her, and stroked her back smoothly the way she likes, and called her "princess," he was lying, lying. Erica feels dizzy with rage and grief; she stumbles on the broken sidewalk and puts one hand on the nearest object—a telephone pole, stained dark-brown and with a numbered aluminum label nailed to it—to steady herself. He had pulled off her shoes gently, one at a time, and said— But this is too much to bear thinking of; Erica takes a breath, lets go of the telephone pole, and walks on.

To protect his ugly, trashy affair, Brian has lied and manipulated her into giving up something she really wanted to do, and needed to do. Then, instead of thanking her for her generosity, he has blamed her for having even thought of it. He has shamed and bullied her; he has managed to make it appear that wanting to hire a housekeeper and take an ordinary part-time job, something thousands of women in America do, is selfish and reprehensible. Again, just as last spring, she has been maneuvered into the wrong; into a deep moral hole.

Turning the corner, Erica sights her car next to another heap of rubbish. It is a shiny bulging tan station wagon which Brian bought last spring, and which she has not yet been able to get used to. It is slow to start, clumsy to drive—and impossible to parallel-park; after trying on one memorable occasion, Leonard Zimmern had named it The Jar of Peanut Butter. Erica, who does most of the daily driving, recently suggested that they might trade it in for a smaller car, like Danielle's Peugeot. This had infuriated Brian, who is suspicious of all foreign goods, and opposed to their purchase on economic grounds. If she didn't like the car, why hadn't she said so before he bought it?—i.e., before she knew. Then Brian had delivered a lecture on responsibility for one's choices and the balance of trade, which ended as usual lately with Erica dug farther down into her moral hole. It is very disagreeable and unattractive there, and Erica knows that she herself is becoming rapidly more disagreeable and unattractive, like most prisoners.

But now, this afternoon, a ladder has been lowered into the hole, and she can climb out. Yes. It is Brian who is guilty now; it is Brian who can be exposed. Erica stands with her hand on the door of the station wagon, thinking hard through her headache. She must climb carefully; she must remember what happened last time, how Brian had eventually turned his guilt into hers. She must be armed against every possible counterattack. She must stay cool and not expose her own weakness—no sobbing this time, no passionate jealousy; no accusations without evidence.

But what evidence has she? Frowning, Erica gets into the hot Jar of Peanut Butter, slides behind the wheel, and slams the heavy door. When she confronts him Brian may deny everything. He may put on his professional manner and say that her accusation is not based on historical evidence, but on malicious secondhand or

*9 2*

thirdhand gossip. He may accuse her, and Danielle, and Danielle's acquaintance, of being malicious, suspicious, credulous women.

She turns the ignition key; the engine, as usual, roars once boastfully and dies. Suppose she is in fact suspicious and credulous. For a moment Erica considers this possibility, and what she feels is not relief. She sees her ladder being pulled up, up, out of the moral hole. If Brian is not guilty, she is as deep in the wrong as ever; and she will be in even deeper if she accuses him falsely. Though she does not yet quite put it to herself in these words, she wants him guilty.

*Arroor, roor, rr* . . . Again the motor gives out. The air in the automobile is hot and thick; the plastic brocade of the seat feels sticky against Erica's thighs, and the wheel is warm and damp. What she needs is more time, more ammunition: she needs to wait and watch Brian, to stockpile evidence and gather her forces before she attacks. There will not be too long to wait, Erica judges; and meanwhile she will have the satisfaction of knowing that whatever Brian may do or say, she is in the right again—triumphantly and thoroughly in the right.

**5**

It is late October. The high winds have begun to blow and the trees to change color and fall apart, and everything in Brian's life is changing color and falling apart and going wrong. His colleagues, against his advice, are altering graduate requirements; his students, against his advice, are altering their consciousnesses—in both cases for the worse. Constantly—at lunch in the faculty club, in class, even in committee meetings—arguments about national or campus politics replace discussions of the matter at hand. The war in Southeast Asia is escalating, and Jones Creek is polluted with detergent.

At home too everything is falling apart. Most obviously the children, whose early adolescent rebellion, instead of running its course, has been escalating. In the past Brian has usually been able to ignore their behavior, but recent changes in his and their schedules have made this impossible. For years he has had no early classes, and therefore has been able to rise and eat breakfast peacefully after Jeffrey and Matilda have left for school. This term he has a nine o'clock. Moreover, the children have now succeeded, after a prolonged and disagreeable contest, in having their bedtime advanced to ten on weekday nights and eleven on weekends. This means that they are always around when he is home; that the radio and/or phonograph is always on, the best chairs in the sitting room occupied, the refrigerator door left hanging open, and the sink full of dirty dishes. Rational protests and attempts at serious discussion of the principles of family living seem to have less and less effect, and Erica is apparently completely unable to cope.

Things have got to the point where there is not just a conflict of generations at the Tates', but a condition of total war. Hostilities begin when Jeffrey and Matilda wake at seven a.m. and continue throughout the day.

This morning it was Jeffrey who started it; he could not find his left sneaker. Explosions of shouting and cursing; banging of doors and drawers above; Erica leaving Brian's breakfast on the stove to run up two flights and scuffle among the foul debris in Jeffrey's closet; two fried eggs rusted to the pan.

Meanwhile Matilda attacked passively, by not getting out of bed. When she finally appeared in the kitchen, after prolonged bombardment, she was dressed for battle. She had recently dyed her hair (and the bathroom wash basin) a vivid and ugly salmon-pink, and was wearing purple flowered bell-bottom jeans and a boy's skimpy sleeveless undershirt, stretched vulgarly taut by her developing breasts. She stood by the sink cramming jam toast into her mouth and exchanging insults with her father, mother and brother. When it was time to leave for school she pretended not to be able to find her social-studies book; Jeffrey simultaneously announced a rent in his jacket.

After the last door had slammed behind them Brian sat down at the kitchen table, already exhausted, though it was only eight a.m. The angry voices of his wife and children rang in his head still, and all around the room, like the echo of bombs and flak, along with his own angry voice:

"I can't find my fucking shoe, that's why!"
"Aw Dad, don't be disgusting. I haven't got time to change. Can't you leave me alone for once?"

"There's some awful stink in here. If you burned something, I'm not going to eat it."

"What's this crap?"
"Hey, Matildy, you really look grungy today."
"Oh, why don't you blast off?"
"Screw you."
"Asshole."
"Shit."

"What's the matter up there, for God's sake?"
"Do you really have to shout like that?"
"All right, Jeffrey. Pick up that disgusting piece of toast you dropped on the floor."
"You'll miss the bus! And don't think I'm going to drive you to school this time. You can walk."

Brian and Erica, like their friends, students and colleagues, have spent considerable time trying to understand and halt the war in Vietnam. If he were to draw a parallel between it and the war now going on in his house, he would have unhesitatingly identified with the South Vietnamese. He would have said that the conflict, begun a year or so ago as a minor police action, intended only to preserve democratic government and maintain the status quo—a preventive measure, really—has escalated steadily and disastrously against his and Erica's wishes, and in spite of their earnest efforts to end it. For nearly two years, he would point out, the house on Jones Creek Road has been occupied territory. Jeffrey and Matilda have gradually taken it over, moving in troops and supplies, depleting natural resources and destroying the local culture.

From the younger Tates' position, however, the parallel is reversed. Brian and Erica are the invaders: the large, brutal, callous Americans. They are vastly superior in material resources and military experience, which makes the war deeply unfair; and they have powerful allies like the Corinth Public School System. The current position of Jeffrey and Matilda is, from their own viewpoint, almost tragic. In spite of their innate superiority and their wish for self-government, they remain dependent on Erican aid and Brian Tate's investments. Worse still in some ways is the barrage of propaganda and lies they have to endure. Brian and Erica keep insisting publicly that they are not trying to destroy Jeffrey or Matilda, but instead fighting to preserve the best, the most enlightened and democratic elements within them. When they hear these lies, the younger Tates naturally feel exploited and furious. They refuse to negotiate, and retreat into the jungles of their rooms on the third floor, where they plan guerrilla attacks.

Brian and Erica are at a moral and psychological disadvantage in the war because they want to save face both at home and abroad. They have been favored by environment and heredity, and wish to think themselves worthy of their good fortune. They therefore desire (against all reason) to enjoy the affection, respect and gratitude of the people they are at war with and whose territory they have invaded; and they never cease to be deeply hurt and indignant that they are not receiving this affection, etc.

Externally too Brian and Erica have a reputation to uphold. For many years they have been generally regarded, and have regarded themselves, as democratic peace- and freedom-loving persons, devoted to decent and humanitarian goals. So great was their need to preserve this reputation that they had never declared war officially, but continued to speak of the conflict as a peace-keeping effort and to insist that they were acting in an advisory capacity. Nevertheless, the true facts are widely known, and have earned them the bad opinion of the rest of their world—including that of other parents who are currently engaged in their own undeclared wars.

Jeffrey and Matilda, on the other hand, do not have to worry about public opinion. They know they are right. They know that any belligerent action they might undertake will be applauded by their contemporaries, some of whom have already gone even further in terms of overt hostility. The magazines they read, the songs they hear, their whole culture supports them. Even on the enemy side there are many who dare to take their part, repudiating natural adult allegiances in the cause of revolution and truth.

As yet, Brian has won most of the pitched battles; but the effort of winning is exhausting his resources, and he knows it. He knows that time is against him, and he cannot win the war. Even now his victories are all negative ones: he has, once more, beaten off an attack on some stronghold, or contained the enemy within the existing combat zone. He can, for example, wearily congratulate himself on the fact that his children do not—as far as he knows—steal cars or bomb buildings or inject themselves with drugs; that they have not got themselves arrested by the police yet, or pregnant. Sometimes Brian wishes they had done so; then at least they would be somewhere else—in jail or an unwed-mothers' home—and someone else would be responsible for them.

What makes the war most exhausting for Brian now is that his ally, Erica, has deserted him. She has declared, not so much verbally as by her recent actions, that she cannot fight any more, that she is giving up the effort. This defection seems to him profoundly unjust; even dishonorable. For years the Tates' domestic life has been governed according to the principle of separation of powers: Erica functioning as the executive branch, and Brian as the legislative and judicial. He has always left it to her to supervise the children in everyday matters. Now when—possibly as a consequence of her management—the children have grown into selfish, rude, rebellious adolescents, she resigns and declares that it is his turn. Which is as if the President and his Cabinet should abdicate and turn over the task of suppressing a colonial revolt to Congress and the Supreme Court.

Under normal circumstances Brian would not have permitted this. But circumstances are not normal; Erica is not normal. For the last six weeks especially she has been behaving in a very abnormal way. She is alternately watchful and abstracted; curious about his work and openly bored by it; overtalkative and silent. In bed she feels peculiar: half stiff, half limp; she comes late with a wrench and an angry cry, or does not come at all. She appears on campus at odd times of day with no explanation, and serves supper up to half an hour late with no excuse. It has not occurred to Brian that his wife suspects him of having an affair, since he cannot imagine she would keep silent about that. What he fears is that she is coming down with a mental illness; and since yesterday, Wednesday, he has feared it more.

On Tuesdays and Fridays, Brian has lunch with Wendy in her Collegetown apartment; on Mondays and Thursdays with his colleagues at the Faculty Club. On Wednesdays, however, he has a class until one-fifteen followed by a committee meeting at two. He therefore buys coffee from the machine in the basement, and Erica packs his lunch (sandwich, fruit, and cake or cookies) in a brown paper bag. At the same time she also packs lunch boxes for the children, washes the breakfast dishes, sweeps the kitchen, and takes out the trash—the bottles and papers and cans to one container, the garbage, in a paper bag, to another.

This Wednesday after his class, Brian returned to the office accompanied by a radical graduate student named Davidoff who had proposed a dubious project for his seminar paper. While outlining his objections to this project Brian sat down at his desk, uncovered his container of coffee, and upended his paper bag. Instead of lunch, what fell out onto the blotter was a heap of coffee grounds, crushed eggshells, orange rinds, crusts of toast stained with jelly, and soggy Frosted Flakes.

"Hey, wow!" Davidoff exclaimed, laughing good-naturedly. "Is that your lunch?"

Equally annoying, and perhaps more disturbing, was Erica's reaction that evening. She seemed to be aware only of the humor of the incident and not of what it implied about her own state of mind. "It was a mistake, that's all," she kept saying, obviously suppressing an impulse to laugh as Davidoff had done, but more ill-naturedly.

"You already said that," he told her. "What I was asking you is why you should make that sort of mistake. What it means."

"What could it mean?" Erica stopped smiling and looked at Brian in what seemed to him a disturbed way.

"Well, that you were disturbed, or unconsciously angry at me."

"Why should I be angry at you?" Erica's tone was ambiguous; for a moment he imagined she knew everything. Fortunately, he was not startled enough to lose the offensive.

"I couldn't say. What concerns me is—" and he went on to list other failings of Erica's which concerned him. But her question has remained hanging in the air ever since, half visible, like a cobweb. It is hanging there now. Suppose she does know, Brian thinks, only she doesn't know he thinks she knows. But then, why doesn't she tell him she knows? If she doesn't know, then her behavior is crazy. Unless of course she is still angry about what she does know, about last spring. Should he admit that he knows this? Brian blinks; he feels as if spiders were at work in his head, spinning sticky gray webs of conjecture from point to point. Or are they in Erica's head?

But these spiders are not the most serious of Brian's troubles this morning. His doubts about his wife's mental condition, the dislike he feels for his children, and his professional irritations and disappointments, all are as nothing today to the problem of Wendy Gahaghan.

To put it briefly, Wendy has recently become preoccupied with the idea of bearing a child—preferably Brian's child. She mentioned this interest at first casually, some weeks ago, in reply to a compliment from him: "Yeah, they're all right—only I sort of wish they were bigger." She smiled confidingly. "When I have a baby, I'm going to breast-feed it for six months at least—that makes your boobs grow, you know." A week later the theme recurred: "Gail says if it wasn't for the population problem she and Danny would have five or six kids. I can groove on that, you know? I mean if you love somebody you naturally want to have as many kids with them as you can; like I'd like to have kids with you."

This remark made Brian uneasy; apprehensive. As a form of

insurance, he told Wendy that he sincerely hoped her friends weren't planning to become parents at once; he elaborated upon the harm which was so often done to society, to their children and to themselves by people who reproduced irresponsibly, before they were economically or emotionally mature. Ecologically speaking, it was just littering—in every sense.

And then finally on Friday, when they last met—and at a very intimate moment: "You know, it's funny how things work out, with heredity. I mean I was thinking just the other day, if you and I had a baby, what it would look like." Brian refused to speculate on the appearance of this hypothetical infant. "I don't know, and I don't ever want to know," he said. Drawing back, he looked at Wendy's smooth, slightly convex belly uneasily, imagining it inflate before his eyes like a pale balloon. "That'd be the end of everything. Anyhow, you don't want to think about babies now, your job is to think about finishing graduate school," he added, smiling uselessly, for Wendy had turned her face away. "Okay?"

A silence.

"Okay," Wendy finally replied, turning back, also smiling. But her smile was not very happy, Brian recalls, and she left soon afterward. Probably he had hurt her feelings.

He had realized this even then, and planned to straighten things out when they next met on Tuesday; but there was an unexpected department meeting. He called the apartment that morning, something he always dislikes doing, and as he feared got only Wendy's roommate. He left a brief, perhaps brusque message —no doubt hurting Wendy's feelings again, for she has not called back. It is now Thursday noon, and she has still not called, nor come around to the office.

What he has to explain to Wendy is that his reaction to her baby fantasy was not meant to hurt, but was natural, automatic. He is too old to have any more children (indeed, he sometimes thinks, too old to bear the ones he already has). But if Wendy has daydreams of becoming a mother, that too is only natural. He has daydreams himself: imagining himself nationally recognized as a political analyst; called to New York or Washington, legally and financially free to enjoy life there; to meet someone perhaps, in certain respects, like Wendy. He has entertained these fantasies as often as Wendy hers, and more foolishly—for she will presumably have children someday, but he will never be famous or free. He will have to sit in this same office until he retires, legally and financially bound to Corinth University and to three people toward whom he feels almost nothing now but obligation: a woman who hates him and is having a nervous collapse, and two revolting (in both senses) adolescents. It is the bitterness of this, perhaps, which made him speak hastily to Wendy, whose life is not over. He admits it. He spoke hastily to her, and harshly.

All right, Brian thinks. I hurt Wendy's feelings. It is up to me to apologize, to point out that I felt no revulsion from her maternal fantasies, only a practical concern that they should not become reality yet. What I should do now is call her up and explain this.

Brian looks at the telephone on his desk, but does not lift it. It is noon, and Wendy is probably at home; but so, unfortunately, is her roommate, Linda Sliski—a skinny, long-haired girl with large hands and feet and a breathy manner, who sometimes trips on mind-expanding drugs. Brian regards Linda with wariness and antipathy, both because of what he knows about her and because of what she knows about him. Wendy insists that Linda is really straight and loyal, that she would never cop out, but he is not convinced. He has a recurrent dread that on one of her trips Linda's mind will expand so far that his name will leak out through the cracks.

Brian avoids Linda whenever possible. If he sees her approaching him on campus he turns onto another path, climbs unnecessary stairs, or abruptly enters the nearest building. In closed spaces such as the coffee shop, he either pretends not to notice Linda or gives her a rapid, hearty "Hello" and moves off as fast as possible. At his earnest request, Wendy has so arranged it that Linda is always out of the apartment when he comes to lunch.

*102*

He feels a suspicious dislike of even speaking to her, however briefly, on the telephone.

Frowning, tightening his face, Brian decides to wait until tomorrow, when he will see Wendy, and not to worry about it meanwhile. Yet when he stops in the department office on his way to lunch and recognizes her handwriting on an envelope among the junk mail in his box, his facial muscles loosen in relief.

"Good news, I hope?" asks Helen Wells, the department secretary, observing this relaxation.

"No, just advertisements and bills," replies Brian. Smiling, he takes his mail back upstairs to read in the privacy of his office, opening it, as always, in reverse order of interest.

Now At Last FUNK AND WHANG PUBLICATIONS Bring You What You As An Educator Have Been Asking For . . .

Dear Friend of American Liberties: On May 16 of this year C. Daniel Farber was arrested following an alleged sit-in and destruction of property at the Clinton County Draft Board. His bail was set at . . .

Dear Brain—
I guess maybe this is the last letter I will ever write you which kind of blows my mind because I figured I would write you and rap with you the rest of my life. Which maybe wasn't saying so much.

The end of everything as you so firmly said so I'm splitting as you know, and want. I would have dug discussing what it means that it happened, getting into why and how but when I tried to bring up the topic I got such bad vibes from you I couldn't hack it. Like Professor Frankel said I have sometimes the difficulty in expression. My hangup. I was too psyched yesterday when you didn't come to take a chance on calling or going to see you in case I might like start screaming and really freak out, which was why I didn't as undoubtedly you know because you know everything. It took me until this morning to stop being childish and personal and laying the blame on you which was a copout because we both knew and said from the beginning that if I got knocked up it was my responsibility or as it turned out irresponsibility. Anyhow I have to cope now. I got pretty flaky waiting for you to call but finally I accepted that you weren't going to, that you had decided. If you know everything then you must be right it would have hurt worse to lay it on the line although I still can't visualize how anything could hurt worse.

I was going to disappear silently like WHOOSH Away Soil and Toil on the TV only I was afraid (and Linda agrees) that if I did you might have some doubts later and get racked up which would be a bad development because the whole idea is for Brain Not To Be Hassled, to be always and more and more calm and productive and together—as much as anybody can be in this American Century—granted that. And to finish your book which will be a beautiful child for you and the world. Don't regret anything not ever I don't. I wanted to love completely and give my whole self to you and I got my wish not the way I thought but that's how it is with wishes. Zed says we all live many different lives and this one is over for me that's all. I want to say besides, think of me some cold afternoons in your office but I know that's an ego trip. Don't think of me just remember how important what you are writing is and now nothing can get between you and it anymore. And take care of yourself.

                                        yours yours yours yours yours

Brian's first reaction to this document is bewilderment, followed, as he reads on, by great vexation of spirit. How can Wendy have become pregnant? Supposedly, she is on the pill; "what it means that it happened" therefore is that she has lost her balance and carelessly, stupidly, fallen off the pill. Next he is angry at his own stupidity, for not having foreseen this, prevented it; then again at her for not having told him, for having been so stupidly inarticulate.

But after all, Wendy admits these faults. He reads her letter over again and is struck by her admission of weakness, her acceptance of responsibility, her generous refusal to blame or involve him. Believing that he knew what had happened, she has waited for him to speak. Since he has not, she accepts it. Without asking for anything, without making a scene, she declares her intention of leaving town, presumably to seek an abortion ("I have to cope now").

For a moment he considers allowing the misunderstanding to continue, accepting her generosity silently and letting her go—but only for a moment. To do that would be both morally and practically indefensible—both bad government and bad politics.

Besides, he wants to see her. He must see her, must clear up the misunderstanding, assure himself of her emotional stability and continuing discretion, assure her of his continuing affection, his emotional and moral support— And his practical support. Legal operations cost a lot of money; illegal ones, not covered by Blue Cross, cost even more. Brian can afford to replace Blue Cross, and it is right that he should do so.

Lifting the receiver, he dials Wendy's number, planning what he will say (Why didn't you tell me— How could you have thought I—). The phone begins to ring. (But there's no need to break off your education, to drop out of school— A short medical leave of absence— Mononucleosis is the usual cover story—) The dead, even burr of a telephone sounding in an empty apartment; three times, four, five. Has she left town already?

He sets the receiver back and begins to read Wendy's letter for the third time. "Zed says we all live many different lives and this one is over for me that's all" he reads; ". . . disappear silently . . . The end of everything . . ."

Brian half starts up from his desk, making the noise "Awff." He controls himself, sits down again. He warns himself aloud not to leap to conclusions, while a voice located somewhere behind his left ear shouts silently into it that time is of the essence if a frightful disaster is to be averted. He dials Wendy's number again, while another voice at the top of his head remarks how in crisis even sophisticated, educated men employ the rhetoric of cheap political melodrama; this fact has interesting historical applications, it remarks.

*Brr, brr, brr.* But perhaps that wasn't Wendy's number. Brian replaces the receiver and consults a student directory. Though the figures appear to be the same, he dials them again, slowly, with fingers which feel swollen. *Brr, brr, brr, brr,* etc.

All right, this is an emergency. He must think clearly, logically. If Wendy is not home, she might be somewhere on campus. Leaving a note on his door, he hastens out and spends the next half-hour in a rapid tour of the university, becoming, in spite of Wendy's declared intention, progressively more and more uncalm and unproductive and apart. He looks for her in the reading room and in the library stacks, in three cafeterias and two coffee shops and the campus store. He looks also for Linda, whom he has so often in the past tried to overlook. But he cannot perceive them, though people in all these locations perceive him. Some of them stare at him, probably wondering what he is doing there. And what *is* he doing there? If Wendy plans to kill herself, or even if she only plans to leave town, she isn't going to be reading in the reserve book room or eating one of her cream-cheese-on-raisin-bread sandwiches in the Blue Cow.

This evidence of his mental confusion makes Brian stumble on the steps of the library. He stops, tries to catch his breath. He must clarify his mind, review the situation as a whole, make a structural analysis, reject extraneous data.

Here in Corinth, because of its unique geological history, the means of suicide are always at hand. Wherever claustrophobia for life strikes, you are seldom far from the easy way, the traditional Corinth University way, out. Two of the bridges over the north ravine, and one over the south, are most popular. But the cliffs are everywhere, and at this time of day more private. Every year a few unhappy students, in the local phrase, "gorge out."

If Wendy has already leaped into one of these deep, fatal cracks in the landscape, there is nothing to be done, Brian thinks as he stands on the library steps panting and sweating, though it is a cool, cloudy day. Nothing to be done even if she is now on her way; there are too many possible spots, he could never find her. But she will be found, soon enough— Found, identified, examined;

found to be with child, his child. The tragic event will be reported as usual in two discreet paragraphs on an inner page of the Corinth *Courier*, read with supper tomorrow by everyone in town, by Erica. His denials. "I haven't seen her, spoken to her—hardly seen her, spoken to her" (more believeable) "since last spring. Of course, I'm afraid, she was always somewhat unbalanced—" Unbalanced, fell easily. The event recorded at greater length, with a recent photograph, in the student paper, read with breakfast next day by everyone; by Linda Sliski. Linda's sorrow, her rage, her consciousness, the expansion of her consciousness into that of others, many others, expanding circles of others.

"Good afternoon," remarks a colleague, one George Chambers, passing Brian on his way into the library.

"Mrm," Brian replies, recalled to public awareness. He holds out his hand, palm up like a beggar, to give the impression that he has paused outside the library only for a moment, to test for rain. It is not raining, but looks threatening. A strong wind is blowing across the quad under dark, smoky, dirty-looking clouds. Rain is promised, lightning, thunder, hail. Automatically Brian begins to walk away from the library toward his office. Publicity, scandal, ruin. George Chambers, a family man of exemplary sensitivity, will no longer wish him a good afternoon, or any afternoon.

Back at his office, panting and slightly giddy, as if he had just climbed a mountain instead of two flights of stairs, Brian again lifts the phone. He dials Wendy's number and lets it ring, eleven times. As it rings he visualizes the apartment. He imagines the bathroom, which has pink walls, white tiles. The sink and tub are antique, rust-stained under the faucets. A razor blade rests on the rim of the tub, which is beginning to fill with blood, and with Wendy's long pale hair. She has just cut her wrists, though inexpertly and perhaps not fatally; but, leaning over the rim, she has already lost consciousness. Slamming his office behind him, Brian half walks, half runs through the building toward the faculty parking lot.

Wendy's apartment is on the second floor of an old frame

house in Collegetown. It is approached by way of a steep flight of stairs, a sort of narrow chute lined in red cabbage-rose wallpaper leading to a glassed door curtained inside with green burlap. Brian alternately knocks upon this door and shakes it by the cut-glass handle, calling out Wendy's name and demanding that she let him in.

No answer. He descends the stairs and goes outside, walking around the building and looking up at the windows of the apartment. It is hard to see anything, for the backyard is on a downward slope and littered with trees and drifts of leaves and rusted play equipment.

Brian begins to climb the fire escape. Breathing hard after three flights, he draws level with Wendy's bathroom. Between pink curtains he can see a corner of the mirror; then as he climbs further some toothbrushes of varied colors. The sink. The empty tub. Of course, he thinks on the way down, Wendy would never cut her wrists; she is afraid of blood.

Standing in the yard, frowning up at the second floor, Brian suddenly sees in his mind right through the brown shingles into Wendy's kitchenette. Wendy is there; she is kneeling on the spatter-pattern linoleum, with her head inside the stove. The vision is so clear that he can even see the two metal racks which normally occupy the oven, and upon which Wendy has in the past broiled Swiss-cheese-and-tomato sandwiches for his lunch. To make room for her head, she has removed these racks and placed them against the wall. Brian hurries into the building again and up the cabbage-lined chute. Again he rattles the door handle, and shakes it.

"Wendy?" he shouts, several times. He tries to think of ways of breaking the door in—difficult because there is no landing—ways of breaking the glass panel. "Wendy!"

"What the hell's going on up there?"

Glancing down, Brian sees in foreshortened perspective a bearded young man—the physics graduate student who lives in the downstairs apartment.

"I'm looking for Miss Gahaghan."

"She's not there, she went out about an hour ago. Nobody's home."

"Are you sure?"

"Sure I'm sure. She had a suitcase with her. What's the matter, you stoned or something? I'm trying to study."

Brian apologizes, thanks the young man, leaves the building. A suitcase, he repeats to himself half aloud. Certainly if you intend to kill yourself you don't take a suitcase. He draws breath. Inside his head he can still see Wendy's kitchen and the two stove racks leaning against the yellow wall, but Wendy has vanished. He can therefore look right into the oven and see what he must have known all along, that it is an electric oven. This evidence of mental confusion, warped memory, appalls Brian. He realizes by what a narrow margin he has been saved from smashing in the door of an empty student apartment; from being discovered in this act, or just afterward, by the bearded young man.

A suitcase. What Wendy intends, just as he had deduced at first from her letter, is to leave town. To do what most girls would do in her situation—that is, go home, to her parents in Queens.

Brian gets into his car; his pulse is returning to normal. All right. To reach New York, Wendy will probably have to take a bus, and to take a bus she will have to go to the bus station. He starts the car and drives across town, fighting an impulse to exceed the speed limit considerably.

The Greyhound station is deserted except for one bored clerk who tells Brian grudgingly that the last bus for New York departed at noon—too early for Wendy, who must have left her letter in his mailbox about that time. The next one leaves after three, nearly two hours from now. He has plenty of time.

Standing in line at the bank, waiting to draw out six hundred dollars (a sum suggested to him by recent articles in the *Village Voice*), Brian congratulates himself on the decision to keep his royalties and lecture fees in a separate account with which Erica has nothing to do. As he moves forward he notices a sign urging customers to Place Your Valuables in Our Vaults. Vaults; Tombs; Wombs. Wendy lying broken on wet rocks; his name printed near hers in the newspaper. But he stamps these irrational fears down into the brown-patterned carpet, repeating to himself "Suitcase . . . Bus."

But if Wendy is still in town, where is she? As he watches Mrs. Morrison telephoning some higher authority to learn if it is all right to give Brian Tate his own six hundred dollars, the hunch comes to him that she is at that occult bookstore, talking to the phony who runs it, telling him everything.

Mrs. Morrison is still on the phone, listening, nodding. The figure, six hundred dollars in cash, has aroused suspicion. She too, or her superior at the other end of the line, has read the *Village Voice*; they know.

The phone is replaced. Is he sure he doesn't want travelers checks? They're so much safer. No? Tightening her lips, Mrs. Morrison begins counting out the money, in tens and twenties— unmarked bills, he hopes. She slides them through the gap in the bars, and Brian folds them into his wallet under her gaze.

The Krishna Bookshop is located at the shabbier end of Main Street, between a Chinese restaurant and an office-supply store. From outside its appearance is drably exotic. The narrow dusty window, like Wendy's day bed, is draped with a fading India-print spread, on which a large Oriental stone idol sits smiling faintly and smoothly. All around him books on occult subjects are haphazardly placed; some standing, some lying, some leaning on one another, as in a partially ruined temple, a miniature Asian Stonehenge.

Inside, the first impression is of dull light, crowded tall shelves, a dirty-sweetish smell of incense. Wendy is not in the room. At a high wooden counter on Brian's right a boy with a skimpy beard is reading, in disregard of the sign on the wall behind him which proclaims in heavy black-script capitals on faded gold:

# IF THE WAY CAN BE EXPRESSED IN WORDS,
## IT IS NOT THE TRUE WAY

In the corner to Brian's left a girl in overalls is sitting crosslegged on the floor; at the far back of the store two men are bent over some papers at a table. One is young and husky, with bushy black hair; the other older and thinner—possibly the proprietor.

Brian feels scorn rising toward disgust—an intensification of the political and strategic advantage he is aware of when entering any store. He is at a political advantage in these situations, like most customers, because he is socially anonymous, while the people in the store are defined, and defined as low-status clerks; and at a special advantage here since he knows who Zed is, while Zed does not know him. He is at a strategic advantage because he can choose whether to buy or not, while they cannot choose whether or not to sell; and strategically invulnerable here, since there is nothing in this dingy place he wants. Except of course information. He selects the girl on the floor as the most normal-looking of the lot, and moves toward her.

"Excuse me," he says. "I'm looking for Wendy Gahaghan. Has she been here today?"

No answer. Brian raises his voice and repeats the question.

Still no answer. The girl does not even look at Brian, though he is standing directly in front of her; she looks through him. A thin, dizzy unease comes over him, a sensation of not being in the Krishna Bookshop, or anywhere.

"Gail can't talk now, she's doing her yoga," remarks the boy at the counter.

"Oh; sorry." Brian moves off, reminding himself that he is still in a state of tension.

"You looking for Wendy?"

Brian admits this.

"I haven't seen her." He lowers *The Zodiac and the Soul* and calls, "Hey, Zed. Has Wendy been in today?"

At the rear of the shop the older man turns and looks for a

second at Brian, with an odd, startling effect like the switching on and off of a strong light. Then he shakes his head, turns back.

"She might be in, if you want to hang around awhile," the boy offers. "She usually comes in the afternoons."

Hanging around, Brian moves along one wall, reading the backs of books. *Demonology Today. The Tarot Revealed.* The very titles proclaim them full of lies, superstition, fear—all that should have been destroyed for good by the philosophical and political enlightenment of the eighteenth century, the scientific and social enlightenment of the nineteenth, but is now crawling back into every corner. The sleep of reason produces monsters, and they are here, invisibly thick in this ill-lit room. That skinny drug addict has brought them here, and with their help he is living off Wendy and other innocent students, poisoning their minds, subverting everything Brian and his colleagues have taught them.

*Wisdom of the Sufi. Psychic Self-Defense. The Book of the Dead.* The information that Wendy usually comes here in the afternoons, something she has concealed from him, is to Brian another proof that the demons of irrationality and self-destruction have their claws into her deeper than he knew. If she does destroy herself, this place must bear the guilt. Some of the guilt. He grimaces, moving along the wall of books. From time to time he glances with distaste at Zed's back, or pats his jacket pocket, where the wallet stuffed full of bills still bulges and glows fluorescently.

Presently there is movement at the back of the room. The heavy young man is getting up from the table, collecting papers covered with figures and diagrams, expressing gratitude.

"Yeh, well, I'd like to go along with you on that; but you know those Mercury and Venus progressions never act much on me," he remarks as he and Zed walk past Brian toward the door. "They don't energize me like the Mars-Uranus aspects do. I guess violence is just my karma." He laughs childishly. "Ready, Gail? Well, see you later."

"Go in peace, Danny."

Zed shuts the door and slouches slowly back down the long,

narrow book-lined room toward Brian. There is something uneasy, even threatening in the approach of this gangling figure, its face obscure against the back-light from the window. Brian's hand goes protectively to his jacket pocket. But as Zed draws nearer and the musty glow from the ceiling fixture strikes him, the threat dissolves. He is revealed to be a weedy, nondescript middle-aged man; tall, pale, balding, with blurry worn features.

"Can I help you?" Zed's voice and manner are mild, almost shy. He is ill-dressed in a tired gray turtleneck sweater and sagging work pants, and looks ill-nourished, even unhealthy.

"No thank you," Brian says dismissively, relieved but rather surprised. From the reports of Wendy and other students he had expected something more than this slack, dim being—something more forcible, even formidable. "I'm just waiting for somebody."

"Ah."

A self-evident failure, Brian thinks, looking him over. A weak, small-town crank. He has wasted his time being jealous of this fellow; Zed doesn't look as if he'd been able to get it up for years.

It annoys him though that the proprietor of the Krishna Bookshop has not been definitely dismissed, but continues to hover about four feet off, not quite watching him, like an intrusive salesperson. "If you don't object, that is," he adds pointedly.

"Oh no. We're all waiting for somebody here, isn't that right, Tim?"

"That's right." An appreciative smile from the boy at the counter.

Cheap profundity, Brian thinks to himself, not smiling. He moves away from Zed. Like that stare he gave me earlier: another trick. Anybody could do it; I've done it myself with students. It only affected me for a moment because I am in a state of tension. He looks out of the window over the head of the stone idol to discover if Wendy is coming along the street.

"I haven't seen you in here before," Tim remarks conversationally, putting his book down and leaning forward.

"That's because I haven't been in here," Brian replies. "But

I've heard a lot about this place," he adds somewhat more agreeably, wondering if and how he should ask what time Wendy usually comes in.

"Oh yeh?" Tim smiles.

Zed shuffles slowly nearer. "And what have you heard?" he asks.

"Various things." Brian frowns; he has no wish to get involved in conversation, but wants to establish his position as a rationalist who has not the slightest interest in the wares of the shop. "For instance, I hear that you believe in devils," he says, allowing a mocking overtone.

Zed smiles. "It seems a mistake not to, given this world."

In other company Brian might laugh and concede the point, but not here. "And God?" he asks coolly.

"Oh yes." Zed has reached the counter now and leans on it with one frayed elbow.

"And where is God, in this world?"

Zed sighs and looks directly at Brian. Again, the flash of light. "I think God is not very interested."

Though this in effect is what Brian himself thinks, that Zed should say it strikes him as phony. He glances out the window again impatiently; surely if Wendy were coming she would be here by now.

"I also heard you were doing a roaring business," he says. Since he has been in the bookshop for twenty minutes and seen no sign of business, this is meant ironically, but Tim takes it straight.

"People might say that, but it's an illusion. We don't make much bread; he"—gesturing with his head—"gives too many books away. Besides, we get ripped off all the time."

"Ripped off?" Brian says, observing that Wendy is still not coming along the street, nor anyone. Only some bits of dirty newspaper are swept past by the hard wind. Perhaps she has left town by the early bus, or got a ride from someone.

"Yeh. We lose a lot of books that way, maybe ten, fifteen a

week. We could stop it—anyhow, cut it down. Only he doesn't want to." Tim laughs, looking at Zed.

"I stop it sometimes," he says. "It depends on the person. And the book."

Brian glances at his watch: two twenty-five. He decides to give her five minutes more.

"Some people only feel good about something they've stolen," Zed continues. "That makes it really theirs. With others that doesn't work. Like Wendy: she'll only pay attention to a book if somebody she admires gives it to her." He glances up at Brian; another, though fainter, flash of light. This effect is due, Brian now realizes, mainly to the fact that Zed has unusually pale eyes, of a watery gray which is almost white.

"Or take Danny, who was just in here," Zed adds. "I wouldn't give Danny any book I wanted him to read seriously. And I'd stop him if he tried to lift one, because he's the type that doesn't value anything they haven't paid a good price for. For Danny, we should mark the books up." He smiles and adds slowly, turning toward Brian, "A lot of Capricorns are that way. Like you."

Brian, who has been gazing out into the street, faces back. "And what makes you think I'm a Capricorn?" he asks.

"I know you're a Capricorn," Zed says slowly, "because I know who you are."

Brian swallows and shifts his feet angrily. It is not only that his anonymity, his social advantage as a customer, has been destroyed. If this white-eyed crook knows who he is, it is because Wendy has explained him, described him. He has been exposed, betrayed— how fully exposed, he has not time to consider now. He recognizes an attack, and knows as a political scientist that the correct strategy is not to stop and analyze it, or even to defend himself, but to counterattack with any weapon handy.

"There you have the advantage of me," he therefore retorts. "I don't even know your name."

A short pause. The opponents look at each other; or rather,

Brian looks at Zed, and Zed looks at a spot some inches to the east of Brian.

"Why, this is Zed," Tim offers cheerfully, gazing from one to the other like a small child who has never seen a machine gun. "He lives here; he runs this place."

"Zed what?" Ignoring Tim, Brian stares at the shabby, phony individual who knows whatever Wendy has told him . . . perhaps everything.

"Just Zed," Tim says.

"That's what you call yourself," Brian says. Zed nods minimally. "What's your real name?"

"You mean, what was my name before I came here?"

"Yeh."

"That's the past. It's irrelevant."

Defensive tactics, Brian thinks scornfully. "Not to me," he insists. "I'm a historian."

"History doesn't interest me any more." Zed smiles weakly but stubbornly. "It's two-dimensional, and I'm not interested in anything now below the fourth dimension." Apparently a joke, since Tim laughs appreciatively. The noise of this laughter irritates Brian; he rolls out his big guns.

"He refuses to admit what his name is," he says, speaking ostensibly to Tim.

Silence. Then Zed looks up.

"If you really want to know," he says in a strained, pale voice, "I used to be called Sanford Finkelstein."

"Sanford Finkelstein," Brian repeats slowly, mockingly. Though he has never to his knowledge heard the name before, he smiles—for the first time in two hours.

# 6

"Sanford Finkelstein—"

For the third time that day, and within the hour, this name is spoken in Corinth—a coincidence which Zed, had he known of it, might have attributed to the Law of Simultaneity as defined by Jung and other writers on the *I Ching*. It is spoken this time by Danielle Zimmern as she and Erica wait in line at the Blue Cow, the campus coffee shop.

Danielle has heard the name herself only the day before, from an emeritus professor in her department: an elderly, gentlemanly scholar whose own name is Jack Shade. In his day, Professor Shade established a reputation for loyalty to the university and original research; he retains both. Unlike so many of his former colleagues, he has not abandoned either Corinth or his intellectual interests upon retirement in favor of Florida and television. He remains in town, and the history and traditions of the university remain absorbing to him.

Learning recently (from the complaints of younger professors) of the appearance in town of the Krishna Bookshop, Shade took the academically unprecedented but for him perfectly logical step of paying it a visit. He had inspected the premises, talked to several customers and finally, triumphantly, identified its proprietor as "one of our alumni—indeed, as it turns out, a former student in my introductory course." Shade's satisfaction at this discovery, and at the spirit of local patriotism shown by Zed's return to Corinth, quite overshadowed any doubts he might feel about the manner of this return.

For Danielle too the significant fact about Zed's name is that she has heard it before. It is, she believes, the name of a graduate student in philosophy nearly twenty years ago.

"I wondered if it was the same guy I knew at Harvard," she remarks to Erica, holding a Styrofoam cup under the coffee urn. "That tall, funny-looking man with the red hair that Ann Hershey used to go out with. Wasn't he from Corinth?"

"Ann didn't go out with Sandy Finkelstein," Erica says, filling her cup in turn. "She went out with his roommate. But he did go to Corinth; it could be the same one."

"He was studying philosophy." Danielle moves along the counter toward the cashier, searching in her memory, and also in the side pocket of her briefcase for a dime. "And he played the piano, didn't he?"

"Yes; quite well." Erica shifts two heavy books on medieval Irish art and reaches into her shoulder bag. "Here, I have change. Let me pay."

"That's all right, I've found it. Yeh; I remember him at some party at Lowell House. Everybody was dancing and he was playing."

The cashier rings up their money; Danielle and Erica move on toward a counter where individual portions of cream and sugar are heaped in plastic bins.

"Sanford Finkelstein," Danielle repeats. "Listen, isn't he the one that ostrich is based on, in your books?"

"Well, I suppose in a way." Erica smiles. "It was the name mostly. Sanford seemed like a good name for an ostrich."

"He looked sort of like an ostrich. Those long skinny legs and neck. And the way his red hair stuck up on top of his head." Both women laugh. "If it's really him, it's funny he should come back here and run a crank bookshop. I thought he was teaching philosophy out in California somewhere."

"The last I heard, he was in Japan."

The coffee shop is crowded; Erica and Danielle end up sitting on a window ledge. Danielle would have been content to share a table, but Erica prefers this, both because it affords more privacy and because it gives a better view of the room, thus furthering the real purpose which has brought her onto campus.

"We ought to go down to that bookstore sometime and see if it's really Sandy Finkelstein," Danielle says, pouring a paper trapezoid of cream into her coffee.

"Mm." Erica stirs sugar into hers with a plastic stick. "Speaking of identifying people," she adds. "Do you happen to notice that girl here?"

"What girl? Oh." Lowering her cup, Danielle scans the room. "No, I don't see her. She was here the other day, though," she adds unhelpfully.

Erica controls a sigh of impatience. This is the third time in as many weeks that she has had coffee with Danielle in order to identify Brian's nameless new mistress. Once she has seen her (ideally, in Brian's company) she can confront him, and she is eager to confront him. The pleasure of being secretly in the right has worn thin for Erica over the past weeks. She is in the right, and Brian in the wrong, but he doesn't know it, or rather he doesn't know she knows. He goes on smugly believing he is getting away with something. And, in fact, as long as she doesn't speak, he *is* getting away with something.

Besides, concealing what she knows from Brian is a kind of lying, and Erica hates lies. She has sometimes told polite fibs, but she disapproves even of this, and avoids it when she can. She has not lied seriously since junior high.

Therefore she has sought the girl, both in Danielle's company and alone, even more conscientiously than she had hunted for Wendee last spring. Again her search has been vain, but this time for the opposite reason. The moon-faced graduate student she is seeking now, with her "stringy bleached hair" is as much uglier than the real Wendy Gahaghan as last spring's quarry was more beautiful.

But though she hasn't been able to identify Brian's mistress, Erica has plenty of circumstantial evidence of her existence. There is Brian's continued air of uneasy, preoccupied self-righteousness; his phony concern for his wife's mental and moral health—intended, she believes, simultaneously to disarm her suspicions, keep her on the defensive, and cover his own guilt. There is his disinterest in making either love or serious conversation. Above all, there is the evidence of his new sideburns.

To Erica's knowledge, Brian has had hair on his face only once in his life before: in the summer of 1952, when he grew a mustache while they were on Martha's Vineyard. After a rather slow start it came in well: glossy, full, seal-brown. He took it back with him to Cambridge for the fall term, where his friends agreed with Erica that it made him look much older, and more serious. But three months later a student organization published a guide to freshman courses illustrated with caricatures of faculty members. In this guide, Brian appeared as a very small man attached to a very large mustache. Over the Christmas vaction he shaved it off.

The mustache had been a deliberate effort; the sideburns appeared deviously. Brian did not at any time declare an intention to grow them; they merely began—as if on their own momentum—edging down the sides of his face a fraction of an inch at a time, like some geological formation. When they reached the level of his mouth they began to put out a sort of horizontal extension or spur on each cheek. They are an announcement to the whole world that Professor Tate wishes now to appear younger, and less serious—to be seen as a "swinger." To Erica, their message is as plain as if her husband had been branded across the face: ADULTERER.

"The vet was over again last night," Danielle says, breaking into these thoughts.

"Oh?"

"He turned up about nine-thirty, said he wanted to take

another look at Roo's sick turtle. But I don't think that was what he really wanted."

"What *did* he want?" Erica turns from contemplation of the entrance to the coffee shop, where Brian's mistress might at any moment appear.

"Sex, I think." Danielle laughs briefly. "Not that he made any move, or said anything. He just sat there drinking beer and telling me animal stories for a couple of hours. But he kept looking at me. You know how it is—you can usually tell."

"Mm."

"Of course I suppose he's lonely too. His wife died last year; or 'passed away' as he puts it. He practically never talks about her. I guess it still hurts him a lot. And both his sons have left home, and all his friends are respectably married. I feel sorry for him in a way. I mean, he's a nice guy, and not bad-looking, if he weren't so dumb and slow. I feel like I ought to tell him he's wasting his time at my house—barking up the wrong tree, to use his phrase. He ought to go after one of these hot little bitches who are just asking for it, like my husband always did." Danielle smiles sourly and gestures around the coffee shop.

"Mm." Reminded, Erica looks again toward the door, in case a pudding-faced bleached blonde of the sort who is just asking for it should enter. Then she looks back at her friend, frowning slightly. Ever since the separation she has followed Danielle's emotional life with anxious concern. First, directly after Leonard moved out, there was a period of stunned despair. This was followed by several months of flagrant and indiscriminate misbehavior with an overlapping series of unsuitable men. (Erica and Brian had divided them into two types: Scavengers and Weaklings. The former were like those gulls which follow in the wake of large departing ships, where it is traditionally easy to pick up leavings; the latter of the doglike variety, drawn to any woman who recently belonged to a successful man by the magical belief that if they rub against her some of his power, his *mana,* will rub off on them.) This period was especially hard on Erica, who found it difficult to hide her disapproval when she dropped in on her friend and found some man she hardly knew—or worse, knew quite well—in a position of temporary intimacy.

Finally, there was a long, severe reaction. Danielle was "through with all that, thank God," as she declared many times with a stoic grin which made Erica want to weep—or possibly go to New York on the next plane and assassinate Leonard Zimmern. If she could help it, Danielle announced, she wasn't going to have anything to do with love, or men, or any of that garbage, for the rest of her life. ("If it really starts bothering me, I can always masturbate.") This dismal state of mind, which shows no sign of letting up, has lasted nearly a year.

"I think he has some idea that I might come across because I'm so weird by his standards. I mean, I'm forty-one, but I have long hair and wear arty clothes and I read books in foreign languages, so I might do anything, even sleep with him," Danielle continues with a half-laugh. 'You're kind of a hippie, aren't you?' he said to me last night. 'I didn't know that when I saw you up at the clinic. The way girls dress these days, you can't tell them apart.' "

"You know, that's true," Erica says, looking around the Blue Cow again. "It's not like when we were in college. When somebody wore jeans and no make-up, instead of the standard plaid skirt and sweaters, and didn't have her hair set, you knew instantly that she was one of us."

"That's right." Danielle drains her coffee cup and sets it down. "It was the men you couldn't tell apart then. They all had short hair and button-down shirts and chino pants. You had to talk to them to find out if they were interesting, or kind of spooko, or just club boys or sheep." She smiles reminiscently, and so does Erica. "Now everything's reversed. I know exactly how antiestablishment my male students are by the length of their hair; but the girls all look alike, whether they're Delta Jello or SDS."

Yes, Erica thinks as she backs her car out of the lot and starts home, it was different then. Better. But it isn't quite true that all the men looked alike. Sandy Finkelstein, for instance, who is now possibly in Corinth—there was always something peculiar about him. He wore ordinary clothes, but they never fit right, perhaps because he was so thin. His pants flapped around his legs, his socks sagged, and his shirts ballooned and fluttered in the slightest breeze, as did his untidy red hair. She remembers him best in Greek class, struggling over sight translations in a room on the third floor of Sever Hall, raising his pale eyes to the ceiling in a pantomime of despair.

After class Erica occasionally had coffee with him on Mass. Avenue; and once Sandy, who was rather pathetically stuck on her for a while, took her to hear *The Magic Flute*. At the end of that year he left Cambridge, but he came back now and then for a visit. He had been at her wedding on one of those trips; not that she'd invited him, but somebody had brought him along. He was rather sweet, really, Sandy—amusing to talk to, and intelligent—but sort of a lost soul even then. It wasn't so surprising that he should end up out of a job, involved in Eastern mystical nonsense. But it was a little sad.

Erica turns north at the edge of campus onto the main road. A hard, high wind is blowing across it, shifting banks of cold-looking clouds. The last she'd heard of Sandy was a picture postcard of some Japanese temple; a shiny color photograph—on the reverse no address, no message, only his name and a haiku he'd copied out, something about crickets. That was several years ago . . . three, four? She tries to recall whether the card was mailed directly here, or forwarded from Cambridge. In other words, does Sandy know the Tates are in Corinth? Were it anyone else she would have assumed not; otherwise they would have called. But with Sandy you couldn't be sure—especially if he has turned into some kind of superstitious eccentric.

If she goes to the bookstore with Danielle, and it really is Sandy, then she will have to invite him to the house, to dinner, whatever he has turned into. But there is no need to do it instantly.

*1 2 3*

Next week would be soon enough, or next month. If he has joined one of those vegetarian religions, it means a special meal, too. Well, that egg curry from the United Nations cookbook is quite good, with walnuts and chutney. Danielle can come, though Brian will not like that; nor will he like the vegetarian curry. He always demands meat for dinner. And Sandy himself will probably annoy Brian, or at least bore him. But perhaps it would not be unpleasant to bore and annoy Brian a little. And when you learn that an old friend is in town, the right thing to do is invite him to dinner, for instance next weekend.

Out on Jones Creek Road the wind is blowing even harder, scraping down the grass in the fields, pulling the few remaining wrinkled leaves from the oaks. As Erica comes up the hill past the latest Glenview Homes, which always look particularly exposed and vulgar from now until the first snowfall, she sees that there is someone, a young girl, sitting on the top step of her front porch next to two suitcases. From her attitude—body huddled against the wind beside a post, head down, eyes shut—it appears that she has been sitting there a long time; or is very cold, or very tired, or both. As Erica's car enters the driveway, however, the girl hears it, and sits upright.

Erica turns off the ignition and sets the brake. Her thought is that this person is at the wrong house; that she has come to visit someone in a Glenview Home. Her suitcases, which are of molded plastic, pinkish tan, suggest this. She has yellow hair, most of which is pulled into braids that hang limply on either side of a round, ordinary Glenview Homes sort of face, while escaped shreds blow across it.

Erica gets out of the car with her books, and walks around it. "Can I help you?" she asks in a neutral, pleasant voice.

Slowly, the girl stands up. She is short—hardly taller than Erica though she stands a step higher—and not quite as young as she first looked. Her eyes are red-rimmed, worn, as though she had a bad cold, or had been weeping.

"Are you Mrs. Tate?"

"Yes." Erica smiles encouragingly, not puzzled, since the name is within view, painted by her in script on their mailbox.

"Mrs. Brian Tate?" she repeats, with a sort of tired eagerness.

"That's right."

"I've come to apologize to you, before I leave town. I'm Wendy Gahaghan."

"Wendy Gahaghan?" Erica shields her chest with the facsimile edition of the *Book of Kells*. Wendee? But she's not beautiful; not even terribly pretty. She's just ordinary.

"Uh huh . . . You know who I am?"

"Yes." Erica has a sense of speaking with difficulty, through her teeth. "I know all about it." She grips the books tighter. It is for this limp, snuffly, ordinary girl that Brian has behaved so atrociously, caused so much pain, so much rage! Wendy looks at her blankly, waiting; it is not clear for what. If she is to be scolded, insulted, even struck, her stance suggests, she will not have the energy to defend herself. Her head hangs sideways. You miserable, cheap, nondescript— But Erica has not been brought up to insult strangers; she cannot voice the words. Besides, if she does insult Wendy, she will be jumping back into the wrong-hole. Wendy came here at last to apologize, and I—

"You'd better come inside," she says.

Awkwardly, she holds open both the screen door and the front door, while Wendy, weighed down lopsidedly with suitcases, plods past her, and stands dumbly in the hall.

"In here." Erica leads Wendy toward the sitting room, where last night's paper still lies on the sofa, and the curtains are due to be cleaned. The kitchen, where she usually sits with Danielle and other friends, is tidier; but Wendy is not a friend, and probably will not notice anyhow.

Abandoning her suitcases in the middle of the rug, Wendy takes the nearest chair, which happens to be Brian's—something she could not have known, but which makes Erica shiver nevertheless. I must not be mean or hysterical, I must behave well and do the right thing, Erica tells herself, sitting down formally opposite

Wendy on a straight chair which she has not sat in for three years. A pause; but she is not obliged to break it.

"I'm not going to take up that much of your time," Wendy finally begins, moving forward to the extreme edge of Brian's chair as if to demonstrate this. "All I wanted to tell you is, I'm sorry for the hassle I've caused around here." She takes a breath.

"Yes," Erica says neutrally. Since she will probably never see her again, she is cataloging Wendy's appearance for future reference: pale round face, conventional childish features, bitten nails.

"I mean, it's racked me up all along what I was laying on you, somebody I never even met, you know?" Wendy's hands are clutched together in her lap; her voice is high, uncertain. A faint New York accent—lower-middle-class. "I used to think how you were living right here in town and you knew all about it. And if you wanted you could probably report me to the grad committee and get me thrown out of school. Or you could come over someday and shoot me. Only you never did, you know?" Wendy's voice catches again. Erica realizes she is not merely guilty and nervous, as she ought to be, but actually frightened.

"No," she agrees, trying to ease the tension a little. "It never occurred to me."

"I mean, what I did to you, it was shitty. Some of the professors around here, their wives probably wouldn't give a damn. But BRIAN." She pronounces his name with a special exhalation of air, of awe. "I mean, if you did shoot me, everybody who knew him would say, 'Well, okay,' you know?"

The idea that Brian is of such unique importance and value that infringement of rights in him would justify murder annoys Erica profoundly, although (or even because) she might have subscribed to it in the past. Naturally, she does not show this annoyance. "I wouldn't know how to shoot anyone," she merely says, smiling briefly.

Wendy smiles back; her smile is timid, grateful. She has small uneven white teeth, like a child.

"The other thing I wanted to say, it's that you shouldn't blame Brian." She takes another breath. "I mean the, uh, you know, relationship wasn't his idea. I like persecuted him into it. If it wasn't for that, I bet he wouldn't have ever got off with any chick."

"Perhaps," Erica says, thinking that Wendy is deceived, for Brian is off with another chick even now, and one reportedly much inferior to her. Her defense does not persuade Erica of Brian's relative innocence, but rather the reverse. It demonstrates that Brian had not only seduced this girl last spring, but had somehow managed to convince her that it was all her fault. Just as he has so often tried to convince Erica that everything was hers. She'd like to tell him—

And she will tell him. I had a visitor today, she will remark calmly after supper tonight, when the children are out of the way, when Brian is fed, relaxed and expecting no unpleasantness. Who do you think it was? she will ask. A visitor to lunch. And then bring up the other one, because it is time for that. Yes.

"Look," she says aloud, speaking for the first time in a normal conversational voice. "Would you like a cup of coffee? Or something to eat, perhaps. Have you had lunch?"

"Oh no, no thank you." Wendy looks frightened again; can she suspect that Erica, having neglected to shoot her, now intends to poison her?

"I haven't eaten lunch yet myself," Erica continues reassuringly, standing up. "I'm going to make myself a tunafish sandwich, and you could have one too if you like."

"No thanks, really. I better not." Wendy also rises. "Hey," she adds, trailing Erica toward the kitchen. "You hafta believe me, you know. I mean about Brian. That he's not responsible."

"Brian is a grown man," Erica says, opening the refrigerator to remove milk, lettuce and a bowl of tunafish-salad mix; and shutting it again with the emphasis her tone lacks.

"But it was my fault really. For months I kept coming around to his office, and he always wasn't having any. He tried to help me get over it, he was beautiful about it, and so patient and intelligent, well you know how he is, but I couldn't. I just cried all the time and kept saying how I was going to have a nervous breakdown if he didn't love me."

"I see," Erica remarks, rinsing two pieces of lettuce in the sink under an unnecessarily hard flow of water.

"But that was straight, you know," Wendy insists. "I figure I would have flipped out pretty soon." She makes the gesture of someone exhausted or insane flipping a pancake, in demonstration. "I was really flaky." Erica takes a loaf of whole-grain rye bread out of the bread drawer. "I'm not getting across to you," Wendy says anxiously. "You're not listening to me; you're just angry."

"I'm not angry at *you*," Erica corrects, opening the mayonnaise jar. "I think it's very honest and decent of you to come and see me like this." In her head, she contrasts the natural whole-grain honesty and decency of Wendy's conduct, her willingness to accept blame, with the slippery opaque homogenized mayonnaise behavior of Brian.

"I had to, because I probably won't be back here for a long while." Wendy shrugs wearily, and leans against a cupboard. Her raincoat has fallen open; under it she is wearing a leather vest and skirt trimmed with long untidy leather fringe.

"You're leaving Corinth for good?" Erica asks, thinking that according to Brian, Wendy had already left town in June. Either he has neglected to mention that she has returned for a visit (by the look of the suitcases, a lengthy visit) or he does not know it.

"Yeh. I hope it's for good." Wendy grins, sighs. "I'm taking the bus to New York this afternoon."

"Ah." In all their years here Erica and Brian have never used the bus, which takes six uncomfortable hours to reach New York, but always a car or the more rapid and expensive plane. "Have you seen Brian?"

"No; not since Monday. He doesn't want to see me again."

"But he knows you're going to New York?"

"He knows I'm splitting." Wendy's voice rises and wobbles as if she were going to cry. "It's what he wants."

Splitting = leaving town, Erica translates. But Wendy also appears to be splitting in another sense, of which her fringed and shredded clothes are the visible sign. Though Brian has long since lost interest in this miserable girl, she still has a crush on him—is even now being cut into shreds and torn apart by this crush.

"And do you want to leave town?" she asks, trying to speak gently.

"I hafta leave town." Wendy gasps, swallows. "Not just on account of what's happened, but if I stay I know I'll hassle Brian and keep him from working on The Book. That's the really heavy thing."

"How do you mean, heavy?" Erica arranges her sandwich on a willow-pattern plate.

"You know—serious. Important. I mean, compared to The Book, none of us are important, you know? Not even Brian, maybe."

"I don't think I follow you," Erica says, turning up the flame under the coffee pot.

"You know his book, on American foreign policy?"

"I know about it, naturally. I haven't read any of it yet."

"But you know what it's about, and that he's going to show how this really beautiful plan Kennan had after World War II was shucked because of selfish establishment politics and intrigues. He's going to explain the whole thing, and if The Book is published in time, and the right people in Washington read it, it's going to really zap them. And that could have a fantastic effect, you know? Like once they realize what happened before, they would reverse their strategy, and stop trashing the rest of the world." She looks at Erica with absolute, almost hysterical sincerity. "There's no way of predicting for sure, but it could happen, you know?"

"I suppose possibly it could," Erica admits, wishing that Wendy would stop asking her if she knows things.

"Well, then. Say The Book wasn't finished, and so our policy wasn't changed and the world was destroyed, all because I wanted so bad to see Brian and get fucked?" Erica flinches at the term;

Wendy, not noticing, moves nearer, gazing at her with intensity. "I mean, what I believe is if you really love somebody you hafta want what's right for them irrespective of if it hurts you personally. Like what my roommate Linda says about Madagascar. The way you know you really love a guy is, suppose he was to get a telegram saying he could have whatever he wants most in the world if he would move to Madagascar, and suppose you got this telegram first. Would you rip it up and destroy his future, or would you give it to him?"

"Mm," Erica says, moving back from this outburst. "It'll be easier for you both if you're in New York," she says, trying to speak in a calming voice.

"It's like the only way. I mean, we both realize if I'm here I won't be able to leave him alone, because I tried that already last summer. I swear to stay away but then I get racked up about something and telephone, you know? Or I freak out completely and go to the office. And even when I'm seeing him it's no good: I want to see him more, all the time, and there's bad scenes, like last month in the coffee shop. It's a bummer, really."

Reminded by the word "coffee," Erica turns off the flame under the pot, pours a cup, and sits down at the kitchen table. But she is also reminded of something else. Coffee shop. Last month. Last summer. A few moments ago she had a vision of Wendy as splitting, torn apart. Now, instead, she begins to see her as several figures coalescing. It is as if she, Erica, had been stunned or drunk for months and was just coming out of it. Like a cartoon character she sits frowning, watching the stars and asterisks fade; three images blend into one. The beautiful blonde she was seeking last spring; the pudding-faced ugly one she has sought all fall; and the weary, overwrought young girl who now stands in her kitchen— can they all be the same person?

Erica shakes her head slowly, to clear it, and looks at the single image. "Let me ask you something," she says, speaking carefully. "Are you a psychology graduate student?"

Wendy takes a moment to register this. "I guess not, not any more," she says then, looking at Erica with a dazed, bitter expression. "I didn't tell them yet, but starting today I guess I'm just a grad-school dropout."

Returning to consciousness, the animated-cartoon cat sees her several vibrating, threatening enemies reduced to one small, almost pathetic mouse—a mouse who has taken her request for information as a catty remark. Brian has had only one affair, and that affair is now over. Both Erica's invisible rivals are simultaneously defeated, rejected.

Erica has always been a good winner: generous, modest, charming. (She is a less good loser, but fortunately she has seldom since childhood been in that position.) She realizes that she does not wish to cause Wendy any more pain than she is obviously suffering now—that she is in fact sorry for her.

"I'm sorry," she says. "I didn't mean— Listen, please, Wendy. If you don't want any lunch, at least sit down. You look exhausted."

"I am sorta spaced out." The mouse slumps into a kitchen chair. "I didn't sleep last night. I figure maybe I'll get some sleep on the bus."

"Are you going home?"

"Uh uh. Not right away. Ma'd be too psyched if I was to just walk in and tell her I quit school and the whole bit. She comes on enlightened, but she's really a pretty square type. I'm going to stay with a married girl friend in Jersey City, she'll lend me some money. And I'll try to get some kind of job when this hassle is over." Wendy puts a hand on her stomach and grins oddly. "Then maybe I'll break the bad news to Ma."

"Mm," Erica says, not listening, trying to arrange her new information. All this time, Brian has had only one affair; but he has had it all this time. When he promised to end it last spring, when he said it was over, he was lying. Only now, only since Monday in fact, is it really finished. And when he blamed her for still brooding about it, last summer; when he wondered audibly if she was mentally unbalanced, this fall— Erica feels as if she were being poured full of boiling soup; a hot furious bubbling and trembling in her chest and arms. What lies Brian has told, what hypocritical pomposity he has shown; what guilt, what awful waste of energy and feeling he has caused her!

Now phrases Brian has used in the past about his affair begin to return. "It meant nothing . . . I don't think about it . . . It just wasn't that important." To him, that is. To Wendy it was important, painfully important—and still is, though Brian evidently is tired of her.

"Why don't you have a cup of coffee," she suggests gently.

"Well. Okay. I mean if it's no trouble."

"Would you like sugar? Cream?"

"Everything you've got, please."

Erica sets her blue enamel sugarbowl and cream pitcher before Wendy, who proceeds to dilute her coffee into a sort of hot ice-cream soda; perhaps it is more comforting that way. And Wendy obviously needs comfort. Brian has refused to see her any more; he is tired of the feelings he has aroused in her. In order that he need not be reminded of them, Wendy is leaving town, dropping out of college. On Brian's recommendation, no doubt.

And now it occurs to Erica, with a black bitterness like her own coffee, that twice this autumn Brian has separated women from their chosen work, merely for the sake of his own selfish male convenience and peace of mind. First, through emotional and moral blackmail, he prevented her from taking that job in the psychology department. Now, presumably by the same means, he is forcing Wendy to leave graduate school.

"Do you really have to quit school right now," she asks, sitting down again. "The term's only half finished. You'll lose credit for your courses."

"Yeh," Wendy agrees dully.

"Can't you wait until the end of the semester? Till Christmas, at least."

"Uh uh." Wendy shakes her head. "I should, maybe; I thought about it, but I know I'm not strong enough to stay here without bugging him. Anyhow I can't afford it now." She takes a breath, then lets it out, seeming to collapse inwardly.

Erica picks up her tunafish sandwich, looks at it, and puts it down. Rage at Brian, who has caused this collapse, pity for herself and for Wendy, rise in her throat, almost choking her.

"Please, have some of my sandwich," she says, moving her plate across the kitchen table toward Wendy.

"I better not . . . Well; if you're sure you don't want it . . . Thanks." She smiles weakly, childishly.

"You're welcome." Erica smiles back. She thinks that she is behaving rather well to Wendy; better than Brian has behaved. Brian has acted very wrongly, with deliberate and unprincipled selfishness. This idea does not completely displease her. In a husband, active is always preferable to passive misbehavior. It is not nice to think that Brian has callously and casually seduced and then rejected Wendy, but what is the alternative? The alternative is to think of him as a passive victim of circumstances, the sort of weakling whose life can be pushed around by sad pale little girls.

"You know, you're a lot different from what I expected," Wendy remarks, looking up from her coffee.

"Oh? How?"

"I thought you'd be much—I don't know—bigger and madder." She takes another bite of sandwich. "I mean, you know, I used to wonder all the time about what you were like. Brian would never rap with me about you. The only data he ever gave out was that you were taller than him. And then one time he was telling me about some fraternity party where these boozed-up guys knocked over a punch bowl on you, and it sounded like you never even lost your cool. So I got this idea you were some kind of frozen lady giant eight feet high."

"I see." Erica begins on her own sandwich. "I thought of you as rather formidable too," she says.

"Really? That's pretty funny." Wendy smiles a pale, distracted smile. "I guess you're the first person who ever . . . thought that. Mostly—" She slows, then stops speaking, drops the crusts of her

*133*

sandwich, and puts her hand on her stomach with an expression of great unease.

"Are you all right?"

"I d'know." Wendy shoves her chair back and stands up. "I guess maybe not. I better—" She looks around the kitchen, takes two steps toward the door, another step back.

"Uh— Can't—" Bending suddenly over the drainboard, she throws up into Erica's kitchen sink, at first in a continuous loud rush, then more intermittently, punctuated with choking gasps of apology. "Oh, shit— Jesus, I'm sorry—"

Erica stands a few feet off, wincing as her whole-grain bread, lettuce, tunafish salad, coffee and cream reappear in the sink, much the worse for wear. I have poisoned her just as she feared somehow, magically, she thinks. But how? "That's all right," she says distantly several times.

Slowly, Wendy leaves off and straightens up, still holding on to the sink. Erica hands her some paper towels, and then a garbage bag; finally she removes the drain basket from the sink and turns on the hot water hard.

"God, how gross. Hey, I'm really sorry," Wendy says, looking at Erica like a sick puppy.

"That's all right." Erica puts the top back on the trash can. "How do you feel now? Would you like to lie down for a bit?"

"Well. Okay, for a couple minutes, maybe I better," Wendy says blurrily. Leaving go of the sink, she staggers after Erica into the sitting room. "Wow. I'm really dizzy." She slumps onto the sofa and collapses sideways in a small heap. Erica hands her a pillow; then she unfolds the crocheted afghan from the rocker and covers Wendy with an elaborate pattern of blue, green and red geometrical flowers.

"I knew I should never have eaten that sandwich," Wendy says meanwhile. "How could I be so stupid, stupid, stupid!" She hits her forehead weakly with one fist.

"I don't see how it could be the sandwich," Erica defends

*134*

herself. "I had the other half myself, and I don't feel ill. Unless you're allergic to fish."

"It's not that. Anything would have done it, the way I am now."

"Mmhm," Erica murmurs sympathetically, though the phrase which has begun to run through her head is *hysterical psychosomatic vomiting.* "Of course this is a difficult time for you." Perhaps Wendy ought not to go to friends in New Jersey. Perhaps instead she should go home to her family and a good psychiatrist.

"Yeh. It's really been a bummer, these last couple weeks. I mean I thought, All right, morning sickness; I can hack it until I get to the city. Nobody told me it could go on all day."

"You. Have. Morning. Sickness," Erica hears herself say in a very cool high voice, the voice of an ice giantess eight feet tall.

"So-called. With me it's not so bad in the morning. It starts about noon and lasts like practically till bedtime. Did you ever have that?"

"No. Not. Really," replies the high voice. "You'd better rest for a while now," it adds, with what strikes Erica as great aplomb. "And I think I'll go and finish my lunch."

"Okay." Wendy closes her eyes obediently.

For a moment Erica stands looking at her. "You're sure you're pregnant, I suppose," she says. Wendy opens her eyes. "Sometimes people imagine—"

"Yeh, I'm sure. I had a test at the clinic. You know, that test where they kill the rabbit." She shuts her eyes again; then she pulls Erica's afghan up over her head and snuggles down into it, disappearing completely. A casual observer might not have suspected there was anyone but Erica in the room, were it not for the two dull-pink plastic suitcases, still standing in the center of the rug where Wendy had dropped them—how long ago?

Walking carefully around the suitcases, Erica returns to the kitchen, where she is surprised to find it is not yet two o'clock. She finishes her lunch by pouring the coffee down the sink and putting the remains of her sandwich into the garbage. Then she sits down, rests her chin on her hand, and tries to order her ideas, which are now tangled together like frozen garden hose, or one of those complicated designs knitted out of snakes in the *Book of Kells*.

Wendy is one person, not three.

Wendy is here, in her house.

Wendy is pregnant.

This last idea explains several things: why Wendy threw up into the kitchen sink, why she is leaving Corinth, and why she needs money. It shocks Erica because of what it reveals about her husband: that Brian Tate, that serious, righteous man, that well-known liberal professor and household moralist, has knowingly and deliberately seduced, impregnated, and abandoned a child.

Wendy is leaving town.

Wendy is going to Jersey City, where a friend will lend her money.

Now a new, terrible idea strikes Erica. She thinks that Brian has not only seduced and abandoned Wendy, he has in effect delivered her into the hands of a Jersey City abortionist. She recalls horror articles in Brian's *Village Voice* in which that very city was mentioned as a center of the illegal abortion racket; descriptions of filthy makeshift operating rooms, bloodstained tables; callous and venial doctors whose names have been struck from the Medical Register because of drink or drugs.

But this cannot be allowed to happen. It must be stopped. If it is not stopped, in a few days Wendy may be lying dead in some slum cellar or alley.

Wendy must not be allowed to go to New Jersey. Probably she ought not even to leave town until she feels better, stronger—until a good, trustworthy, sympathetic doctor has been found to help her.

But who is going to find such a doctor, and how? And where is Wendy going to stay meanwhile? Who is going to take care of her? Her Ma is apparently no use; and it is clear that Brian has no intention of taking any responsibility; that he has made no move to do the decent, civilized, generous, right thing.

Erica looks out of her kitchen window. The strong cold wind is still blowing, bending the trees between her yard and that of the new Glenview Home next door. Heavy flat clouds slide by rapidly, slate-gray, smoke-gray. Time is passing, and somebody must do something. She, Erica, must do something. She must do the right thing.

### Three Telephone Conversations

1.

"Hello."

"Mrs. Tate? This is Dr. Bunch."

"Oh, hello, Dr. Bunch. I wanted to see you, but your nurse said you were going away this weekend, she suggested I call Dr. Keefe, but I don't really know him, and the problem is . . . Well, the problem is we have a friend, a graduate student at the university; it's her I'm calling about actually. You see, she's in trouble."

"Trouble? What type of trouble?"

"I mean, she's found out she's pregnant . . . And she's just terribly unhappy about it. You see, she's studying for a degree, and if she has a baby she'll have to leave school, and her whole future will be disrupted. So she came to me, today, and I thought you might have some idea about what she could do. You might know where someone in her condition could go, or someone who could help her."

"Hm. Well. Has this pregnancy actually been medically confirmed?"

"Oh yes. She's had a test. With a rabbit—"

"Hm. Of course this is a difficult experience, a shock—"

"Yes, it's very—"

"—and probably there hasn't been time for you to seriously consider how very wrong, not to say hazardous—"

"I know it's hazardous, Dr. Bunch; that's the whole reason I'm calling you. You see I have to find someone decent and competent to help her, because if I don't she'll probably go to some awful quack abortionist in Jersey City or somewhere, she might do anything, really, she's so depressed, so exhausted, miserable—"

"How old are you, Erica?"

"Forty, last month, but I don't see—"

"And how many children do you and Professor Tate have?"

"Two. I know what you're going to say, you're going to say that this child deserves to be born as much as they did. But when a child is unwanted, when it just interferes with everyone's life—"

"Please listen to me for a moment, Erica. You're a relatively young, healthy woman. You and your husband have a secure income and only two children. You're upset now about this pregnancy, you think that you don't want another baby, perhaps that you're too old—"

"But *I'm* not—"

"—or possibly your husband doesn't want it—"

"Dr. Bunch, it isn't—"

"—or both of you, but believe me, I've seen many cases of this kind, and in my experience these late children, these 'little afterthoughts' as I call them, are often in the end the greatest source of satisfaction of all to both parents. Now, I suggest that you make an appointment for next week with my—"

"Dr. Bunch, listen! You think it's me who's pregnant, but I'm not, really. It's this student—"

"If it's a student, why doesn't she go to the Corinth clinic?"

"Because they won't help her at the clinic. She's already been there, and they—"

"If you're not personally concerned, Mrs. Tate, I frankly don't understand why you would want to involve yourself in something like this. Abortion is not only against the law in this country, it's a serious crime, and you're proposing to make yourself an accessory to a crime. Why should you take any such responsibility? This student, if she exists, must have a family, friends— And how about the father? Isn't he able to help? Would he be willing for example to marry her? Who is the father?"

"What?"

"Who is the father of this baby?"

"Uh I don't know him. I mean the girl, my friend, doesn't know who the father is. It might be anyone of several people; students, you know. There's nobody she can really go to, except for money that is. I mean you don't have to worry about that, about money. If you could help her, I'm sure—"

"You're asking me to perform an illegal operation, is that right?"

"I'm not asking you to perform it. I'm just asking you to recommend—"

"Mrs. Tate. In my eighteen years of practice, nineteen next July first, I've had many, many patients come to me with this same problem. Most of them have claimed they were just asking for a recommendation, and almost all of them begin by saying they are inquiring for a friend—"

"Dr. Bunch—"

"—when it is quite obvious to me from everything they say that there is no 'friend.' Do you have any tranquilizers in the house now, Erica?"

"No, I—"

"Well then, I'm going to write a little prescription for you; I'll call it in to the Country Corners Drugstore, and it should be ready for you to pick up in about an hour. I want you to take one every four hours; and then tomorrow morning, when you feel more yourself, when you're calmer, you can telephone this office and make an appointment for next—"

"But I'm already myself. I don't need a tranquilizer, I'm quite tranquil, considering everything, but I'm honestly not expecting a—"

"I can't discuss this matter any more with you, Erica. I have other patients waiting."

"But, Dr. Bunch!"

"Good-bye, then. Don't forget to pick up that prescription."

## 2.

"Brian Tate here."

"I've been trying to reach you all afternoon. Where have you been?"

"I was out of the office. What is it? Is something the matter?"

"You're asking me if something is the matter? That's funny, really."

"Erica, please. I've had a difficult day. Tell me what you called about, if it can't wait until I get home."

"It can't wait, because you're not coming home today. That's what I've been calling you about, to tell you not to come here. I've packed your Gladstone bag, I put in two shirts and an extra pair of slacks and—"

"What do you mean, you packed—"

"—and your shaving things and some underwear, and I already took it up and left it in the office with Mrs. Wells. I told her you were leaving town and you would pick it up later."

"Now wait a moment. What do you mean, leaving town? I'm not going anywhere until the APSA meetings next month."

"I don't care where you're going. I don't care anything about you, or what you do any more, I just don't want you to come here, that's all."

"Now listen, Erica. Try to get control of yourself—"

"I have got control of myself. I've got a good deal more control of myself than—"

"Erica, look, I'm leaving the office now, and I'll be home as soon as—"

"If you come anywhere near this house, I'm going to tell The Children everything you've done."

"The Children, what do you mean, tell—"

"Because I think they're old enough to know. And please don't start again on the apologies and excuses. Don't tell me this time how important I am to you and how I have to learn to forget and forgive and not act irrationally and brood about events in another less important separate area of your life which didn't mean anything. I've heard enough of your political speeches, and so has Wendy."

"Wendy?"

"Yes, Wendy. In case you want to know, she came to lunch here today."

"Oh, hell."

"You didn't think she would do that, did you? You thought she would just get out of Corinth quietly and obediently, not asking for anything, not blaming you for what you've done to her, and to me. And she probably would have, that's what's so awful, and terrible."

"Wendy was there at the house? When did she leave? Was she going to New York?"

"No, to New Jersey."

"New Jersey?"

"Yes, she has friends there. You mean you didn't even know where she was going?"

"No, I—"

"And you didn't care. You thought you could throw her out like an old pair of pajamas you were through sleeping in, and you weren't going to concern yourself with where she went or what happened to her. You didn't care whether she might be dead by this time next week."

"Dead! What do you mean, dead?"

"And don't bother to put on that concerned public voice. You know quite well what I mean. You know what the statistics are on illegal operations in Jersey City, you read that article in the *Village*

*Voice*, but you don't care. As long as she leaves your sphere of operations and doesn't bother you any more, you don't care."

"That's not true. I've spent all afternoon trying to find Wendy, trying to help her. I've been at the bank taking out money, I've been to the bus station, to her apartment, and all over town, all over the campus looking for her, calling her friends, for Christ's sake, I've been doing everything I can—"

"Everything you can? You want me to believe that for months you've used this girl like a pair of dirty pajamas, and now, suddenly, today—"

"Erica, please listen to me! I didn't know about any of this until today. I didn't know Wendy was pregnant until I got a letter from her at the office, this noon."

"You'll excuse me if I don't believe that."

"Well it's true, whether you believe it or not. And I didn't tell her to leave town, that was her idea, I didn't know anything about her plans, I didn't think she was going to go to you and make trouble—"

"Wendy didn't come here to make trouble. She came because she wanted to apologize to me, because she at least has some sense of guilt, some sense of decency, and since she thought I already knew all about her—"

"How could she think that? I never said anything that could make her think— At least, not since last spring. Erica, listen. I'm coming home now, and we can work out—"

"I don't want to work out anything with you."

"All right, if you feel that way now, I can understand that, but at least we can talk—"

"And I don't want to talk to you. I don't know why I'm talking to you now, it's a waste of time talking to someone who does nothing but lie and make excuses."

"Erica, please listen—"

"If you really want to do something, Brian, you might try to find a decent doctor who would be willing to help Wendy. And don't bother calling Dr. Bunch. I already tried him."

"You mean someone in New York."

"New York, or Corinth, or Albany or Boston or Puerto Rico, it doesn't matter."

"But there's no point in that, Erica. Even if I could locate someone, I still can't get in touch with Wendy. I don't have her telephone number in New York, I mean New Jersey."

"I know how to reach her."

"You do? Good, give me the number."

"I'm not going to give you anything. Wendy doesn't want to speak to you, anyhow."

"But—"

"If you find a doctor, you can call me. Otherwise, I don't want to hear from you again."

"But Erica! . . . Erica? . . . Are you there? Don't hang up . . . Oh, shit."

## 3.

"799-0579."

"Leonard? This is Brian Tate."

"Well, good evening, Brian. Are you in the city?"

"No, I'm in Corinth."

"Ah, Corinth. And how is everything up there? How is my ex-wife, and my ex-children?"

"They're well, as far as I know; I haven't seen them recently—"

"And how are you, and all your relatives?"

"Fine, thank— Well, not so fine, actually. Something's come up, that I wanted to consult you about."

"Of course. Listen, Brian, can I call you back in about half an hour? I have a friend here now."

"Yeh, all right— No, wait a minute; I'm not at home."

"Not at home? Where are you, then?"

"I'm at a motel."

"A motel, in Corinth?"

*144*

"Well, just south of Corinth. I believe it's in Hesiod, actually. It's called the Twin Birches Motel."

"You're in a motel, hm. It sounds like you've got a problem."

"Yeh."

"All right, give me your number."

"It's— No, I'll call you back. I'm in a pay phone."

"In that case, maybe you'd better tell me about it now. Inez, honey, could you excuse me a minute? This is an old friend calling from Corinth, and he's got a problem . . . No, you don't need to leave, just move over to the other side of the bed so I can reach the phone a little better . . . Okay. So what's up up there? What are you doing in a motel, did Erica throw you out?"

"Yes, as a matter of fact she did."

"That surprises me. I would have said it wasn't in Erica to do anything so vulgar, so obvious, so lower-middle-class. But we live and learn. And why did she throw you out?"

"Well, it's complicated. I don't want to go into the whole thing now, I just . . ."

"Was it for the obvious, vulgar reason?"

"What? I'm afraid I don't understand you. I've had a hell of an exhausting day."

"Let me put it this way. I take it you're not alone now."

"What? Oh no, that's all right, no one can hear us."

"I mean, there's somebody with you, isn't there? Not in the phone booth, in the, what was it, Twin Bitches Motel."

"Twin Birches. No, I'm here alone."

"I see. Excuse me. I mean, I don't see. You're not drunk, by any chance?"

"Not as far as I know. I wish I was drunk. That's an idea. Maybe I should get drunk."

"All right, Brian, hold on. I'm listening to you . . . So what's your problem?"

"It's— Leonard, can your girl friend hear me?"

"I don't think so. She's not listening, anyhow; she's reading *Art International*."

"It's— You know I'm counting on your discretion about this."

"Yeh, all right. Go ahead."

"I mean, if what I'm going to tell you should get out, if it was known around the university, it would really screw things up for me."

"It won't get out. Don't worry."

"The thing is— Couldn't you ask her to go into the other room for a few minutes?"

"There is no other room. You've seen this apartment, haven't you? I can't afford two rooms on what my ex-wife leaves me. Do you want me to ask her to go into the bathroom?"

"No; never mind. You know, Leonard, I want you to understand that I wouldn't have called you if I wasn't really up against the wall, or if I had any other way of getting the information. You understand that, don't you?"

"For shit's sake! What information?"

"I don't want to relate the whole history. What I wanted to ask you. What I called about, is. I need to locate an abortionist."

"I see . . . Well, you surprise me more and more. Hold on. Let me think a moment . . . How soon do you need this information?"

"As soon as possible. There's a chance the, uh, girl might do something rash, she's in kind of a disturbed state now of course, she's very young, quite emotional . . ."

"Very young. A student?"

"No. A graduate student."

"Well, congratulations . . . It's not going to be all that easy, you know. I've never had this particular problem myself, touch wood. I'll have to make inquiries."

"All right. But you can find someone?"

"I don't know yet. I think I might be able to get you a name. But it'll cost you."

"I have some money, I already went to the bank this afternoon."

"How much?"

"Six hundred dollars."

"Better make it a thousand."

"A thousand?"

"If you don't want any mess. I can probably lend you the rest, if you need it."

"No. That's not necessary. I—"

*"Your time is up, please signal when through."*

"All right . . . I don't need any money, thanks."

"Okay. Can you call me tomorrow morning, say about ten, at the university?"

"At the university?"

"You have my number, don't you, it's—"

"I have it, I only wondered—"

*"Your time is up, please signal when through."*

"All right, goddamn it! I was saying, I wondered if your switchboard girl might—"

"Forget about that. This isn't Corinth, nobody here cares how many students you knock up. And try to relax, friend, okay? It's not World War III."

# 8

"How is everything?" Erica asks in a low anxious voice, coming into Danielle's house and shutting the door behind her against the morning frost and damp thin mist.

"All right."

"Where's Wendy?"

"Still asleep." Danielle gestures toward the ceiling, toward her spare room, where Wendy has been staying since yesterday afternoon. Erica had thought first of keeping her at home until she felt better and the arrangements for her operation had been made. But Erica's house is not a good place for Wendy. First, because it contains Jeffrey and Matilda. Meeting them would certainly be upsetting to Wendy—and still more upsetting for the children if they were to learn who and what Wendy was—something she might very easily reveal by mistake in her present state.

Even more dangerous was the possible reappearance of Brian. Erica had told him to stay away, but there is no guarantee he will do so. It was very likely that he would suddenly decide to come home to get clean shirts or argue his case. This would be bad enough if Erica were there; worse if Wendy were alone. Brian has already done her serious emotional damage, and might do more.

But Erica could not stay home with Wendy night and day; she had to shop for groceries, buy Matilda a Halloween costume for tonight, deliver two drawings to the Community Art Show and Jeffrey to the dentist. At Danielle's, however, Wendy would be safe from Brian; and Danielle's children would be incurious, since there was often some old acquaintance or student of their mother's staying in the spare room.

"How is she?" Erica asks.

"Still pretty exhausted. She went to bed early, but I heard her moving around much later." Danielle, who is dressed to go out, picks up her briefcase from the table, then sets it down. "Listen, I spoke to Bernie last night, after you called."

"Oh, good. What did he say?"

Danielle shakes her head. "Not much. He doesn't know of anybody he could recommend. He doesn't like the whole idea, anyhow: he thinks Wendy ought to go into a home he knows of and have the baby, give it up for adoption. He gave me the address." Danielle shrugs. "Anyhow he won't do it himself. When I asked about that he got quite angry, angrier than I've ever seen him. He said, 'I wouldn't even consider it. I'm a veterinarian, and this is a woman, not a pet chow.'"

"He could do it, if he wanted to."

"I guess so. But he won't. I don't think he'd ever break the law; one of his brothers is a cop, you know." Danielle makes a face. "Maybe he's right about the home. It'd be safe at least."

"But Wendy wouldn't want to leave school, not for such a long time."

"I don't know. I think probably she'll do anything you tell her. Especially if she thought it was good for Brian and his Great Book." Danielle grins shortly. She pulls a red flowered scarf from the pocket of her raincoat, shakes it out, and ties it over her hair. "I have to get up to school—I should've been there an hour ago. But listen, if you still think Wendy ought to have the operation, I could ask my sophisticated friend in the philosophy department—"

"No, don't do that yet," Erica says. "I heard from Brian this morning; he gave me the name of a doctor in New York he says is supposed to be reliable."

"Oh yeh? Well, okay. I'll be back in my office after twelve if you need me for anything. Tell Wendy to help herself to whatever she wants to eat. Roo fed the bacon I was saving for her to Pogo; typical, huh? But there's plenty of eggs, and some coffee on the stove."

Alone, Erica takes off her raincoat, thinking hard thoughts about children: their ingratitude, their greed. This morning there had been another hateful scene about steak sandwiches, the third in a series of such scenes. Matilda had become shrill; Jeffrey loud and coarse:

"Can we go out tonight for dinner, at least?"

"Aw shit, why not?"

"That's no reason. You said you were too tired yesterday."

"You said the next time Daddy was away you would take us to the Faculty Club and we could have a Supersteak Sandwich, didn't she?"

"I don't want you to make me one at home. The kind you make are always foul."

"You always promise you'll do things for us but you never do, you're just lying."

"I won't be quiet. Liar, liar, liar."

What is so deeply unfair is that this scene, and the others—her anger and guilt, the children's anger and disappointment—are all Brian's fault. She would be perfectly willing to take Jeffrey and Matilda to the Faculty Club, were it not for the possibility, indeed the probability, that Brian will also be there and not, as she had told them, in Detroit, Michigan. Liar, liar, liar.

Erica hangs up her coat and goes into Danielle's kitchen, where she switches on the light and begins to make breakfast for Wendy. She is frowning, thinking hard thoughts about men.

*150*

Danielle's house is built close against a steep wooded hill. The front rooms are large and sunny, with a winter view across the valley and the lake. But the kitchen at the rear is dark, cramped, overhung—almost a basement. It is impossible to work there without artificial light; but as Danielle often points out, this house like most houses was designed and built by men.

It is true, Erica thinks: men run the world, and they run it for their own convenience. It is a man who is responsible for Wendy's present condition—for her exhaustion, her desperation, her danger. And the two women who are trying to rescue her from this condition cannot do it on their own; they must beg and plead for help from other men.

Erica turns Danielle's stove to medium high. The iron snail of the electric coil slowly flushes a sullen red-black. Hateful, she thinks, hateful that women should have to appeal to their natural enemy in such a matter (and in vain)—that they should have to expose themselves to the pompous assumptions and disapproval of a country doctor like Bunch; to the self-righteous anger of such a person as Bernie Kotelchuk.

It is Danielle who has had to bear Dr. Kotelchuk's anger, since he is not aware of the connection between Erica and Wendy, whom he believes to be one of Danielle's students. But Erica feels his words striking at her through Danielle, like invisible machine-gun bullets, wounding them both, weakening their resolve. Women are emotionally soft still; so long dependent on male approval that they are influenced even by the opinions of men they despise.

The stove brightens to a grainy vermilion. Erica melts butter in a frying pan and breaks two eggs into it. The golden, nourishing, domed yolks quiver against each other and come to rest, surrounded by the thin, gluey viscous whites; like semen. Meanwhile upstairs at the top of the house in the spare room, floating in a bowl inside Wendy, there is something similar.

It would be better, much better, if Erica or Danielle could find someone to help Wendy; if it were possible to refuse to tell Brian where she is or what she is going to do; to renounce his assistance entirely, to break off all connection with him, to hang up when his voice sounds inside the black plastic cannon-mouth of the telephone and leave him altogether alone and in the wrong, where he belongs. But time is passing. The eggs are swelling and congealing in the frying pan; Wendy is pregnant, and every moment, even now while she lies unconscious overhead, she is becoming more pregnant. And the more pregnant she becomes, the more dangerous an operation will be.

The truth is, even the best possible operation is dangerous, Erica thinks, lowering two slices of raisin bread into Danielle's toaster. The most skillful, legal, routine operation, for example an appendectomy, in the most modern hospital, can go wrong. Too much anesthetic may be given, or too little; there may be shock, infection, complications. And this is where there are many skilled persons and complex equipment, where there is no greed or fear of the law, no need for haste and secrecy . . . Perhaps after all it is better that the responsibility of finding an abortionist, and the blame afterward if anything does go wrong, should rest upon Brian.

Erica sets a tin tray on the counter and lays on it a plate, a white paper napkin and three sharp metal implements: a knife, a fork, a spoon. The result is unpleasant. It is not improved when she slides Wendy's two fried eggs onto the plate, and one breaks in the process, bleeding gluey yellow. The raisins in the toast look like black scabs, and the coffee, smoking darkly, is—

But she must not give way to morbid imagination; she must be calm, cheerful, rational when she goes upstairs. Erica adds sugar and milk liberally to the bloody coffee, takes two deep deliberate breaths, and picks up the tray.

"Wendy?" There is no answer to her knock; Erica enters the spare room, which is dark and rather cold. She sets the tray down and raises the blind, which has been lowered so far that its end lies limp on the radiator. Even then the room is grayed, obscure; white mist presses up against the glass.

"Wendy?" No response. In a cage by the window some

shredded newspapers and shavings begin to squeak and rustle about; one of Roo's gerbils raises its muzzle and front paws. "Would you like some breakfast?"

"Wha?" The voice comes not from the pillow, which has been abandoned at the bed head, but out of a snarl of sheets and blankets halfway to the foot.

"It's quite late, you know."

The mound of bedclothes moves, and Wendy puts her head out from it. "Erica? Wha time is it?"

"About eleven."

"Oh, wow." Wendy squints, rubs her eyes, and sits up on her haunches, in a short crumpled cotton nightgown. She looks plump, worn and not quite clean, with unshaven prickly legs and stained feet. Her hair, snarled with sleep, hangs like limp shredded wheat.

"How do you feel?" Erica asks.

"All right, I guess." Wendy grins feebly. "Hungry."

"I brought you some breakfast."

"Breakfast? Great." She smiles as the tray is lowered onto a chair by the bed, not seeing there what Erica sees. "Hey, raisin toast, fantastic."

Squatting on the rim of the bed, she pushes her hair out of the way and begins to eat, while Erica stands watching, planning what she is about to say. Wendy—or no, better she herself—must call the number Brian gave her and make an appointment for as soon as possible. Brian will provide the necessary cash from his famous separate account, but will not be told where or when the operation is taking place.

Someone will have to go to New York with Wendy; her roommate, or the friend in New Jersey. Erica wants to help; but to accompany Wendy on the long bus ride to the city, to walk the Manhattan streets looking for the address, to sit in the waiting room while behind a closed door the bleeding fried eggs— No, she can't do that, that would be going too far, in every sense. And besides, she has to stay with The Children.

But if she is afraid just to go to New York, to wait in the next room, what must Wendy feel? At the moment, apparently nothing. She is eating with small eager bites, shoving egg onto her fork with a piece of toast, lifting it, chewing.

Erica opens her mouth, but something keeps her from speaking: reluctance to interrupt Wendy's innocent enjoyment, or perhaps the social rule—learned so early it is almost instinctive—that nice people don't discuss medical problems during meals.

Wendy drinks from the mug, sets it down, and wipes her mouth with the back of her paw.

"How come you're so good to me?" she asks. "I mean," she adds, since Erica does not at once reply, "considering what I did to you, it really kind of zaps me out, all this."

"But you didn't do anything to *me*," explains Erica, sitting down across the room in Leonard's former desk chair and rotating it toward the bed.

"Sure I did."

"Not to me personally. You didn't owe me anything—you didn't even know me then."

"You think that matters?"

"Of course." Erica does not add the moral—that now Wendy knows her and thus owes her—she barely even thinks it.

"But still." Wendy grins uneasily. "Why should you want to help me?"

"Well. Partly because I think women have to stick together. Like Danielle said yesterday: we're all members of an underprivileged majority, and if we can help each other we ought to." Wendy's plate appears to be empty. "Are you finished with breakfast? Would you like more of anything?"

"No thanks. That was great." Wendy sags back against the wallpaper, hitching up one shoulder of her nightgown.

"You're welcome." Erica transfers the breakfast tray to the desk and sits down in the bedside chair. "I've been doing some research," she begins in a reassuring voice, "and I think I've finally got some results."

"Results?" Wendy looks perplexed, not reassured.

*154*

"Yes, I've heard of a doctor now, in New York, and I thought I might call him—"

"You don't have to do that, I—" Wendy interrupts.

"I know I don't *have* to do it," Erica interrupts back. "But I want to do it." She smiles kindly. "And I think I should call now, this morning, because it's really better not to lose any more time, and make an appointment for you."

"I don't know if I wanna see him." Wendy huddles her knees up to her chest and pulls the nightgown down over them to her feet, so that her body is enclosed in crumpled cotton like a small bundle of unhappy washing.

"But this is a very good man; he's supposed to be extremely careful, reliable—" She speaks gently, not allowing any vexation to show.

"I don't mean that. What I mean is, I'm not sure I wanna see any doctor now. I think maybe I hafta, like, go through with it."

"Go through with it? But what on earth for?" Erica forgets to modulate her voice.

"Because maybe I should. See, the thing is." Wendy fixes her eyes on Erica. "Last night, well I guess early this morning really, about five, I woke up. And I couldn't get back to sleep again, I was so psyched up about everything. I thought how I was making all this grief for you and Danielle, and what I ought to do is just go down to the Greyhound station and take the next bus to New York whenever it was. So I got up and dressed and went out. It was pretty freaky really, because it was still completely dark, and more or less raining. I was walking along not paying much attention where, and then the street stopped and there I was right by the edge of the gorge.

"And I thought, Why not? I thought how I wanted to make Brian so happy and give him everything, but all he'd got from me actually was a lot of heavy trouble so that he like never wants to see me again. And if I went and had the abortion, I would be like ripping off all this bread from him, hundreds of dollars." Wendy's voice weakens; she lowers her face to her knees. "Well, anyhow, it seemed like the fastest way to solve everybody's problem," she says hoarsely. "And I thought, God will forgive me; he'll understand. I mean if he exists.

"So I sorta got up on the wall," she continues from behind her knees, in the thin confiding voice of a schoolchild describing her trip to the park. "I can't stand heights usually, you know. I don't even like crossing the bridge to campus. That open grid really freaks me out, and if I look down, everything starts to spin. But it was so dark last night I couldn't see anything; I could hear the water running, but I liked that. I mean it seemed right, you know? The end of the year, rain falling, leaves falling, water falling. I thought how I'd kind of loused up in this incarnation, and maybe next time I'd be reborn as something easier like a cow or a tomato plant." Wendy grins.

"Well, so I was sitting there on the stone wall, getting really soaked, shivering. But I thought how it didn't matter because I wouldn't have time to come down with flu or anything. I hung my legs over and squinted down between them into the gorge, to make sure there wasn't anything in the way like a tree or a rock, because I didn't want to miss and just get smashed up. And then I happened to look across to the other side and there was a light on in one of the dorms. Somebody was still awake studying; or maybe they had got up real early. I remembered reading how John Stuart Mill used to rise before dawn to work on his philosophy by lamplight. And Brian—at Harvard he used to stay up studying almost all night sometimes, you know? And then it hit me that maybe I wasn't important, but here, inside me"—Wendy lowers her knees and lays one fist on her nightgown—"there was somebody that had half Brian's genes, and maybe it was destined to be as brilliant as him; maybe a great genius. And years from now some night when everybody else was asleep they could be sitting up at some university working and studying. Only if I got off that wall on the wrong side, they would never get the chance." Wendy's last words catch in her throat and come out damp; she begins crying.

"I'm sorry—I had no idea," Erica says, moving from her chair to the bed. She reaches across it and touches Wendy's shoulder, smoothing it lightly but firmly as if she were making pie crust. "Danielle said you were restless, moving around last night, but I didn't know—"

"It's okay," Wendy gasps. "It's just that. Brian. I remembered when. He was telling me that." She swallows with apparent difficulty. "I mean, like I knew all along he didn't love me the way I love him, I could accept that, but I never thought he'd— Hey, this is sort of freaky," she says in a different tone, looking up and focusing on Erica. "I mean, talking to you this way."

"That's all right." Erica is still sitting on the edge of the bed, but she has stopped patting Wendy's shoulder since it occurred to her that Brian also had patted this shoulder at one time; or rather many times.

"But listen." Wendy makes an effort to steady her voice; she swallows hard. "What I hafta ask you is, do you think I could be right? About the baby. I mean, did you ever feel the same about your kids, that their lives are very valuable, more than most, because of their heredity? Not only Brian, you know, but all those judges and people in New England history that he's descended from. I mean, his kids might grow up to be important people, maybe very brilliant, great human beings."

"Yes," Erica admits. "I thought something like that once, when Jeffrey and Matilda were babies." She does not add that she is almost sure now neither of them will grow up to be great human beings, or possibly even human beings. It would probably seem only one more reason why someone else (Wendy, for instance) should try to reproduce Brian's valuable genes.

"So you think I should go through with it?"

"I'm not sure," replies Erica, who is sure but wants to give the impression of reflection, and to marshal her arguments. "It's a very serious responsibility," she says. "I mean, you can't just have a baby. That's only the beginning; it's a lifetime job. A child needs more than good heredity, it needs a stable family, parents who—"

"But I don't want to raise it myself," Wendy interrupts. "I just think maybe I ought to *have* it, you know?" She sits forward. "There are homes you can go away to; Danielle said last night she might know of one. There was this place out on Long Island a friend of mine in high school went to. They took care of everything and found people to adopt the kid. Do you think it could still be running?"

"I suppose it might be," Erica admits.

"It would be sort of a drag, because I'd have to stay there for like four or five months. My girl friend said they were always lecturing them and showing them these gross-out films on drugs and VD, and they made her go to church every day and take sewing lessons. But maybe I could work on my thesis some, at least do the reading. The place Sharon went was free, too. That'd be cool, if I could find a place like that, so I wouldn't be ripping off Ma or Brian."

"You mustn't worry about that," Erica says firmly, standing up. "You mustn't even consider it. Brian can certainly afford to pay for the operation."

"But that's not fair."

"Of course it's fair."

"But it's not his fault; it's my own stupid fault. There was this all-night party and I missed a day and a half and then I thought I could make up for it by taking two pills at once, because I'm so stupid." Wendy shows signs of beginning to cry again seriously.

"Please, Wendy. Don't upset yourself," Erica begs her. "There's no use thinking about that now." These remarks are not effective. "I'm sure it can't be good for the baby," she tries.

"No." Wendy attempts to control her gulping sobs. "Yeh."

"You're overtired, that's what it is. Why don't you go back to sleep for a while? Danielle's children don't come home for lunch, so you can get a good rest. Come on now. Lie down."

"Okay." Wendy uncurls and subsides onto the bed, then half rises again. "You know what I want to do. I want to go down to the bookshop," she announces.

*158*

"Bookshop?"

"The Krishna Bookshop. Do you know it?"

"I've heard of it."

"I want to talk to Zed. Do you know Zed?"

"No," says Erica, who has not thought of Sandy Finkelstein once since she found Wendy on her porch.

"You oughta meet him, he's out of this world. I mean like literally. He's a renunciate; he's renounced all material goods and possessive relationships. He doesn't even drink coffee. He's been on the Path for years. You know, the spiritual Path."

"I see." Erica has a vision of Sandy on the Path: it appears to her as a narrow dirt track, overhung with brambles, winding up haphazardly through a steep dark wood.

"He's helped me a lot, you know. He's very wise."

A new and disagreeable possibility occurs to Erica. "Have you told him about all this?"

"Uh uh. I haven't seen him since I found out for sure. Well, he sort of knows I'm in love with somebody, but he doesn't know who it is. He's not interested in details like that, only in your spiritual development . . . I think maybe I'll go down there this afternoon and get him to look at my chart."

"Chart?"

"My horoscope. Zed's a really heavy astrologer."

"Please, Wendy, don't do that," Erica asks. "I mean, too many people know about this already."

"But Zed wouldn't tell anyone. He's a fanatic about keeping secrets; he's a double Pisces, with practically all his planets in the twelfth house."

"All the same, I'd rather he didn't know. Not yet, anyhow. Please."

"Well. Okay." Wendy lies down again with a small sigh.

"Here's your pillow."

Erica covers Wendy, lowers the window shade and carries the tray downstairs. The plate is empty now except for a sticky yellow smear and some dark broken crumbs, and there is only a dirty sludge in the mug; but she does not like it any better.

She sets the tray on the kitchen counter and looks at the telephone beside it. Should she call that doctor now and make the appointment? Danielle is probably right: Wendy will go to New York if Erica tells her to. But if she goes only because Erica tells her to, whatever happens there will be Erica's fault. It is all so difficult, so complicated. If she had refused to speak to Wendy yesterday, as some—perhaps most—wives would have, Wendy would be in Jersey City, and everything would have been over soon one way or another. But it is too late for that now.

Sometimes a miserable refugee cat or dog, abandoned by its owners, appears in your yard. If you keep your door shut until it goes away, nobody will blame you. But suppose instead you take it into the house, feed it, find it a place to stay. From then on you are responsible.

Of course sometimes the stray cat runs away again, as had almost happened last night. If Wendy had gone then, taken the bus to New York before anything more could be done for her, it would have been distressing; but also a kind of relief. There would have been no more responsibility and blame then for Erica and Danielle—only for Brian. If Wendy had done something awful and stupid (Erica does not think "killed herself") there would have been unending guilt for him. All the rest of his life Brian would have carried this guilt on his back, like a phantom knapsack full of wet broken bloody rocks. No, no. Even now, she cannot wish him that.

But whatever happens in New York, there will be something in the knapsack. At the best, something halfway between a dead fish and a dead baby. Brian will haul it to campus, into his office and his classrooms; at night he will drag it home again. The ghostly knapsack will be propped against the wall of her sitting room, a dim, uneven canvas shape; later it will lie collapsed, almost but never quite empty, in a dark corner of their bedroom; all night, night after night, year after year.

*160*

No, Erica resolves, settling the perforated chrome basket into Danielle's sink to block the drainpipe, she cannot do that to Brian—or to herself. She cannot call that doctor—some other solution must be found. She turns on the water and squeezes out detergent, slides the frying pan into the hot suds, and begins to clear off Wendy's tray, on which the surgical implements are beginning to turn back into ordinary tableware.

Suppose Wendy goes into a home. That means that for months she will be in some ugly institutional building somewhere in the state, forced to sew and sing hymns with a lot of other stupid, unhappy girls, all of them swelling larger and larger like balloons. Next spring sometime the balloon will pop, and a child, Brian's child, will be released into the world. Official persons will take it away and give it to strangers, among whom it will continue to exist, imagined but always unseen, for the rest of Erica's and Brian's and Wendy's life. All of them will have many years to think of this lost, unknown baby—child—boy or girl—man or woman. Is that any better? No, it is almost worse.

There must be some other way, Erica thinks, frowning and chewing the inside of her cheek as she rinses the dishes under the tap and sets them to drain. Suppose someone they knew were to adopt Wendy's baby; someone really intelligent, kind, responsible — She tries to think of such persons, but no name comes to mind.

What if she, Erica, were to take the baby, to adopt it herself and bring it up, as E. Nesbit did with her husband's illegitimate children, passing them off as her own? Admirable, noble, generous, romantic, Erica had thought when she read of this. To have a baby again—its plump face, its solid small weight against her left shoulder, its small fat hands catching at her hair— "Is that the right thing?" she asks, whispering the words aloud over the sink, above the white sudsy water. There is no reply; instead, as if she had opened a box of insects, a cloud of buzzing, biting problems and complications rises up, filling the kitchen with the whirr of wings.

First, could she get away with it? E. Nesbit and her husband were radical bohemians living in a big isolated country house; the

Tates are part of a small-town academic community. Is she going to pretend to be pregnant, buying phony maternity clothes, wearing an ever-larger pillow under her skirt for the next six months? Could she successfully fake a confinement and appear to go into the hospital, so that none of her friends suspect how admirable, noble, etc., she is being? If they don't suspect, of course, they will probably pity her for having been careless enough to become pregnant again at forty, and/or condemn her for deliberately adding to the population problem. Those who know the family best may be surprised that the Tates want another child, after two such evident failures.

Perhaps it would be better to say that they were adopting a baby, though this too will require justification—indeed an elaborate rationale; and even then some people may wonder whose child it really is. Either way it means months, years, a lifetime of lying.

And what will Jeffrey and Matilda think when the baby appears? What is she going to tell them; or how is she going to deceive them?

And it is not only the deception, but the possibility of being found out in it. Too many people already know about Wendy, and it would be foolish to expect that none of them will pass it on, or will add $1 + 1 = 1$ if a baby disappears from Wendy's stomach and simultaneously appears in Brian's house. Even more likely is that Wendy will disclose the truth herself. She may think she feels nothing now, but maternal instinct may catch up with her. Then she will want to see her child, to visit it; perhaps she will desperately want it back.

Even if Wendy were to forget the whole thing and move to Alaska or Hawaii, there would always be the apprehension that she might return, the knowledge that the child is really hers. And is Erica sure she can love Wendy's child through years of Infant and Child Care: years of damp diapers, jars of strained apricots, broken push toys and bedtime tears? Can she swear that she will never blame its childish misbehavior on heredity?

Yes. She can swear this. But what about Brian? Even if he

agrees to let her adopt Wendy's child, how will he act toward it? Bad enough if he were to favor it over the others; still worse if he should particularly dislike it.

The crowd of buzzing complications are beginning to fly back victorious into their box, taking with them the tiny pink winged vision of a baby. Erica realizes that with the slightest encouragement she too could start to cry right here; to sob and shake. But she cannot allow herself that. She must remain calm and think clearly, because, at last, she has an important decision to make.

First, she must give up the idea of taking Wendy's child. Considering everything, especially considering Brian, there are too many problems. She would prefer not to consider Brian; she would rather not think of him at all, but that is impossible. He cannot stay in "Detroit" forever; he will have to come home, and she will have to see him. At first, just as before, he will be solemn and contrite. He will accuse himself, and figuratively pour ashes upon his head, but in reality his hair will remain quite shiny and smooth, sideburns and all. Then he will begin to explain how the affair with Wendy meant nothing to him and was not important; how the child means nothing and is not important. Gradually his smooth, shiny air of self-esteem will reappear. He will begin to think that it is time for Erica to swallow his version of events, and to forgive and forget again. Presently, if she does not do so, he will begin to feel righteously aggrieved.

Erica rinses Danielle's frying pan under hot water and sets it upside down on the drainboard. She turns off the tap and lifts the metal basket from the sink. There is a sound of choking from below; the dirty water, floating gray curds of detergent, quivers as it is sucked down into the drain, which swallows it finally to the dregs with a nauseous gulp.

Looking ahead, down into the long dirty dark drainpipe of the coming winter, Erica can imagine that she might one day be able to accept what has happened; that she might be able to forgive. But the person she will forgive is not her husband Brian Tate, but a weak, shallow-minded, self-justifying middle-aged man of the same name. Such men often become involved in messy, loveless adulteries; and they are forgiven, because nothing better can be hoped from them.

But Brian will not only expect to be forgiven, and to have his version of events listened to and believed. At some time during this process he will want to move back into the house on Jones Creek Road, and presently he will want to move back into the bedroom. He will expect Erica to make love to him; to love him, although it has been proved he does not love her, or anyone.

And this is impossible. Erica can never like, much less love the person her husband has turned into. The very most she will ever be able to do is to pretend to tolerate him, to remain silent as he rehearses his excuses and false protestations of love, to wait and watch for the next sign of deception, to lie still under him at night with her teeth together. Lies, more lies, years of lies.

It is so much easier for Danielle. She does not have to have Leonard in the house; she need only see him a few times a year. She can say what she thinks of him without risking criticism, because everyone knows now what he is really like. And it is easier for Leonard too: he need not be reminded every day of how shabbily he has behaved. Really it is more charitable to let a man like that live where his faults will not be so glaringly obvious: among other shallow, undependable people who will forgive him because they are no better themselves. Or perhaps among naïve people who still believe in him, who accept his pretensions, as Wendy does Brian's—and thus possibly motivate him to live up to these pretensions.

Wendy still thinks Brian a great man, a hero; she thinks that the book he is writing will be a great book. This need not be wholly naïveté: very likely, when Brian is with her he plays that part, or more than plays it—he really is serious, dignified, affectionate, etc. Brian always behaves best when people are watching him, especially people he does not know too well; and after all, it has taken Erica herself nearly twenty years to find him out. If Wendy were to know him as well— A faint idea, like the shadow of a small fast plane or a large bird flickering in weak sunlight high over a field, crosses Erica's mind at this moment, and is gone. But Wendy will never see Brian as he really is now; she will go through life mourning him as a lost hero.

Whereas Erica, very soon, will have to see Brian again. If she puts it off much longer she will seem hysterical, unforgiving; everyone will blame her. Then she will have to let him move back into the house. And when she does so, it will become a sort of prison.

She remembers a conversation she had once with Sandy Finkelstein, coming home from *The Magic Flute* on the streetcar along Mass. Avenue. He had been reading Dante's *Inferno*, and was saying how he didn't think the sinners in the first circle, in the whirlwind, had it so bad, because they were with someone they loved passionately. The real hell, he said, would be to be with someone you couldn't stand. "Or someone you once loved, but now you hate them," Erica suggested. "Like my mother. That would be the worst."

In that same conversation Sandy had said what really gave him the horrors was all those people drifting outside hell in that sort of dirty fog, the ones who did neither good nor evil, but were for themselves.

There must be some other solution for all of them, Erica thinks; some way out of that fog. A moment ago there was a sort of idea in her mind . . . She looks out the kitchen window into the misty narrow backyard. The shadow of the idea is returning; nearer this time, darker, more distinct— Yes. Now she recognizes it.

Teachers, especially university professors, often have an elective affinity with their subjects. Whether through original tropism, conscious effort or merely long association, language instructors born in Missouri and Brooklyn look and act remarkably like Frenchmen and Italians, professors of economics resemble bankers, and musicologists are indistinguishable from musicians. The similarity is usually only one of style; indeed most professors, at least at Corinth, tend to regard with suspicion and hostility any colleague who leaves the academy to practice what they preach.

These affinities also profoundly influence the functioning of the various Corinth University departments. They determine, for instance, which academic issues will take the longest to resolve and arouse the strongest feelings. Members of the math department tend to quarrel over the figures in their annual report, and members of the English department over its wording. In Psychology, analysis of the personality traits of candidates for promotion sometimes ends in ego-dystonic shouting; and the controversy over the new men's washroom in the Architecture Building (during which two professors who had not designed an actual building in twenty years came to blows) has already passed into university annals.

But it is among Brian Tate's colleagues that the effect of the law of affinities is most strongly felt. Since every member of the political science department is in outward manner and inner fantasy an expert political strategist, every issue provokes public debate and private lobbying. Even when there is little at stake, eloquent speeches are made; wires are skillfully pulled and logs rolled out of simple enjoyment of the sport.

In the past Brian has played the game with as much zest as any of his colleagues. Today it seems petty and tiresome. The transactions of the Curriculum Committee, of which he is chairman, appear vain playacting, and the question it is discussing very trivial compared to that on his own agenda, viz.: How is he going to cope with his wife's crazy demand that he divorce her and marry Wendy Gahaghan?

The issue which is now before the committee, and which has been before it for an hour already, plus nearly as long on Tuesday before the whole department, is known as the Pass-Fail Option. It first appeared last week in the shape of a petition signed by thirty-two undergraduate majors in Political Science, nineteen in other departments, four teaching fellows, and three persons giving the names of "Thomas Paine," "F. Kafka" and "Janis Joplin." These fifty-eight real and imaginary persons demand that students in political science courses be allowed to choose whether they shall receive a letter grade or merely an indication that they have or have not passed a course.

In practice it is likely that the Pass-Fail Option would have little effect. The experience of the history department last spring suggests that the only students who will opt for it are those who would prefer the euphemism Pass to the letter C. Nevertheless, the matter has provoked great controversy: Brian's colleagues have made long and sometimes emotional speeches containing phrases like "freedom of conscience," "academic integrity," "evasion of responsibility" and "moral cowardice"—the last two of which he has heard in another context recently, in fact only a few hours ago, when they were used by his wife to describe his conduct to Wendy.

Brian's committee, which is supposed to study the petition and make recommendations to the department, is divided on the issue. Each of the four other members has, as usual, taken up a philosophical position which he is arguing in his characteristic style. For not only do professors resemble their subjects; these resemblances are subdivided within each department. Just as some instructors in art history take on what they imagine to be the appearance, manner and opinions of Renoir, and others what they imagine to be those of Jim Dine, so each of Brian's colleagues imitates a school of political thought, if not a specific politician.

John Randall, the grand old man of the department, last survivor from the days when it was known as the Department of Government, appears to Brian in the role of Cordell Hull. He is a large stiff elderly man, somewhat pompous and slow on the uptake, but with remarkable staying power; a Hegelian who lectures on political philosophy, often quoting by memory from Plato. It is John Randall's view that if they admit the Pass-Fail Option, they will be breaking their moral contract with the university and failing to recognize true excellence. Students at Corinth are created equal in opportunity to attend lectures in Government (as he still calls it), but not equal in ability to comprehend these lectures. The petition should therefore be rejected, politely but in a firm and dignified manner.

Brian's principal enemy in the department, C. Donald Dibble, also opposes the petition, but more violently; just as he has for years opposed every proposal and blocked every suggestion for curriculum change made by Brian. It is largely due to him that the committee has accomplished almost nothing since September. A tense, talkative, rather paranoid bachelor, Don Dibble designates himself in interviews, of which he gives many on varied topics, as a "radical conservative." Brian has privately designated him as Metternich. Dibble is a political philosopher of a more recent school that Randall's, but he also quotes Plato frequently—and in Brian's view deceptively. He has been trained at the University of Chicago to hunt out the basic political principles which are hidden in the undergrowth of even apparently obscure events. Occasion-

*1 6 8*

ally he fails to flush any significant issues from the shrubbery, and refrains from involvement in the ensuing discussion; but not today. Hidden in the Pass-Fail Option, Dibble has discovered a wedge-shaped animal something like an elephant. If his colleagues let it into the department, he insists, they will be abdicating the responsibilities of power and yielding to mob pressure. Presently larger and larger elephants will enter behind it, and trample them all to death, which will be no more than they deserve.

Chuck Markowitz, the youngest member of the committee, appears in the role of Castro. He is an awkward, engaging young radical who is also extremely well read. Normally Brian feels rather fond of Chuck, but today he is impatient with him. For one thing, Chuck is not only in favor of granting the demands of the petition; he is probably responsible, at least in part, for its having been written in the first place, and thus for the special departmental meeting on Tuesday which prevented Brian from having lunch with Wendy, and all the trouble which has followed from that. It is his fault that the five of them are sitting in this room now instead of attending to their personal or academic business. More generally, Brian holds it against Chuck that though over thirty he affects the costume of a radical undergraduate, and has allowed his hair to grow out until it resembles a small dirty black poodle dog sitting on top of his head.

Chuck's remarks in favor of the Pass-Fail Option are extensive and predictable. He dwells upon the stupidities and inequalities of the present grading system, with illustrative anecdotes; he extolls the superiority of independent study, and the success of free universities. "After all," he concludes, grinning engagingly, "how can we really know what some kid has learned in our course? How do we have any right to grade him?" The faces of the other committee members harden at these words, and they silently give Chuck's speech the grade of B-minus.

Last to speak, as usual, is Hank Andrews, a skinny pale clever man who is Brian's best friend in the department. Andrews has long ago adopted for himself the role of Machiavelli. In meetings he plays the part of the detached scientist, observing and occasionally manipulating political forces out of pure intellectual curiosity. It is impossible to guess what side Andrews will take on any question, since he is as likely to be motivated by cynical amusement as by either interest or principle. Today, after appearing to hesitate for some time, he has finally come out in favor of the Pass-Fail Option—largely, Brian suspects, in order to cause trouble. Andrews declines to consider any of the larger issues involved. He merely points out in his dry way that the Option has been allowed by several other departments with apparently little effect, and that the petition has been signed by over half their own majors. If its demands are not met, considerable ill feeling will be felt. There will be mutterings about monolithic bureaucracy; snide or angry letters and editorials will appear in the student newspaper.

When Andrews ceases speaking there is a clamor of exclamation, among which the words "truckling" and "expediency" can be heard. The other three professors begin to repeat the arguments they have already put forth, and to make the points they have made half an hour ago or on Tuesday. Brian does not listen to them; he hears other voices arguing, demanding.

He should have suspected trouble from the way his wife sounded on the phone this morning—from the tension in her voice, the unnatural pauses. But he was unprepared for the assault which began when he opened the front door of his house an hour later and they met face to face—Erica's white as if lit from within by fever, with wide ignited eyes. Her Jeanne d'Arc face, he had called it once: the face of a woman fighting, as she believes, for unselfish ends, fanatically certain she is in the right. When Erica herself is injured she merely becomes cross and depressed; but she can rise to flaming indignation over any injury, or possible injury, to a child. The younger the child, the hotter the flames. He has not seen them blaze this high since just before Matilda was born, when she battled two doctors and the management of a large hospital for the right to have the baby stay with her after birth instead of in the hospital nursery. "Do you know what the babies do up there in that place?" he remembers her demanding in a raised voice as they stood in the admitting office with her pains coming every eight minutes. "Each one is isolated from all human contact in a kind of horrible plastic cage. The lights are always on, glaring down into their eyes twenty-four hours a day, like some North Korean military interrogation, and they *cry,* that's what they do, twenty-four hours a day, except when they're too exhausted even to cry, for five days and nights. That's their introduction to this world."

Today there was the same high fervor in her voice as she told him he had to marry Wendy—not so much for Wendy's sake as for the sake of the almost nonexistent infant. And also, according to her, for his own. "You see, Wendy *believes* in you," Erica explained, walking rapidly up and down the sitting-room carpet. "She thinks—no, it's more than that, she *knows* you are a great man and that you are writing a great book. And I don't know that, not any more. But I do know it's wrong to hold on to a man you don't believe in, when there is someone else who does."

Brian had tried to argue calmly with her, to explain that she mustn't involve herself in his mistakes; but he couldn't get her to listen, or even stand still. "I don't agree that it's not my concern," she insisted passionately while he followed her up and down the long room. "That's what the 'Good Germans' said. After all, Wendy came to me; I have to help her. I don't want to be like those people in Dante who did neither good nor evil, but were always just for themselves."

After this interview there followed another just as bad, or worse, with Wendy at the Zimmerns'—where it turns out she has been staying ever since she disappeared—and in the oppressive presence of Danielle Zimmern. Danielle as well as Erica has known all along that Wendy never left Corinth, but she has concealed this from him. In the same way, she and Erica have concealed from Wendy that he has been anxiously and continually seeking her. For Erica, in her present emotional state, there is perhaps some excuse. For Danielle, none.

Considering Danielle, Brian grimaces so that Chuck Markowitz, at whom he happens to be gazing, stumbles over a sentence. He thinks that he has never really liked Danielle; he has suspected that she does not like him, and now he is sure of it. Very likely she is behind the whole thing. She has somehow convinced Erica that the Jeanne d'Arc thing to do is to give him up, or in less noble language throw him out. She wants him out of the way so that she, Danielle, need not see him any more, and so that Erica also will be a divorced woman. Misery loves company, especially ideological misery—and for some time Danielle has sounded more and more like an ideologue. Since Leonard left she has nursed a grudge against men, which she has recently attempted to generalize and dignify as radical feminism. If he didn't know what he knows about her promiscuity at the time of the separation, he might wonder if she were a lesbian. And after all, promiscuity proves nothing; it might even suggest that Danielle cannot really love any man. No doubt she is attractive in a way—but isn't there something heavy, something bovine (or "oxlike" might be a better word) about her good looks? He remembers that when he danced with her at parties it sometimes seemed as if she were trying to lead, and he was always uncomfortably aware that she must weigh nearly as much as he.

For months Brian has hardly spoken to Danielle; but now she has somehow forced herself into his private affairs and is standing over them like a policewoman, so that he hardly dared touch Wendy when they met today, and did not dare kiss her. Yes, a policewoman; or an MP guarding prisoners of war—for, seen together, she and Wendy might have come from different countries, even different races. He recalls with a pang how small, soft and young Wendy looked, hunched on the Zimmerns' grotesque Victorian sofa with her bare feet up and her pink freckled arms wrapped protectively around her knees. She seemed reduced in size—not only in relation to the oxlike Danielle, but in contrast to Erica, whom he had just left. On one of her plump feet there was the angry, scraped mark of some recent injury. Her eyelids drooped, and her face was the weary, flattened face of child refugees in news photographs.

Danielle did most of the talking during this scene, telling Brian what he was to do and when. Wendy hardly spoke, except to say how grateful she was to Danielle, and even more to Erica—how fantastic Erica had been, what a really cool person she was. And then, even less confidently, almost whispering: "I was thinking, what Erica says about kids needing more than just good heredity. I mean that's straight, you know? I wouldn't want just anyone to have this baby. It'd have to be somebody that could understand it and educate it right. Kids are so impressionable, even bright kids. I mean, suppose they gave it to Republicans or something: its mind could get all warped like. That's why I gotta do it myself."

Still, subdued though she was, there is no doubt that Wendy was pleased, even overjoyed by the idea that he might marry her. Like a refugee in a first-aid station, afraid to test her sudden luck, she did not ask if he really would do it; she only looked at him—dumbly, longingly.

The arguments of the committee are subsiding. Hank Andrews turns toward Brian, who has said nothing for the last half-hour, and asks his opinion. There is a pause while everyone waits for him to step forward in his usual role of George Kennan—to make a structural analysis of the conflict and propose a compromise which all of them can, though grudgingly, accept; that is why he is chairman.

But today Brian has difficulty remembering his lines. To gain time he asks that Chuck read the petition again. He rests his forehead on his fist and gives the impression of a person listening, while he looks around the table at his colleagues, imagining what political advice they would give if they knew of his own dilemma.

Chuck-Castro might advise him to leave Erica because she represents middle age and the past as against youth and the future. On the other hand, with his belief in freedom of choice and suspicion of all institutional structures, he is hardly likely to recommend a forced marriage to Wendy. He will probably encourage Brian to assert his right to self-determination; to resist the attempts of other persons to lay their trip upon him, or force him into their bag.

Randall-Hull will also stress individual freedom, along with individual responsibility. He will enjoin Brian to stand on principle: to uphold his public reputation as a man of moderation and integrity, and to honor his past commitments—with specific reference to those made in 1950 in Cambridge, Massachusetts.

As for Dibble-Metternich, he will see in Erica and Danielle's plan what he has detected in other instances: a monstrous conspiracy of women. Or if not a conspiracy, a hysterical revolt against male authority and (on Erica's part at least) against their own best interests. He will demand that Brian suppress this revolt by any means possible, not excluding physical force.

Brian cannot guess what advice Andrews-Machiavelli would give him, though he is sure to recommend guile rather than oratory or violence. Very possibly he would suggest that Brian attempt to divide and conquer the three adversaries who are now joined against him.

The reading of the petition is almost done; it is time for Brian to speak. Luckily, the issue is comparatively simple. As in most cases, it is a matter of containment, of separate spheres of influence. The Pass-Fail Option must itself be made optional, with each instructor deciding whether or not to allow it in his courses. Wearily summoning up his usual casually authoritative manner, Brian suggests that they recommend this to the department. And, after some routine oratory, his suggestion is accepted.

Brian tries to accelerate the rest of the meeting, but it is past four when he returns to his office. He shuts the door but does not turn on the light, so as not to be interrupted while he plans his counteroffensive.

Fortunately, he has not yet committed himself to any position.

*174*

Although stunned by Erica's assault, he had somehow retained his presence of mind: he had not said anything unforgivably insulting. More important, though moved by pity and concern for Wendy, he had not promised her anything.

He must begin, Brian decides, by taking what he imagines to be Andrews' advice: he must separate his opponents. First, and most important, he must separate Wendy physically from Danielle so that he can talk to her alone. Even so, the interview will not be easy. Wendy will be disappointed, badly disappointed; and hurt even more than she has already been hurt—he can see her face now, her bruised bare feet. But she is not the only one; Brian himself feels a kind of sick physical despair to think that never again— Her bare legs, her wide small rump—

But why never again? a voice remarks in his head. After all this is over, after Wendy has been to New York—and this must be arranged for as soon as possible— Of course they will have to be extraordinarily discreet from now on, he will tell her. He will hold her strongly, speak to her gently, explain what is best for all of them. He will speak of her graduate fellowship, of Erica's precarious mental condition, of his book. "Trust me," he will say; and perhaps, quietly, he will point out how much trouble and pain there has been because she didn't trust him—didn't confide in him and let him take the responsibility, make the decisions. And she will trust him; she will be grateful, because in spite of her panic and errors of judgment it is not "the end of everything," and he still cares for her, wants her.

Brian sits down at his desk in the fading light and dials Danielle's number; but at the sound of Danielle's voice he hangs up. He looks at the phone, considering whether he should call again and demand to speak to Wendy. But perhaps it would be better to see Erica first, to get that over with. Then he can phone and suggest that Wendy meet him somewhere. If he can't get past Danielle, he will go to the house and remove her—by force if necessary, as Dibble would recommend.

The interview with Erica will be in some ways even more

painful, and certainly more difficult, as Erica's feelings are more complicated. Wendy loves him; Danielle hates him. But his wife is caught in a cross fire of emotions; not only love and hate but jealousy, pity, shame, fear—he can see her now driven back and forth between them from one end of the sitting-room rug to the other. He sees her white feverish face—and next to it, Wendy's face, staring at him with the same distracted fixity. The two faces, the four eyes, move together and merge into one.

The unwelcome thought comes to Brian that two women who were in reasonably good shape when he met them are now, somewhat as a result of his actions, on the verge of nervous collapse. That he hasn't intended this, that he is in fact extremely fond of them both, would be no defense to anyone who knew his history; and if he does not act now with great decisiveness and diplomacy, everyone will know it.

Erica will be hard to deal with, even to speak to at first. He must be prepared for this. She will perhaps always be convinced that she was right, just as she still believes she was right about rooming in. (Even now she sometimes harks back to this, blaming Matilda's problems on the fact that her mother was overruled by the Boston Lying-In Hospital thirteen years ago.)

And once Erica realizes that she has been overruled again there is no guarantee that she will accept it gracefully; that she will cease hostilities and let him move back into the house. But why should he need her permission? Is it not his house, with the principal, interest and taxes paid out of his earnings?

If he tells Erica that he is coming home today—better yet, if he just comes home—she may not like it; but what can she do about it? She may sulk, but she is not going to call the police or become violent. Danielle Zimmern once threw a can of Snow's New England Clam Chowder at Leonard (she missed), but Erica has never within his memory raised her hand against anyone. When the children were too young to reason with, she would pick them up and carry them into another room away from some forbidden

*176*

object, rather than slap them—sometimes over and over again, with a stubborn womanly patience he could only marvel at.

Even after he has reoccupied his own territory there will be difficulties in pacifying the natives. He must resign himself to a long, hard campaign. He must arm himself this time with better arguments, including those suggested in imagination by his colleagues. He must, like Chuck, defend self-determination; like Randall he must speak of responsibility—of his and Erica's moral obligation to carry out their sworn promises to each other, to society, and above all to Jeffrey and Matilda. He must point out to Erica that her plan was not only against her own interests—which in her present martyr's mood will hardly weigh with her—but against the interests of The Children. How could she think of exposing them to so much pain, disruption and scandal?

These arguments must convince her, since they are true. But even if they do not, eventually the argument, and the proof, that he loves her and prefers her to Wendy and all other women, must prevail.

Of course as long as Erica goes on seeing the abhorrent Danielle, his campaign will be twice as difficult. He must begin as soon as possible to separate them, pointing out at every opportunity—but subtly—how aggressive and unfeminine Danielle is, how hostile she has always been to men, and specifically to him. Erica is loyal to Danielle out of habit, because they were in college together, and such habits are hard to break. But she must realize that people change, not always for the better. After all, Danielle is not the only possible friend in town. Among the wives of his colleagues there are many pleasant, normal women.

It is quite dark in Brian's office when he leaves, but outside the air is still saturated with dull gray light. The clouds hang low, heavy and fuzzy, though it is not actually drizzling. As he stops for the traffic signal by the bridge, he suddenly sees a very peculiar, unpleasant thing crossing in front of his car: a sort of faceless, headless dwarf in black galoshes with a dirty burlap bag pulled

*177*

down over most of its body. Though this formless thing does not seem to notice Brian, who is also protected from it by the metal armor of his Karmann Ghia, his breath stops; he feels shock, dread. Then, ahead, coming toward him along the sidewalk in the damp dusk, he notices two more uncanny dwarfish figures: one red with horns and the other wrapped in a sheet. Of course; it is Halloween. He breathes. The light changes and he drives on, passing on his way home other children dressed as skeletons, pirates, Mickey Mouse, Dracula, Batman, and other conventional monsters.

It is still light enough for him to remark again how disreputable his yard looks. The grass is strewn with broken twigs and damp leaves, and in places with rotting wormy apples. Even more offensive are the overturned cans by the drive, spilling wet papers and bottles and foul sodden garbage into the gravel and grass. The dogs of Glenview Heights have been at their trash again, and no one has done anything about it.

Trying to set aside his disgust and anger, to compose himself for the coming battle, Brian enters the house. He is aware first of rock music soaking down from above; next that all the lights are burning in the empty kitchen, the refrigerator door is partly open, and there is food abandoned on the table: a box leaking crackers, a carton of milk souring, smeary jars of peanut butter and jam.

"Erica?"

There is no reply. He turns off the light, slams the refrigerator door, and walks through to the sitting room. Slouched down on the sofa, reading a comic book and eating a leaky sandwich, is a skinny adolescent boy with thick wire-rimmed spectacles, long dirty blond hair, and acne.

"Jeffrey. Is Mom home?"

Jeffrey looks up briefly, chewing, and returns to his comic.

"Please answer me when I speak to you. And take those muddy shoes off the table."

"I did answer you."

"Excuse me, you did not."

"I shook my head," Jeffrey says in a sullen argumentative voice, not moving his feet. "That's an answer, isn't it?"

"Not a very polite one." Brian waits, but his son remains silent. "Where is she, then?"

"Idunno," Jeffrey mumbles, spitting crumbs. "She wenout."

"Mm." Brian paces back the length of the carpet and looks out the window, noticing—as he would have noticed sooner if he were in a calmer state of mind—that Erica's car is not parked in the driveway next to the overturned cans.

"Jeffo, I'd like you to do something about the yard," he announces, attempting to speak pleasantly, even humorously. "I've only been gone two days, and already the place looks like a suburban slum."

"Yuh," his son mutters, not glancing up.

"The lawn needs to be raked. And there are a lot of twigs and branches down; you'd better stack them by the back wall. The leaves and apples can go onto the compost heap. And I'd like you to pick up that garbage. Those idiot dogs have got into it again, because somebody forgot to put the rocks on top of the cans . . . You know," he adds conversationally, "it seems to me you shouldn't have to be told about this sort of thing. You're getting old enough now to take some responsibility for the place, to notice when you come home from school if something needs to be done, and attend to it."

There is no visible response to this speech. Jeffrey turns a page of his comic book.

"So come on, now," Brian continues, speaking louder and a little less pleasantly. "Go outside and get started on the job, before you forget."

Finally his son looks up. "Wouldja stop *persecuting* me, okay?" he asks in a tone of deep grievance. "I'll do it later."

"I want you to do it now." Brian keeps his voice even with difficulty. "And while you're at it, you can clean up that mess you left in the kitchen."

"I didn't leave any mess!" Jeffrey slams his comic down on the sofa. "Why do you always blame everything on me, huh? If there's any crap in the kitchen, it's Muffy's crap. Whydoncha ask her to clean it up?"

Brian represses a comment on his son's choice of language. "All right, I will. And you get to work on the yard, okay?"

The rock music intensifies as Brian climbs the stairs; soon he can make out the words, which express crude, clamorous physicality. He thinks, as he has thought before, how disagreeable and unsuitable such music is for a thirteen-year-old girl. Matilda is presumably still technically inexperienced; but shut up for hours every day with those obscene noises, how can she retain any real innocence?

On the third-floor landing the frenetic pulsing and shouting are intolerable, and his knock inaudible. So, apparently, is his voice.

"Matilda? Are you there, Matilda?"

Receiving no answer, Brian opens the door. A fat witch is in the attic bedroom, standing with her back to him before a mirror. She wears the traditional filthy black skirt and cape, with peculiarly stringy and shiny long black hair falling from under a tall cardboard hat.

"GOTCHA BOOM BOOM," screams a hoarse licentious male voice from opposite speakers, as if summoning the fat witch to a Black Mass.

"Matilda!" Brian shouts.

The witch turns. Beneath the pointed hat and straggling black plastic hair is a plump young painted face, chalk-white and hideously asymmetrical. One eye has been outlined and rayed in electric blue and black so that it resembles a huge spider; the other eye is Matilda's.

"Would you turn that record down, please! I'd like to speak to you!"

With an air of sulky weariness the witch crouches and reduces the volume minimally. "GOTCHA Boom Boom . . ."

"I wanted to ask you, Muffy— I said, turn it down so you can hear what I have to say."

"I can hear you now."

Exasperated, Brian crosses the room and turns off the record player. "Boommmmm."

"You're ruining my Stones record!" Matilda wails, snatching the tone arm off.

"And you're ruining your hearing, playing the phonograph so loud, do you realize that?" he retorts. "I've already told you, and I'm sure your mother—"

"I can hear better than you can," Matilda interrupts spitefully, turning her back on Brian and continuing with her make-up.

"That's not the point, Matilda. It's a gradual process." No response; his daughter is frowning close into the mirror, blackening her brows and lengthening them until they meet above her snub nose in a hag's scowl. "Your hearing may be all right now, but if you don't take care of it, by the time you're my age you may be sorry." No response. Matilda begins to smear her other eyelid with blue grease. Presently, when both eyes are spiders, she will go out with a shopping bag and show them to the whole neighborhood. "You know, Muffy, a witch doesn't have to be grotesque. You're an attractive young girl; I should think you'd want to look pretty when you go trick-or-treating."

Though he has spoken mildly, Matilda's reaction is a howl. "Aw, cowplop! What's the good of trying to look pretty, long as I've got these?" She rounds on him, grinning fiendishly to reveal a mouthful of metal braces laced with damp rubber bands. "And I'm not going trick-or-treating. What do you think I am, a baby?"

"Then what are you dressed up like that for?"

"I'm invited to Elsie's slumber party."

"Oh? And what is a slumber party?"

"Don't you even know that? You have a party, and then you sleep overnight."

"Overnight? You're too young to stay out overnight."

"Mom said I could." Matilda pulls the bottom lid of her right eye down hideously while she lines it in black crayon.

"Well, I say you can't." Brian makes a mental note to speak to Erica. If she gave any such consent, it must have been in a moment of distraction. "If you want to go out in the neighborhood that's all right, as long as you're home by nine," he adds generously.

"But I already told Elsie I'm coming!" His daughter's voice rises steeply.

"Then you'll have to tell her you're not."

Under the witch's hat and hair, Matilda's pudgy thirteen-year-old face takes on the foul expression she has painted onto it. "I don't have to do what you tell me," she declares. "You're not my boss." As if to prove this she squats down in her black skirt and restarts the phonograph.

"No, but I'm your father, and I want—" Brian begins, but he is shouted down by sex-crazed voices as the volume rises: "awah booM BOOM GOTCHA!" He is aware that he should turn the machine off again, should carry the battle with his daughter through; but a feeling of disgust and exhaustion has overtaken him. Erica is responsible for this insurrection; let her handle it. He turns and leaves the room.

As he descends the stairs, pursued by the lewd shouting and panting, he thinks how when he first met Erica her two favorite albums were the Bach double-violin concerto and some old English ballads sung to a dulcimer, of which he remembers best a song about a fair maid who followed her true-love to the wars. He can remember Erica shyly and eagerly setting the heavy waxy old black 78s on a wheezy phonograph in the living room of her Radcliffe dormitory for him to hear. She would go with him wherever he chose to go, the song seemed to declare, some weeks before Erica herself declared it; her life would flow after and into his as Bach's second violin gracefully echoed and joined the first. A choking feeling comes over Brian; he leans for a moment against the stairway wallpaper, but Matilda's infernal music drives him on down.

*182*

In the sitting room Jeffrey has not moved, except to slump lower on his spine behind *Plastic Man Comics.*

"I thought I told you to clean up the yard," Brian says, standing over him.

"S'too dark out," his son mumbles through an apple core. "Do it tomorrow."

"I want you to do it now."

"I said I'd do it tomorrow, awright?" Jeffrey brays, finally looking up at his father with an insulting stare. Brian stares back, not moving. "Wouldja leave me alone now, so I can read?"

Brian feels a pounding in his chest. "You're not reading!" he explodes. "You're just rotting your mind with childish trash. When I was fifteen I read Gibbon, but I haven't seen you with a book, outside of homework, for weeks. Do you have any homework today, by the way? . . . Jeffrey, I asked you a question."

"Oh, why don't you fuck off."

"Don't speak to me like that." He pulls *Plastic Man* out of his son's hands.

"Gimme back my comic!" Jeffrey yelps, rising angrily, clumsily. Over the summer he has grown to be nearly as tall as Brian, though he probably still weighs twenty pounds less. If it came to a physical struggle— Brian holds the comic behind his back, gripping it tighter.

"I'll give it back after you've done your work."

Jeffrey glares, and begins a threatening gesture, but does not carry it through. "Awright, awright," he growls. "If you'll get the fuck out of my way."

Having won, Brian overlooks the obscenity; he stands aside, and Jeffrey slouches grumbling from the room.

Five o'clock; and Erica is not back yet. Brian frowns and goes into the kitchen to check his watch. The sight of food still spoiling on the table reminds him that he has neglected to tell Matilda to clean up, or to ask when her mother will be home.

His Timex is accurate, but the times are out of joint. He feels exhausted, persecuted; his heart is still pumping. Brian has never cared much for children in general, but for years his own children have been the exception. He has treated them affectionately, seriously, fairly. Then why should he now have a son like Jeffrey, so sullen and selfish: a son who when other boys are out raking leaves or playing football sits slumped on his plastic spine reading *Plastic Man Comics?* Why should he have a daughter like Matilda, so painfully different from the gentle pretty daughter he had wanted and expected: a pudgy, whiny, sulky child who battens upon the commercial screams of sexual delinquents while disguising herself as a witch?

Suddenly the idea comes to him that it is not a disguise—that the scowling adolescent hag upstairs is Matilda's true self, just as Jeffrey is in some profound sense a plastic man; that all the monstrous children he passed this afternoon on his way home, dressed as devils, ghosts, Dracula, etc., have merely made their real natures visible, this one day of the year.

As he walks about the kitchen waiting, very impatiently now, for Erica, Brian thinks how unfair it is that he should be insulted as he has just been by his children, and threatened—yes, even physically threatened, there was that in Jeffrey's voice and stance. And Jeffrey is still growing; presently he will be taller than Brian and weigh more. Matilda also is beginning to grow; she is already large for her age. It is not beyond the bounds of possibility that one day Brian Tate will be the smallest person in his family.

That he should have to listen to the daily insults and threats of these monstrous adolescents, to live in the same house with them— The irritated muttering in Brian's head halts. Another clearer, louder voice remarks that he does not have to live in this house; that in fact all those concerned are concerned to put him out; that he is there now to argue and plead to be allowed to remain "for the sake of The Children." That is, for the sake of Jeffrey and Matilda, who obviously would not care if they never saw him again.

He must be crazy. Why should he do anything for the sake of such children? Why should he stay here to be insulted and threatened by them; to be scolded and blamed by his wife?

Considering what she has made of them, what right has she to judge him? Let her cope with what she has created; or rather—to be charitable—failed to prevent. Let him go where he is wanted, listened to, passionately loved.

Brian looks out the window again, but this time to make sure his wife is *not* coming home. Hastily, before she can do so, he retrieves his briefcase, raincoat and overnight bag, and leaves the house. Jeffrey is in the side yard, raking up apples with the wrong, or garden, rake, which is very bad for the lawn; but Brian does not stop to correct him. He gets into his car, starts the engine, and drives off into the damp, cold, darkening afternoon.

# 10

It is the day after Thanksgiving. Erica is up in the storeroom sorting clothes: putting summer dresses away in cloudy plastic bags and taking winter skirts and coats out. She is alone in the house, for Jeffrey and Matilda are in Connecticut with Brian's mother and aunt; but she is not lonely. She has not been lonely, or depressed or unhappy, for nearly a month.

At first she had hardly believed her feelings; she kept waiting for the reaction. Instead, day after day, there was only the euphoria of freedom—joy and relief at having Brian out of the house for good—in every sense *for good.* Cleaning out his chest of drawers, she felt no nostalgia—only a faint distaste for all those identical rolled dark-brown Orlon socks clustered together like horse droppings, for the pale shirts ($14\frac{1}{2}$–32) pressed bone-stiff in their cellophane bags. She took everything out and packed it into cardboard cartons; then she scrubbed the drawers with detergent and hot water, and relined them with fresh shiny blue-flowered contact paper. She dusted and waxed the empty bookshelves in the study.

Suddenly there was so much space in the house! She could walk through it, from room to room, and make everything right everywhere. She could take down the ugly yellow-varnished antique maps Brian had hung in the hall; she could move the best reading lamp, which he had somehow appropriated, back into the sitting room where it belongs. She could trade in the ugly, clumsy Jar of Peanut Butter for a nice little blue VW station wagon that can park anywhere.

She can do what she likes now in her house; she can wear what she likes and cook what she likes. Brian will not come home at five-thirty tonight or any night to criticize the salad dressing or blame her for Jeffrey's table manners or the fact that the plumber hasn't come yet to fix the drip in the downstairs bathroom. She needn't ask his permission to buy new curtains or have Danielle to dinner. And she doesn't have to plead and reason with him if she wants to take a part-time job: all she need do is call the placement office as she did last week and say she can start on Monday. It vexes her that the job she has started is not as good as the one Brian forced her to decline: November is the wrong time to seek employment, and the best they could offer her was fifteen hours a week of typing and proofreading for a science journal. Still, it is a start.

More important, she has begun to draw seriously again. There is gradually taking shape in her mind a new children's book, about a hare who lives in the northern forest, and turns white when the snow comes. She is not sure of the plot yet, but she has already completed some of the illustrations: large, delicately detailed ink-and-wash drawings.

Thinking of her book, Erica turns to the attic window. This is the one room which still has a view uninterrupted by ranch homes; it looks away from the city of Corinth over rising fields and woods bleached and stripped for the coming winter. As a local painter once remarked, nature is an instinctive psychologist of color: in summer she soothes the eye with cool greens and blues, but when the weather turns cold she puts on warmer hues. The late autumn landscape is all done in beautiful pale reds and browns, freckled

*187*

with white from the first light snow. She must draw her next scene like this, from a height, with an oak tree there, the road there, the long field sloping up—

Erica rests her elbows on the sill, looking out over the lovely empty world, contemplating with wonder her own state of mind. She had expected to feel some moments of painful satisfaction at having made the right decision about Wendy, but not this continuing joy. Is it true, after all, that virtue is rewarded?

Of course there have been some difficult moments. But she would not have had it otherwise: without them, her happiness might have seemed too dreamlike; almost unreal.

Many of these moments have come about because she is still outwardly living a lie, though not one of her own choosing. As yet the real story behind the separation is known only to Danielle and to Wendy's roommate. Everyone else in Corinth believes that the Tates have parted because of mutual dislike. It is Brian, of course, who has invented this fiction. He has made her promise to conceal the truth until after their divorce—in order to protect Wendy, he claims. But it is really himself he wishes to protect, for Wendy has no social shame, and would be proud to announce her condition from the steps of the college library through a microphone. Erica acceded to her husband's demand very reluctantly. In her view it was not only dishonest but foolish. It would not prevent scandal, but merely postpone it—and very likely accentuate it. For now, when the real facts are uncovered, one of them will be that Brian and Erica have been lying to all their acquaintances for several months.

Already many of these acquaintances are not satisfied with the report of mutual incompatability; they want to know the details. Was it sex? money? relatives? drink? They have invited Erica to lunch and to parties in order to pursue the investigation. Usually she has gone, and smilingly endured their covert or overt scrutiny, their pitying and prying remarks; she has met their tactful or tactless inquiries with calm self-possession. This restraint was painful at first, but she kept silent by reminding herself that her inquisitors would learn the truth soon enough. Then they would remember how she had said with a fine smile that this separation was the best thing for everyone. By now she no longer regrets her promise to Brian; she feels as if she were walking through the world carrying within her a wonderful secret, which like Wendy's child grows larger every day.

Concealing the facts from her own children has been harder. She and Brian had given out the official version together at a special family council; they had decided beforehand, not without acrimony, what to say. Brian had wanted to break the news gradually, and speak now only of a temporary separation. But she had insisted that even if they didn't tell the whole truth, they must not tell any lies which the children would remember later. They mustn't promise that the separation would be temporary; Brian musn't say that he had to be alone because of his work. She had spent wearisome hours convincing him of this, and more hours devising honest but evasive answers to every question she imagined the children might ask.

When the council finally took place it was anticlimactic. Brian and Erica made the short, neutral statement they had agreed upon; Jeffrey and Matilda received it stolidly, without apparent curiosity. Pressed for an opinion, they became even blanker. Their father was going to be away from home for a while—but he had been away before, lecturing and at conferences; and this time he would still be in town and would see them regularly. So what was the big deal? It was okay by them. No, they had no questions.

During the next few days, however, both Jeffrey and Matilda approached their mother separately. Erica had anticipated and even hoped for this. When Matilda asked how long Dad was going to be gone, she had her answer ready ("I can't say now. It depends on a lot of things . . ."). As she spoke she looked at her daughter and felt, for the first time in months, a deep rush of natural sympathy—not so much maternal as simply female. As a child, Muffy had been strikingly pretty, like her mother: slim, graceful, elfin. Now, at thirteen-and-a-half, she was pudgy and shapeless.

Her beautiful pale brown silk hair had been split and roughened and streaked orange by cheap dyes; her mouth was full of orthodontic hardware. But beneath this appearance, beneath the badly patched jeans and the baggy sweatshirt with ZOWIE! printed on it in comic-book lettering, was—or one day would be—a woman like Erica herself. Like Erica—or Danielle, or Wendy—Matilda would grow up, fall in love, have children, and be disillusioned by some man.

And this man already existed, somewhere in the world. At that moment, wherever he was—standing in line for a Thanksgiving film matinée in some small town or big city, walking in the country, playing football in a vacant lot, or in some college stadium—he was slowly moving, walking, running toward this house, toward Matilda. It might take him a long time, but eventually he would get there, and get at her, and it would all begin over again.

". . . so we just have to wait and see," Erica concluded, touching the shoulder of Matilda's pink ZOWIE! sweatshirt gently.

"You think Dad could be gone a month, maybe?"

"He might." Erica smiled, conscious of all she could not say now, would be able to say later.

"If he doesn't come back—" Matilda looked up at her intently, as if she had understood somehow, instinctively—as if she knew that Brian would not come back, and was glad of it.

"Yes, ducky."

"Well then, Mummy." Muffy's eyes lit, and she spoke with her old warm, childish eagerness. "Can we get a TV?"

"Certainly not." Erica ceased to smile.

"Why not? You said it was Dad who didn't like TV."

"He doesn't like it, and I don't like it." Erica tried to control herself and speak more evenly.

"You said you didn't care."

"I did not, Matilda."

"You did too. Anyhow, what about majority rule? It's two against one now, because Jeffrey wants TV too . . . Oh yeh? . . . You always give us this bullshit about fairness and democracy, but you don't mean it . . . phony . . . mean . . ." She continued in this manner for some time, becoming first whinily insistent and then abusive, finally referring to her parents as "senile freaks."

Erica managed to remain calm, even forgiving. She looked at the mouthful of metal and rubber from which this abuse was issuing and thought of the fairy tale in which every word the ugly daughter utters comes out a toad. It was really as if Muffy had fallen under a bad spell—the spell of Brian's lies. If Erica could have told her the truth she would have had other things to think of than TV, and this bad unreal scene would not be taking place.

When Jeffrey accosted her a few days later Erica was more on her guard. He appeared at the kitchen door when she was cooking supper, and barked, "Hey. What's for eats tonight?"

"Kangaroo burgers, baked kangaroos and kangaroo sticks." This was an old family joke, meaning that the answer to a question was obvious, just as now: the hamburgers were simmering in onion sauce on the stove, the potatoes visible through the oven door, and she was at that moment scraping a carrot under the tap.

"I just asked," Jeffrey grumbled, not smiling. He slouched into the room and remarked in the same noisy, offhand way, "Listen: this business of Dad moving out. I don't get it."

"Really?" Erica stopped scraping. "What don't you get?"

"The whole scene. I mean, you don't fight or anything, like Joey's parents."

"People don't have to fight to be better apart for a while."

"But what's the hassle then? How come you can't hack it with Dad?" Jeffrey continued in the hip speech he has begun to affect. "I mean, he zaps everybody sometimes, but he's not basically such a bad cat."

"I'm afraid I can't explain it to you now." She smiled at him, conscious of exerting calm patience.

"When can you explain it?" Jeffrey began to drum with the joined fingers of one hand against the counter, an irritating nervous gesture that he must have picked up from Brian.

"I don't really know." She shut off the faucet and laid the wet carrots on the cutting board which Jeffrey had made for her in seventh-grade shop, when he was all right and everything was all right. "It depends on a lot of things—" But Jeffrey, unlike his sister, did not wait to hear the prepared speech through.

"Yeh, you said that already." His adolescent voice broke awkwardly. "Only you never tell us anything. It's just, like stupid."

"Please don't interrupt me, Jeffrey. I'm telling you something now. I was saying that when two people have differences, they may not know right away whether—"

"What differences, man?"

"—whether they will turn out to be unimportant, or not; they may need time to think things over and consider them," she continued, chopping the carrots into small strips with a knife. "That's why we all have to—"

"Oh, fuck it," Jeffrey exclaimed. He turned and left the kitchen loudly, and Erica did not forgive him as she had forgiven Matilda.

Nor does she forgive him now. For one thing, he is older than Matilda: he is fifteen, not a child. He should realize that there might be things she cannot tell him yet; he should have the tact— And why should he assume the separation is her fault, that she cannot "hack it"—whatever that means—and tell her that Brian is not a bad cat?

That's what you think, Erica says to herself, reviewing the conversation as she looks out the attic window over the winter landscape. And it occurs to her that Brian is, precisely, a bad cat; she recalls a specific former local cat, a sneaky prowling tom named George who lived on Jones Creek Road when the Tates first moved there. George, who belonged to a nearby farmer, habitually killed songbirds, and twice in rapid succession knocked up the Tates' Flopsy before they had her fixed. Flopsy died of old age and overeating two years ago; and George is dead long since, his back broken by a truck hauling out dirt from the first of the Glenview Homes, but Erica has not forgiven him.

Jeffrey blames her already, she thinks, though he knows nothing about the separation. When she can answer all his questions, will he change his mind? She is not sure. Beyond the clumsy childish egotism he shares with Matilda, another manner has begun to appear: a noisy male coarseness of speech and gesture. Picking him up after school, she has seen him (before he saw her) in a group of loutish half-grown boys, all laughing grossly and shoving each other as a group of girls passed. She has found a magazine called *Penthouse* among the candy wrappers and grit and wads of used tissue under his unmade bed. Perhaps, even when he knows the truth, Jeffrey may think his father not such a bad cat.

But Matilda will understand; as time passes she will understand better and better what Erica has done, and sympathize more and more with Wendy, a woman like herself; indeed a girl not much older than she.

The shadows of high clouds pass over the fields beyond Erica's attic window, stippling the ground with paler and darker patches of light, like an impressionist painting; and a similar effect of light passes over her mind as she thinks of Wendy. She smiles, recalling Wendy's affection, her continuing eager gratitude, her appreciation of the obstetrician recommended by Erica, and of Erica's understanding when she has morning sickness or cramps in her legs (appreciating it even more because Brian is impatient with such complaints); her new look of health and enthusiastic happiness. Perhaps at times Wendy's happiness is too enthusiastic: the truth is that, unlike Erica, she is a good loser but a poor winner. In defeat she is gentle and resigned; in victory she has a tendency to exult, even to crow. But, considering everything, Erica does not find this very hard to overlook.

What disconcerts her more is Wendy's blind admiration of Brian. That she should love him and believe in him is of course desirable; but she seems to have no ability to judge him in anything, let alone oppose him. And without this moral independence it will be hard for her to be a really good mother, for there are moments when even the best husband must be overridden. (Erica recalls, as she often does, how Brian once tried to make her leave for a weekend in New York although Jeffrey looked flushed and had a low fever. "It's nothing," he had insisted; but it was German measles.)

It is clear to her already, though not to Wendy, that Brian is not sufficiently aware of his responsibility to the baby; that his attitude toward it is impatient and peevish. For instance, Wendy tried recently to talk to him about names. She wanted to give the child a unique, meaningful name; among those she and Linda liked, she said, were Laurel and Lavender. Or if it was a boy, perhaps Sage. "Why not Spinach or Cabbage?" Brian had scoffed. But Wendy attributed his callousness to the fact that she had approached him at a bad moment. ("It was all my fault really. I'm so dumb; I'm always interrupting him when he's trying to concentrate.")

She will have to stand by Wendy after the child comes, to watch over them both. The prospect makes her smile firmly and nod her head. Then she frowns, recalling that it is almost a week since she last saw Wendy. They had planned to meet for coffee on campus Tuesday, but at the last moment Wendy couldn't come because Brian needed her to read proofs of an article out loud to him. Erica suspects this excuse; but she does not suspect Wendy. She believes that Brian heard of their appointment and invented the need to read proofs; she thinks he is deliberately trying to discourage their meeting for some reason—perhaps social embarrassment, perhaps mere jealous spite.

Men are often jealous and suspicious of friendship between women, though they value it among themselves. According to Danielle's feminist friends, this is because it contradicts their idea of women as lacking the political virtues, as desiring neither liberty, equality nor fraternity. ("You notice you never hear anyone talk about *sorority*.") We are held to be capable of devotion to our husbands and children, but catty and competitive with all other women, without true affection for them.

Whereas the truth is, as anyone can see, that women are far

better friends to each other than men are. We are not naturally so selfish and aggressive, and we do not have to be. Brian is directly in competition with his "friends" in the political science department here, and indirectly with those elsewhere. Or, if they are much older (or younger) than he, he looks to them (or they to him) for professional advantage. Only rarely, as with Leonard Zimmern, can he have a friendship untainted by either rivalry or calculation —and then it must lack professional intimacy, for Leonard is in another field. Women, however, are all in the same field, yet not in competition. Brian must hoard his ideas for publication; but if she passes on a new recipe she earns her friend's gratitude and loses nothing.

Another cloud passes over the sun, shadowing the view. Erica recalls that her children will be arriving on the bus from New York in less than an hour. She must finish up here, hang the winter clothes in the proper closets, put on her coat, and drive downtown. Conscientiously, she follows this program. But at the bus station she is informed both by a hand-printed sign on the counter and by a rude young man behind it that the 3:20 from New York will be an hour late.

To pass the time she decides to go to the library. Leaving her car, she walks up the shabby end of Main Street, by cheap small groceries, bars, beauty shops, garages, a Chinese restaurant and a narrow store she doesn't remember having noticed: the Krishna Bookshop.

Erica halts. For weeks, in the retroactive amnesia which follows upon shock, she has forgotten Sandy Finkelstein. Now she remembers that her old Cambridge acquaintance, or someone else of the same name, is the proprietor of this shop. Beyond the printed sign hanging inside the glass door (YES, WE'RE OPEN) is a narrow room lined with bookshelves, occupied by two people. One is a girl with fuzzy hair in a duffle coat; the other a man. His back is turned to Erica, but something about the uneven droop of his shoulders, the way he now reaches up one long arm for a book, seems familiar.

Erica pushes the door open. The man glances around at her briefly, nods—but with no sign of recognition—bends to retrieve a book he has just dropped, turns back, and continues his conversation.

She advances two steps into the store, and stops beside a colored astrological poster, uncertain. That man looks too old, too bald; also he didn't seem to know her. Perhaps she only imagined it was Sandy.

Talking rather excitedly (something about the new moon) the fuzzy-haired girl walks past Erica to the front desk, followed by Sandy's aging namesake. She hands him money, receives change and the wrapped book, and leaves with friendly exclamations:

"You oughta come out to the farm again for dinner, okay? How about tomorrow?"

"I'll be happy to, if I can get a ride," Zed says in Sandy's voice—gentle, light, dry.

"Oh, no problem. Mike or Stanley oughta be coming in with the truck sometime. I'll tell them to stop on their way home and pick you up, okay?"

"Fine."

But if it really is Sandy, he is sadly changed. He looks tired out, shabby, in poor condition. His face, with its blurred pale scarecrow features, is badly creased around the eyes; and the thick energetic red hair which was one of Sandy's few good points has faded and slid down off his head, as if with exhaustion. It lies now in dingy rusted curls around the base of the freckled crown.

"See you tomorrow, then."

"Peace, Jenny."

Jenny makes a peace sign in return, hunches her shoulders under the heavy coat and goes out. Zed follows her to the door and reverses the sign hanging on it so that the other side faces out (SORRY, WE'RE CLOSED). Then he turns and stands with his back to the door, looking across the shop at Erica, smiling, but very slightly.

*196*

"Aren't you Sanford Finkelstein?" she asks, also smiling, mainly with embarrassment.

"I was."

"You *were?*"

"Are you Erica Parker?"

"I was." Erica smiles fully, then laughs. "Sandy—" She moves nearer, holding out her hand. Zed hesitates, then takes it with his, which feels dry and cold.

"I'm awfully happy to see you again," he says.

"Yes, so am I." This was one of the nicest things about Sandy, she recalls: his childlike directness. But how changed and worn he is! He looks older than Brian, though he must be four or five years younger, and his freckled skin is lined and gray. She might not have recognized him on the street, except possibly for his eyes, which are still pale and wide under sandy eyebrows with an expression of perpetual surprise. "How long has it been, eight or nine years?"

"Nearly ten. We met at the ballet in New York just before Christmas in 1959."

"Did we?" Erica frowns. "Yes, I think I remember. What ballet was it?"

"The Nutcracker. You had on a purple dress and were with your son, and another little boy named Freddy and his mother. She was very pregnant."

"Emmy Turner. That must have been just before she had Hannah. What a fantastic memory! You probably still know all those Greek verbs, too, that I've completely forgotten."

"Some of them."

"I thought you were in Japan."

"I was in Japan."

"But you came back."

"Apparently."

Erica laughs again; she recalls this tone, and looks at Zed with reminiscent affection. "You know, you've been here all year, and I never knew it until about a, week ago," she says, altering the time out of politeness.

"Yes. I thought that."

"You thought that? You mean you knew I was here in Corinth?" He nods. "You should have called me." He shrugs. This too she remembers about Sandy: his shyness and lack of social initiative. He was always willing to accompany her wherever she happened to be going, at any time—to Sage's grocery, the library, the Fine Arts Museum in Boston, or Filene's Basement—but he seldom suggested any excursion himself; and when invited to a party he usually did not come.

"I don't like telephones. Evil spirits of the air, a friend of mine in Tokyo calls them."

"But in Cambridge—"

"I didn't like them then either. I never phoned if I could help it; I always came over to Edwards House to see you, if you remember."

"You didn't come to see me here." Erica smiles, but she is thinking that perhaps this was just as well. The effect on Brian and the children of this pale, shabby ghost from her past; their probable impatience and irritation, even rudeness; the probable effect of this rudeness on him—

"I don't like automobiles." Zed glances toward the street, where automobiles are parked, with a grimace she remembers well. "No. That's not the whole truth. I thought of calling, or getting somebody to give me a ride out to your house. But then I thought, If it was meant to happen, it would happen. God's will." He smiles oddly, and looks at Erica. "Would you like some tea?"

"Yes, that would be nice."

"It'll take a few minutes." Zed goes to the back of the shop and passes behind a curtain made of faded orange-striped madras bedspread. There is the sound of water running unevenly. She waits, looking at the shelves which line the room, the books with odd titles and obscure publishers, a notice announcing classes: MONDAY—ASTROLOGY. WEDNESDAY—BEGINNING MEDITATION.

"You give lectures here, as well as selling books?" she says when Zed reappears.

*198*

"Not really. Seminars. I don't perform like Levin or Jaeger. I couldn't if I wanted to; and I don't want to. Though that's what they'd like, most of the people who come." Zed grins.

"Because they're lazy, you mean?"

"Not so much lazy as intellectually passive. A lot of kids get interested in mysticism because it looks like a way out of all the pressure that's on them. A way out of the system."

"And they're wrong?"

"No, they're right. But that doesn't mean there's no work involved. Not just study—they don't usually object to that; they're used to it. They'll do anything you tell them, really. Except think." Zed smiles. "They have this idea that the Path is a sort of conveyor belt that'll carry them along to enlightenment without any serious effort on their part. If they have questions, they think all they have to do is ask me."

"But if you know the answers—" Erica tries to keep irony out of her voice. She doesn't want to mock Sandy; she is sorry for him, and mildly curious.

"I don't know the answers," Zed says impatiently. He sighs and leans back against a shelf, where his elbows make two indentations in a row of works on alchemy. She can see the nearer one, white and knobby, through a raveled hole in his gray sweater. "I tell the kids who come in here, 'Don't lay that guru trip on me. I'm not qualified.' I know something about meditation, and I can tell them what books to read, and what not to do if they want to get onto the Path, and that's about all. If they want a real teacher they've got to go somewhere else: to the Zen Center in Rochester, or to New York. Or the Far East. There's the kettle." He straightens up.

This time Erica follows him down the dingy narrow room and past the bedspread to another even narrower and dingier room. Shelves and cartons of books take up most of the space, along with a narrow studio couch. In one corner there is a paint-streaked sink with dishes and pans stacked on the ledge beside it, and a row of canned goods, tomato soup and peas and applesauce, above.

*199*

Hanging from nails are what must be Sandy's clothes: a long overcoat, two long-armed wool shirts and some crumpled striped pajamas.

"Do you live here, too?" she asks.

"It's convenient." Zed shrugs. "And cheap." The kettle is wheezing and spitting; he lifts it from the hot plate and tries to pour into a teapot on the shelf above. "Oh, blast."

As the hot water slops over, and he grabs for something to mop up with, Erica remembers another afternoon tea nearly twenty years ago. Sandy is sitting opposite her at one of the small square tables in Schrafft's on Brattle Street. In front of each of them is a glazed paper doily with spiderweb designs punched out in opposite corners, and a cup and saucer with a green *S* monogram in Gothic script. Sandy raises the dark-green teapot and tilts it over her cup, and its oval top falls off, slopping hot water on the varnished wood. She can hear him cry "Oh, blast," just as he did now, and see him lifting aside the cups and the silvery aluminum sugar bowl with its two handles like arms akimbo, and the plate of cinnamon toast cut into four parallel strips; mopping up awkwardly with his own and then her paper napkin; finally bending under the table to retrieve the top of the pot, because no one in rural Waterford, New York, ever taught him that you don't pick things up off the floor in restaurants.

It is not, however, an instance of Proustian recall, the discovery of a lost memory. Erica has thought of this scene many times, because it took place during the most important conversation of her and Sandy's acquaintance. The subject of this conversation was, Whether it is worth doing anything after you realize you will never be first-rate at it. Or, as he put it—referring to a philosophy essay on which he had labored for three weeks—"if you know it will always be an A-minus, never an A. Once you're sure of this, shouldn't you just quit the field?"

But Erica, who had the same problem, found herself taking the other side. As Sandy rose into view above the table again with his red hair awry and the top of the teapot in one hand, she heard her own voice maintaining a position she had not, up to that moment, known she held. You didn't leave the field, she insisted; you only moved to another part of it, where the ground wasn't so hard. Take her cousin at MIT. He couldn't do theoretical physics as well as some people, but he would still be a good engineer. Or suppose, like her, you knew you probably weren't going to become a first-rate painter, she went on with conviction, gazing across the damp table at Sandy. You didn't give up art. Instead you concentrated on what you could do, didn't he see? Which in her case was small amusing line drawings.

"Yes; I see," Sandy had replied; and for once he seemed to be considering Erica's argument seriously, as possibly true and not just an expression of her own opinions. This was rare; in spite of his chronic shyness and naïveté, it was difficult for anyone to make an intellectual impression on Sandy. Perhaps, as a rural small-town boy, he had picked up the automatic agrarian suspicion of all theorizing.

Subsequent events seemed to prove that this time, though, he had been convinced. Not only did Erica follow her new rule from that day on—Sandy also seemed to be following it. The trouble was, he didn't seem to know where to stop. Leaving behind the heights of logic and metaphysics, he moved down to the less difficult slopes of ethics and aesthetics; then, the next year, still lower, to the history of philosophy, with special emphasis on the Oriental tradition. After finishing his degree, he associated himself with less and less reputable institutions, finally ending up with a part-time appointment in a California city college.

But no matter how far he descended, Sandy never seemed to reach his level of competence. Probably this was mostly due to self-doubt rather than lack of ability, Erica thinks sadly, watching him now as he spoons sugar clumsily from a cardboard box into a stained cup with no handle—why doesn't he just pour it? Sandy had a good mind, and he always worked hard. But even now, on the lowest and muddiest slopes of philosophy (if it can still be called that), even here, in this dingy shop surrounded by half-literate tracts and astrology posters, he doesn't feel competent. It is really pathetic. For over a year he has been living in this dismal back room on Iona canned peas and Heinz vegetarian baked beans, too shy to presume on their past acquaintance, thinking perhaps that she wouldn't want to see him now he has sunk so low. Something must be done about this.

"You must come to supper sometime soon," she therefore says, following Zed back into the shop and watching as he sets his improvised tea tray (a length of unpainted shelving) on the counter by the door.

"I'd like to." He unfolds a metal chair for Erica and takes the stool himself. "I have a class tonight, though, and tomorrow I'm going out to Vinegar Hill—the commune. I could come on Sunday," he adds hopefully, handing a thick crockery cup full of dark reddish tea across the counter to Erica.

"Sunday, then." Though she had in mind a date further off, Erica smiles with some kindness.

"If you're sure you want me. I'm a vegetarian now, you know."

"That's all right. I'll make a cheese soufflé or something." Yes; and without having to worry any more about how the soufflé, or Sandy, will irritate Brian.

"And I haven't any car. But don't worry about that. I'll get out there somehow."

"Mm," Erica says, not really listening; it has occurred to her that there is something she must tell Sandy. "Brian won't be there, you know," she begins, her voice faltering slightly. "He and I . . ."

"Yes, I heard about it."

"Oh? I suppose everybody has, by now. There's so little to talk about in this town . . . How did you hear about it?"

Zed pauses, looking at Erica over his mug. "Wendy told me."

"Ah." Erica tries to swallow this information, which tastes unfamiliar and hot, like her tea. She sets the cup down. "You know the whole story, then?"

"Just what she's told me." His manner is vague, mild; but

Erica is not fooled. She recalls how after quizzes in Greek class, when she asked Sandy how he'd done, he would reply in the same vague, self-deprecating tone. He knows everything.

"I haven't seen her for a while," he adds. "I may not be up to date."

"Neither have I." Erica looks at the floor, considering. Brian would be furious that someone like Sandy should know his story; yet she cannot blame Wendy for confiding in him. It was always terribly easy to tell things to Sandy, even things you wouldn't tell your best friend; perhaps partly because he was so dim and out of it all.

"She admires you very much, you know."

"Yes." Erica lifts her face, on which a look almost of pride has appeared. "It was all an awful muddle really. I just tried to sort it out the best I could."

"Wendy said you were incredibly kind to her. She thinks you're a fantastic, beautiful person." Zed smiles. "She admires Brian too—maybe even more," he adds in a different tone.

"Oh yes, she thinks he's—" Erica begins shrilly; then stops herself, for she has resolved never to criticize Brian to anyone except Danielle. "I don't blame Wendy," she continues more evenly. "Not for anything really. She's a nice girl. A little naïve and weak, that's all . . . You're shaking your head. Don't you agree?"

"I was shaking it at them." Zed indicates the door of the shop, outside which two young people are standing. As Erica watches they turn away with disappointed expressions. "But I don't agree, not exactly. After all, weakness can be a strategy like any other."

"A strategy?"

"Or say a *modus operandi.* I see it here in the store all the time. And I know from my own experience. If you give up the struggle for conventional goals—money, status, power—a lot of energy is released, for one thing." He refills the cups, and continues, speaking more slowly, "Also, you have certain tactical advantages. The battle isn't always to the strong, as we learned in History I. The weak have their weapons too. They come and collapse on you, like defeated nations, and you have to take care of them. 'Oh! What shall I do now?' they cry. So you tell them what." He grins mockingly. "Then they go and do it, and whatever happens after that is your responsibility. I've had to make myself a rule: never give advice to anyone."

"Yes, but she was so helpless—so desperate really," Erica says, almost to herself. "She couldn't—I had to—" she utters, and stops.

"I know that." Zed looks at her. "I don't mean it's calculated," he continues. "Or even conscious, most of the time. But it works. How do you think Wendy got what she wanted from Brian in the first place? Essentially it was the same as it was with you. She went into his office and fell apart. Typical double Cancer."

"She fell apart," Erica repeats, passing over the astrological joke, if it was a joke. She has a vision of Wendy crying and vomiting into her kitchen sink.

"It didn't work for a long time. Your husband kept giving her the wrong advice, the kind she didn't want. He told her to find other interests, study harder, try cold showers—"

"But she didn't take that advice." Erica frowns; she feels a little dizzy.

"Oh yes she did. She took it, but she kept coming back again and saying it hadn't worked. That's how it's always done. It's a very old strategy, thousands of years old— It's the standard method for getting into a Zen Buddhist monastery, for instance; I've used it myself." Again Zed glances past Erica to the door. The two young customers have returned, with a third, and are gesturing through the glass; one holds up a book. "Just a second; I'll tell them to come back later." He stands up.

"No, don't do that," Erica says, looking at her watch. "Let them in; I have to leave now anyway to get my children." She begins to gather her things. "I'll see you on Sunday."

"Well. All right." Zed goes to the door, motioning to the people outside with the patting gesture that means "Wait a moment." "What time shall I come?"

"About seven? Then I can give the children their supper first."

"Fine."

"And I'd better tell you where I am, and how to get there; it's a little complicated. If you could give me a piece of paper, I'll draw a map."

"You don't need to do that; I know where you are," Zed says, turning his sign so that CLOSED faces in again, and unbolting the door. "I've always known where you were."

# 11

In the vestibule of the Frick Museum, shortly past noon on the day after Thanksgiving, Brian Tate strolls back and forth, occasionally glancing at two carved chests and a small bronze sculpture group depicting the triumph of Reason over Error. From time to time he pats the front of his jacket in a quick, concerned way which would inform an experienced pickpocket (who fortunately is not present) that a large sum in cash is concealed there. He is dressed more soberly and formally than usual, and his expression is one of confidence and well-controlled tension, like an officer directing a military operation—in fact, very like that of General Burgoyne in Reynolds' portrait, which hangs in one of the rooms he has just passed through.

Already today Brian has accomplished much. He has risen early, forced Jeffrey and Matilda to rise, breakfast, pack, and leave his mother's house in Connecticut; he has driven to New York, garaged his car, bought Cokes and snacks for the children, put them on the bus for Corinth, and seen it depart—completing all these maneuvers in such good time that he was half an hour early at the Frick. His first action there was to make a quick reconnaissance of the galleries in case Wendy had arrived even earlier. But the museum is unusually empty; it is an unpleasant day, promising cold rain or sleet, and there are only a few well-dressed old ladies and ill-dressed art students wandering about.

Brian has chosen the Frick as a rendezvous for several reasons. First, it is easy to find and convenient to the address he and Wendy must proceed to later. Second, it is one of the few remaining places in Manhattan where it is possible to sit down in pleasant surroundings without buying food or drink. Also it provides the first comer with something agreeable and educational to do while waiting, instead of wasting time. Even more important, it is never crowded. The Met and the Modern are mobbed by humanity during vacation, and among these mobs some of Brian's students or ex-students are statistically likely to appear. The Guggenheim is quieter, but its design is unsuited to a meeting—besides, it always makes him dizzy, as if he had been swallowed by a concrete snail.

Beyond its practical advantages, the Frick Museum has an important symbolic function—a lesson to teach. More than any public collection can, it stands for a way of life: for elegance, art, taste and civilized living conditions—in fact, for all that Wendy has to gain by having finally listened to Reason. In these high, airy rooms is the concentrated essence of everything lacking in her background and education—a sample of what he will show her next summer when they go to Europe. Wendy has never been abroad except for a three-week tour which seems to have consisted mainly of driving through foreign cities during heavy rain in sightseeing buses crammed with American students, all singing popular American songs. She has never met any Europeans except hotel managers and shopkeepers; never been to Sadler's Wells or the Prado, or eaten in a good French restaurant. All this, and much more, he can give her, will give her—as otherwise he never could have, for as he and Erica proved years ago, it is neither economically or socially possible to tour Europe with a small child.

For Brian, the last four weeks have already been an education: not in art history or European civilization, like that he plans for Wendy, but in her own field of social psychology. As his separation from Erica became known to all his acquaintances, and his attachment to Wendy to some of them, he has learned firsthand what is meant by "role typing" and "social cathexis."

Marital difficulties, he has discovered, are socially equivalent to a childhood or trivial illness—colic, chicken pox, flu. Everyone who hears of them is openly concerned; they express mild regret ("Sorry to hear about you and Erica") mixed with curiosity ("How is it going?") and a compulsion to relate their own experiences with the same ailment ("You know Irene once moved out on me? Yeh, she took the kids and went to her mother's for three weeks") and to offer advice ("That's how women are; you have to give them time to cool off").

Adultery, on the other hand, is a social disease. Like halitosis or the clap, it is what only your best friend or worst enemy will mention, though everyone talks about it behind your back. Brian can therefore only guess how widely his affair is known, or how it is generally regarded, though he is aware that both his best friend in the department (Hank Andrews) and his worst enemy (Don Dibble) think less of him for it.

Not all Brian's lessons in social psychology have been as hard as this. He has found it a great relief not having to face, every day, Erica's spoken and unspoken reproaches; and an even greater relief to get away from Jeffrey and Matilda—from their noise, their rudeness, their greed. He recalls something Leonard Zimmern said long before his own divorce: that most men don't want to leave their wives half so much as they do their adolescent children.

Now that he has vacated it, Brian realizes he has been living in a hostile camp, among people who at best tolerated, at worst exploited and defied him, for a long while—in a sense, all his life. What amazes him most is that this discovery has come so late; for instance that he could have lived forty-six years without knowing what it is to be really loved. His parents' affection, though genuine, was always conditional on good behavior; as was that of his other relatives and his teachers, from nursery to graduate school. The girls he knew before marriage were all self-seeking: even when they claimed to love him, they strove to withhold some part of themselves, either physical or emotional, according to current social custom, in the hope that he would commit himself further to obtain it.

As for Erica, Brian has always known that she cared less for him than he did for her. From the start he was the one who loved, while she allowed herself to be loved. That was her nature, he had told himself. It was not as if she preferred someone else; indeed she very evidently preferred him. Brian could accept that; did accept it for nearly twenty years—until he met Wendy, who never judges him, withholds nothing, cares more for him than for herself.

Of course this unconditional love has disadvantages. Sometimes Brian feels like a man with a new, overaffectionate pet, whose constant and obvious devotion is half a source of satisfaction, half an embarrassment. He cannot romp with Wendy as often as she, or he, would like—he has to conserve energy for his work. He has had to teach her to restrain herself in public: not to lick and paw him; to sit, quietly, and not disturb him when he is working. But overall her effect has been energizing, even exhilarating. He has not perhaps spent as much time on his book as he should, but what time he has spent has been productive.

As he paces the hall of the Frick, Brian glances alternately at a guidebook he has purchased, and into the galleries, planning what he will show Wendy, and in what order. The dining room, with its rather simpering portraits of English beauties, can be skipped. The two smaller rooms beyond—all light, elegant eighteenth-century French furniture and decorations—seem at first glance just right to begin with: a pleasant if frivolous contrast to the gray, dirty city outside. But after a second look he rejects them. There are altogether too many babies in the painted wall panels by Boucher. Indeed, the panels of the inner room, which represent the arts and sciences, are entirely peopled by babies: plump, coy infant poets; chubby infant astronomers and musicians—figures which cannot help but recall Wendy's obsession with the possible genius of her unborn child.

Better to start across the way, in the Fragonard Room, where the panels portray an elegant pastoral love affair, and the only children present are winged cupids. It is not the sort of art Brian usually pays any attention to, but today one of the paintings, titled "Reverie," catches his eye. This shows a very pretty young girl, fair, round-cheeked, sitting dreaming at the base of a tall sundial in a relaxed attitude. He has often seen Wendy sit so, on the floor in his apartment, with her head tilted back and one arm flung out along the couch. Indeed, Wendy could almost have posed for this picture, in the proper fancy dress, with her hair curled and lightly powdered.

When they are abroad next summer—or even this weekend here in the city if she feels well soon enough—he must take Wendy shopping. He doesn't know much about women's clothes, but he is aware that hers are not only ridiculous but unbecoming. The heavy leather browns and tans of her American-Indian getup, the dirty yellows and reds of the East Indian prints, are suited to women of a darker complexion. Wendy ought to wear rose, creamy white, lavender, like these French girls whom she resembles; also her clothes should fit, rather than hang. Something might be done about her hair, too.

Looking at the painting again, Brian feels, as the artist clearly intended him to feel, both romantic and sensual. The girl is young but not, to judge by her pose and hints in the other panels, innocent. Her charmingly but almost indecently low-cut dress suggests experience, and so does the way her knees are spread under the long draped skirt, and one hand placed strategically in her lap. The thick column of the sundial, with its round tilted top on which a naked cupid marks the hour of noon, is surely phallic. An observer is meant to imagine himself stepping up over the carved and gilded frame into that leafy sunlit garden, lifting those folds of pink and white silk . . .

He checks his watch. Wendy is nearly due, so he returns to the museum entrance, but she is not there. This irritates Brian, who dislikes waiting for women at the best of times, and has suggested that she arrive early. Now there will hardly be time for them to look at anything seriously before their appointment with "Dr. Friendly." (Impossible to guess what impulse of self-deception or black comedy had made the abortionist choose this alias.)

Brian walks back through the rooms toward the West Gallery, where the most important works of art hang. It will be a relief when this day is over, he thinks; when this month is over. Reason has fought a hard battle; Wendy's mind, under the veneer of education, is illogical and stubborn. She may look like a graduate student, a liberated woman, but basically she is no different from the girls in the Fragonard Room: feminine, emotional, driven by instinctive forces beyond her own control. Though exasperated and exhausted by the struggle, he knows he cannot really blame her—that is what women are born for, as the numerous simpering madonnas on these walls testify, from Byzantine icons to Renoir. He recognizes the strength and inevitability of Wendy's wish to have a child; but he is determined not to become personally involved in this process.

The logical conclusions of his argument have not escaped Brian. Fond as he is of Wendy, he knows that their relationship cannot be permanent. Eventually she will need to have children; she will marry someone nearer her own age. Eventually he will return to Erica and his family—probably when Jeffrey and Matilda are somewhat older. But not now; not yet.

He walks down the long gallery inspecting the paintings. Wendy's attention should be called to the Rembrandts and the Goya; the rest can be passed over more rapidly, since they will not have much time now. But as he dismisses them Brian notices one picture which appears to his heightened and impatient perception almost symbolic: Veronese's "Allegory of Vice and Virtue." It seems to him that the features of the handsome youth who is rising from his seat beside Vice into the embrace of laurel-crowned Virtue (but looking back over his shoulder) might be his own at an earlier age. Virtue, who is somewhat taller than the young man, wears an expression of calm and loving solicitude. Though he has evidently sinned with plump, blond Vice, she intends to take him back; she wraps her blue mantle around him forgivingly and protectively.

Erica should see this painting; there is a lesson there for her. But she would not heed it; she has not forgiven him yet and may never forgive him now. Most wives would be relieved and grateful for what is about to take place, but he knows Erica will be furious. She will pretend regret for the baby, but Brian suspects that all along the baby was just an excuse to get rid of him. Otherwise, why should she have been so eagerly self-sacrificing, so willing to dispose of him "for his own good" and the good of another woman's unborn brat? Tall, cool, unforgiving, this modern Virtue spurns the hero; she turns away and wraps her satin cloak around herself.

Brian checks his watch again and realizes that Wendy is now almost fifteen minutes late. He walks rapidly back through the rooms. In the front hall he pushes through the turnstile and goes to the door, but Wendy is not coming along the street in either direction. Something has delayed her: her mother? the bus? It is annoying, because they are due on Park Avenue at Eighty-seventh in three quarters of an hour.

Perhaps he should call, just to be sure. He goes back into the museum, receiving a sour look from the guard at the turnstile, and finds the public telephone, which is not well located for seeing Wendy if she should come in. His dime produces no dial tone, and after losing twenty cents he notices a discreet *Out of Order* sign in italic penmanship. Swearing, he makes another even more rapid tour of the galleries, and again returns to the front door, squinting through the cold drizzle along Seventieth Street for a phone booth. There seems to be one at the far end of the block and across Madison Avenue; but if he goes to it he may miss Wendy. And since this is New York, it is also likely to be broken.

Feeling more and more irritable, Brian turns back into the building for the third time. As he clicks through the turnstile the guard, a tall cavernous figure in the style of El Greco, addresses him. "You going in or out, mister?" he asks sarcastically. "This ain't the subway."

Ignoring the remark as it deserves, Brian continues with an air of purpose to a room called in his guidebook the Living Hall, which is strategically located so that anyone visiting the Frick must pass through it to reach the major galleries; it also commands a view of the courtyard in case Wendy should choose that route. This room is dominated by an imposing fireplace, over which looms El Greco's "St. Jerome as a Cardinal"—the guard at the entrance transfigured. He points sternly to an illuminated page of his Vulgate. The text is indecipherable, but from its location in the volume and his expression, it must be one of the more hysterical prophets. "This place is damned, and all its inhabitants," he seems to inform Brian.

On either side, Holbein's Thomas More and Thomas Cromwell face each other across the empty marble hearth: the scholar, saint and gentleman's son from Oxford; and the son of the Putney brewer, the shrewd, hard politician who in a few years will destroy him.

Neither More nor Cromwell are looking at Brian, but as he stands there he feels their attention—even, before long, their disapproval. The expression of More, who had been one of his early heroes, combines sorrow and resolution: it is that of a Harvard professor who finds himself forced to fail a once-promising student. Both as a fond husband and father and as a loyal Catholic, he cannot sanction Brian's recent behavior. His grief at seeing him there on the carpet, with a wad of twenty-dollar bills where his heart should be, is restrained but profound. In a moment he will repeat sadly, almost to himself, the words from his *Utopia* which he knows Brian once copied onto the flyleaf of a Coop notebook with secret high resolve:

> For it is not possible for al thinges to be well, onles al men were good.
> Whych I thinke wil not be yet thies good many yeares.

As for Thomas Cromwell, he has little interest in past promises, or in moral questions. This hard-headed administrator, with his heavy ringed hand and his narrow moneylender's eyes, has no time for such nonsense. He measures value in terms of accomplishment: deals made, problems solved, opponents eliminated, cash coming in. At certain moments in his career, for instance at long-winded departmental meetings, Brian has silently called upon this man, who in an incredibly short time and almost single-handed brought the English church under submission to the state. Sometimes the ghost has responded; has given him the energy to interrupt tedious arguments and propose cutting through petty scruples and red tape. But Cromwell's attitude toward Brian today is one of cold scorn. He condemns him as a clumsy and impolitic small fool who has allowed mere women to get the better of him; who has failed to make it either as a good man or a bad one. "You still think that little whore is coming, do you?" he asks suddenly, hardly moving his tight lips.

Disconcerted, and not only that he should imagine a picture to speak, Brian turns his back on the three portraits and looks at his watch. It is twenty minutes to two; unless Wendy arrives almost at once she will be late for her appointment. For the first time it occurs to him that something has gone seriously wrong. Wendy has come down with the intestinal flu since he spoke to her yesterday, or she has been mugged by a mugger on her way from Queens to Manhattan.

He starts back through the galleries, forcing himself not to hurry, even pausing at moments in front of some painting. The Fragonard girl is still dreaming of her lover below the sundial; but this time she has a different look. Her abandoned pose, the swelling of her breasts (now too large to be properly contained by her silk bodice), and a fullness in the face which he has lately noticed in Wendy, all suggest the same thing: that she is already, as she would put it, *enceinte.* And is not the naked cupid above, whose shadow falls toward the number XII, unmistakably demonstrating that it is too late?

Brian pushes past St. Jerome at the turnstile and out onto the damp cold front steps, where for some time he paces back and forth, continually consulting his watch and becoming damper and

*2 1 4*

colder. Finally, at three minutes to two, he makes a rush through the drizzle toward the distant phone, looking back over his shoulder at intervals. Reaching it, he hesitates, wondering how long Dr. Friendly will wait for his thousand dollars (minus the two hundred he has already received)—fifteen minutes, surely?—and decides to call Wendy's house first.

This telephone seems to work, but Brian hesitates; he stands listening to the dial tone, reluctant to dial, to speak to Wendy's mother again. He has never met Mrs. Gahaghan, and does not want her to hear his voice too often. Also he feels uncomfortable because when she does hear it she responds as if he were Wendy's age, rather than only two years younger than she. But the phone is humming, time is passing, and he is cold. He dials the number.

"Hello?" The formal, wary, falsely genteel voice of Mrs. Gahaghan.

"Hello, is Wendy there?"

"Gosh, I'm sorry." Her tone changes to one of informal, good-natured regret. "Wendee's already gone back to college."

"Already gone?" Brian feigns surprise, for this is what Wendy had planned to tell her parents. "When did she leave? . . . You see, I was planning to meet her," he adds.

"Oh, dear. You were expecting to meet Wendee *today?*"

"Yes, about half an hour ago." Brian tries to project a light, careless tone through the electrical connection.

"Oh, dear me. I'm awful sorry. I guess she must of forgot about it. She left right after breakfast for the university, she got a ride with her roommate Linda, do you know Linda?"

"Yes, I know Linda," Brian says through his teeth.

"She was planning to take the bus, see, but then last night Linda was over and she'd heard of a ride back to college with some friends, of course that's much nicer than the bus, and Wendee hasn't been feeling very well this vacation and she wanted to get back to her work, she has an examination coming up, I'm sure you know how that is, and I'm afraid she didn't think— I know she'll be very sorry when she remembers—"

During this speech Brian holds the telephone farther and farther away from his head, causing Mrs. Gahaghan's apologetic quacking to dwindle to a distant twitter. When she runs out of breath he brings it back. "Yes . . . Thank you . . . No, that's quite all right . . . Don't worry about it," he says, and hangs up.

For the next hour, like Burgoyne at Saratoga, Brian does not allow himself to speculate on what has happened. He concentrates on arranging the practical details of his retreat: telephoning Dr. Friendly, canceling the hotel reservation, returning the two tickets to *Little Murders*, and getting his car first out of the parking garage and then out of the Friday afternoon Manhattan traffic.

But once he has crossed the George Washington Bridge and turned north on the thruway, there is plenty of time to think. There is time to rehearse his conversation with Mrs. Gahaghan; and also his conversation with Dr. Friendly, in the course of which the doctor reminded him 1) that he, Dr. Friendly, is a very busy man who has given up one of his few opportunities to spend time with his own family on a national holiday in order to help Brian out; 2) that he does not do this sort of thing for money, but because he believes in Human Rights; and 3) that he has, nevertheless, extremely heavy expenses. Brian would have liked to make an abrasive remark at this point. Instead he controlled his tongue, and—with considerable effort and the promise of an additional fee—managed to arrange another appointment for the following week.

As well as rehashing the past, Brian has time to think about the future. He curses aloud as he contemplates the student conferences and the committee meeting that must now be canceled, the new hotel reservations that must be made, the twenty-dollar bills that must be withdrawn from the bank; the renewed negotiations with Wendy, who will have to be convinced of the reasonable thing again, and driven to New York again. This time he must keep her away from Linda Sliski, and from Erica and Danielle. He must not let her visit her family; he must not let her out of his sight for a moment.

Brian feels an angry exhaustion, a kind of battle fatigue—almost a desire to give up the struggle. But he cannot afford to give it up. If Wendy remains pregnant she will expect him to marry her. Erica will expect this too, and so will Danielle, and Linda, and presently Mrs. Gahaghan, and all Wendy's sisters and cousins and aunts. He can imagine how they will all set upon him, using every unfair weapon in the female arsenal: tears and scoldings, injured looks and righteous nagging, sexual blackmail and moralistic whining and threats of suicide. He can see them now in his mind, a band of harpies charging toward the New York State Thruway over the nearest icy hill—hair flying, claws outstretched—followed by dozens more, hundreds, a whole monstrous regiment of women.

The men of his acquaintance will not stand with him against this onslaught, though they will censure him if he goes down before it. Brian recalls the earlier imaginary unanimous opinion of his colleagues on the Curriculum Committee that for him to break off his long-standing alliance with Erica Tate and suddenly form one with Wendy Gahaghan would be morally and politically indefensible. In a few cases this opinion will make no difference; whatever he does, Hank Andrews will remain his friend, and Donald Dibble his enemy. But if he marries Wendy, Hank's wife (an elegant shy young woman who quietly admires Erica) will not invite them to dinner very often. John Randall's wife (a well-bred elderly beauty who is a famous local gourmet cook and has always been fond of Erica) will probably not invite them to dinner at all. Chuck Markowitz and his wife will perhaps still invite them; but since Lily is a militant vegetarian, her dinners will consist, as usual, mostly of steamed wheat and raisins and fried eggplant, a type of nourishment he already gets too much of from Wendy and her friends.

Essentially, all Brian's colleagues will think less of him if he leaves his wife and children for Wendy—including those who might condone a discreet affair. A few may envy him sexually, but not very much, and not for very long. As soon as Wendy's pregnancy becomes public knowledge even they will look down upon him, and laugh silently, as he would do in their place.

And if Wendy remains pregnant and he does not marry her, he will also be censured, especially by members of her generation. When his students and graduate students find out (and some of them will inevitably find out, or at least hear rumors) they will think him selfish, untrustworthy, uptight and square. In other words, whatever he does, he will be condemned and ridiculed by at least half the world.

By the time Brian is a hundred miles out of New York the repetition of these ideas and recollections has become intolerable to him. It is for this reason that, somewhere near Liberty, he stops for two bedraggled young people holding up a damp-stained cardboard sign reading CORINTH U. As a rule he declines to pick up hitchhikers—not as a precaution against robbery, but because he prefers his thoughts to their conversation.

In the rear-view mirror, as he slows down, he can see the two students jogging toward him along the dirty shoulder of the road through the rain. They are about the same size and wear the same anonymous, androgynous jeans and boots and parka, making it difficult to tell of what sex they are, even when they reach the car.

"Hey, thanks." They pile in behind with their knapsacks, breathless. "We thought nobody was ever going to stop. How far you going? . . . Corinth? Wow, beautiful." Brian identifies one by its rudimentary pale mustache as male; the other by its voice—a warm, dominant contralto—as female.

"You still pissed at me, Sara?" the mustache asks as Brian swings back onto the highway.

"I never was pissed at you," Sara replies with dignity. "I just think you were being chicken-assed . . . We had this bad experience just now, dig," she adds, sitting forward behind Brian so that he can see her in the rear view mirror; she is very young, slim, boyish and intense, with a lot of dark red-brown hair and matching red-brown eyes under heavy straight brows. "We got a ride outside the city with these two greaser-type guys in a truck. They were into a six-pack, and pretty soon they began giving us a hard time because we wouldn't drink. Especially Stanley. They were picking

on his hair and saying how they'd thought he was a cute chick."
Brian moves his head to get another view of Stanley, who indeed
would have been good-looking if he were female, but makes only a
soft, nondescript young man. "Then they started saying how they
were going to pull off the road and give him a haircut; and
me—well, you know the kind of shit." Sara clears her throat.

"So when they had to slow down for the construction back
there, we opened the door and jumped out," Stanley explains.

"That was lucky," Brian says.

"Yeh, except then we had to stand in the fucking rain for
about an hour, not getting any rides," Sara complains, "because
Stan said no more trucks. He had like suddenly got this stereotype,
see. Every time we saw a truck a mile off we had to put our thumbs
down . . . I don't see why *you* were so unglued," she says to him.
"All you would have lost is hair. I could have got the clap from
those guys."

"Yeh, maybe," Stanley growls faintly.

"Anyhow"—Sara turns back to Brian—"you like saved our
lives, or at least our relationship. If you hadn't come along when
you did, I would have stopped anything on wheels."

"You wouldn't have got into a truck alone," Stanley states.

"The hell I wouldn't. Well, maybe I wouldn't now," she admits
crossly. "But after we finish karate I'm going to go anywhere I
fucking feel like."

"You're learning karate?" Brian shifts his head so he can
address both of them.

"I'm thinking of it," Stanley says, smiling nervously. "I don't
want her to beat me up."

"I could beat you up now, Stanley," Sara says. "I could break
your arm with the side of my hand, if I wanted to. Lesson Four."

Brian laughs, partly to ease the tension between his passengers.

"You think that's a joke," Sara says, leaning forward again.
"You think it's pretty funny for a woman to want to learn karate."

"I think it's not absolutely necessary for you to know how to break a man's arm." Brian smiles at Sara in the rear-view mirror, but her expression only becomes more belligerent. The premonition comes to him that he is about to hear a speech on the New Feminism. "Though I suppose in certain situations it might come in useful," he adds, hoping to head the subject off. "If you were living in Manhattan, now—"

But it is too late. "You think that, because you're a man," Sara informs him. "You're used to the idea that women are the weaker sex, and you want to keep it that way."

"No, I—"

"You don't want us to learn karate, it really scares both you and Stan shitless, because for thousands of years you've kept women down basically by the threat of physical force and violence."

"Now, really, I—"

"I know what you're going to say, you're going to tell me you never hit a woman in your life, but that's because you never had to, you got your way without it. You don't have to physically hassle them, all our social institutions do it for you. Like for instance—"

For the next hour and a half Sara lectures Brian and Stanley on the subject of women: their natural physical, psychological and moral superiority to men; the manifold injustices they have suffered in the past; and their right in the present to equal pay, equal educational and vocational opportunities, free day-care centers, and abortion on demand. (Brian finds this part of the lecture especially annoying). At intervals she takes various paperback and magazines and newspaper cuttings out of her knapsack and reads aloud to them from Simone de Beauvoir and other lady authors. Occasionally Brian tries to change the subject; or to declare that he is already in favor of equality between the sexes, but Sara will have none of that. "Sure, you say so, but you don't really mean it. It's the same with Stanley. He thinks he wants to get rid of all that chauvinist shit, but he can't—it's in too deep, from his conditioning. Like that stupid crack he made about karate."

In the rear-view mirror Stanley's face twitches, but he does not protest. Really, Brian thinks, he is a pretty miserable, low-spirited imitation of a young man. Somebody ought to tell him so, to shame him out of his passivity and knock some guts into him. Brian is beginning to understand why the drunken truckdrivers baited Stanley, and threatened to cut off his long limp curls. If he, Brian, were two big greaser-type guys instead of one small professor, he too might— And Sara? Yes, why not? A good hard fuck, to shut her mouth for a while.

Picturing this scene in his mind, Brian continues to drive as fast as prudent in the direction of Corinth, and to give the impression of listening to Sara. He does this last so successfully that, having concluded her sermon, she becomes quite affable, even confiding. She and Stanley tell Brian of their difficulties with some members of their commune who are heavily into nudity ("Okay, so that's their trip, except then they want the heat up to seventy-five all the time, and the rest of us swelter; besides, it really kites the gas bill") and others who shirk KP. As they approach Corinth, Sara, who is a science major, asks Brian's advice: is there some course in his department he could recommend to fill her distribution requirement? (an impulse of malice comes over him, and he recommends Donald Dibble's Constitutional Law course, smiling to himself as he imagines the inevitable collision of views.)

Leaving his grateful passengers at the bottom of a muddy farm road, Brian drives on into town, to the apartment building where he has been living for the past month. Alpine Towers (more literally Tower, for there is only one as yet, though others are threatened) is brand-new, blatantly modern. Most of the apartments are rented furnished, in the bland indestructible style of airport motels. After four weeks, Brian still often feels that he is in a motel. At other times he feels he is living in one of a rank of post-office boxes—which, from the outside, the tall, flat building with its squares of glass and pressed-metal plating closely resembles. Some of the boxes are empty, some crammed full, and they are constantly emptied and refilled; because of its unusually small rooms and large rents, there is a rapid turnover of incoming

Corinth faculty and outgoing husbands. It is the only building in town which always has a vacancy.

Brian lives alone in the Towers. He has not allowed Wendy to move in with him, though she spends most of her time there. At this stage, he has explained to her, it would not look well. Besides, the apartment is not large enough for two people—or even for one: the closets are inadequate, and apart from the Living Area there is only a tiny ill-lit bedchamber. But Alpine Towers is just a few blocks uphill from Wendy's room in Collegetown, so it is easy for her to go back and forth.

As Brian had expected, his apartment on the sixth floor is dark; Wendy is afraid to face him. Presently he must try to locate her, but not yet; not tonight. It is nearly nine o'clock; he has driven for over eight hours today and eaten nothing since breakfast. His body demands a hot shower, a hot dinner and at least eight hours sleep.

Throwing his coat on the Danish-anonymous couch, Brian makes himself a strong Scotch and water. He takes one gulp, sighs loudly, and carries the drink with him into his bedroom, switching on the light and tossing his suitcase onto the bed, where it falls heavily against a big heap of blankets which was not there when he left, for Brian always makes up his bed tightly every morning as he was taught in the Navy.

"Uhhh."

"Hey! Wendy?"

The blankets churn and shift; she raises her face, which is puffy and streaked with dirty tears.

"Well?" he says in an exhausted, exasperated Navy voice.

"I'm sorry." Wendy struggles to a sitting position. "I didn't think you'd be back this soon, and Linda's having a blast."

"I see," he remarks, in the tone of one who does not see.

"I blew it, Brian."

"So I gather." He comes further into the room, causing Wendy to draw back across the bed with a frightened expression.

"I couldn't hack it, that's all," she mews. "I couldn't."

"You.could.have.let.me.know." Brian is aware of controlling his anger, ejecting his words slowly like separate cold lumps of metal.

"I was scared to." Wendy smiles rapidly and nervously; she is up on her knees now, and he can observe that she is wearing only an oversize faded white sweatshirt printed with pink peace symbols.

"You.ran.away.because.you.were.afraid.of.a.minor.operation." He fires another round.

"It wasn't just that. The whole thing freaked me out. Like you know how I was all last week. And yesterday was worse. I mean you know, Ma and Pa and Brendan and Jakie. And then my sister and her husband drove in from New Jersey with the baby for Thanksgiving dinner, and we had the whole family-of-origin scene. All of them smiling and passing me the gravy and asking how I enjoyed my courses, on account of they didn't know that I was about to commit a murder. Because that's what they'd think it was. I realize it's just my same old parochial-school hangup, the return of the repressed. I know that. Only it really racked me up.

"But I was still convinced to do it. Then last night Linda came over, and I was rapping to her about it, and she said, why didn't we consult the *I Ching*? So we found the book up in my old room; and the first time I threw the coins I got hexagram number forty-two: Increase. I mean, wow."

She looks up at Brian expectantly, but he makes no response. "The thing is, you know," she continues, "with the *I Ching*, lots of times you get an answer that's really hard to connect to your personal situation: it's all about the emperor and the great stream. But this was so right on. Increase! I mean, that's what I'm doing, right? And the Judgement said, get this: 'The satisfaction of the people in consequence of this increase is without limit.' You understand? That means it's going to work out really fine for everybody."

"I understand, yes," Brian says, holding his tone steady. "You're telling me that you decided to change all your plans, and

*223*

screw up your life, and mine, because of the way three pennies fell on the floor of a bedroom in Queens."

"I didn't decide—" Wendy's voice trembles.

"No, I don't think you did. You don't really believe that kind of superstitious crap. Linda might, her head's so fucked up, but not you. The truth is you just hadn't got the courage, or the integrity, to stand by your decision." Wendy edges away from the machine-gun fire along the bed, her back against the wall. She has begun to sob intermittently, but Brian has seen too much of her tears over the past month to be impressed. "You hadn't even got the decency to let me know. Instead you had to sneak out of town." Wendy has reached the end of the bed; she stands up against the far wall, looking damaged.

"But if," she whimpers. "If it's, you know, God's will."

"God's will!" he repeats grindingly. He feels rage burn up inside him, as if a match has been put to powder, fusing all the anger he has tamped down over the past twenty-four hours: anger at his mother, his aunts, Jeffrey, Martha, the guard at the Frick, Mrs. Gahaghan, Dr. Friendly, the parking-garage attendant, the clerks at the hotel and theater box office, Sara, and Stanley. He rounds the bed toward Wendy, who is weeping steadily now.

"Stop that stupid noise." He raises his hand; Wendy, anticipating the blow, crumples with it to the floor. Though he has barely touched her, she does not get up or move, but lies there in a heap, sobbing monotonously.

The fire blazes on; Brian prepares to strike again, more effectively, then pauses. It is partly the inhibition of which Sara spoke, a moral and social block against hitting a woman, especially a pregnant woman, a mother. But even more, it is a sense of futility. He sees himself and Wendy again as the sculpture in the Frick: Reason conquering Error. To an observer there would be no doubt which of them was victor, which vanquished. Brian stands upright, fully dressed, his arm raised, his square jaw set, and a righteous frown on his brow; while Error, half clothed, huddles under his feet, abject and trembling.

But appearances can lie; art does lie habitually. Brian knows from twenty-five years of teaching that Reason often fights a losing battle, and it is proved again here. All his arguments, his month-long logical analysis of the situation, were not worth three cents to Wendy once his back was turned. She lies there now looking weak and disheveled and defeated; he can curse her, strike her again, throw her out of his apartment, and she will not resist. But such tactics will not save him. He is joined to Error through his own flesh, as the figures in the Frick are cast of the same bronze. To separate them will take craft, skilled force, patience.

"Come on, get up," he says therefore, nudging Wendy's bare flank gently with his foot. "Don't lie there crying. I'm not angry at you; everything's going to be all right."

# 12

The one ugly part of the Tates' pretty old farmhouse is the cellar. It is almost entirely below ground level, dark and usually damp, with mottled walls of a sour gray cement which will not hold paint, and a web of rusty pipes and hot-air ducts and wires hanging from the low ceiling. In the least damp corner, raised off the gritty cement floor on soggy two-by-fours, are the Maytag washer and dryer.

Erica is in this cellar on a Monday afternoon in December doing the laundry, which should have been done days ago, when she was in no condition to do it. For a week she has given in to her own bad feelings; she is almost literally washed out, as if she had climbed into the Maytag and let hot rage and soapy self-pity slosh over her, swishing her back and forth in the dark, draining her finally with a hard sucking noise and leaving her as she is now: limp, wrinkled and wrung out.

She still feels wrung out, but the chore cannot be put off any longer, for the weather has suddenly turned worse, as everything has turned worse. Erica cannot feel the wind down here, but she can hear it beating around the walls ·with a noise like hostile laughter. The basement air is at once chilly and stuffy, as if it had been left too long in a refrigerator.

It is Brian's fault that she is here, because when he came last Sunday to take the children out to dinner he asked if she could find his old Navy shirts—which she later discovered, dirty, in Jeffrey's closet. "It's getting pretty fucking cold for this time of year," he explained in the new youth-culture manner he has recently grown to go with his new sideburns and way of life. She should have screamed at him, Find your .own old shirts! But she was too stunned; she merely smiled tightly and agreed to look. She went on behaving as she had been behaving for weeks: as if theirs was the most civilized, high-minded, mutually agreeable separation ever seen in Hopkins County. And this although Brian had just given her news that made the separation, and all her plans and efforts and sacrifices, meaningless. Laughable, even. For over a month she had been a romantic and moral heroine; now, with one stroke, he had turned her into a character in a cheap farce.

But for over ten minutes, until Brian and the children drove off, she went on smiling, conversing—like those figures in cartoons who go on running in the air after they have passed the edge of the cliff, or had the bridge blown out from under them—until the glance down, the double take. Then they crash. As she had crashed after she was left in the empty house with the news that Wendy was not going to have her baby.

Brian had announced this calmly; almost as if he were not concerned. But of course he must have arranged it all; must have been trying to arrange it for weeks. She had been naïve not to have known that he would do this if he could. Naïve and stupid. The wind whuffles against the house, choking with laughter.

And of course Brian knew what it would mean to her. That's why he told her when he was about to leave, when the children were practically within hearing—so that she dared not respond. Because he is a coward, afraid to face the consequences of his acts, as Danielle said.

Erica doesn't blame Wendy; she knows how Brian must have bullied and argued her into it, probably with some of the same arguments he used here in this house when Erica wanted a third child: overpopulation, financial responsibilities, his age. She can imagine too how he must have underplayed the risk of an illegal operation at this point—the pain, the danger. "But isn't it too late for that?" she had whispered when he told her. "Wasn't it very dangerous?" "No," Brian replied smugly, standing there in her dining room in the new dirty-tan Student Shop duffle coat fastened with imitation clothesline and clothespins, which he has bought to go with his new sideburns and manner and way of life. "Not too late."

And why shouldn't he look smug? He has won; his lies have come true. There will be no inconvenience in his life now, no night feedings or diapers, no use for clothespins except to decorate his coat. There will be no inconvenience to his reputation either: almost no one will ever know that Wendy had been pregnant; no one but Danielle and Linda Sliski and Sandy will know what Erica had planned to do for her. And if she were to attempt to tell anyone else, to explain how this separation had been different from all others, how she had arranged it herself out of unselfish motives, probably they wouldn't believe her. They would think she was deluding herself, or trying to delude them, or both, like— Like—

Like Lena Parker, her mother. Erica lets an armful of crumpled wash slump toward the floor, and stands there. For twenty-eight years, ever since she was twelve, she has been running away from Lena Parker and everything she represents. Now she has circumnavigated the globe and run back into her mother's arms. She too has a husband who has ambiguously left home; she too can loudly justify herself, and claim more freedom of choice than she really had.

At least Lena isn't alive to see it, to add her rationalizations to Erica's, to say what she would be sure to say about the separation: that it was best for everyone; that Brian was never "right" for her daughter. "A man married to his work, who does not know how to enjoy, how to laugh!" as she had once exclaimed.

But no doubt Brian is laughing now. He has won: he has destroyed Wendy's child; his own child; her child.

*228*

Stooping wearily, Erica picks up the clothes she has dropped, and climbs the cellar stairs to the dining room. She sorts the clothes, folds them, and climbs two more flights to her children's rooms. Jeffrey's looks as if it had been recently burgled: the bed is torn apart, drawers are wrenched out and overflowing, books and magazines thrown about. She begins to tidy up, for the third time in a week, then stops. What is the use? Let him live in filth and chaos, if that is how he chooses to live. She sets her mouth and shuts the door behind her.

Matilda's room, across the landing, is somewhat neater, but equally painful to enter. The bedcovers have been more or less pulled up, the drawers are shut—but in the corner behind the door is an ugly heap of debris. It has been there for two days, since Saturday morning when Erica sent the children upstairs to clean their rooms. Jeffrey was back almost at once (obviously having done as little as possible), but Matilda delayed. Presently, while Erica was ironing, she became aware of distressing sound effects overhead: banging and splintering. Setting the iron on end so fast that it spat water, she ran upstairs, calling her daughter's name.

"Yeh, what?" Matilda held her door open two inches, scowling through the gap.

"What's going on up here? I heard dreadful noises."

"I'm cleaning my room, like you told me to."

"Cleaning your room? It sounded as if somebody were breaking things. Let me see."

Matilda said nothing, only stood aside so her mother could enter.

"Muffy! What's happened? Your weaving loom is all smashed —and your planetarium."

"You told me to get rid of all the crap I didn't want to play with any more. You've been hassling me about it for weeks."

"I didn't say for you to destroy everything. Oh, look at your ballet scrapbooks! And that beautiful map of Fairyland, that you used to love so much." Erica felt like weeping. "And the dollhouse, it's all smashed sideways. How could you do something like that?"

"I was sick of it," Matilda cawed. "Can't I do what I like with my own stuff?"

"No, you can't." With difficulty, Erica kept her voice under control. "Somebody else might have wanted these things, didn't you ever think of that? We could have given them to Celia Zimmern." No answer. "Don't you touch anything else! Do you hear me?"

"Ookay," Matilda sighed theatrically—her new victim-of-injustice manner, which Erica finds almost more infuriating than the old sulks and screams.

Not all the remains of Matilda's destructive fit are still in her room. Erica has carried what was beyond repair out to the trash can, leaving only a few toys which are undamaged or salvageable: some hanks of colored yarn, a few old picture books, and parts of a plastic Blue Willow tea set—the one that Muffy and Roo used to set out on the grass in the orchard for dolls' tea parties, with one of her striped linen dishtowels for a tablecloth, and apple-juice tea and animal crackers.

And the dollhouse. Once an elegant Colonial mansion, with real turned white wooden bannisters and flowered wallpaper and a pink-and-yellow celluloid fanlight over the door, it looks now as if it had been hit by a hurricane. The roof is unhinged and gaping, the windows sprung out of their frames; furniture and rugs and dishes and doll people have been shaken into the corners of the rooms, which are compressed into ugly parallelograms. Gripping the open sides of the house, she tries to straighten it out. But as soon as she lets go, the beaverboard and wood collapse again with a nasty creak.

Erica feels her head filling with anger and tears. The selfish destructiveness of her daughter, the loss to Celia—and not only Celia, there would have been lots of children, generations of children, who would have been very, very happy to have all those nice toys. Someday, if Wendy's child had been a girl, and been born, instead of being scraped out of her by some greedy crooked doctor and flushed down a drain in New York—

Erica sinks onto Matilda's braided rug, beside the beautiful Colonial dollhouse which Matilda has turned into a broken home—as if one weren't enough for her. This whole house is a broken home now, she thinks—as if some stupid teenage giant walking over the world had picked it up and then, losing interest, flung it aside. Like Matilda, she doesn't want to play with it any more; but it is all she has.

Her head aches with tears and rage, but she mustn't cry again, it will only exhaust her, and besides it is useless. Even if her broken home could be repaired, she wouldn't want it now. She doesn't want her husband back, though the cause for which she sent him away is lost; because who could possibly want someone like that, so selfish and cruel and cowardly and weak and dishonest? What she wants is her old friend Brian Tate, the honorable, strong, brave, kind, generous young man she married. But that is impossible. There is no such person.

Against our will we are dragged through time, by time. Eventually Matilda will become a woman, and be restored to her; but Jeffrey will grow into a man and join the enemy. Because men are the enemy. The Hens are right about that, if nothing else.

Erica has been with Danielle to two general meetings of WHEN, which she found mildly interesting, and to a "rap session" sponsored by them, which she found appalling. She agrees with the Hens in principle, but not in practice—politically speaking, she supports their Declaration of Independence, but not most of their Constitution. She isn't sure, for instance, that she believes in day-care centers. Mothers have a duty to their young children which shouldn't be made too easy to evade.

It also seems to Erica that many of the Hens, though they criticize men, are trying to become like them in all the worst ways—taking on their most unpleasant qualities. They are loud, aggressive, competitive: the woman at whose house the rap session was held, for example, talks about female solidarity, but practices the sort of one-upmanship usually seen only in men. If you tell her that Jeffrey won't pick up his room, she doesn't reply "So aggravating" or "I know, Billy's just the same," but "Oh, really? Billy's always been very good about that. Maybe it's because when he was little I began to teach him . . ." etc.

Another unpleasant male characteristic many of the Hens display, and which more than anything else has made Erica determined not to meet with them again, is coarseness of speech. They use the sort of language she abhors in her children, but in an even worse way. It is bad enough to hear Jeffrey speak of his "fucking homework" and call his teacher an "ass-kissing idiot"; far worse to hear educated women use these adjectives as verbs to describe actual occurrences—to listen while they speak in clinical detail of matters which should remain private.

But the whole feminist campaign, in Erica's opinion, is a mistake. The Hens have identified the enemy correctly, but their battle plan is all wrong. They want to scrap the old code of good manners: they don't like to have doors and coats held for them, or seats offered on crowded trains. They reject these gestures and all that they imply. But in repulsing the traditional attentions of gentlemen, in refusing to be ladies, they are throwing away their best, perhaps their only defense against the natural selfish brutishness of men. Impulsively and foolishly they are abandoning the elaborate system of fortifications which was built up and maintained by their mothers and grandmothers over centuries.

Today, everywhere, Erica thinks, men must be laughing uproariously as they see us dismantling our own defenses from within—removing the elaborate barbed-wire entanglements of etiquette, tearing down the modest walls which for so long shielded our privacy, and filling in the moat of chastity with mud. In a provincial academic town like Corinth the destruction of the fortress is not yet far advanced, or very visible. For years, secure in a rather old-fashioned marriage, Erica· was hardly aware of it. But it was going on all the same; now she sees it everywhere.

The behavior of men to women living alone, for instance.

Erica had heard about this from Danielle, but she had misinterpreted it—or rather it had been misinterpreted to her. After Leonard left, a year and a half ago, a series of semidetached husbands began to appear at the Zimmerns' house, offering to replace him temporarily. Erica had reported this phenomenon, rather indignantly, to Brian. But Brian explained that these men came because Danielle had, explicitly or implicitly, invited them—because she was, as he put it, "broadcasting." And Erica believed him, because he too was a man.

But she knows that she is not broadcasting now. The station has gone off the air, perhaps permanently, and yet these same men, or others like them, have begun to appear at her house, ostensibly to borrow tools or bring their children to visit hers. Others have tried appearing in the university building where she now works and suggesting coffee, or, more crudely, driving her home from dinner parties in the wrong direction and then suddenly stopping the car. But though their means differed, their ends were identical. As she said to Danielle, they only wanted one thing. (Danielle's response, as rather often lately, was not satisfactory: "Hell, I don't know. I used to think, if they only want one thing, the poor bastards, why not give it to them?")

What infuriates Erica most about these men is their patronizing attitude. They all seem to believe, and some have openly, jokingly declared, that they are doing her a favor. When she declines this favor they smile knowingly and renew their attack, for they assume she must be in a state of sexual starvation, and would be grateful for the opportunity to have intercourse with them.

Needless to say, Erica was not grateful. The surprised politeness with which she had at first received these men's attentions was quickly replaced by cool disinterest. If they were still not discouraged she showed moral indignation. This was not well received. When Erica explained that she had resolved never to do to another woman what had been done to her, or reminded her suitors that they were married, some of them laughed and asked when she was going to start living in the modern world; others sighed and began to complain in a disgusting way of their wives' sexual inadequacies. One or two even became sneering: they said or implied that if Erica didn't want them she must be frigid, and it was no wonder Brian had left her.

Another thing which dismays Erica is that several of her unwanted suitors are the husbands of acquaintances whom she had always believed happily married—who no doubt still think themselves so. She feels a painful sympathy for these deluded women, and it has occurred to her that it might be right to tell them the truth about their husbands, but so far Danielle has dissuaded her. ("Believe me, they won't thank you. Maybe if it was a real affair they might want to know, some of them." She smiled cynically. "But not a business like this. Even if they don't blame you for the whole thing, they'll dislike you for it, and take your name off their party list. Or else they won't believe you. Hell, you remember that time Ruth Taylor came around and said she thought I ought to know that Leonard had tried to feel her up at the English department picnic? I practically threw her out of the house.")

Erica is still not sure Danielle is right, though. Her friend is negative about everything lately; she has become so bitter that it is almost painful to visit her. Roo and Celia are not happy either. It is going to be a sad Christmas for them. Not only did Leonard refuse to invite them to New York, he has also declined to come to Corinth to see them until after New Year's Day, claiming that he has to work on an important article. ("Important article, my foot," Danielle said. "It's some girl's ass that's the important article.")

Moreover, Danielle has just had a very bad experience, one which might have sent a less tough and experienced woman— Erica, for instance—into a nervous collapse. This event had occurred last Friday, when she received an unexpected visit from Dr. Bernard Kotelchuk, the veterinarian who had treated Pogo in September. Dr. Kotelchuk had called occasionally since then to see his former patient and the rest of the Zimmern menagerie; he had become popular with Celia and Roo, who has nicknamed him "St. Bernard." Erica had met him only once; he appeared to her as a large, doggy, coarse-looking, inarticulate man of about fifty who smelled faintly of disinfectant and was losing his hair.

Last Friday Dr. Kotelchuk arrived without warning at the peculiar hour of 8:45 A.M., just after Danielle's children had left for school. He had hardly been in the house ten minutes when, as Danielle put it, "he practically raped me on Roo's bed with six gerbils watching." "I fought him off as hard as I could at first," she told Erica. "It wasn't so easy; he must weigh about two hundred pounds. I was going to knee him in the groin like in that self-defense book, but then it occurred to me that he had probably saved Pogo's life, and if he wanted sex that badly, why should I make such a fuss about it? I mean it didn't really matter to me; it didn't hurt or anything. So I stopped fighting him and lay there, and it was just like nothing was happening. The only thing I thought was, Well, at least I've still got that loop inside me; I won't have puppies."

Yesterday evening, in answer to Erica's anxious inquiry, Danielle insisted that she was all over the incident; but Erica doesn't believe her. No matter how experienced you are, that isn't the sort of thing you recover from in a few days. And when you are already as badly hurt by men as Danielle has been, it could have lasting psychological effects.

For a long while Erica has hoped that Danielle would recover from her bitterness toward the other sex with the help of some kind, sensitive man who would be wise enough to approach her gently and slowly. What happened Friday seems likely to set this recovery back months, perhaps years—assuming recovery is possible. Or that there is anyone in Hopkins County worth recovering for. Erica remembers how she used to think that Danielle and the Hens were prejudiced against men. Individually they might have had bad experiences; but not all men were like the ones they have known, she can remember saying to Danielle. Brian Tate, for example, was not like that; he was decent, serious— Of all the women she knows, she had been the most deceived, just as now Wendy is the most deceived.

*235*

One of the most miserable hours of the past miserable week was the one Erica spent having lunch on campus with Wendy. It had been a long time since they met. For some weeks Erica had kept expecting to run into Wendy, and Brian, at one of the many parties given at this season. She had explained to all her friends that there was no reason not to invite both her and Brian, and she was sure that she would be able to meet him calmly, and behave in a generous forbearing manner when he showed up with his pregnant hippie girl friend. But she was given no opportunity to exercise this forbearance; and she realizes now how naïve it was of her to have imagined that Brian would ever choose to appear in public with a pregnant hippie.

It was dreadful just to look at Wendy now; to see her no longer confident and blooming but sallow, weary, with a nervous tremor in her voice. Worse still was the way she parroted Brian's arguments, acquiescing in her own defeat. She didn't reproach him for anything—only herself, for having caused him inconvenience. "I mean, I've got years to have kids," she bleated, pushing aside a half-chewed cream-cheese sandwich. "But if Brian doesn't finish his Book now, when it's published it could be too late to save this country. I could like kill myself when I think how much time he's already lost because of my stupid behavior." And Erica could not find it in her heart to tell Wendy that she *was* like killing herself; that no book was worth this double human sacrifice. That would only make her more tense and unhappy—as tense and unhappy as Erica is herself.

Pity and self-pity are catching up with her again as she sits on the floor in her daughter's room, tempting her to get into the washer again, to give in to despair. She must find something useful to do quickly. She remembers the rule a counselor at camp once taught her: whenever you feel awful, go do something for somebody who feels worse. Psychologically cynical, perhaps—but over the years Erica has found it effective. Now, for instance, she could pack up what is left of Matilda's toys and take them over to the Zimmerns'. The dollhouse, too; even if it can't be repaired, at least it will be out of her sight.

Erica finds Danielle at home in her kitchen, where she is cutting the meat off the roast chicken they had last night for Sunday dinner, and looking rather better. Her hair has been washed and brushed, and she has on a new red ribbed sweater.

"Look at all that," she says, gesturing with her knife. "I can't plan meals right yet; I still think in terms of a normal family. And I keep forgetting about Roo and her stupid diet."

"I know." The strain at the Zimmerns' has been increased recently by Roo's conversion to vegetarianism. Not only did she refuse to eat any roast chicken, she did her utmost to prevent anyone else doing so. ("Do you know how they kill the poor, poor chickens?" she asked, staring emotionally at her mother, her sister and Erica in turn. "They grab hold of them and screw their poor heads tight into a sort of big vise, like the one in Industrial Arts, and then they take this big, sharp, bloody ax—" But at this point Danielle sent her daughter out of the room.)

"She told me this morning she can only have unfertile eggs for breakfast. Where the hell am I supposed to get unfertile eggs?" Danielle laughs.

"I thought all eggs nowadays were unfertile," Erica says, trying hard not to think of Wendy's fertile egg.

"So did I. But apparently not, at least not at the Co-op. Here, let's have some coffee, it's pretty hot. I can't keep up with her any more. The rules keep changing too fast."

"Thank you . . . But that's how it is with everything. You know what I feel sometimes?" Erica adds, sitting down on a kitchen stool and warming her hands on the mug of coffee. "As if I'd got into a time machine, like in one of Jeffrey's science-fiction stories, and been shot forward into the wrong time. Nineteen sixty-nine—it doesn't sound right, it's a year I don't belong in. It doesn't even feel real. Reality was when the children were small, and before the housing development."

"And before Lennie and Brian left home. Yeh. I know what you mean."

"You see, we know all the rules for that world," Erica goes on. "Where to shop, what to read and talk about and wear, whom to have for dinner and what to serve, what kind of sandwiches to make for each lunch box, everything. But now we've got moved into nineteen sixty-nine by mistake. The A & P has burned down and you can't park on campus any more and everybody's children have got big and awful. Everything's changed, and I'm too tired to learn the new rules. I don't care about nineteen sixty-nine at all. I don't care about rock festivals or black power or student revolutions or going to the moon. I feel like an exhausted time traveler. All these new developments they have, maybe they're interesting or depressing or amazing, but they have nothing to do with real life."

"Future shock." Danielle laughs.

"I want to go back where we belong, back to when we were first here, and you used to bring Roo and Silly over to play dolls' tea parties with Muffy." Erica looks at her friend for the confirmation and humorous sympathy she has learned to expect, but Danielle is busy again with the dismantled chicken. "How are Roo and Silly, I mean Celia, anyhow?"

"Fine. They're all excited because Bernie promised to take us out to the country this afternoon to see his neighbor's stables."

"Bernie?" Erica sets her mug down. "Do you mean Bernie Kotelchuk?" Danielle nods. "I thought you weren't ever going to speak to him again."

"Yeh, I know. But when he came over last night, after you'd gone— Hell, you know, what happened before, it was partly my own fault." Danielle stops chopping chicken and turns to face Erica, leaning back against her kitchen counter. "I mean, I told him when he got here there was nothing doing, that the other day was a big mistake. He took it very well. He said okay, sure, he understood; he even apologized. He said he hadn't planned to lay a finger on me when he came to the house that morning, but when he saw me with my hair down and barefoot, and only what he called my 'nightie' on, he lost control of himself. It never occurred to me I wasn't dressed properly. I mean, my nightgown's not transparent or anything—it was the red one, you know, that I wear around the house all the time."

"The long sort of Hawaiian mumu, with the big white flowers?"

"That's the one. Utterly decent. Hell, it was invented by missionaries in Hawaii to cover up everything. But apparently Bernie was brought up in a different tradition, Polish or whatever it was. Respectable women don't go around barefoot in their nighties. If I didn't want to screw, I should have put on a flannel bathrobe and pink fuzzy slippers before I let him in . . . Well, anyhow he apologized. And he looked at the turtles, and I put Celia to bed, and then Roo went to bed, and we sat around, and I poured us some Scotch—you know all those ladies in Brookdale who want to marry Bernie and keep having him to dinner with elaborate food, baked ham and three kinds of pie, only they never give him anything decent to drink . . . Well, there we were . . . So it happened again."

"You mean—"

"Yeh." Danielle looks away, then back, smiling with something almost like embarrassment. Erica does not smile. It is bad enough that her best friend should have been raped once by a stupid, coarse, red-faced veterinarian. That she should passively let it happen a second time worries Erica even more. She decides to speak out.

"You know, you don't owe that creep anything just because he looks at sick turtles and once took care of your dog. After all, that was his job. I think you should tell him to stay out of your house. If he has to sleep with somebody, why doesn't he go and sleep with one of those women who are always feeding him out in Brookdale?"

Danielle shrugs. She puts the cut-up chicken away in the fridge and moves onto a stool opposite Erica. "He can't, unless he plans to marry them," she says. "And even then probably not until after the ceremony. He explained it all to me last night. Those people operate on a different system. They're all good churchgoing widows and spinsters who were friends of his dear departed wife. They play by the old rules and don't commit fornication."

"But that's not your fault! You don't have to let him use you sexually just because nobody else he knows will."

"He doesn't use me, really." Danielle looks down into her coffee and then up again, almost defiantly. "I mean, it wasn't so bad this time. In fact"—her face reddens—"it was sort of fantastic. I was surprised."

"I should think so."

"He was pretty surprised too. But appreciative. He wants to take me out to dinner tonight at the Gables." Danielle half laughs.

"Are you going?"

"Hell, sure. Who would turn down a meal at the Gables?"

"I don't know," Erica replies, thinking that she would, but trying not to let any note of disapproval into the tune of her voice. She reminds herself that the men with whom Danielle was briefly involved after Leonard left also had faults. Some were opportunistic, others neurotic. But at least they were all presentable, intelligent men: lawyers, artists, professors—not Polish veterinarians.

"Of course I can't really talk to him," Danielle adds, as if she had heard Erica's thoughts. "If I mention anything I'm teaching, he just looks dumb. And politically he's hopeless: a grass-roots agrarian populist. But hell, I'm sick of talking to men. Once you start talking to them the next thing is you begin to get emotionally involved, and I'm not interested in getting involved with any man. I don't have to worry about that with Bernie, because he doesn't want it either. Basically he's a pretty domestic type, even kind of romantic. He'll probably end up with one of those nice women out in Brookdale. But right now he's not ready for that; his wife has only been dead about a year. It's just a physical thing between us: I need it and he needs it, and that's all."

"Mm," Erica comments, thinking in spite of herself that Brian last spring had used almost these same phrases to describe his feelings toward Wendy.

"And I really don't like masturbation," Danielle confides in a lower voice. "I tried it a few times, but I could never get much out of it. I couldn't come or anything; I just always felt nervous and silly, you know?"

"Mm," repeats Erica, who has had the opposite experience.

"Bernie and I talked it over," Danielle continues. "I told him, no sentimental lies, no commitments, no promises." She pushes her heavy dark hair back and her jaw forward.

"I see." Erica knows that Danielle wants her to accept, if not approve, this plan of finding temporary sexual gratification with Bernie Kotelchuk. But how can she? It is so flat, so grossly practical—as if Danielle were to announce: "I want a piece of meat, so I'm going to the grocery." Better, surely, to make out with what is already in the cupboard, or to become a vegetarian.

But she is anxious not to hurt her friend's feelings, so she says something vague, and then, inventing a dentist's appointment, declares that she must leave, in order to prevent herself from saying anything more—or worse, having to meet Bernie Kotelchuk. In a flurry of false haste, she scrambles on her coat and boots and scarf and gloves and literally runs from the house. She starts the car fast and, in case Danielle is looking, heads it downtown.

It is a heavy, cold, unattractive afternoon; the clouds hang close over the bare trees, like a huge sodden canvas tent; the wind, still blowing hard, beats and slaps the empty branches about. Erica feels like weeping for Danielle, who has been so beaten about and exploited by men—and by her own dependence on them. Gripping the cold wheel with her driving gloves, she promises herself that she will never, never let herself be so exploited. In spite of herself her eyes begin to fill with tears. Never, never—

She stops for a red light, blinking. She is downtown now, but what is she doing there? There must be something useful, some errands, or Christmas shopping. In the past Erica had always finished this task by the first week of December, but this year she is far behind, partly because she can't decide what to get for anyone, especially the children. Brian told her yesterday that he is thinking of buying them each an expensive AM/FM radio, something she considers quite unnecessary, indeed an ill-concealed bribe. Not to mention the additional noise these radios will cause in the house, where of course Brian is not living at the moment.

Brian feels guilty toward Jeffrey and Matilda, but not any longer toward Erica. He thinks he has done her a favor by arranging the murder of Wendy's child, and he proposes to do her another soon by moving back into her house and bedroom. For surely that is what he had in mind last night when he said they must have a serious discussion soon. Like her unwanted suitors, he would be first incredulous and then abusive if she said she didn't want him; that she doesn't want to live in the modern world with a modern man.

But she cannot sit crying in traffic. Perhaps if she were to park and walk past the stores . . . and there is a space across from the post office. She backs into it, gets out, walks away—then returns and feeds a series of pennies into the metallic head of the parking meter. Jeffo and Muffy used to love to do this for her when they were little; they loved the story she had invented for them about how all the meters in town belonged to a big family of underground aluminum giraffes, and late at night when nobody was looking they would pull their heads back down through the pavement and play together under the city. But the last time she had referred to this fancy, about a year ago, she had been badly snubbed: "Oh, Mother, must you be so stupid?"

The giraffe smacks its cold metal lips on each coin, *pst, pst, pst,* and sticks its round metal tongue farther out. Erica walks away from it toward Main Street, looking into shop windows. But instead of useful purchases, everything reminds her of what she wants to forget: a real estate office "Photo Gallery of Desirable Homes"; in the window of the savings bank, fourth-grade clay artifacts from the school Muffy and Jeffo once attended, where they had made the same loving lopsided bowls and glazed blue animals for her; the gift-shop display of Great Artists' Puzzles, featuring a Renaissance nativity in sawed-up wooden fragments.

Across the street it gets worse. The department-store windows are vindictively symbolic: on one side an imitation ideal family— hers of five years ago—in matching ski outfits sprinkled with soapflakes; on the other, four grinning young people in party clothes. The display case flanking the front entrance is full of men's shoes and boots drawn up in rows at different levels, decorated with argyle socks and plastic holly. They are glossy, heavy-soled, brutally new, ready to stamp and kick and tread on women—

She is not right today, in her head. It is abnormal to feel referred to and mocked and threatened by window displays. That is paranoia, delusions of reference. She must go into the store like a normal person and buy something. But after waiting for fifteen minutes at a counter, elbowed and shoved by other shoppers, only to learn that they are out of Matilda's size in skating tights except for Baby Pink, Erica has a feeling of exhaustion and revulsion and leaves the store. She walks away from the happy plastic family, taking deep breaths of the clammy December air and trying to calm herself.

Main Street has been elaborately adorned for the holiday season, with garlands of sham grass-green fir and colored bulbs looped from one lamppost to the next, and fat red and silver letters spelling MERRY CHRISTMAS hung across the street. The store windows are also decorated, but in two contrasting styles. As Sandy said last week, two different deities are worshiped in America at this time of year; and each Corinth merchant has chosen which he will enthrone. Some windows, therefore, feature nativity scenes, softly lit and trimmed with straw, silver-paper icicles, and stars: homage to nature, rural simplicity and maternal love.

But most of the shopowners prefer another god. They have erected altars, not to a poor young woman and her baby, but to a rich fat old man. In spite of his evident high spirits, he has certain unpleasant characteristics. He is not especially kind to animals, for instance. The family in the bookstore window share their lodgings affectionately with two Steiff cows and a donkey; but in the stationer's next door a life-size cardboard cutout shows the old man wearing a velvet suit trimmed with animal fur. He has large leather boots too, and cracks a long whip over the flanks of his team. He does not favor the working classes, but brings most of his gifts to the rich. He is a pagan God—Jove, perhaps—whose worshipers have placed his image before their shops to bring not spiritual blessings, but material abundance. At the same time he is also Bacchus: look at the heavy belly, the red drunkard's complexion; hear his manic laugh, which is broadcast continually by a speaker over the entrance of the cut-rate drugstore: "aHo Ho Ho! aHo Ho Ho!" And he has a good reason for his merriment: he has won now, he has defeated the Virgin and Child, and is on his way to Erica's house with his sleigh full of unnecessary expensive objects.

But does she have to let him in? Can it be right, really, to take back into her house the sort of Santa Claus that Brian has proved himself to be? If she allows it, she is condoning all he has done; she becomes an accessory after the fact to his crimes. And what about the moral effect on Jeffrey and Matilda? What about poor Wendy; how will she feel, having made this sacrifice?

Besides, there is Brian's work. He needs time alone in order to finish his Great Book, and if he does not get it he will eventually blame her and the children, even if it is not their fault but his own.

No, no, Erica thinks, turning and walking back up Main Street, almost the one person empty-handed in the crowd of package-laden Christmas shoppers. Brian must not move back into the house. She must prevent it, for his own sake, and the children's sake, and Wendy's. It will be difficult: he will try to persuade her, to reason with her. He will speak of his affection for her, his duty to The Children; of the relation between broken homes and school failure. He will try to make her feel guilty.

*244*

But she must not listen. She must lock her doors against him, even literally if necessary (it wouldn't be a bad idea to have the locks changed), and if he tries to get down her chimney, she must build up the fire.

# 13

Early March. In Corinth it is still winter; week after week cold clouds hang over the town like wet dirty laundry. A rare bright morning may release some mud and a few crocus shoots, but the air remains raw; every night the earth freezes hard.

Out on Jones Creek Road the Tates' lawn is still spread with lumpy layers of crusted snow like an ill-frosted birthday cake—the one Erica made for Jeffrey this week, for instance—and a damp gusty wind wheezes across it at the house, as if a large child with a bad cold were trying to blow out the lights. Erica can feel this wind up in her bedroom, where she is dressing for Danielle's party.

She has just recovered from a bad cold herself, one which began over a month ago and hung on, with headache, sniffles, clogged nasal passages and loss of appetite. She would have got over it if she could have stayed in bed for two or three days, Erica feels sure; but a woman living alone with children cannot stay in bed even for one day.

Tonight will be the first time in more than a month that she has attended a formal social event—both from choice and because she hasn't been asked out much lately. Even when she is well, going to parties alone is difficult—especially since Christmas, when the weather turned bad and physical problems (icy roads, stalled cars, children sick at home) were added to the social ones. More and more, it has come to seem not worth the effort.

At the same time there have been fewer parties for Erica to go to. For a month or so after Brian left she was a local tragic heroine—or at least a disaster victim; she had more invitations than she could accept. Now the flurry of sympathetic and curious attention has died down, and she is just another single woman, easy to overlook when making up a list—especially if she declined your last invitation. There are already too many extra women in Corinth: spinsters, widows, ex-wives. One cannot have them all at once; they must take turns, and be grateful.

An extra man, on the other hand, is always welcome. Erica suspects, though she has no evidence, that she has been left out of many parties because people are having Brian instead. And why not? He is more successful than she, more important, better company because he is in better spirits—even, in a way, nicer. The most depressing discovery Erica has made in the past four months is that ill fortune is bad for people's character. It makes it harder to be good-natured, either in word or deed. Sometimes she hears what hardly sounds like her own voice nagging the children or complaining to Danielle, and is horrified—and how often does she not hear it?

Ill fortune makes it harder to do anything creative, like cooking a birthday dinner for Jeffrey, or working on her painting. As for the book about the white hare, she has had to put that aside completely. The idea of being alone in the country in the winter, which seemed so lovely last autumn, has become a cold, exhausting reality of clogged driveways, frozen engines and overlapping family flu.

Dressed in a blue-lace bra-slip, Erica stands frowning in front of the bedroom closet, trying to decide what to wear to the party. There is not much choice, though for years this closet was overcrowded. Now it is not only Brian's things that are gone; Matilda has permanently borrowed many of her mother's clothes. It is a year since Erica bought a new party dress, and none of the old ones seem right for the occasion. The pretty mauve-and-brown plaid is now unfashionably long, the black wool too plain and gloomy. Both the paisley print and the glossy brown silk are too low-cut for her present circumstances: decolleté on a wife merely enhances a husband's reputation; on an ex-wife, it vulgarly proclaims availability. If the wearer is not yet divorced, or even legally separated, that only makes it worse: by baring her flesh she is inviting all comers to adultery rather than simple fornication.

Erica has been stuck in this uneasy, embarrassing state, this limbo between married and single, for four months. Not on purpose: she is eager to be unwed, to be disconnected from what Brian has become. She knows couples—for instance, the Zimmerns—who have gone through months of legal and financial squabbling and seemed to enjoy it. But Erica has always despised such squabbling. She does not want to argue about who pays the auto insurance or the orthodontist's bills. Besides, there is no need to argue about such matters. Erica knows that her proposals for a settlement are very reasonable, even generous—because her lawyer, a lady named Clara Dickson, has told her so.

Brian claims that he does not want to fight over details either; he tells Erica that he too is impatient for an agreement. But at the same time, through his lawyer, he has made one difficulty after another. His first counterproposal, according to Clara, was so impossible that there was no point in going over its terms with Erica. Supposedly, a compromise settlement is now being drawn up, but not very fast. Whenever Erica calls the office Clara tells her that she has not been able to reach Brian's lawyer on the phone, or that he has been out of town and has not yet answered her last letter. "Jack Lucas *does* seem to be dragging his feet," she admits cheerfully. "I can't explain why, unless possibly Brian doesn't really want a separation."

But Erica is not cheered by Clara's cheer, and does not for a moment believe her explanation. She believes that Brian, with the help of Jack Lucas, is trying to wear her and Clara down, to force them to agree to his terms. He wants to keep as much money for himself as possible, out of selfishness and greed, so that he can buy new inappropriately youthful clothes and a new stereo system and go to Europe with Wendy this summer. He wants to reduce her (and Jeffrey and Matilda) to poverty, out of greed and revenge; to punish her for having tried to do the right thing and make him do the right thing.

What she cannot get over is that he seems to have no sense of duty or obligation toward his family. His lack of moral responsibility for Wendy's child seems to have been extended to his own children. For example it had not occurred to him to propose taking them for even part of the summer vacation, and he was almost indignant at first when she proposed it. And this although he claims that Jeffrey and Matilda have improved greatly in the past few months, becoming (in his view) quite easy to cope with.

It is mean and hypocritical for Brian to say this; because he does not really have to cope with the children at all, since he is never home. He has been able to de-escalate the war with Jeffrey and Matilda, to withdraw his troops from the occupied country and establish friendly or at least neutral diplomatic relations. Erica, however, has had to stay on the ground, fighting a losing battle and maintaining a precarious puppet government, with only very minimal and intermittent air support from her former ally.

She has often heard how loyally and affectionately children have rallied round and supported their mothers after a separation. Indeed, Roo Zimmern had done so, though only eleven at the time. But Jeffrey and (worse) Matilda support, or at least prefer, their father, who now makes almost no demands on them and enforces no rules, whom they see for only a few hours a week over expensive meals. During these excursions they are on their best behavior, and Brian returns them afterward with an air of self-satisfaction, praising their improved table manners and their knowledge of current events.

At home, however, the children are as bad as ever, or worse: more foul-mouthed, untidy, rebellious and disobedient. No matter how reasonably and tactfully Erica approaches them, they refuse to do any work around the house, or to keep decent hours. They read after bedtime with a flashlight under the covers, and on weekends they stay out until eleven o'clock or later with their friends, God knows where, doing God knows what. When she asks what and where they mutter rudely or do not reply at all. But when Erica doesn't answer their questions or is not home when she has said she will be, they complain, and are righteously indignant.

Sighing, setting her lips, Erica slips the plaid jersey (which she has not worn since Christmas) from its hanger and over her head. The fine pale wool settles loosely about her hips—too loosely; the wide ruffled collar hangs limp. In these last months she has lost weight. She straightens up and sticks out her chest, but the neckline still gapes, and folds of extra stuff hang about the waist.

Pulling the extra material around to the back as much as possible, Erica crosses the room to her dressing table, sits down, and looks into the glass, smiling slightly. For forty years she has had a happy relationship with mirrors. She regarded them with delight from the very beginning; the walnut-framed oval mirror in the front hall, to which her father held her up as a laughing baby; the long narrow mirror fastened to the back of her mother's closet door by metal clips which rattled as if with applause as, aged seven or eight, she paraded before it in Lena Parker's late 1930's fashions and wedgies. She liked the heavy triple-plate glass of stores: Manon's and Altman's in White Plains, later Filene's and Jordan Marsh, more recently Lord & Taylor's and Bloomingdale's on trips to New York; the neon-bright mirrors of bathrooms; the round and square and oval bits of glass dimmed with powder in a long series of compacts. All these, and many, many more, reflected Erica flatteringly, for she had from babyhood the sort of smooth beauty which adjusts effortlessly to its frame. Brushing her teeth in the dorm bathroom at college, she was all pink innocence; in the smoked glass of a Greenwich Village boutique, draped in a fringed shawl, she became dark and mysterious. She felt at ease even with the mirrors most women avoid. In the harsh light of public washrooms she was merely interestingly pale; and the stained greenish glass of old bureaus, mercury-speckled like stagnant water, showed her as a green nymph rising from a pond.

Now, on this cold March night, Erica sits before the mirror she knows best, and for the first time in weeks looks close into it, smiling gently, anticipatively. A woman whom she scarcely recognizes looks back at her, first with a blank, then with an injured and startled expression. This person is whey-faced, middle-aged and skinny, with a hollow goose-flesh chest above her ill-fitting, inappropriately girlish dress. Her dark hair has been chopped off too short above a too-long neck, and what remains shows crinkled threads of gray. The stranger's nose is pinched, her mouth tight. Only the eyes—large, gray, thick-lashed—are familiar to Erica, and now they blink and turn in nets of tiny wrinkles, like caught fish.

With a fishlike gasp, Erica rises and backs off from the dressing table; and as she moves away the image she knows reappears: the familiar tall, elegant, pretty young woman in her pretty ruffled dress. It diminishes, leaves the glass, and reappears across the hall in the bathroom mirror, smiling with relief, drawing nearer, larger, leaning into the hard neon light over the sink, staring; then putting up both hands to shield its face, which has become, and remains, white, thin, creased.

Erica feels dizzy and frightened; she wants to scream at the mirror, to weep. But instead she swallows, sets her jaw, and returns to the bedroom, where she pulls off the ruffled jersey and zips herself into the high-necked black wool. The bedroom mirror approves, if grudgingly; it reflects a slim, pale woman with neat small features, somberly dressed, not in any way ridiculous. She ties a rose-and-white silk scarf (bought in Paris long ago in a better time) around her neck to disguise its thin length and the severity of her costume. Then she rolls the ruffled dress into a ball and shoves it far down inside a cardboard carton marked RUMMAGE at the back of her closet.

Hastily now, for it is growing late and she has promised to be at Danielle's before the other guests come, Erica returns to the bathroom to see what can be done with make-up. Again she stares close into the glass. She feels lost, dispossessed of her rights. She remembers a remark of Leonard Zimmern's—that if Martians ever came to America, they would conclude our religion to be the worship of the pretty young woman, for she or her image is everywhere: at political rallies and parades and sports events; on billboards and packages; presiding over every public ceremony and every exchange of goods. For over twenty years she, Erica, was one of the incarnations of the goddess. Now the spirit has departed from her.

She must camouflage the loss, but is uncertain how to begin. Brian prefers the natural look, and as a natural beauty it is years since she used anything but a little rose lipstick and blue eye shadow—not even mascara, for her lashes and brows are naturally thick and dark. She owns no other cosmetics. But Matilda has recently begun to accumulate all sorts of bottles and tubes; they fill a shelf of the cabinet already. Opening a jar almost at random, Erica smears a thin pink paste, smelling faintly of medicinal soap and designed to cover adolescent acne, over the fine dry creased surface of her skin. The stuff coats her eyebrows and eyelashes; she wets them to remove it, and when this is ineffective, colors them brown again with Matilda's mascara, and rubs her own blue shadow over her lids. She outlines her mouth with the eyebrow pencil and paints it rose-mauve. Then, stepping back, she looks into the glass. The total effect is somewhat masklike and artificial, and the pink paste has turned her eye shadow an odd, bruised lavender—but at least she does not look quite so old. She fluffs her hair out with her hands and goes to tell the children she is leaving.

Matilda, by the sound of it, is in her room. Erica climbs the stairs and knocks loudly on the door; when there is no answer she pushes it ajar. Matilda is lying on her bed with her eyes shut and a school text open face-down on her stomach; the hoarse screams of a rock group issue from opposite speakers. Erica looks from one to the other with a sense of fatigue. For the last month Matilda has been complaining that her own phonograph is lousy and is messing up her records, making it necessary for her to play them downstairs in the sitting room. The house has resounded with frenzied thumping and shouting, and the angry voices of Jeffrey and Matilda quarreling over when, how loud and for how long she could use the machine, while Erica struggled to control her own voice and act as referee. Finally, in a moment of exhaustion, she told her daughter to take the family stereo upstairs. The result has been that Erica cannot play her own records, and there is a constant faint background of bad music throughout the house at all hours.

"Matilda!"

"Yeh." Matilda half opens her eyes. Though both children have continued to change for the worse, the change in her has been the most upsetting lately. A few months ago she was a plump, sulky child. Now she is a sulky adolescent, almost embarrassingly developed for a thirteen-year-old. None of her clothes fit or suit her, and none of her old friends. Boys, some of whose voices have already changed, have begun to phone, asking for "Tilda." She has been forbidden to date until her fourteenth birthday, next month; but she goes for long walks after school and has been seen in disreputable hamburger joints in Collegetown. Erica wonders at intervals if she ought to speak to her seriously about birth control.

"I'm going to Danielle's party now. I want you to have your bath and be in bed by nine-thirty. This is a school night." The last sentence sounds suddenly loud, for the record has ended.

"Yeh." The tone of Matilda's voice suggests that she has no intention of being in bed by nine-thirty. She raises her head. "Hey, you look flaky."

"Flaky? What does that mean?" But another disc has begun to blare from both sides of the room; Matilda has shut her eyes again, and her mother lacks the energy to pursue the question. She stops on her way downstairs at another mirror, but can see nothing flaking. Perhaps it was a kind of compliment?

Jeffrey is in the kitchen eating again and possibly doing his homework; at least there is a book propped in front of him.

"I'm going out now. If you need me for anything you can call

Danielle's house. And I'd like you to be in bed at ten, please; this is a school night . . . Jeffrey, really. You might answer me."

"What for?"

"So that I'll know you heard me." Erica strives to keep her tone friendly.

"How could I not hear you? You're standing right nexta me."

"It's a matter of good manners." No reply. "And Jeffrey, you really shouldn't eat so many chocolate cookies; they're bad for your skin. If you're hungry, why don't you have some fruit? An orange, or one of these bananas. Jeffrey?"

"Look, why don't you blast off?" her son growls. "I thought you said you were gonna."

Erica opens her mouth to expostulate, then shuts it because she is not sure she can do so calmly. She might shout, might howl, lose control of herself. To avoid this she retreats to the front hall, where she puts on her coat and boots. Carrying her shoes in a plastic bag with the legend *Superbread* printed on it, she leaves the house, not even slamming the door behind her.

At Danielle's all the lights are on, and through the porch window her living room has the bright, empty, pre-party look of a stage set. Danielle, in her red mumu, opens the door.

"Yes? Oh, Erica, come in. I was afraid it was Mrs. Heyrick again."

"Has she been complaining?"

"You said it. I thought I'd head her off; I told her this afternoon I was having a party so she could make all her fuss then. But she was just over ten minutes ago asking if it was possible for me not to play the phonograph because her husband doesn't feel himself."

Danielle laughs roughly. For over five years, ever since the Zimmerns moved to Corinth and into this half-house, she has been at war with the owners of the other half, an elderly couple named Heyrick. Battle was joined almost at once, on a hot September morning when Mrs. Heyrick, from her front porch, observed Silly squatting in a bed of petunias with her skirt lifted.

"What are you doing, little girl?" she cawed, rising to her feet.

"Watering the flars," replied Silly, then aged three.

After going indoors to skewer a small veiled hat to her hair, Mrs. Heyrick proceeded down her front walk, along the street under the elms and up the adjoining walk, where she rang the doorbell and informed Danielle that this was a nice neighborhood and that her daughter was old enough to know better and to wear panties.

The resulting conflict had continued ever since, finding new grounds without wholly abandoning the old ones. It waxed and waned with the seasons: during the winter months there was usually a cooling-off period, with only occasional skirmishes about noise and the removal of snow; as temperatures rose and the un-nice behavior of the Zimmerns and their friends became more visible, it heated up again.

Had Erica and Brian found themselves in such a situation they would have moved out as soon as possible; but the Zimmerns declined to do so. Leonard, who while he lived in the house took an equal share in the war—and in Erica's opinion sometimes went out of his way to provoke it—considered it a matter of principle. "Not on your life," he exclaimed once when she suggested moving. "Why should I let a couple of senile anti-Semites turn my family into Wandering Jews?"

Since Leonard left, active hostilities have been carried on principally by Danielle and Mrs. Heyrick, a scrawny lady with a penetrating whispery voice and a large collection of small hats. Mr. Heyrick plays only a supporting role, his frequent ailments serving as ammunition for his wife.

"How's everything going?" Erica asks, following Danielle into the kitchen, where platters of party food are ranged along the counter.

"Not bad. I forgot to get more flour, so I decided not to bother with those cheese puffs. There's really nothing much for you to do—well, maybe you could cut some rye bread. Here. Roo's made all the dips, that was a big help. She's trying to bribe me." Danielle grins at her daughter, who is scraping out the blender and licking the spatula. "She wants to start a gerbil factory in the sewing room."

"Really?" Erica looks at Roo, who is silent.

"I told her, Yeh, that's fine, but where am I going to sew? Also I don't want a couple dozen gerbils running around the house; two is bad enough. And don't tell me you'd keep them in their cages," she adds, as Roo opens her mouth to protest. "Pretty soon you'd feel sorry for them and let them out for exercise, just like you do now with Victoria and Albert."

"If you would buy me a horse, I wouldn't want to raise gerbils," Roo says abruptly.

"That's silly." Danielle stops slicing a red Edam cheese. "You know I can't afford to buy you a horse."

"I do not either know it. You always say that, but it doesn't mean anything. You have hundreds of dollars, I saw your bank book. If you thought it was really important, you would do it."

"Why do you want a horse so much, Roo?" Erica asks, more to relieve the atmosphere than out of curiosity, for what Leonard has called Roo's Houyhnhnm Complex is of many months' standing.

"Because horses are the most noble, beautiful, wonderful thing in the world. I wish I'd been born a horse."

"You have riding lessons now, don't you?"

"Yes," Roo admits. "But—"

"More than lessons. She can go out to the stables any time she wants," Danielle explains, arranging half-moons of red-rimmed cheese on a plate. "St. Bernard fixed it up with his neighbors."

"But isn't that enough?" Erica asks.

"No." Roo speaks with intensity. "I want a horse of my own. That's another reason I want to start breeding gerbils, see, so I can save up for one faster."

"You're not going to make much money on gerbils," Danielle says, starting on a block of pale-brown goat cheese. "Already they're advertising them in the paper for five dollars a pair, when Victoria and Albert were twelve from Contemporary Toys last Christmas. Everybody has gerbils now, and they're all breeding. In a few months people will be giving them away. Anyhow you know how you are, Roo—you'll get attached to all those dozens of babies, and you won't want to sell any of them."

"I will too. As long as I know they're going to good homes. And I'm not going to start with dozens. I just want to keep the litter Victoria has. Why can't I do that?"

Danielle sighs. "I haven't time to argue about it now; I have to get dressed. Don't cut any more bread, Erica, that's plenty. Come on upstairs with me. There's something I want to tell you."

In the bedroom, as Danielle drops her shoes and begins to pull off the flowered gown, Erica approaches the Victorian chest of drawers and its wide mirror, raising her hands in a pretense of tidying her hair. The first glance is reassuring: at three feet the slightly yellowed glass reflects a very pretty, slim young woman. Only as she leans forward over the chest is the image flawed, the face seen to be finely wrinkled around every feature under a pink dusty coating of Matilda's acne-proof paint. Close up against the glass, Erica looks as if she had walked into a spider's web.

"You know Bernie went to the Co-op with me today, to help carry home all the food and drink for tonight. We got some of that new Chilean wine, I don't know how people will like it, but I think . . ."

Though she has turned away from the mirror, Erica is still not listening seriously. She is not very interested in exotic wines, and still less in Dr. Bernard Kotelchuk. Instead she is studying her friend to see whether she too has become suddenly old. As usual, Danielle is without ordinary modesty; as she pulls off her black tights and unhooks a worn leopard-print bra (36 C) it is possible to make a complete survey. Even at close range her face, with its strong, simple lines and high color, seems merely weathered, as if she had just come in from outdoors. There are shallow folds on either side of the generous mouth and between the dark brows, but no wrinkles. But Danielle's body looks heavy, used. The full breasts have begun to descend; there are broken veins in the brown thighs and lumpy rolls of flesh over the hips—and the broad curve between them, once as smoothly tan as a sand dune on a summer's day, is marbled and puckered with the scars of appendicitis and childbirth.

Women age like wild apples, Erica read once. Most, fallen under the tree and ungathered, gradually soften and bulge and go brown and rotten; and that is what will happen to Danielle. Others hang on to the branch, where they wither and shrink and freeze as winter comes on. That is how it will be with her.

"Anyhow, the big surprise of the day was," Danielle continues, with a pause and deepening of her voice which finally reclaims Erica's attention, "he wasn't joking; he was serious. St. Bernard really wants to marry me." She grins and pulls open her top drawer.

"No! Actually?" Erica laughs. "You mean he proposed to you formally in the Co-op liquor store?"

"That's right." Sitting on the edge of the wide bed, Danielle bends and begins to ease on her pale-gray pantyhose.

"How bizarre." The proposal surprises Erica; not because of Danielle's ruined beauty (her friend is still far, far more attractive than Bernie Kotelchuk deserves), but because it is incongruous with her idea of his motives. As she imagines he would put it: Why buy a cow when milk is so cheap? "Whatever did you say?"

"I told him I'd think about it." Danielle stands and pulls the cloudy gray nylon up to her waist, veiling the damaged summer landscape of hips and belly. "After all, it's a long time since I had that kind of proposal." She laughs a little uneasily, and shrugs first one and then the other shoulder under the straps of a white-lace bra.

"Mm." Erica frowns; she doesn't like to hear her friend mock herself.

"There'd be some advantages to it, you know," Danielle continues from within the new dark-red brocade dress she has made for this party. "I'm used to Bernie now; I'm even kind of fond of him. And of course the girls are crazy about him. If I got married, we could all move into his house in Brookdale; Roo could have her horse; and there's lots of kids in the neighborhood for Celia to play with, so I wouldn't have to drive her everywhere like I do now. And I'd never have to speak to Mrs. Heyrick again." Danielle pulls her dress down and turns to Erica. Her expression is almost but not quite serious.

"That would be a great advantage, of course," Erica says, giggling. "The only trouble is, you'd have to speak to all his Brookdale friends and neighbors instead."

"I know." Danielle makes a face. "All those pie-baking women that knew his wife. They'd never forgive me for marrying him."

"Never." Erica is still laughing.

"And they're not the only ones. My parents would be hurt because he's not Jewish. Especially my mother." Danielle has stopped laughing. "And you can imagine what Leonard would say."

"I can." Though Danielle had never mentioned Bernard Kotelchuk, Leonard has somehow learned of his existence. Since January, when he discovered a reprint of one of Dr. Kotelchuk's articles on the diseases of young swine in Roo's room, he has referred to him as "the pig pediatrician."

"I wonder why he asked you to marry him?" Erica continues, since her friend is silent. She has no hesitation about speaking this way, for Danielle has declared several times that she is merely making temporary use of Bernie; and even more often that she has no intention of ever marrying again—that she considers it a stupid, antiquated and exploitative institution. "Maybe he thinks he should offer at least once to make an honest woman of you. He must know you'd refuse."

"I thought of that too," Danielle says after a slight pause. "I asked him if it was that. But he insists he's in love with me."

*259*

"In *love?*" Erica giggles again.

"Uh huh." Danielle finishes zipping up the back of her dress and sits down again on the bed. "Well, you know, he hasn't had much experience for a man his age. I used to think that when he praised me, when he told me how great I was in bed for instance, he was just being polite. I would think how I was probably a poor substitute for his wife Marnie, whom he always spoke of with such awe and restraint.

"But the truth seems to be she was really rather a bitch. Not in ways anybody could see; but she was always getting at Bernie in private because he drank and smoked and didn't go to church enough. He says he used to envy his friends who could grumble about how their wives burned the dinner or dented the car or couldn't manage a budget. But Marnie was a superb housekeeper, and an elaborate cook. She braided her own rugs and canned her own tomatoes and baked her own bread and spent all her free time doing good works. Everybody thought she was just about perfect. Bernie never told them she didn't like to make love and thought he was a weak, corrupt, unreliable man who was a bad influence on his own sons. Partly he agreed with her, that's the really sad thing. Sometimes when he was out of town he'd get drunk, or once in a while pick up a girl in a bar. Marnie never said anything, but he was always sure she knew. 'How could she know a thing like that?' I asked him. 'I don't know, but she did,' he said. 'She used to tell the boys she had x-ray vision and could see right into their brains.'"

"That's rather creepy," Erica says, feeling distaste for both characters in the story. "And does he still get drunk and pick up women?"

"I don't think so. He didn't enjoy it much even then, he told me. He says he's never known a woman who liked sex the way I do."

"Really."

"Well, it *is* good." Danielle laughs with uncharacteristic embarrassment. "It's funny, but he suits me better than even

*2 6 0*

Leonard did. Of course Leonard was amazing in bed, but he was so unpredictable. He was always wanting to do something new. I used to like that too, but it didn't always work out. Maybe I'm just getting old, but it's nice to know what to expect, and not have to keep trying uncomfortable positions somebody saw in a book on Oriental art."

"I know what you mean," Erica says, in full agreement for the first time in the conversation. "I feel exactly the same."

"Another thing, I think Bernie's lonely," Danielle continues, standing up. In front of the mirror she releases her dense dark-brown hair from its tight ponytail, and starts to brush it back and out from her head, so vigorously that the air in the bedroom crackles. "Both his sons are away now, and he doesn't like living by himself. I'm afraid if I don't marry him he'll find somebody else."

"Well, if he does, so can you," Erica says with some enthusiasm.

"Maybe." Danielle pauses, holding her brush out at the end of a stroke. "You know that old saying, about how men are like buses? And if you miss one, don't worry, because there'll be another along in a few minutes. Yeh, maybe. For a while. But as it gets later they run less often."

"Yes—well." Erica laughs uncomfortably. "I don't know. You've always found them without any trouble whenever you wanted them."

"That's different." Danielle opens her make-up drawer. "If you just want to screw, there's always somebody around. That's all right for a while. But you get tired of all the coming and going." She pencils her emphatic dark brows even darker. "I'm like Roo; I sort of want a horse of my own."

"Not a farm horse, though." Erica smiles. "Not that Bernie Kotelchuk really reminds me of a farm horse, he's more like—" She breaks off, noting Danielle's expression in the glass. Perhaps it is just the effect of holding her facial muscles stiff while she outlines her eyes; all the same, Erica does not go on to say that what Dr. Kotelchuk reminds her of is a farm dog, that she can see him as this dog: a large old St. Bernard padding along a country road on a cold late winter night to where Danielle is waiting for the next bus—trudging up to her over the snow, slobbering over her, offering her his cheap domestic brandy.

"I know you don't fancy him much," Danielle says, thickening her already thick lashes with mascara.

"It's not that." Again Erica looks into the mirror where Danielle is framed by mahogany Victorian scrolls and leaves. With her hair down and her face made up, in the mahogany-red dress, she is still a very beautiful woman; much, much too good for Bernie Kotelchuk. "What I think is—" Downstairs the bell twangs. Danielle turns her head.

"Oh, hell, there's someone already. Roo, honey! Could you answer the door? Say I'll be right down." She steps out of the mirror frame and goes to feel in the closet with one foot and then the other for her black silk pumps.

"I'll be with you in a few moments," Erica says, moving toward the bathroom. While her friend clatters downstairs, she locks the door and inspects herself in both mirrors: the small one over the sink and the long one on the door. The result is the same. Up close under the light her face looks like a stone rubbed with pink chalk, powdery and worn. But as long as she keeps a certain distance from people—a bit over two feet—she will seem perfectly normal, though a little pale.

This shouldn't be too difficult tonight; indeed in some cases she will have cooperation. Among those who are sure to keep their distance are the men who tried to get too close last fall. Corinth being the size it is, Erica has not been able to avoid these rejected adulterers completely—especially since many of their deceived wives are close acquaintances who would be surprised and hurt if she dropped them without apparent reason. Several of them are coming tonight; and she will have to speak to them in a friendly, open way, and to their husbands; not showing what she knows, not knowing what she shows—and moreover, not knowing what they, or anyone at the party, know about anything.

*262*

Officially, for instance, Brian isn't living with Wendy, but alone. Erica, according to her promise, has never contradicted this, though surely by now some people must have heard the real truth, or part of it. But she has no idea who these people are. Which of Danielle's guests still believe the official version, which know the whole story? And which, aware of Wendy's existence but no more, regard Erica as yet another middle-aged wife whose marriage has failed—another deserted woman whose husband has, as Leonard Zimmern once put it, traded in a forty for a twenty?

The doorbell rings again; more voices below. Erica looks for a last time into the two mirrors and, sighing, leaves the bathroom; she descends the stairs, fixing a social smile on her chalky face.

Already the rooms are filling; Danielle is an impulsive last-minute hostess, and has invited most of her freshman seminar, all the members of her feminist rap group, and several neighbors. But the bulk of the party is composed of her colleagues in Romance Languages and their spouses. These tend, as usual, to cluster in tight small groups, laughing and speaking rapidly in foreign accents, and occasionally in foreign tongues. Erica passes among them, smiling and nodding; pausing sometimes for a few words, but always keeping her predetermined interval of two and a half feet. It is not as easy as she had hoped, because of the Romance Languages habit of standing rather too close—close enough to breathe, and in some cases spit, on one's companions. But Erica manages it. Over the last months she has learned to keep her distance with everyone—a distance not only physical but psychological.

For years she had enjoyed and excelled at that sort of harmless flirting which is not intended to lead to assignations and fornication but is only a pleasant way of passing time and informing the other person that they are attractive. Now the gay, confiding manner which she used to put on for parties is as inappropriate as a low-cut dress—and for the same reasons. It makes women look at her with wifely suspicion; it causes men to move deliberately and crudely toward her—or worse, deliberately away, with an expression of No Thanks.

"Hiya, Erica!" Chuck Markowitz, one of her former pursuers, greets her noisily, not at all abashed—perhaps not even recalling the day last December when he came up the road from his Glenview Home with his new snow blower, offering to clear her driveway after the first big storm of the winter. Since Chuck was a neighbor, a junior colleague of Brian's and about ten years younger than Erica, she accepted gratefully and without suspicion. Even afterward, when he was having coffee in her kitchen and complaining humorously about family responsibilities (his wife Lily was then eight months pregnant with their second child), she remained off guard. She was therefore first flabbergasted, and then very angry when he put down his cup, leaned across the table toward her and said, "Hey, Erica. You, uh, wanna make out?"

"Hello, Chuck. How are Lily and the baby?" Though she has not spoken to him face to face since December, Erica has often driven by the Markowitz's Glenview Home and seen Chuck working with his snow blower, pushing before him the large machine with its bright-red nozzle extended and spurting snow, its vigorous mechanical noise. Occasionally he has called and offered again to clear her driveway; naturally, she has always refused.

As soon as she politely can, Erica disengages herself from Chuck. Smiling and nodding at arm's length, she makes her way through Danielle's guests toward the dining room, where Dr. Bernard Kotelchuk stands behind the long oak table pouring drinks with large gestures, a loud red tie and an offensive hostlike manner.

"Good evening, Mrs. Tate! How're you doing tonight?"

"Fine, thank you." She smiles thinly, irritated to be addressed as "Mrs. Tate," though aware that his intention is not facetious, merely formal.

"What can I give you?"

"Some white wine, please."

"Coming up."

Erica moves away with the glass, sipping sparingly from it: not only is she aware that she will have to drive home—she knows that she is being watched. Because of her separated condition, if she seems to be even slightly high both men and women will look at her with suspicious pity: is Poor Erica starting to drink?

The party is in full blast now, its density and volume increasing every moment. Nervously scooping up cheese dip with a cracker, though she is not hungry, Erica scans the room. Years ago, and again for a time this winter, she went to every party with the fantasy that someone would be there—"someone" whom (though they had never met before) she would recognize—who would recognize her.

Foolish; pathetic. As usual, she knows every grown man present tonight, and doesn't want to know any of them better. Most of them are out of bounds anyhow, being married—as is most of the male population of Corinth over thirty. Among the remainder there are two or three men (not now present) whom Erica has finally decided she might be willing to go out with. It is not that her opinion of men has altered, or that she has any desire to become romantically involved. But it would be nice sometimes to have a respectable, attractive escort to concerts, films and art shows.

As yet, however, none of these men has offered to escort her. The only man she has gone anywhere with for nearly three months is Sandy Finkelstein, who is neither respectable nor attractive, though he is—just as, long ago, in Cambridge—usually available. There are problems even with Sandy: he can't afford to go to anything that costs money and will not let her pay for him; he has no car and his appearance is weird. Last Sunday at the afternoon concert he wore a secondhand Army overcoat he had bought for two dollars, and a red knit hat with a long tail and tassles like one of the Seven Dwarfs.

Erica thinks of something Danielle once said: that what men do if they can afford it is take a naïve young woman, give her a couple of babies and a big house to look after, and then after fifteen years of hard work they discard her. By that time she's used goods; damaged merchandise. Nobody wants her any more. Except maybe the sort of man who buys day-old bread and gets his clothes at church sales.

But she must not think that way. She is at a party, where people have come together to have a good time. She scans the room, looking for someone to talk to; but they all seem to smile and then turn away, avoiding her. It is a strange sensation. For years, as a beautiful, happy young woman, she was the object of general admiration and attraction; last fall when Brian first left she was also surrounded, wherever she went, by interested sympathizers and wolfish husbands. But now her story is no longer news, and as a lonely middle-aged woman with moral principles she is dull, an embarrassment. As Danielle said, it gets later and the buses run less often—finally not at all.

Taking a deep breath, suppressing these thoughts, she scans the crowd again and then moves through it toward Clara Dickson, her lawyer—also once Danielle's. Indeed Clara, a motherly broad woman, long happily married, has helped to end most of the local unhappy marriages Erica knows of.

"Hello, Clara. How are you?" Good manners demand that she should not ask instantly whether Jack Lucas is still dragging his feet about the settlement; Erica begins the conversation by inquiring about Clara's many grown and successful children. Before she can finish this polite ceremony they are interrupted by neighbors of Clara's who are remodeling a house on the lake and intend to explain the process room by room. Discouraged, smiling chalkily, Erica drifts away, waiting for a better opportunity. She moves through the guests, keeping a becoming distance, stopping at intervals to smile, deplore the weather, and parry inquisitive remarks with conventional answers. ("How are you these days?" "Oh, fine." "Well, what's new with you?" "Oh, nothing much." "And how is all your family?")

In the front room, away from the bar, the crowd is thinner; in the hall there is only one person: a tall, very shabby, dim-looking man standing by the stairs reading a magazine.

"Sandy." Erica smiles. It is a relief to see anyone who knows her story and won't ask questions, and it is mildly pleasant to see Sandy. "I didn't think you were coming."

"Neither did I." Zed puts the magazine down.

"I'm glad you came." Erica smiles, but with mixed feelings. She had asked Danielle if she could invite Sandy—for his own good, so that he might again meet people of his own age, background and intellectual sophistication. For in spite of his shabby appearance he is an intelligent and sophisticated man; he has been kind to her this depressing winter, and Erica wants to repay him—to restore him to his right place in the world.

But now that he is here, Sandy looks incongruous and uncomfortable. He has put on his only respectable shirt—a frayed white oxford button-down, an apparent survival from his years of teaching—and a narrow, limp black knit tie. The effect is somehow to make him seem even more of a dismal outcast than he does in his secondhand pants and sweaters.

Still, since he *is* here, he can't spend all evening in the hall reading the *New York Review of Books*.

"Have you had anything to drink yet?" she asks. "There's tonic and orange juice if you don't want liquor, or I could make you some tea."

"No thanks. I'm not thirsty."

"Well then. Come and talk to someone." Erica reconnoiters the crowd in the next room and selects a professor of French named M. Alain who is known for his good will. She propels Zed to his side, introduces them, and suggests the neutral topic of Japanese theater, a sample of which has just been presented locally.

Cheered by having accomplished a good deed, Erica heads for the kitchen to see whether she can do another. She finds Danielle simultaneously spreading pâté on squares of toast and talking on the phone.

"Yes . . . All right . . . You're welcome, good-bye." She puts the receiver down with some force. "Dhhh. That was Mrs. Heyrick again. She wants to know can we please, please, be a little less noisy. Mr. Heyrick has a migraine headache."

"He would," Erica says, thinking that she too has a headache. "Can I do anything?"

"Yes. We're running out of glasses already. Everyone must be leaving them around."

"I'll go and see what I can find, and wash some."

"That'd be great. I didn't think so many people would come."

Why not, you invited them, Erica thinks as she returns to the living room with a tray and begins to collect used glasses. She has nearly a dozen and is on her way back when the front door opens and a person Danielle hasn't invited enters—not Brian, but the next-worst thing: his lawyer, Jack Lucas. Jack is accompanied by, and has evidently come with, a friend of Danielle's named Nancy King. Erica looks at them with a heavy, angry feeling, for Jack is not only Brian's lawyer and hence her enemy, but also one of the unattached men she had in years past flirted with and later chosen as a possible escort. She had even, before Brian went to him, had the fantasy that Jack would refuse to take the case out of admiration for her. That he should come with Nancy is another blow—for until recently Erica has never had anyone else preferred to her by those whom she preferred.

"Erica!" Nancy whinnies, galloping toward her and pawing her arm. "Lovely to see you. It's been years. You know Jack, don't you?"

"Of course we know each other," Jack cries, smiling broadly and hobbling up as fast as possible. He is literally dragging his feet, or at least one foot, which is in a cast as a result of one of his continual skiing accidents. "How are you, Erica?"

Jack leans forward; guessing his intention, Erica tries to retreat, but there is a wall behind her and her hands are full; she can do nothing but turn her head at the last moment, so that Jack's belligerent kiss explodes damply on her cheek.

"Must get these glasses back, Danielle needs them," she insists, escaping. She hastens into the kitchen to complain to her friend ("You might think he would have known—would have had the good manners not to—"). But Danielle is not there.

She washes and dries the glasses and takes them back to the dining room, where Danielle is laughing with Bernie Kotelchuk in a noisy group. Frustrated, she takes her complaint back across the room.

"Jack Lucas just came in," she announces to Clara in an angry whisper.

"Oh, yes?" Clara turns toward her, smiling. "That's nice."

"I don't think so. I think it's extremely rude. He must have known I'd be here."

"Heavens, Erica." Clara shakes her head, laughs gently. "If Jack or I couldn't go anywhere we might meet someone we've got a case pending against, we'd both have to stay home most of the time. In this town."

"I suppose you're right."

"Of course I'm right."

"Mm." Erica hesitates. "But now he's here, will you speak to him?"

"Why, of course I'll speak to him!" Clara stops smiling. "Jack and I are old friends."

"I mean, about the agreement. You can ask him why he hasn't answered your last two letters."

"I couldn't ask him that now," Erica's lawyer says firmly. "This is a social occasion." She gives Erica a smile of maternal disapproval mixed with pity, as if she were a child who wanted to bring up some silly old quarrel at a party. "Why, hello, Nancy. How are you?"

"Beautiful." Nancy, who is of course also one of Clara's former clients, embraces her warmly, while Erica slides away, feeling worse than before.

The front hall, where she goes to recover her composure, is again empty except for Zed, who is now crouched on the rug reading one of Danielle's books.

"Sandy?"

"Hello." He straightens up, smiling sheepishly.

"You're not enjoying the party. Didn't you like Monsieur Alain?"

"He was all right. But then these other people came up. A very angry man who was always laughing, with a bristly beard and a sad wife. I forget their names."

"The Diacritis," Erica supplies with a sigh. "He's the chairman of Danielle's department."

"I see."

"But what happened?"

"I said something he didn't like. He was complaining about how hard it was to stop smoking. When he goes to a party where there are people like Monsieur Alain with cigarettes, he gets very angry and wants one too. He asked me what I thought he should do about it. I suggested he might stop going to parties, or else, what a Zen Master told me once, he could try to experience his desires fully without satisfying them. Then he figured out I was the nut who runs that bookshop, and started to abuse me." The telephone in the hall beyond Zed begins to ring. "So I got out of his way. Do you think I should answer that? . . . Hello . . . Yes, just a moment . . . It's the next-door neighbor. She wants to speak to Danielle."

"Oh, Lord. I'll get her."

Erica makes her way back through the party, delivers the message, and returns. "Danielle's busy now, she says to tell Mrs. Heyrick she'll— Sandy! You hung up on her."

"She hung up on me." Zed grins. "She was worried because there's a car parked in front of her driveway. She was afraid there might be a fire or some other emergency and she couldn't get out. But I told her she needn't worry, because both the lights are in watery signs tonight, and Jupiter is conjunct Uranus. Only good adventures can happen."

"Oh, Sandy. How could you make fun of her that way?"

"I wasn't making fun of her."

"But that's what she'd think. She must be furious." Erica looks toward the wall which divides the two halves of the house, imagining Mrs. Heyrick in the room beyond, which is the mirror image of this one; she is standing facing Erica, furious, in her perpetual hat. What is to be done now?

She looks into the living room. In the far corner, Danielle is laughing tipsily and leaning on Bernie Kotelchuk, who is even more red-faced than usual—obviously drunk. A feeling of exhaustion, disgust and hopelessness comes over her.

"Where are you going?" she adds, as Zed moves past her toward the hall closet.

"Away."

Erica opens her mouth to protest, shuts it, opens it again. "I'll drive you home."

"You don't have to do that, Erica," he says in a strained voice. "I can walk."

"It's too cold out. I'd like to get away for a while anyhow." She swallows. "I'm not enjoying this party much either."

"Oh?"

"I'll tell you about it on the way downtown."

It is not only cold outside, but starting to snow. The hill is already slippery, making conversation difficult; by the time they reach the bookshop Erica has only half expressed her resentment at Nancy and Jack.

"Would you like to come in and have a cup of tea?"

Erica hesitates, checks her watch. It is not yet ten. She feels cold, damp; her mind is clogged with depression. There is nothing to go home to except the mess Jeffrey and Matilda will have made of her house, especially her kitchen; and she doesn't want to return to the party, where Mrs. Heyrick and the Diacritis have probably already begun to complain to Danielle about Zed and ask who on earth brought him. "All right. For a few moments."

# 14

Across town on the same cold March evening a very different social event is taking place in the apartment of Linda Sliski, Wendy's nominal roommate. Danielle's party is brightly lit and everyone is standing up, talking loudly. Here it is smokily dim; the few guests are sitting or lying silently on the floor, passing around a joint. When it reaches Brian he does not take a drag, but hands it on to Wendy, who is leaning against his leg with her head on his raised knee.

It is peaceful here, warm; a little too warm and too peaceful for Brian, who can't get any conversation going and whose left leg is starting to ache. But he is willing to ride with it; more, it is a matter of pride with him to do so. He believes that a political scientist, like a politician, should be able to fit into a wide range of social scenes.

It is as well that he feels this, for he has had few opportunities of late to attend more conventional parties. Like Erica, he has noted a falling off in his social life. However, he is aware of the correct explanation, which is that—in spite of their protests that this is an amicable separation—nobody wants to ask them both to the same party, because it is not the custom. The custom is to keep them separate; to invite the estranged husband to small dinners as an extra man, because he cannot cook for himself and is probably starving; while the estranged wife is asked to large cocktail parties for visiting celebrities, on the grounds that she needs to meet people.

In the case of the Tates this policy is irritating to everyone. Brian already feels overfed by Wendy, but would welcome the opportunity to have a few drinks and some interesting conversations before returning to Alpine Towers. Erica, on the other hand, does not want to meet visiting celebrities, and cocktail parties come at the worst time of day for her—the children's supper hour. After serving the pizza, spaghetti or hamburgers they demand, she would be delighted to go out to a civilized meal, but nobody asks her.

Wendy is not so much irritated as depressed. She becomes weepy every time Brian goes out to dinner without her, and she believes he isn't invited to large parties to which he might bring her because people disapprove of her and don't want her in their houses. As for the hosts at these dinners and parties, they also are irritated and depressed because so many of their invitations are refused.

Brian cannot return even those invitations he does receive, because his apartment is too small and too full of Wendy. Nominally she is still living with Linda, but she is seldom there, and over the past months there has been a steady movement of her clothes and personal effects into Alpine Towers. By now it would be obvious to any guest who happened to open the bathroom cabinet or the coat closet that some woman is more or less in residence. Moreover, if he turned Wendy out while he entertained she would be hurt, while if he did not it would amount to openly declaring that they are living together.

Though he hasn't been asked to Danielle's party, Brian is well aware of its existence. Several of his acquaintances have mentioned it, adding naïvely, or maliciously, that they hoped to see him there. His lawyer, Jack Lucas, even suggested that Brian might like to tag along with him and his date. Needless to say, Brian refused. He has never in his life liked to "tag along," and if he were to do so in this instance, Danielle would probably ask him to leave.

Moreover, Brian is tired of Jack Lucas and his interminable negotiations. Leonard Zimmern—whom he saw recently in New York—has advised him to discharge Jack. ("Sure, he's a nice guy; that's the whole trouble. A divorce lawyer isn't supposed to be a nice guy. You want fast action, go to Frank Panto. That's what I should have done, but I was too dumb.") As yet, Brian has hesitated to take this advice. He is unacquainted with Frank Panto; but like everyone else in Corinth, he knows the name. It often appears in the newspaper, in reports of trials for burglary, forgery, rape and drunken driving—and is always taken as a sign that the defendant is guilty, but having retained Panto, may with luck get off.

Brian does not like the idea of thus admitting guilt. On the other hand, he is weary of hearing from Jack that Erica's lawyer has not yet answered his last letter or returned his phone call, or has done so only to propose ridiculously unfair terms. Leonard also has an opinion about these proposals: "Six hundred a month? You know what they're trying to do, those harpies, don't you? They're trying to emasculate you, to cut off your balls. They want to get at you through your superego and destroy you economically. Clarabelle tried the same thing on me, but I finally beat her down."

At times Brian thinks his friend may be right about Jack's incompetence and Clara's malice. More often, though, he suspects that Jack and Clara are in collusion—that they have agreed to delay the Tates' divorce as they have in the past delayed the Zimmerns', and others', in the hope that time may effect a reconciliation. They may not have discussed it openly, but they are old friends, and understand each other almost without words. ("Real shame about the Tates." "Mm, yes." —A procrastination of six months or more.—"Not exactly surprised re the Farrells." "No; about time, some might say." —Formalities concluded in two weeks.)

*274*

Though he suspects this, Brian has not yet challenged Jack on it, for in a way the delay is useful to him; it sets up a blockade between him and Wendy's wish to get married. Actually she has not spoken of marriage in some weeks, but he can feel her desire for it all the time, just as he now feels the warm, heavy, slightly numbing pressure of her body against his leg.

There are other disadvantages in being legally separated. It is expensive, for one thing, and will be inconvenient and embarrassing if/when he decides to return to his family. He hasn't given up the idea of such a return, though he tends to imagine it as taking place further and further in the future. He certainly doesn't want it now, and Erica doesn't want it, though it would be in her best interests. Living alone hasn't been good for her; she has been ill often this winter, and looks thin and strained. Last Sunday when he went to pick up the children this appearance was so pronounced that Brian could not help commenting: "You're very pale. Have you got another cold?"

"Yes, as a matter of fact," Erica replied bleakly.

"You're overworking yourself, that's what it is. If you gave up that ridiculous job—"

"If I gave up that ridiculous job," she interrupted in a thin, strained voice, "I couldn't buy groceries."

Brian has managed not to brood about this conversation by telling himself that he is giving Erica so much of his salary now that it is he who can hardly buy groceries; that she is still living in a large comfortable house and not in a cramped apartment. He has repeated to himself the words of Leonard Zimmern: "You've got to be tough, or they'll get you down with their female pathos and whining. Erica was never ill when I knew her."

These techniques have been partly successful. Brian does not feel consciously guilty; he doesn't even think about Erica very often. But he has bad dreams. Often they hark back to his war experiences, and repeat the nightmares he had just after his tour in the Pacific on a DE; nightmares involving confused orders and water and sticky darkness and loud noises. Only now Erica is in them. Last week he had one in which she appeared with large wings, perched on the porch roof of the house on Jones Creek Road, like a figure in Renaissance painting. It was a cloudy evening in this dream and the air was full of a dangerous wailing noise like antimissile missiles which made him gasp and cry out, waking Wendy. "Hey, Brian? What's the matter? Is it one of your war nightmares? Wake up! What happened, tell me about it."

And Brian told her, ill-advisedly. For after she hugged and soothed him she asked, "How come you always dream about Erica? Maybe you're still in love with her."

"I'm not in love with her," Brian insisted. "I wish she'd get the hell out of my dreams." Wendy remained silent, unconvinced. "She had wings like a harpy," he added, and went on to relate this to Clara Dickson's impossible demands.

But Wendy was not persuaded. "I d'know. Maybe she's asking for so much bread on purpose, to zap the proceedings. On account of she wants you back, account of she's still in love with you."

"Erica is not in love with me," Brian insisted with still greater conviction. "As a matter of fact, I don't think she's ever been in love with me." In the dark, Wendy murmured doubtfully. "Look, let's go back to sleep. I have two classes tomorrow."

"Okay. I'm sorry. It's just—I mean, shit, you never dream about me."

"I don't have to dream about you," Brian said in his fondest tone, and with an appropriate gesture. He could feel her relax then; she returned the gesture, laughed warmly, and flopped back onto her stomach. She always slept that way, often with one fist in her mouth, like a child; and now, like a child, she was asleep again in a few moments. But Brian lay awake for over an hour, while the wailing noise of his dream came and went in his mind.

The joint comes around to Brian again: a thin, wrinkled cigarette, pinched and wet at one end. Again he passes it on. He has no moral objection to marijuana, but he dislikes its effects. When he smokes grass he enters into a dull, stupid, sensual state in which the world is brightly colored and flattened out like the sort of abstract painting he finds most boring. He has the sense of being slowed down and speeded up alternately: a minute passes infinitely slowly, and quarter-hours disappear between two sentences. Wendy and her friends, with their childish sense of an infinite future, may think this amusing; but Brian finds it disagreeable: he does not wish to have big bites of time taken out of his life. Still worse than these sensual distortions is the intellectual effect of the drug. Meaning and order are blurred, and rational argument and comparison become impossible.

Besides, it makes social life boring. When drinks are served, people become more lively and communicative; they talk and move around more. Grass has the opposite effect: look at Linda and her guests, lying about for the last half-hour almost silent, like cows on actual grass.

Brian is seriously concerned about Wendy's constant use of marijuana. She and her friends cannot seem to get together socially without lighting up a joint, and hardly a day goes by that she doesn't smoke at least part of one, often (as now) mixed with hash to make it stronger. Possibly the stuff is harmless in small amounts, but what is a small amount? Without federal controls, how can anyone know how much they are getting? Also, he has read that the effect may be cumulative over months or years. Besides, it is a drug, and leads to stronger drugs: to LSD, speed and heroin; to addiction, weird delusions, mental and moral collapse, overdose and death. Nobody has proved that marijuana itself is not addictive, at least psychologically. And apart from everything else, it is illegal. It is distributed by criminal organizations part of whose profits go to bribery, corruption and possibly murder; and the use of it makes one a criminal. Right now Wendy and her friends are breaking a federal law. They could be arrested and tried and sent to jail; and so could he, as an accessory. Probably the judge would be especially hard on him because of his age and position.

Brian sighs and reaches past Wendy for another can of beer, and as he does so her peaceful bovine smile is replaced by a look of anxiety. He knows what this means: she is worried about his constant drinking. She has discovered that he and his friends cannot seem to get together socially without opening a bottle; that hardly a day goes by when he doesn't have at least a glass of vermouth before supper, often mixed with gin to make it stronger.

In fact Wendy thinks of alcohol much as he thinks of drugs. In her view, grass makes you relaxed, happy and at peace with the world; it refines and heightens perceptions. Alcohol blurs the senses and causes you to become noisy and violent. Besides, everyone knows the stuff is addictive. A small amount—a can of beer or a glass or two of wine—might be harmless, but it is apt to lead to the use of stronger and more dangerous drinks: to loss of physical control, shouting, fighting, vomiting and fatal auto accidents; eventually to impotence and visions of snakes and cirrhosis of the liver. And apart from everything else, it is a gross commercial rip-off. A bottle of whiskey costs six to eight dollars, and a lot of that is taxes, which means it goes to supporting corrupt government and killing people in Vietnam.

The door bangs open, admitting two more of Linda's friends: a pretty, sturdy girl with a Jewish Afro hairdo, and a bearded young man. Both are already known to Brian: the young man is the graduate student in physics named Mark who used to live downstairs. He now lives in a commune with the girl, Jenny, a Corinth undergraduate with whom he is having a relationship, but not a really meaningful one. As Wendy has explained to Brian, "In a relationship you're just screwing the guy. In a meaningful relationship you're screwing him and also he's your best friend."

"Hiya, everybody." Jenny pulls a poncho over her bushy head. Beneath it she is dressed in a style Brian recognizes but still finds odd. Unlike Wendy, with her mixed East-West Indian costume, Jenny and most of her undergraduate friends get themselves up as poor cowboys and dirt farmers. They wear heavy boots and faded, patched jeans, with a man's shirt or sweater. For parties the sweater is replaced by a fancy low-necked blouse trimmed with lace or bright embroidery; necklaces and long earrings are added. But the jeans and the boots remain, making these girls look mismatched at the waist, like the cardboard figures in a game Brian had as a small child.

"How's everything?" Linda raises a limp bony arm and hand from the floor, where she is lying prone.

"Lousy." Jenny waves away the joint one of the other guests has offered her and sits down next to Brian, reaching for a can of beer. "I'm really disgusted at this university."

"Oh, yeh?" Brian shifts position, relieving the weight on his leg, and turns toward Jenny with pleasure—not only because she is very pretty, but because he may now hear something of interest. Also, he may be able to help. In the last few months he has counseled Wendy's friends on a variety of problems: academic foul-ups, hassles with landlords, job applications, draft resistance. His advice is valuable to them, partly because of his greater knowledge of university procedures, partly because of his greater experience of the world. "What's happening?"

Jenny frowns as she pulls open her beer can, but is silent.

"It's that man in your department, that Professor Dibble," Mark explains. "He sort of keeps insulting women in his lectures."

"Not sort of," Jenny says. "He does it blatantly."

"Ah." Brian is familiar with this problem; more, he is in a sense responsible for it. It was he, after all, who last Thanksgiving suggested to a hitchhiker that she enroll in Dibble's course. Sara had not only acted on the recommendation, she had passed it on to friends and members of her commune. As a result, at least three militantly feminist students are taking Poly Sci 202. They have not found Dibble sympathetic, nor he them; Brian has already heard complaints from both sides.

"I figured he was going to be bad when we got to the Nineteenth Amendment, but I didn't think he'd be this bad. I mean, he's really a fascist chauvinist pig. Some of the things he's said, I didn't think I'd ever hear them in an American university; they sound like *Mein Kampf*. And you can't reason with him."

"You've tried?"

"Oh yeh. Pat and Sara tried to talk to him after class, and I went to his office twice this week. The first time he wouldn't even speak to me because he had some meeting, and yesterday he made me wait about half an hour and then gave me five minutes. And he was like really insulting. He said he was surprised an attractive young woman like me should be associated with such a foolish cause." Jenny imitates Dibble's supercilious look and prissy manner, then scowls darkly. Neither expression is able to disguise beauty so remarkable that even a woman-hater like Dibble was aware of it—the full young mouth, the very full young breasts unconfined in the flimsy embroidered blouse.

"Disgusting," caws Linda, of whom such an insulting remark will never be made. "You know what you ought to do, you ought to stop going to his class."

"That's what Pat said. She thinks we should just drop the course and write Dean Kane telling why. But I don't know. It seems like sort of futile to me. I thought maybe we should try to organize a boycott." She turns to Brian. "We could call a meeting of the women in the course and try to get them all to cut class, and send a letter to the *Star* about it. What do you think? But why wouldn't that work?" (for Brian is shaking his head).

"It's wrong politically," he explains. "Negative tactics. Let me ask you one question: What do you want from Dibble?"

Jenny takes a breath, raising her breasts. "We want him to listen to us, and stop saying denigrating things about women, and apologize publicly—at least correct the lies, like when he told the class that women's IQ stops at age twelve, and—"

"Exactly," Brian interrupts. "But Dibble doesn't listen to you, and he won't pay any more attention to a letter in the *Star*. And I doubt it will help if you cut class. How many girls, excuse me, women"— he smiles at Jenny—"are there in 202?"

"I don't know exactly. Maybe twenty."

"And how many of them would join you, do you think?"

"All of them, I hope," she says warmly. "Or almost all. There's always a few Aunt Toms in every bunch."

"Hm. But all right. Suppose you did get real cooperation. I know Don Dibble. He wouldn't care if every female student quit his courses. And he'd be quite happy to fail ten or fifteen of you for unexcused absence. Or at least lower your grades. No." Brian shakes his head once more decisively. "There's no point in removing women from the course. What you want to do is bring in *more* women." He glances around; everyone looks puzzled except Jenny.

"You mean, we should ask our friends to come to class—a whole lot of them—fill up the room." She rises to her knees, the light of battle beginning to shine in her big brown eyes. "I get it! Then when Dibble starts his stuff we can all look angry—groan and hiss—interrupt even—stamp our feet—" She laughs eagerly.

"That's right." Brian smiles at Jenny, thinking that she has a lively mind and, for one so young, a good grasp of the principles of political action. Then he looks down at Wendy, whose face is still clouded with incomprehension. It occurs to him, not for the first time, that if he had consciously set out to leave his wife for a student, he could have done better in terms of both brains and looks.

"You can get everyone you know," Linda says, sitting up. "I'll come, and I could ask Marilyn—"

"More than that," Jenny interrupts. "I'll go to the next WHEN meeting and ask for volunteers. Then we can organize them into shifts, and have signals— It's a great idea. Wow, thanks!" She turns toward Brian and suddenly embraces him, kissing his cheek; her large warm breasts are briefly pressed against his shirt.

"You're welcome."

"Fantastic," Wendy seconds adoringly, embracing and kissing him from the other side. Brian hugs her back; but he cannot help noting the physical contrast, and wondering why, for the second time in his life, he has become involved with a relatively flat-chested woman. It is not as if he preferred small breasts. But his life is not over yet. Perhaps eventually, he and Jenny . . .

·    ·    ·

*281*

"It's easy for Brian. He only has to see them once a week."
Erica stops, hearing the shrill complaining tone of her own voice.

"Ah." Zed hands her a mug of mint tea.

"He never disciplines them," Erica continues, for after all she has to complain to someone. "He just takes them out to dinner and lets them order whatever they want: pies, Coke, steak sandwiches and greasy French fries; he never makes them have milk, or vegetables. So of course they think he's keen." Holding her mug, she sits down on the thin, lumpy day bed in the back room of the Krishna Bookshop. "I know all about it, from my own childhood."

"Mm." Zed has perched opposite her on the rubber top of a kitchen stepladder, with his worn tweed jacket hung around his shoulders like the wings of a skinny bald bird.

"Only in my case it was worse. I hardly ever saw my father after he went into the Canadian Army; so I not only preferred him, I thought of him as an ideal hero. All through high school, whenever I was unhappy or felt my life was unjust, I had fantasies of how he would come to rescue me. Or sometimes I imagined how I would go to England or France or Canada to find him, and we would have a romantic reunion."

"And then, when he came back?" Zed prompts after a pause.

"He didn't really. He came less and less; after I was fourteen, not at all. I pretended to the girls at school that he did, though, sometimes," she adds, looking down. Then she looks up, but his expression has not changed—it is still gentle, impartial.

"I went to see him once," she continues. "It was in spring vacation, my second year at college. I told my mother and everybody that I was invited to visit a friend in Detroit. Then I bought a bus ticket to Ontario, and wrote and told him I was coming, too late for him to stop me. Or really, too late for his wife Myra to stop me; I'd decided that it was all her fault, that she'd been keeping us apart for years, saying spiteful things against me, even tearing up the letters I wrote him every Christmas and birthday, which would explain why he never answered."

*282*

"And how was it when you saw him?" Zed asks after another pause.

"It was awful . . . Not that he was any of the things my mother said—he wasn't hateful, or cruel, or cold-hearted, or neurotic. But he seemed to be . . . I don't know . . . a Canadian. A middle-aged Canadian businessman, with a large wife and three small children. Quite good-looking—I knew that already; I'd always thought of him as the handsomest man in the world. But he was a lot older than his photographs; and he was tired, and worried, and not very successful or well-educated. He didn't read much. He liked watching hockey, and camping— Nothing to do with me, that was the main thing. But there I was." She laughs, not very successfully.

"At first it was really terrible. My father and Myra thought I must have come to ask for money, so they were very stiff and cautious, and took pains to show me how hard up they were—cotton-flannel sheets on the bed, and corned-beef hash for dinner, and a lot of talk I didn't understand about Canadian taxes. Once they found out it wasn't that they were nicer to me, but puzzled. When I left two days early they were very relieved, and even friendly. They took my picture in front of the house and gave me a box of maple-sugar candy in the shape of maple leaves, each in a little green pleated paper cup."

"I bet you didn't eat it."

"No." Erica laughs. "I gave the whole box to Marian when I got home."

"Did you tell her where it came from?"

"I never told anyone." She laughs again briefly, like a cough. "I felt too stupid, going all that way for nothing . . . That last night, in their spare room—only they didn't have a spare room, it was the oldest boy's really, with newspaper-supplement photographs of Canadian sports stars tacked to the wallpaper—I thought— I lay awake, and I thought that the reason my father never came back to rescue me all those years was, he didn't want to." Her voice is strained. "He didn't want the responsibility of children. He was really more or less a child himself."

"Yes."

"And I lay there in the bed, sort of diagonally across it because it was too short, one of those youth beds; and I made up my mind then that I would never be like that; and I would never marry anyone like that, anyone who wasn't dependable and grown up, no matter how handsome and nice he was . . . Oh, Sandy. Please don't laugh at me."

"I'm not laughing."

"But you know, Brian wasn't like my father when I married him," Erica insists, sitting forward on the day bed. "He was serious, and responsible. I don't know what happened." She looks down into her mug of mint tea. "He changed. I suppose people do change."

A silence. Then Zed says, "Brian didn't change. He's always been the same. A typical double Capricorn; he needs to appear responsible and serious in the eyes of the world. But most people are like that. They want to look good. You're eccentric; you want to be good."

"I'm not eccentric," Erica exclaims, setting down her mug. "I'm quite a conventional person really. At least, I've certainly never thought of myself as unconventional." She gives the last word, which was one of her mother's terms of praise, a particular bitter intonation.

"Oh, Erica." Zed does laugh now, out loud. "Don't give me that. The conventional thing for you would have been to refuse to divorce Brian and refuse to speak to Wendy."

This speech seems a little overfamiliar, even rude. But Erica decides to excuse it; after all, Sandy is a very old friend. "Maybe so," she says. "At least, that's what I guess Brian expected me to do. Really, what I think he wanted was to keep us both," she adds.

"He would." The tone in which Zed utters this reminds Erica of what she has once or twice thought: that Sandy not only does not care very much for Brian, but for some reason actually hates him. "With his Capricorn moon where it is."

Erica does not comment. She frowns slightly, sits back. "Do you really believe all that?" she asks, in a cooler voice. "About the movements of the stars influencing people's lives?"

"Not the stars, the planets." Zed also shifts position: he moves his feet to the top step of his ladder and rests his elbows on his knees.

"But it seems so deterministic." She smiles now, glad to have changed the subject. "I look at the horoscope column in the paper sometimes—I suppose everyone does—and it's always about how if you're born in September, you're very fussy and critical, and you can't do anything about it, especially not on Wednesdays."

"Those daily columns are a fraud. Dangerous, even; most serious astrologers despise them. The point of astrology is that every individual is unique. Of course, there's fate—your planets— but there's also human will. You can't reverse your nature, but you can use it for better or worse. That's very comforting; it provides both encouragement and an excuse, whichever you need at the time."

"Yes." Erica laughs. "But all the same— What good does it do, really?"

Zed smiles at her between his long narrow hands. "You're still asking that. I remember back in Cambridge it was one of the things about you that most impressed me. I was less morally ambitious than you, even then. I didn't aspire to do good; that seemed too difficult. I only wanted not to do harm." He sighs. "Even that— I think sometimes I ought to close this place down and just do charts."

"You think you're doing harm here, in the bookshop?"

"Hard to say." Zed has been unknotting his old black knit tie; now he pulls on one end, dragging it out from under the frayed collar. "It was all right at first. But now there's too many people coming in all the time wanting me to solve their life problems—answer their spiritual doubts, tell them what to do, what to think. They write down whatever I say, including all the stupid things, and repeat them back to me. I don't know how much longer I can take it. I'm not like your husband; I don't like to be worshiped. It gives me claustrophobia."

Erica laughs, starts to speak, and stops. She has always despised people who mock and disparage their ex-spouses, and has a horror of becoming one of them. Months ago she resolved never to speak against or even discuss Brian's character with anyone but Danielle; she has cut off many conversations beginning "You know, I always thought Brian was—" with a cool "I'd rather not talk about him, if you don't mind." She is too fond of Zed to say this to him; instead she looks at her watch, sighs a little, consciously, and stands up.

"You're leaving?"

"I think I'd better; it's nearly eleven. I should go back to Danielle's party—I sort of promised I'd help her clean up when it's over." Erica sighs again less consciously. For the first time in almost an hour she has remembered the woman she saw in the mirrors: worn, creased, no longer really pretty. It is this creased unpretty person who must return to the party, and stay there perhaps for hours.

She lifts her fur coat from a stack of book cartons and begins to put it on; Zed scrambles off the ladder and attempts to help. "Here. Let me."

"That's all right." Erica fastens her coat; she picks up a long rose-colored mohair shawl which has fallen to the ground, shakes out the dust, and wraps it around her head and shoulders. Zed, apologizing for the condition of his floor, follows her to the front of the darkened shop.

"It's still going on," she exclaims. Beyond the black silhouettes of books, the shopwindow is gray and clotted with wet flakes and clumps of snow.

Drawing back the bolts, Zed opens the front door on a solid

block of heavy, exploding snow. Erica's car, a few steps away under the street lamp, is a blurred white mound.

"Oh, heavens! Look at that." She takes two steps out into it; is at once surrounded, blinded; retreats. "The street hasn't even been plowed. What am I going to do?"

"You could wait here awhile, and see if it stops," Zed suggests, shielding his face with one arm.

"Maybe I'd better." Erica steps back into the shop, stamping her boots. "I wonder how long it's going to last. Did you hear any weather reports on the radio?"

"I don't have a radio." He shuts the door—the first time unsuccessfully, for snow has blown into the frame; then with a slam.

"I could call Danielle, I suppose." Erica remembers that Sandy also has no telephone. "Is there a phone anywhere near here?"

"There's one in the Chinese restaurant. But it's probably shut by now."

"You ought to have a phone." Zed makes no comment. "Well, I expect if Danielle looks out of her window she'll realize what's happened, and ask someone else to help her. Her friend Dr. Kotelchuk, for instance." Erica pulls off her shawl, which is filmy with moisture. "I mean her suitor," she adds, loosening her coat and following Zed to the back of the shop.

"I can't get over that, you know," she continues. "Did I tell you he proposed to her in the liquor store at the Co-op? I mean, really." She laughs.

"He should have chosen a more romantic scene?"

"Yes, why not? At least a more private one. Wouldn't you?"

"I've never proposed to anyone," Zed says, taking Erica's coat and laying it carefully over the cartons for the second time. "But yes; I suppose I'd probably wait for more auspicious circumstances. Of course that way you might miss your chance. Would you like more tea?"

"Yes, thank you." Erica pulls her shawl around her shoulders. It is growing chilly, for Zed's landlord, economically, only provides heat during business hours. "The whole idea is impossible, really," she continues. "How could anyone want to marry a man named Bernie Kotelchuk?"

"Or Sanford Finkelstein." Zed is stooped over the sink, rinsing out their cups; his voice is flat. "Maybe that's why I—"

"It's not the same thing at all," Erica lies gaily, inwardly reproaching herself. "Not at all."

He shakes his head. "It's a ludicrous name." His voice mixes with the wet uneven sound of water running. "I've always disliked it."

"So you changed it."

"Yes." He turns off the tap.

"Why did you choose the name Zed? What does it mean?"

"Nothing. It's the last letter of the alphabet." He opens a tin and spoons tea into the pot.

"I understand why you might not like Finkelstein," she says. "But what was wrong with Sanford, by itself?"

"I don't know." Zed looks round, shrugging his bony shoulders. "Perhaps it had become too familiar—too closely associated with a famous character in literature."

"I don't remember any Sanford in literature," Erica says, puzzled. "Whose books is he in—Henry James's?"

"Yours."

"Mine? Oh. But that wasn't— I didn't mean—" She hears her voice rise falsely, falter. "It was just a name."

"You turned me into an ostrich."

"I'm sorry," Erica says, alternately meeting and dodging his half-smile. "It just seemed the right sort of name— He was a nice ostrich, you know." She looks guiltily at Zed, who is taking a box of wheat-germ crackers from the top of a bookcase. In her mind she sees superimposed the colored drawing in which she had depicted Sanford with one long, knobby leg up, helpfully reaching down

*288*

some chocolate cake which the mother of Mark and Spencer had concealed on a high shelf.

"I didn't think you'd ever see those silly books," she says. "Nobody does usually, unless they have children; and I didn't think you'd ever have children."

"No," he agrees in a strained chirp.

A short silence. Erica reproaches herself again, more severely. Zed, his back turned, does something with a plate. "I'm sorry," she repeats. "I didn't mean— Do you mind that very much, not having children?"

"I used to." He turns around. "That's not true; even now sometimes, when I see little kids— But I realize it doesn't matter . . . God's will." He shrugs again. "Creating beings who resemble you physically—that's the lowest form of immortality. It's a joke—a pretty bad joke, sometimes."

"Yes." Erica thinks of Jeffrey and Matilda, both of whom have been said to resemble her.

"It's better to have spiritual children. Like Sanford."

"Maybe so . . . You didn't mind really, did you? About the books, I mean."

"No. I was glad to know you still thought of me sometimes."

"But I did, you know," she protests. "Not just because of the books."

"Really." Zed raises his eyebrows. "I thought of you too, sometimes," he adds mockingly, leaning back against the bookshelves.

Erica smiles with relief, and the beginnings of a flirtatious manner. "That reminds me, Sandy. There's something I've been meaning to ask: Did you know Brian and I were living here when you moved to Corinth?"

"No, I—" He hesitates. "Yes, I knew. That's why I chose it." From his expression it is impossible to tell if this is a joke.

"I thought you came back because you'd been to college here."

"It was a sort of double feature." He grins.

"But then you were in town for months, and you never called us or anything," she complains coquettishly. "And Brian said he came down here once, last fall, and you didn't want to tell him who you were." Erica smiles; she is enjoying herself. "Anybody would think you were trying to hide from me."

"Not at all, I—" Again he falters. "That's not true either. I don't know what's the matter with me; I haven't told any lies for quite a while, but I seem to be lying to you. What happened was, I knew Brian when he came into the store, but he didn't recognize me—he only saw me a couple of times years ago, when I had more hair. I didn't want to give him my name because I thought he'd remember it and tell you, and I didn't want that. I wanted it to happen the right way. Like you said about Dr. Kotelchuk proposing in the liquor store." Zed smiles.

"I don't think you wanted it to happen at all," Erica protests. She hugs her rose-colored stole around her shoulders, delighted to have rediscovered this old, charming, light-hearted self. "When you'd been here absolutely for months without calling. I don't think you have any idea what you want."

The kettle is boiling; he turns to fill the pot. "No," he says over his shoulder. "I know what I want."

"And what's that?" She is almost laughing.

"You." Zed turns his head, giving her, for the first time, the pale intense stare with which Brian and the habitués of the Krishna Bookshop are already familiar.

"I—" Erica's laugh is extinguished, leaving her mouth empty. "Sandy, that's absurd," she says in the tone of one gently rebuking a child. At the same time, almost unconsciously, she gets up off the day bed and puts a chair between herself and Zed. "I mean, heavens, you've known me for twenty years."

"I've wanted you for twenty years," he says stubbornly.

An involuntary satisfaction rises in Erica. She stamps it down, hard, realizing that she has brought this declaration on herself. Because there is nobody now she can safely flirt with, she has been flirting with poor old Sandy; provoking him to console her for having had an awful time at a party and for feeling creased and plain.

"You can't mean that literally," she insists, smiling, holding on to the back of the chair. "You must have had affairs."

"Yes," Zed admits after a slight pause. "But not very many lately. And not very successfully."

"I thought you gave all that up along with meat and telephones," she says, attempting a light manner.

"No . . . But none of them ever were quite real to me, you know. You're the only woman in the world, as far as I'm concerned. The others always seem to me like imitations—bad copies."

There is no doubt now that he is serious. But Erica forbids herself to be pleased or flattered. "Oh, Sandy. That's just silly," she announces sharply to both of them.

Zed says nothing to this, and makes no move. He leans back against the bookshelves in his old white shirt, with his bony shoulders raised. Most of the light has gone out of his eyes. He is not going to make any move, she thinks with some surprise; she is quite safe. She sighs with something like relief.

But this relief is followed by shame. Sandy is one of her oldest friends; he has provided her with countless cups of coffee and tea, listened to her worries about final examinations and faulty plumbing, lent her books, carried her groceries, loved her for twenty years. And how has she repaid him? She has used his name as a joke in some silly children's stories, made him go to a large bad party, and first provoked and then insulted him. No wonder he looks at her now with mute pain and reproach, like a large scrawny wounded bird, shot out of season.

Somehow she must make amends. She comes out from behind the chair, toward him.

"I'm sorry, Sandy," she says, putting her hand on his arm. To her distress, it is actually trembling under the shirt. "I didn't mean—"

"That's all right." He smiles painfully, indicating that it is not all right. Erica feels terrible. What can she do? Like Brian in a similar situation, it occurs to her that if she were to kiss Sandy affectionately he might feel better. She approaches the gesture awkwardly, for she is unused to taking the initiative and has not kissed anyone in months. Another difficulty, one which has not occurred in twenty years, is Zed's height; she has to stand on tiptoe to reach his cheek.

His reaction to the kiss is odd: as she comes near he almost flinches, then he looks surprised; finally he smiles, but stiffly.

"You're not angry?" she asks.

Zed shakes his head unconvincingly. Obviously he does not believe either in her apology or her affection. He believes that she finds him and his feelings "absurd" and "silly."

How could she have said those words, been so thoughtless, so unkind? How can she take them back and heal the injury she has given?

But even as she asks this, the only possible answer occurs to Erica. That it will require greater self-sacrifice than anything she has done yet first frightens and then begins to convince her. If you know of someone who wants your old clothes, your day-old bread, it is wrong to keep them selfishly in the cupboard; she has always believed this. For years she used to save all their stale bread, and once a week she and Jeffo and Muffy would go down to Reed Park and scatter it in the bird sanctuary.

Zed has still not moved. He stands there against the shelves of books with his wings hunched, not even looking at her, simply waiting for her to go away. Instead she takes a step in the other direction, toward him.

"Sandy, my dear. What's the matter?"

He turns his head, looks down, hesitates. Perhaps, now he sees her so close, so creased, even he doesn't want— Then slowly he straightens up and moves nearer; she sees in close-up his ill-shaven, freckled, tired scarecrow features; his pale eyes with their reddish rims and orange lashes. Nearer still— She closes her eyes, improving the view.

At first it is hardly like being kissed at all; then Zed, with a clumsy, half-blind gesture, pulls her closer and shifts his mouth so that it meets hers more accurately. Erica remembers the look in his eyes a few moments ago; she remembers the birds in the park, how impatient and greedy they always were, how they would press close to her and her bag of bread, flapping and squawking; she remembers Brian, and waits for Sandy too to crowd, to grab.

But he only holds her, stroking her face and hair, kissing her gently and intermittently. Gradually she relaxes, rests against him. She sighs—not in protest, but Zed releases her, blinking and putting out one hand to feel for the shelf behind him.

"Sandy? Are you all right?"

"Yes. No. I feel dizzy." He laughs. "I feel— As if I'd got a birthday present I'd given up expecting."

"Did you have a birthday recently?"

"What? My birthday— It was last week."

"I'm glad." Erica looks up at him in a way which would have informed Brian, or any other man, that he should kiss her again. But Zed doesn't move. He has no idea of how large a present she intends to give him. She will have to tell him—to show him— But now she is embarrassed; she steps back, looks around the room. "Is it still snowing, do you think?" she asks.

"Let's see." Zed lifts the curtain to the front of the shop. "No. It looks as if it's stopped." He walks between dim bookshelves to the door and peers out. "And the street's been plowed. You can go now. I'll get your coat."

# 15

It is a cold, shiny April morning. In his apartment at the top of Alpine Towers, Brian Tate is having a leisurely breakfast: English muffins with marmalade, scrambled eggs, and coffee made in a filter pot the way he has finally managed to teach Wendy to make it. It is one of the few things he has managed to teach her—for on close acquaintance, Wendy's malleability has proved just as intractable as Erica's stubbornness. She will agree to anything, accept his opinion on any matter; but a few hours later she will meet Linda or some other friend, hear a lecture, read a magazine article, and change her mind. To keep her on the right track, he would have to stay with her twenty-four hours a day.

Brian has no desire to do this; in his view they are together too much as it is. Three weeks ago Wendy's roommate Linda took up with, and into her apartment, an intense, homeless, bearded young man named Avery. Since then Wendy has been living full-time in Alpine Towers, an arrangement which Brian finds less than satisfactory. He can remember Leonard Zimmern saying cynically that there were only two infallible ways to get over a woman: one was to cut the relationship off completely, cold turkey, never to see her, telephone her or write to her again; the other, equally effective, was to see her all the time.

The idea that one should preserve some modesty, some privacy, even under the most intimate conditions, had been Erica's native creed. It is foreign to Wendy. Every day now Brian can observe her sitting up in bed to blow her nose; brushing her teeth over the sink, her mouth full of foamy pink spit; washing out her dirty panties at night. If he had allowed it she would have used the toilet while he was shaving. Also she is letting her appearance go, putting on weight; in the last month or so she must have gained five pounds. Her breasts are larger, which is all right; but her waist is also thicker, giving her figure a coarseness not at all to his taste.

But even if Wendy were more modest and as slim as before, Brian might still be sick of her. His theory had been right, after all: the way to cure a passion was by satiating it. Mere consummation was not enough; as long as the affair remained secret, the necessary stimuli to desire were there: absence, anxiety, delay, solitary longing.

Now the lovers are in full possession. They can see each other all day long. They can have breakfast together, and lunch, and dinner, and breakfast . . .

In the house on Jones Creek Road the children were always around when Brian got home; he could seldom speak privately to Erica until late at night. But he and Wendy are alone constantly, and always in each other's presence, for the apartment has only one usable room. She doesn't seem to mind this; probably she finds it comfortably familiar, having grown up under equally crowded conditions. She also, as far as he can tell, feels no slackening of romantic love; indeed she claims to adore him more than ever. When he suggests that she might look for another place to live she becomes weepy and helpless, insisting that there are no apartments at this time of year and that she will try even harder not to disturb him in his Work.

Meanwhile, she continues to disturb him—especially when she is trying not to: when she is tiptoeing around the apartment, opening and shutting the refrigerator with elaborate precaution, crawling under his desk to unplug the radio so she can drag it over the rug into the bedroom with her—for like his children, Wendy seems unable to study unless she is simultaneously eating and listening to bad music. In order to get any work done, even to grade papers, Brian has to retreat to his office on campus. Like Jeffrey and Matilda, Wendy is driving him out of his own house.

Brian sighs heavily. He has come to realize belatedly that in love, as in war, whatever is the greatest difference between the principals becomes the central issue. When they are alike except that one is male, the other female, the relationship takes its ideal form. But if there are other important differences—class, race, color, religion, nationality, education, etc.—then the lovers will find themselves polarized around these differences rather than engaged in the natural sexual contest.

There are many differences between him and Wendy, but the greatest is that of generation. He had been born twenty years sooner and had certain interests, habits and attitudes; he found the interests, habits and attitudes of Wendy and her friends tiresome. Last week, at a particularly disorganized and frantic graduate-student party, when he refused to try to dance in the current disorganized and frantic style, even Wendy had turned on him, crying plaintively, "Why can't you swing a little?" "Because I don't want to swing," Brian replied. "I'm not a child. I don't want to swing, or slide, or go on the teeter-totter."

He sighs and unfolds this morning's student paper. Beyond the usual depressing international news, which he has already heard on the radio last night, nothing catches his notice except for another letter complaining about Donald Dibble's course. It is the fourth or fifth such letter to appear in the *Star*, and not very original or well written; but Brian reads it carefully, for he has a personal interest in the controversy.

Since Linda Sliski's party there have been several develop-ments in the war between Dibble and the local feminists, in which Brian has played an important advisory role. His original sugges-tion that more women should be brought into Dibble's class was adopted enthusiastically. Over that first weekend Jenny was able to enlist five or six sympathizers, including Linda and Wendy. They crowded into the room on Monday and sat in a clump at the back. If Dibble had had the slightest political sense he would have avoided saying anything to provoke them; he would simply have waited them out. But he made an antifeminist remark, or what could pass for one, and the girls at the back began to whisper and groan half audibly. On Monday night Jenny and Sara went to a WHEN meeting and asked for recruits; and at Wednesday's lecture there were a dozen superfluous women who did not wait for offensive statements but started groaning and booing when Dibble spoke favorably of the Republican party, causing him to slam down his text and notes and, in a trembling voice, request all auditors to leave. When they did not move he stuffed his books and papers into a briefcase and walked out of the room.

But Dibble was by no means defeated. When Jenny and Sara arrived at next Monday's lecture, followed this time by nearly twenty extra women, they found a monitor at the door with an official class list and orders to admit only students legally enrolled in the course. Baffled, the leaders of the protest returned to Brian for counsel. They were confused and angry; a few wanted to take some drastic action against Dibble, to arouse public opinion on a wide scale.

In fact public opinion was already being aroused; the dispute had become a matter first of departmental and then of university gossip, and was now even known to people outside Corinth. Leonard had called Brian from New York for details. "We've had the same thing," he reported. "The local Hens objected because Jane Austen, the Brontës, et cetera, were taught by men, who couldn't possibly understand, bla bla bla. But as I said to Irv here, you have to get tough and hold the line, or you'll be in for it. Next you'll have the Gay Power boys picketing Comp Lit because Proust and Gide aren't taught by faggots."

But Brian felt some sympathy for Jenny's cause. After all, Dibble probably had made some foolishly unprofessional remarks.

*297*

He was a boor and a reactionary and Brian's long-standing enemy, while Jenny was a beautiful young girl who admired him and would be grateful if he helped her to defeat their common adversary; Brian had already imagined some of the forms this gratitude might take.

He did not get tough with Jenny, therefore, but tried to calm her down and persuade her that the protesters should make their next move through official channels, presenting their case in a letter to the acting chairman of the political science department, with carbon copies to Dibble and the dean. Vague complaints would not be enough, though; what they needed was evidence: direct quotations from Dibble's lectures insulting women.

As a result of this conversation Sara and Jenny, who were the only leaders of the protest now enrolled in the course, began attending it with tape recorders hidden in their bags. They sat in the front row, but at opposite ends; this was necessary because of Dibble's habit of walking nervously back and forth the length of the podium as he spoke. Jenny concealed the microphone in her blouse; Sara, less generously endowed, in the bib pocket of her overalls. But results were disappointing. Dibble had finished discussing the Nineteenth Amendment, and almost all he did for two weeks was to refer once to Prohibitionists as "hysterical old-maid schoolteacher types" and to pronounce the name "Eleanor Roosevelt" in a sneering tone.

Examination of the past lecture notes of sympathizers was more productive, however; and best (or worst) of all was a recording secretly made by Linda Sliski when calling on Dibble in his office under pretense of getting information for her Ph.D. thesis. "If you want my frank opinion, it's a waste of time to teach girls political science," Brian heard his colleague announce on Linda's tape recorder—as he had heard him often in meetings. "Do you know what percentage of our female graduates go on to make any use whatever of their expensive education?" Dibble's voice, converted by the machine to an unpleasant low quacking, continued quoting figures until it was interrupted by Linda's equally unpleasant high bleat accusing him of specious logic and reactionary bias, and informing him that she, at least, had every intention of putting her education to use, and that she had no intention, Professor Dibble, of becoming a mere housewife and bringing more children into a world like this one, and that he might not have a very good opinion of her capabilities, but she would like him to know that she had an A- average and had just been appointed to a position at Ohio State University. This information, or perhaps the realization that Linda was on the verge of tears, caused Dibble to laugh in a way Brian knew well, and to remark, "You got an assistant professorship at Ohio State? Well, you'd better hang on to it. There's a fashion now in some schools for hiring women, but it won't last."

Hearing this conversation replayed, Brian had a strange giddy sensation—an intoxicating sense of power. Almost without effort, he had set the two people in Corinth he most disliked upon each other. He had chosen their battleground and their weapons; now he could sit behind the scenes and hear them attack each other, saying things he would have liked to say himself.

This feeling of power was increased three days ago when Brian was called in for consultation on the dispute by Bill Guildenstern, the acting chairman of the department. Like many acting chairmen, Bill was an ambitious, cautious, personable young man; an executive type, devoted to the smooth functioning and greater glory of the department, but without strong opinions of his own. His policy has been to consult the senior members of the staff individually on any problem which arises (he is too shrewd a politician to consult them en masse), and then present his decision as a consensus. Brian, as a former chairman, is often consulted.

"I'd like to get your opinion of this," Bill said, holding out to Brian a letter he had seen before, now signed by eleven members of Dibble's course and eighteen non-members, all female.

"Certainly," Brian agreed. He pretended to read the letter, making appropriate noises. "Mm, hm. Well, it seems to be fairly temperate and straightforward, as these things go," he remarked, not unnaturally, for he had seen the original draft and told Jenny to tone it down. "But I expect Don is somewhat heated about it."

"Boiling," Bill replied.

For a moment Brian allowed himself to enjoy a vision of Dibble in his office, opening a copy of this letter, reading it, boiling. "Ye-es," he said, frowning so as not to smile. He turned back to the second page, to the demand for a public apology from Dibble plus equal class time for a speaker of their choice. If he wished Brian could advise granting this demand, causing Dibble to boil even harder. But, like Bill, he had to consider the public reputation of the department, to avoid uproar and scandal. It was time to return to the policy of containment.

He could of course, and perhaps should, recommend the usual delaying tactics: suggest that the matter be referred to a committee which would be unable to reach its decision until the term was over. But this would mean in effect a total victory for Dibble. It would be deeply discouraging to Wendy and pretty Jenny and all their friends. Moreover, they would see it as a failure not only of their cause but of Brian's advice and political know-how.

For all these reasons, he had decided on a compromise. It was clear that the demand for an apology must be forgotten. ("Apologize!?" Bill reported Dibble as shouting. "Those spoiled brats ought to apologize to me.") There should be no interference with lectures, but Dibble should be asked to announce optional class meetings during reading period (now only two weeks off) in which the feminist viewpoint would be presented. And as Bill nodded, smiled, expressing approval of this solution, Brian felt again the intoxication of political power. He thought that now he understood why someone might wish to become a double agent.

He was not surprised to discover that Bill Guildenstern had taken his advice. But he was rather startled yesterday when he heard that Dibble had refused even this favorable compromise. Wendy and her friends, quite naturally, were not only surprised but indignant. At about noon Sara and Jenny appeared in Brian's

*300*

office, one white with anger, the other almost weeping. He tried to calm them, to tell them that nothing much was lost—that they could still go ahead and hold meetings in reading period without Dibble's permission. Jenny seemed partly convinced, but not Sara. "You know something?" she cried passionately, clinging to the back of a chair with her small white fists as if it were a podium, and looking more than ever like a young boy revolutionary. "If we were blacks, instead of women, they wouldn't dare give us this kind of crap. Anyone, anyone has more status in this society than we do, more respect!"

"Blacks do not have more status," Brian corrected her. "The establishment is just more scared of them. If you were black, they'd be afraid you'd bomb Burnham Hall, or hold Dibble hostage in his office."

"Yes! That's what we should do," Sara said stubbornly. "Only we've got no guts. We've let ourselves be brainwashed too long." She gave Brian an accusing, discouraged look, such as another woman might give an incompetent repairman, and turned back to Jenny. "Come on, let's split. We've got to get that meeting organized."

From the departmental point of view things have turned out for the best, but Brian regrets that the protest has ended in a rout. Sara had held her meeting last night, and Wendy dutifully attended the first two hours of it. (Brian, as usual, did not go; he would have been unwelcome, not as a professor, but as a man.) She reported that there was a lot of discussion still going on when she left, but no plan of action. Brian was not surprised; women alone can never really get a cause together. It is not only that they are too gentle, but also, as he has read recently, that they lack the male bonding instinct, the tradition of cooperation against a common enemy.

Wendy has poured him another cup of coffee, and is cooking herself a brownish mess of health-food cereal and nuts and raisins when the telephone rings. It is Linda, breathlessly asking to speak to her.

"For you." Brian holds out the receiver.

"Hi . . . What? . . . Oh, wow! . . . Fantastic . . . No, we didn't hear the radio . . . Gee. I don't know. Wait a sec." She turns around. "Linda says they've taken over Dibble's office! She's going over there now, and she wants me to come with her. Oh, hey, isn't that far out?"

"Taken over his office?" Brian drops the *Times,* causing the Cosmopolitan Girl on the back page to become smeared with egg and marmalade, and stands up. He is torn between reluctance to speak with Linda and wish for information. But he recalls her habitual inaccuracy, and the first impulse wins. "Tell her you'll call back. And turn on WCUR."

"I'll call you back . . . As soon as I can. . . . She says she can't wait," Wendy reports, hanging up.

". . . more bulletins as they are received," the radio announces. "And now a message from Bud Wordsworth, president of the Savings Bank." Brian turns down the sound, knowing from experience that this pompous commercial will last sixty seconds.

"They've taken over Dibble's office," he repeats. "How many of them?"

"About twelve or fifteen, Linda said. Nearly everybody who stayed at the meeting last night. She would've been with them, only she had to teach her eight o'clock class. Hey, isn't it just fine, though?"

Brian does not reply, but checks his watch: it is quarter after nine. "And what's Dibble doing?" he asks.

"Nothing, I guess. He was talking on the phone for a while, but then they cut the wire."

"You mean he's in there with them?"

"Oh, yeh." Wendy grins. "That's the whole idea. Sara was talking about it last night, but I didn't think she'd convince them. They're holding him hostage, like you told them to." She gazes at Brian proudly.

"Oh, Christ." A vision comes to him of Donald Dibble at his desk, surrounded—indeed jostled, for the room is hardly ten feet square—by angry girl students. Again Brian has the sense of his own power to affect circumstances; but this time it is the uncontrolled, ignorant power of the sorcerer's apprentice.

He turns the radio up again, hearing first that savings are grow-power for our community and then that everything Wendy has said is true. He learns that although campus patrolmen have been called to the scene, no action has yet been taken against the demonstrators; and that neither William Guildenstern, chairman of the political science department, or Ned Kane, dean of the Humanities, has made any statement.

An undertone of amusement in the voice of the campus reporter causes Brian to realize for the first time that there is a humorous, even farcical side to the situation. Whatever happens now, Dibble's goose is cooked. For the rest of his life he will be known locally as that professor who was imprisoned by a gang of girls. People will make jokes about it, including people who know Dibble well enough to suspect that the worst thing he could imagine is to be locked in a room with fifteen women. For the first time since Linda's call Brian smiles, then laughs aloud.

But of course to Dibble it is no joke. Or to Bill Guildenstern. "I'd better get up there," he says. "Come on. Leave the dishes, for God's sake."

"You realize I don't want you to go into the building," he informs Wendy as they ride down in the elevator five minutes later.

"But I told Linda," Wendy mews. She is now dressed for revolutionary action, in jeans and boots and an old fringed cowboy jacket with peace symbols blazed on the lapels. Her pale, fine yellow hair is loose, her eyes bright. "I promised her—"

"I don't care what you promised Linda," returns Brian, who has also changed his clothes, though in the other direction, replacing his cord pants and knit jersey with a suit, shirt and tie in anticipation of his interview with Bill and Ned Kane. "I don't want you involved in this misguided affair."

"Misguided?" she wails. "But it was your idea!"

"It was not my idea," Brian corrects her as the elevator comes to rest with its customary cough and bump. "I've never recommended political violence of any sort," he continues, determined to make it clear that the occupation of Dibble's office cannot be blamed on him. "As soon as you do something illegal you're in the wrong, and then, even if you win, you lose morally."

"Yeh." Wendy stops in the foyer. "That's what Zed says. Every time you do a violent act you lose a year on the Path, he says."

"Does he." Brian holds the outside door open and motions her through, suppressing further remarks which occur to him in the interest of expediency. Nevertheless it irritates him profoundly that Wendy should still refer her opinions to a middle-aged life dropout who has fused his mental circuits with religious nonsense and drugs. It does not improve his estimate of this creep that he should turn out to be an old Cambridge acquaintance of Erica's.

It is obvious as they turn onto campus that something unusual is happening. The parking lot by Burnham Hall is full of official-looking cars, some without U stickers, and as Brian pulls into a fortunately vacated space he sees two men getting out of a panel truck with what looks like a portable television camera. On the side of the building facing the quad there is a small but growing crowd of spectators and journalists. He follows their gaze to the second-floor window of Dibble's office, but can make out nothing past the glare of sun on glass.

Cautioning Wendy again not to follow him, he enters Burnham. There are more spectators in the hallway; he pushes through them with difficulty and expostulation, thinking as he often does that students seem to be getting larger and ruder every year. He explains his way past two campus cops guarding the stairs and another at the top. At the far end of the upstairs hall he can see a crowd of people, all men. He recognizes some of them: two boys from the campus paper whom he knows, Jenny's bearded friend Mark, and the sad hitchhiker Stanley. He does not approach, but

*304*

turns into the department office, where Bill is in conference with representatives of the administration and the Safety Division.

"Ah, Brian." It is a sigh of relief. "Excuse me a moment, gentlemen." Bill draws Brian aside into his secretary's office (now empty) and in a tense and distracted manner attempts to fill him in: Dibble has been imprisoned for over an hour now. Several people have tried to talk to him on the phone and persuade him to make what is after all a rather slight concession, but without success. Now the line has been cut, and the gang of male sympathizers will let no one through. Worse still, both Dean Kane and President Backson are out of town.

Having no one to pass the buck to in this, his first serious crisis has obviously been too much for Bill. His voice rises and falls nervously as he speaks, and he keeps patting his upper arms with both hands as if to assure himself that he is still there.

"I know some of those kids," Brian volunteers finally. In contrast to Bill he feels quite calm. "They might let me in. But it's no use my talking to Don; he hates my guts. Why don't you try John Randall?"

"I called him." Bill almost groans. "He won't have anything to do with it—says the protesters have forfeited their rights by taking illegal action."

"Uh huh." It is what he would have expected from Randall.

"Of course there's the Safety Division," Bill admits, anticipating a recommendation Brian is not going to make. "But that might be dangerous." Pat, pat.

"You think they'd hurt the girls?"

"I don't know. Maybe the girls would hurt the cops. But either way— You can imagine the news stories. We've got to get Don out of there; when I spoke to him on the phone half an hour ago he was already hysterical."

"You want to get Don out." Though Brian speaks slowly, plans are rocketing through his brain. There is a way, he is sure. Somehow the scene outside on the quad under Dibble's window is part of it— Yes.

"I have an idea," he says. "Wait—not here." He gestures with his head toward Helen Wells and the secretaries in the outer office. Helen has been with the political science department longer than he, and the others have always seemed nice, obliging girls. But they are women, and one of them may be a spy. He draws Bill back into the chairman's office, and leaning close across the table where the other men are sitting with worried expressions on their faces, outlines his plan.

Fifteen minutes later Brian emerges from a custodian's closet in the basement of Burnham Hall. He looks slightly odd, for he is wearing Bill Guildenstern's raincoat which is much too long for him and would ordinarily also be too wide. Now, however, it fits snugly over the fifty feet of heavy knotted rope that is wrapped around his body under his suit jacket, giving him the outward shape of a fat man or a pregnant woman.

On the stairs to the first floor he meets Hank Andrews.

"Well! You've heard the good news, I take it?" Hank grins and leans against the banister. But Brian has no time for conversation.

"Yes, I'm on my way to see Don now." He suppresses the impulse to confide in Hank, promising himself that later he will explain everything, accept his friend's congratulations.

"You're going into Don's office?" Hank frowns. "I wouldn't do that, if I were you . . . They won't let you in anyhow," he adds more easily.

"I think they may. I know some of them."

"Even so. I don't advise it."

"And what would you advise?" Brian asks impatiently. He advances to the next step, bringing his head on a level with Hank's.

"I would suggest that you follow the example of Our Leader: leave town at once in any crisis." Hank's tone is so serious that Brian decides he is joking.

"It's too late for that; I've just promised Bill I'd do what I can. He's quite *non compos*," he adds, smiling.

"You might have a sudden illness." Hank puts his hand on Brian's shoulder, an unusual gesture.

Brian stops smiling. Usually he enjoys his friend's jokes and respects his opinion; now he remembers that Hank has always avoided responsibility—he recently refused again to be considered for chairman, for instance. He thinks that although Hank is six feet tall, he is a passive intellectual, a coward, who would not dare conceive or carry out Brian's present plan. "I'll see you later." He goes up another step; now he is taller than Hank.

"Seriously," Hank continues. "Let Bill worry— Hey, what've you got there?" he asks as his hand slides off Brian's shoulder and down over the bulge of knotted rope. But Brian does not reply, or even look back as he ascends the stairs, two steps at a time.

Nine o'clock classes are ending, and there are even more people in the hall for him to push through. The cops do not question him this time; perhaps they have already been alerted to what will soon happen.

Upstairs the sympathizers are still on guard outside Dibble's office, accompanied now by a reporter and photographer from the local paper who take notes and snap Brian's picture. As he had anticipated, he has little trouble persuading Mark and Stanley to let him speak with the protesters. But when Sara and a girl named Pat, who resembles her, come out into the hall, it is nearly impossible to convince them to give him some time alone with Dibble.

"We can't talk if you're all in there, you must see that," he insists, wishing he had pretty Jenny, or even Linda Sliski, to deal with instead of these militant tomboys. "Dibble's got to have privacy to negotiate, to save his face—"

"We're not interested in saving his ugly face," interrupts Sara's confederate, a skinny small girl with long mouse-colored braids.

"But you've got to consider what effect all this has on him. Dibble's not a well man," Brian improvises. "He has heart trouble."

"Dibble couldn't have heart trouble," Sara retorts. "He has no heart. You should have heard some of the things he said to us in there."

"He called us stupid, spoiled little girls," Pat volunteers indignantly.

"He told Linda she was a denatured female, and he said he was going to see she never held another academic job in her life."

"Very aggravating." Brian prevents himself from smiling even slightly. "But the question is, do you want to win this battle, or don't you? Are you going to let yourself be distracted by propaganda, by name-calling and threats? I think at least you should tell them all in there that I've offered to talk to Dibble, and put it to a vote," he adds, seeing Sara hesitate.

"Well. Okay. Come on, Pat."

For some minutes Brian waits in the hall, listening to the sounds of argument from behind the door and wondering if Mark or Stanley or the others notice anything suspicious about his appearance. Finally the door opens; Sara beckons to Brian and tells him it has been decided that he can see Dibble alone, but only for ten minutes. Behind her the other protesters crowd out into the hall—a small mob of badly dressed, angry-looking girls. All of them stare at Brian, a few with looks of distrust.

"Where's Wendy?" Linda asks him, also distrustfully.

"Outside." Brian pushes forward through the crowd to avoid further questioning, keeping both arms pressed against his body to prevent the rope from unwinding.

"Ten minutes," Sara warns him.

"He's not going to listen to you, you know," Jenny says, touching his arm earnestly. "He's all freaked out."

"Could be."

Brian smiles at her, shrugs, and enters Dibble's office, shutting the door firmly behind him. Both the room and its occupant look definitely deranged. The drawers of the filing cabinet are pulled open, with papers and files scattered on the desk and floor. There are female boots and coats piled everywhere, and a white, obsessed expression on Dibble's face as he rises from behind his desk, fixing his eyes on Brian and speaking in a thin, hoarse caricature of his normal voice.

"I know what you're here for, Tate," he cries. "I know you're responsible for this outrage, and let me tell you it doesn't surprise me, oh no, I'm not at all surprised." He shakes his head several times. "But it's no use your coming in here. I'm not going to negotiate with any little rabble-rouser, oh no, oh no." Again he shakes his head very rapidly, like a wet dog. "I have no interest whatsoever in negotiation. I've already made my position, my position quite clear. I expressed myself clearly to Bill Guildenstern, I think. I told him, I said, if you have any slight regard for academic frin— principles of academic freedom, any professional integrity or loyalty—"

Brian does not attempt to interrupt, or make the persuasive speech he had thought of as Plan One; he realizes that Jenny was right, and besides there is not enough time. He begins to unbutton Bill's raincoat, Plan Two.

"—loyalty to your profession, any conscience or any rudimentary conscience, which quite frankly I doubt, and I say the same to you, because you are certainly quite well aware of the legal sanctions which can and should have been imposed at once, several hours ago, at the earliest possible moment, against these disgusting —" Abruptly Dibble ceases speaking. An expression of astonishment, then of panic comes over his face as he observes Brian removing first his jacket, then his sweater. "Wha! Why the hell you doing?" he brays, backing into the corner as Brian approaches.

"I'm going to get you out of here," Brian replies in a low, controlled voice, leaning toward Dibble. "Don't shout like that, just keep talking normally." He throws his jacket on a heap of girls' coats. "Can you climb down a rope?"

"What?"

"A rope," Brian repeats patiently, feeling behind him for the loose end. "I said, can you climb down a rope?"

Dibble turns, following Brian's gaze. "You want me to climb out that window?" he asks in a shrill half-whisper.

"That was the plan I suggested to Bill and Chief Beaver." Brian hauls a rough, heavy loop of knotted rope around his body. It is hard work, and slow—too slow for the time they have. "I told them I thought you'd be able to manage it." He drops the rope and tries to push down the whole coil at once.

"You told them? I could, I suppose," Dibble says, with some vanity—he is known to spend several hours a week in the college gym, jogging and at times lifting weights. "But it's unnecessary. Quite unnecessary. All that's needed is to alert the Safety Division, they're quite well equipped for emergencies, they have mace now, since the trouble last year— It would be a very simple matter— Tear gas too I believe. They should have been called in at once."

"Bill won't take responsibility for sending in the cops. He's waiting until Dean Kane gets back tonight," Brian explains, struggling impatiently with the rope. Though he sucks in his breath and shoves down with all his strength so that the coarse knots dig into his hands, he cannot budge it. "If you want to stay here with those girls until tonight, you can," he pants angrily.

"No." Dibble glances rapidly from window to door. "But in my opinion—"

"Then shut up, please, and take hold of this." Brian throws the free end of the rope across the desk. "We haven't that much time." Backing away, he begins to rotate, unwinding the rope. "You've got to pull . . . Harder . . . That's right."

He continues to turn: past the bookshelves, the littered desk, the window, the gaping files, the door; past Dibble, who pulls on the rope while continuing to expound his opinions, of which Brian catches isolated phrases each time he comes around:

". . . moral cowardice . . . utter stupidity . . . in my view . . ."

At last the rope is free. Brian halts, breathless; but the room still turns. He is dizzy, almost nauseous. He puts a hand to his head

*3 1 0*

and staggers toward Dibble's desk, now covered with coarse serpentine loops.

". . . feeble-minded administrators . . . unprecedented . . ."

"Just a sec." Brian blinks, swallows. "All right. Now we'll fasten this end to—" He pauses, looking around the spinning room. He had planned tying the rope to one leg of the desk, but Dibble's modernistic desk has no legs. "—to that pipe there," he improvises, pointing upward.

Unfortunately the ceiling in these old buildings is very high, while Brian is short. To reach the pipe he has to put a chair on the desk and climb up on it.

"Wait. Now, hand me the rope. No, damn it, the end."

". . . impudently reading my private correspondence . . . valuable manuscripts . . ." Dibble continues, automatically handing up the rope. Brian is not listening; he is still very dizzy, conscious of moving slowly, of time passing rapidly, of the door with its two long rectangular panels of opaque glass and the heavy shadows of the crowd waiting behind it in the hall— If they should open that door—

". . . utterly intolerable . . . legal action . . ."

Finally the rope is fixed, the knot secure; Brian tests it with his full weight as he climbs down. Four minutes left. Hastily, he clears the sill, knocking books and coats to the floor.

"Okay." He shoves up the heavy, dusty sash. Cold air enters the stuffy office, clearing his head. The sun shines brilliantly.

". . . the admissions office . . . responsible alumni . . ."

Brian hauls the rope toward the window and begins shoving it out, knot after heavy knot; he is feeling better.

". . . insulting . . . determination . . ."

There is a shout from below. Glancing down through the still-bare trees, Brian can see people moving, pointing—

"Come on," he says to Dibble. "You'd better go first."

"I—"

"Quick, damn it." He pushes a chair toward the window. "Before they catch on."

Reluctantly, Dibble clambers onto the window sill. He squats there, a large, long-faced, pink-complexioned man with a stunned, furious look in his eyes, clinging to the rope with one hand and the raised sash with the other.

"Uh, I don't exactly—"

"Hurry." There are more shouts now; laughter; an uneven cheer.

Dibble ducks under the sash and puts his other hand on the rope. His long, pink face appears on the outside of the glass, the mouth working. "You sure it'll hold?"

"I tested it," Brian says impatiently. Below on the quad the cheering grows; he can see figures running toward Burnham Hall across the muddy grass. "Go on. No, wait, damn it, you've got to turn around. Face me and get your feet— Okay. Watch out for that branch. Now."

Slowly, Dibble edges himself down over the broad stone sill. There are people at the windows of the adjoining building now, laughing and calling encouragement; people on the pedestal of the statue below. Some, with cameras, are already recording his faltering and protracted descent.

Now Brian climbs onto the window sill. Holding the rope, he crawls under the sash and stands on the ledge outside, waiting for Dibble to reach ground, for he is not sure the rope or the pipe will bear both their weight. His heart is beating fast; he is exhilarated.

He checks his watch: two minutes left. He has won; he has carried out his plan, and with time to spare.

Tremendous cheering and waving below now, as Dibble nears the ground. Hands stretch up to him; flashbulbs go off. Dibble's picture—and his!—will be in the local newspaper, perhaps even on television. Brian's exploit will become part of Corinth history. Smiling, breathing deeply, he takes a few fatal seconds to look over the broad bright quadrangle to the library tower, landmark and symbol of the university; then down at the crowd, in which he recognizes several faces, including those of Wendy and Bill

*3 1 2*

Guildenstern. Moving his arm from the elbow, he gives them a modest wave.

Suddenly, from behind, there is a howling, trampling noise; cries of "No! Stop!" Brian swings around, kneels down on the stone ledge, and starts to lower himself out over it, feeling for the knots with his feet—

But he is too late. Sara, scrambling over Dibble's desk to the window, catches him by one arm. He wrenches away, but at the same moment two larger girls grab him, the first by his shirt, the other, very painfully, by his hair. Since he is holding the rope, he has only one hand free to push his assailants off, while they each have two; and Sara is clawing at his free arm again.

"That's it. Hang on to the bastard," she hisses as still more protesters lay hold of Brian, and all of them together drag him across the sill, into a room full of screaming women and exploding flashbulbs.

"All right, all right!" Brian shouts, feeling for the floor with his feet and pulling his arms free. Someone slams down the window behind him.

"You let him get away! Whadda you do that for?" Pat screeches.

"You cheated us!"

Brian takes a deep breath, reminding himself that though outnumbered, he is superior in age, sex, status and political astuteness to the angry young women surrounding him.

"I can explain," he says loudly, deliberately. "If you'd all just calm down and listen to me—" He looks around, searching for a sympathetic face, a weak link in the circle; finding one: Jenny, whose expression is less angry than confused.

"Let me explain." He smiles at Jenny, whose huge eyes are blurred with tears. "I had to get Dibble out of here. He's a very ill man; something serious could have happened to him," he insists, putting his hand on Jenny's soft arm. "You see—"

"Yes?" Jenny turns toward Brian. Seizing his chance, he

pushes her aside and makes a break for the open door, the friendly—or at least neutral—male faces beyond in the hall. But his foot catches on a pile of coats, and he stumbles.

"He's not explaining anything, he's trying to escape!" squeals Linda Sliski. "Stop him, everybody!" And she takes her own advice, giving Brian a vicious shove sideways.

"No! Damn it, this is ridiculous," he explains. "You don't understand—" He is down on one knee now; he tries to rise, but several girls are in the way.

"Oh no you don't, you dirty fink." Sara grabs hold of him again. "Shut that door!" she barks.

"Hey—wait—really—" In a blaze of flashbulbs, shouting, and struggling, Brian is pushed heavily to the floor, knocking his head on the edge of a chair. Three of the protesters, braying, holding him down; and pretty Jenny, in a painful reversal of all his fantasies, sits on him. The door to Dibble's office is slammed; is locked.

A week later. The crisis is over; Corinth University is back to normal. Brian has in a sense recovered from his captivity: his bruises have healed; the lump on his head is subsiding. In another, more serious sense, he will never recover.

His opinion of women, for instance, has been permanently altered. Previously, generalizing from his mother and Erica—whom he now realizes to be exceptional—he had believed them to be essentially different from men: weaker and less rational, but also gentler, finer, more sensitive. The two hours he spent imprisoned in Dibble's office were a revelation. It was not only the recriminations and the tears (Jenny's) which he had to face, though they were bad enough. ("You know what it's like to be nagged and scolded by one woman for an hour?" he said to Leonard Zimmern on the telephone that evening. "All right, multiply that by two hours and fourteen women.") Far worse was the aggression, the coarseness, the brutality. The protesters refused to listen to his arguments or explanations, finally even to allow him to speak. ("If you don't shut your big mouth we'll gag you," Pat had threatened.) Also they

*314*

would not let him see Bill Guildenstern or anyone from the dean's office, even in their presence; they would not bring him anything to eat or drink; and when he announced a need to visit the washroom they suggested he piss in Dibble's wastebasket.

While Brian remained captive a bitter debate was taking place in the department office. Frightened by the latest turn of events, and the increasing convergence of sightseers and journalists on Burnham Hall, creating the impression of a public demonstration or riot, Bill was trying to negotiate a settlement with Dibble. But Dibble was not feeling conciliatory; indeed his demands had escalated. Instead of the "bumbling campus cops" he was now insisting that the university send in armed state troopers to clear his office and "teach those vicious juvenile delinquents a lesson." The suggestion that somebody might get hurt in the process seemed to delight him. After two hours of discussion Bill had got nowhere, though he had been joined in his effort by several representatives of the department and the administration, and finally by a long-distance call from Dean Kane, who spoke to Dibble from Austin, Texas, for twenty-five minutes without making any impression on him.

Outside Bill's window the large crowd was beginning to churn and shout. Several posters had appeared, the red paint not yet dry on some of them; struggles were starting between members of the Safety Division and some students who had brought a ladder, and others armed with water pistols. The mood of the mob was light-hearted, but it might turn nasty at any moment. Bill got back on the line to Dean Kane in Texas and secured his permission to concede to the protesters.

Two hours after he had entered Dibble's office, Brian was released. He had, and still has, the small satisfaction of having his strategy adopted; and the greater though more private satisfaction of knowing that his old enemy is about to abandon the field—for J. Donald Dibble, overruled and as he thinks betrayed by his chairman and dean, has tendered his resignation from the university.

*315*

But this gain is as nothing to the loss—to the realization that the fate Brian had amused himself by imagining for Dibble is to fall instead on him. It is due in part to a journalistic accident: the fact that one of the shots of Brian struggling with the protesters happened to come out well. In a week rather low on news, this striking photograph was seized upon by the editor of the Corinth *Courier* and reproduced across four columns on page one. It was almost a classic image of the women's-liberation threat, at once comic and symbolic: a small middle-aged man, his face expressing fear and outrage, being wrestled to the floor by long-haired young Amazons.

The following day the picture appeared in the *New York Times*, accompanied by a photograph of Dibble's escape and an account of the crisis. The story was picked up by a news service, and by the end of the week had been carried nationwide—though in most cases the photo of Dibble, which only showed a man climbing up or down a rope against a building, was printed much smaller or not at all. Several papers, apparently finding the facts too complex, omitted mention of Dibble entirely, giving their readers the impression that it was Brian Tate who had offended so many young women. And such is the power of the graphic image that even those who were able to read something like the true story laid down their papers thinking of Tate as a violent opponent of the new feminism—otherwise, why were all those girls attacking him?

Already the effects of all this are beginning to manifest. Brian has been claimed as an ally by Corinth antifeminists, several of whom have telephoned to congratulate him on his stand. Encouraging letters have begun to arrive from persons he has never met, both in Hopkins County and elsewhere. A few of these letters are brief and rational; but most are long and hysterical, expressive of fanatical misogyny. ("Jesus will Bless you for your Sufferings at the hands of those Filthy Bitches, those Foul Jades of Satan's Womb—for they are not True Wombmen but Barren

Whores . . ." predicted one such letter, typed on the stationery of an Oldsmobile agency in southern New Jersey.)

Not all Brian's fans are male; he has received many sympathetic letters from self-styled "old-fashioned" women, some of them members of an organization he had not known existed called Happy American Homemakers. Two of these hinted strongly that if Brian were ever to find himself in Cape Neddick, Maine, or Wichita, Kansas, they would be happy to make him at home.

All these letters Brian has been able to read with ironic detachment, if not with indifference. What he finds harder to take is what he calls his hate male—all from women. It ranges from the hurt queries of former favorite students and female relatives (including his mother and aunt) to ugly postcards and thick letters from angry feminists, abusing and cursing him—sometimes in language far stronger than that of the Oldsmobile salesman. These letters and cards come to the political science department, where the cards at least can be and probably are read by Helen Wells and her three assistants before they are placed in Brian's mailbox. Because of the story in *Time*, where Brian's name was irritatingly modified by the adjectives "small, square-jawed, recently separated," they often remark that it is no wonder his wife threw him out. Another frequent theme is the supposed insignificant size or absence of his sexual organs. Reading this mail, Brian often thinks that if he were not already convinced of the basic aggressiveness and coarseness of women, he would be so now.

Apart from this unpleasant correspondence, Brian has had to endure many inquisitive telephone calls and proposals for interviews ("My Woman Problem" was the title suggested to him by one free-lance journalist who had a "connection" and hoped to get the resulting article into *Penthouse*); also the mock jovial remarks of colleagues, the glances and whisperings of students, and the sniggering recognition of people in local stores and gas stations ("Say, aren't you the professor who . . .").

Other wars end eventually in victory, defeat or exhaustion, but

*3 1 7*

the war between men and women goes on forever. Now, through a journalistic accident, it is as if Brian has stepped in front of J. Donald Dibble on that perpetual battlefield, deflecting onto himself both the jeers of the public and the armed wrath of the American bitch-goddess in all her forms. Meanwhile Dibble, the real enemy, escapes. He has received many fewer letters, almost none of them abusive; soon he will be on some other campus, his part in the crisis forgotten.

But Brian must remain in Corinth, where recent events will pass into university history, and that garbled news story, that vulgarly comic photograph, will haunt him for the rest of his life. In a horrible way, he has got his wish; the spell spoken over his cradle has come true, and after trying for forty-seven years he has become a famous man.

# 16

Mid-April; the hard bright cold has broken, and it has been raining for nearly a week. The ditches and creeks and gorges are full of churning milk chocolate; the new grass is plastered flat against muddy lawns; clouds hang low to the ground. In the house on Jones Creek Road cold water streams down the windowpanes; water drips through the roof of the back porch, just as it did last autumn. Brian promised to fix the roof then, but he did not. He will probably never fix it now.

Erica cannot afford to have the porch roof repaired, or the electric frying pan; she cannot pay to get the fender of the station wagon straightened out where some clumsy and dishonest person backed into it in the university parking lot last month, and then drove off without leaving a note. She is barely able to meet expenses on what Brian gives her, although she is now working twenty hours a week at a very demanding job. She cannot afford anything nice any more: roast beef, or a new novel, or trips to New York, or tickets to the concert series; she hasn't bought a new dress in months.

And except for the children, who complain about how dull meals are, nobody notices. Nobody seems to think it strange that Erica doesn't have her car repaired or wear a new dress or go to concerts any more. She is no longer one of their company, a member of the local academic aristocracy, but a leftover housewife and ill-paid editorial assistant. Brian, however, has kept his position as a professor, and become in addition a man-about-town. Also, since a week ago Thursday, a national hero of reactionary antifeminism, with his photograph in every newspaper in America.

In a way it is unfair that Brian should have this reputation. He had gone beyond his obligation to the political science department in trying to rescue Dibble, who is a very disagreeable person and has never done anything for him. Besides, it is bad for Brian's or anyone's character to be punished for doing the right thing, while they are rewarded for, or at least get away with, their misdeeds.

But in another sense it is only poetic justice that her husband should take Dibble's place as a feminist scapegoat; for Brian has also injured women, not in the abstract, but specifically and personally. It is only right that they should take revenge on him; and that everyone should see what he is really like under his mask of rational virtue.

And in fact, judging by the remarks made to Erica by her acquaintances, everyone does see—with the single exception of Wendy Gahaghan. Although her former roommate and best friend, Linda Sliski, received an ugly bruise on her leg while struggling with Brian, Wendy remains loyal to him. Of course Wendy's capacity for dumb devotion was apparent from the beginning. There was a time when Erica thought Brian deserved such devotion; when she felt guilty for not providing it herself, and eager to pass on the task to someone else. She still feels guilty; but now because she had encouraged Wendy to believe in a false god, and thus given Brian what he had always wanted and no longer deserved—what in the long run can only be bad for him, and worse for her.

With a sigh, Erica drags the pail out from under the kitchen sink and fills it with hot water. It is her day off, but since she cannot afford help, she usually spends most of it cleaning house. She has to hurry today, because she is meeting Sandy at noon. She adds detergent and scouring powder to the pail, wondering why she is doing this, when nobody will care if the floor is dirty. The children never notice; and Sandy isn't coming here, and if he were wouldn't notice either. This is discouraging, though in a way nicer than Brian—who always noticed, and sometimes complained.

Sandy is nicer that Brian in many ways, Erica thinks, lifting the pail out of the sink. He is kinder and more considerate, with a better sense of humor, and he knows much more about gardening and carpentry and art and music and old children's books. Though he has refused to attend any more parties, he will go with her to places and events Brian used to scorn: an art opening or a tour of the new fire station or a house sale or a bird walk. This is important, now that Jeffrey and Matilda are rudely unwilling to accompany her, and Danielle more and more often busy with her boring Dr. Kotelchuk.

Sandy is an agreeable companion on all such excursions. His work at the Krishna Bookshop seldom seems to get in the way—though he has warned her that it may do so this summer, when he and his students begin working on their "meditation center." They have already bought land about twenty miles from Corinth in a barren wooded area, and are planning to clear it and build a cabin with their own hands, including Sandy's hands. For a moment Erica gazes out the kitchen window across the fields to the west, in the direction of the proposed meditation center, frowning. Then she opens the cellar door to unhook the sponge mop from the wall within, and shuts the door quickly so as not to be reminded that the cellar also needs to be cleaned.

Putting the mop into the pail to soak, she sets the kitchen chairs on top of the kitchen table, thinking that in spite of his odd beliefs Sandy is easier to talk to than Brian. He does not, as she had feared he might, try to convert her to his faith; he never lectures her or tells her what to read or what to think. He listens much better than Brian; also he has a wonderful memory and can tell amusing stories about his childhood and his adventures in California and the Far East.

Erica sloshes the mop up and down in the sudsy water and begins mopping the floor in shiny overlapping strips. For the hundredth time in six years she thinks what an expensive mistake it was to buy these red vinyl tiles, which looked so good in the store but faded to a dirty pink within the first year and showed every spill and speck of dust from the start. Then, for the hundredth time in six weeks, she thinks of something Danielle said about Sandy: that he is not only nice but "too nice to be a man."

Recently Erica has had proof of the truth of this statement, though perhaps not yet conclusive proof. But she might have suspected sooner—even on that first snowy evening in the bookshop, when Sandy did not press his advantage as most men would have. Or she might have guessed in the following weeks, when he seemed quite content with gently enthusiastic kisses and hugs of the sort an affectionate child might lavish on a new pet.

Erica noticed this hesitancy, this childish diffidence—but it pleased rather than troubled her. She thought that Sandy was too much in awe of her to hope or expect that she would sleep with him; that he wanted to spare them both the embarrassment and pain of a refusal. No doubt he had suffered refusals before; had, perhaps often, been laughed at and rejected. Certainly something like that must have happened to make him hesitate, even turn away from life. But knowing what men are like, Erica knew that instinctively Sandy must want more. It was her duty to give it to him—to convince him that her friendship and charity were real. Nor would hers be a shallow, soup-kitchen kind of charity: she did not mean merely to fill a temporary need, but to deconvert Sandy, to bring him back into the world in every way and show him that it was real and good, so that he would give up his pathetic empty asceticism.

With all this in mind, Erica chose her time and place carefully. She had given Sandy his unexpected birthday present impulsively and under poor conditions. Now that he was, in both senses, going to receive the present of his life, it should be under the best possible circumstances and in the most attractive gift wrapping. It must happen in her own house, for motels were sordid and the Krishna Bookshop grungy and cold—and when there was no chance of interruption. Therefore she waited until the children had gone to Connecticut with Brian for spring vacation, and the place was empty.

Erica, like the rest of the nonacademic help at Corinth, had no spring vacation to speak of, but she did have Good Friday off. She made a light but elegant lunch (avocado salad, shrimp bisque, white wine) and cleansed the relevant parts of the house. She changed the bed in the spare room, putting on fresh sheets with a pattern of wild roses, and drew down the blinds three fourths of the way, so that parallelograms of sun fell on the carpet and a warm, watery light suffused the rest. She did not dress up—it seemed too obvious, and she had nothing really nice to wear anyhow—but she took a shower and put on a clean garnet-colored sweater and black wool slacks, and under them her best lavender-lace bra and panties. Then she got out her diaphragm, which had become quite stiff and dry with neglect under its coating of talcum powder, but seemed on inspection to be intact—at least it didn't leak under the faucet—and put it in with an extra large helping of jelly, bought with some awkwardness the day before at a drugstore where she was unknown.

Everything was ready. And for the first hour, everything went as she had planned. She kissed Sandy even more affectionately than usual when he arrived, though his face was unpleasantly blotched with cold from the time he had spent trying to hitch a ride out to Jones Creek Road. She served lunch, turning the talk lightly toward love, teasing, reminiscing. There was a significant moment when she made some generalization about men, and Sandy, smiling, protested, "You can't say that."

"I can too."

"Speaking from wide experience, I suppose."

"I've never had any experience, except Brian," Erica replied.

"But a woman just knows." And she laughed gaily, glad to have told Sandy what would make the gift he was about to receive more valuable.

It was not difficult after that to make clear what she intended; to move from the kitchen to the sitting room and then upstairs to the study. In the warm confusion of that move, and the chill of what followed, she forgets details. One exchange remains, when after gently helping her out of her clothes, Sandy pulled off his own shabby garments. In spite of their last, close embrace, she was startled, almost frightened by what she saw: the long white narrow torso; the burning bush of wiry hair—not faded with time like that on Sandy's head, but still bright vermilion—and what rose from it.

"You," she half whispered, extending her hand, but not to touch. "That . . . I mean, isn't it awfully large?"

"Just average, as far as I know."

There was a silence while both thought the same thing, about Brian.

But Erica's confusion and distress at that moment were nothing to what came after. First misunderstanding and misguided reassurance—for, thinking that Sandy hesitated out of considera-tion, she kept murmuring that it was all right—until at length she moved her hand and discovered that it was not all right. She can hear her own squeak of exclamation now: "Oh! What's the matter?" and Sandy's reply, muffled and bleak: "I don't know."

Next the clumsy straining, the bleats of distress and failure. Renewed effort; renewed failure. Then Sandy pulling away, sitting back between her legs, his face reddened, saying, "It's no good."

And finally she recalls the excuses and explanations, overlap-ping and contradicting each other. "I didn't expect . . ." "You know, I was afraid of this." "We waited too long." Erica, out of hope and faith and charity, accepted these excuses; offered some of her own. She soothed and comforted Sandy, assuring him that she understood, that she wasn't angry, or upset, that it would be better next time.

*3 2 4*

But it was not better next time. It was worse. At the mere sight of Erica naked at night in a university office (her children were back from vacation, but she had a key to the building where she worked), Sandy sagged and shrank in every part. He sat down on the extreme edge of the black plastic couch belonging to the editor of *Current Organic Chemistry*, next to Erica's cold feet; his arms hung limp between his legs, and he spoke in a withered version of his normal voice. "Venus square Neptune again. I suppose it's some kind of sign."

This time Erica did not reassure and comfort him. Instead, all the misery and self-doubt that had been churning below the surface of her mind for the past four days boiled up and over. Her laughter was sour, almost hysterical, as she told Sandy that he must have made a mistake. Obviously he did not want her, or love her.

"No," he whispered from the end of the couch. "I love you too much."

Erica did not believe him. She thought that Sandy had, as he had said before, waited too long. The Erica he loved was a beautiful young girl; at the sight of her creased face and middle-aged body in close-up, desire had left him. She sat up, reached for her clothes, and began to dress wearily, thinking that Sandy might have known, or at least guessed, that this would happen again—that he might have known the first time. She began to feel aggrieved at him for having allowed these two embarrassing and sordid scenes to occur, scenes in which she had offered herself and exposed herself and been rejected. It was too late now. This ugly, humiliating, ludicrous thing had happened, staining this day and their friendship like the big splotch of strained-lamb-with-vegetables Jeffrey had once spat onto one of the illustrations for *Sanford's Busy Day*, so that she had to draw the whole page over.

But she could not draw this over; it would be in her life forever. And what made it worse was that she had brought it on herself, by trying to make love to somebody so ugly and peculiar and hopeless. A sort of fury came over her as she looked at Sandy, who was still sitting at the far end of the couch, his knobby white back bent as he pulled on his socks. She wanted to scream, to hit him, to beat his bald head and stooped shoulders with her fists. She was shocked by this impulse, however, and at once suppressed it, reminding herself that Sandy was not only her old friend, but a pathetic, unhappy person who deserved pity. All the same, he might have known. At least the second time—

"I should have known," Sandy said suddenly, echoing Erica's thoughts as he had a way of doing—in happier moments she had considered it a sign of their psychic sympathy. "I figured out a long while ago, anything I really wanted I couldn't have. It's my destiny."

"That's stupid," Erica exclaimed. A new idea had come to her; she paused with one bare leg up, dangling mauve tights. "You know what it is, you're doing this to yourself. It's a self-fulfilling prophecy. It's not your destiny or anybody's destiny to fail. Everyone's entitled to some success, some happiness."

"No." Sandy, who had ceased dressing while she spoke, let out a long sigh and began dragging down his gray turtleneck sweater. "Not everyone. Not by a long shot. What you don't realize yet, Erica, is that the devil is in charge of this world.

"It's obvious, once you look at it," he continued, smiling briefly and sourly. "Suppose you were the devil, and you wanted to make mankind as miserable as possible. At first you might think of afflicting them all with everything you could lay on: war and unemployment and heroin addiction and cancer and political torture and starvation and blindness and deformity and radiation poisoning. Have everyone in the world suffer, all the time.

"But that's too easy. If the human condition is miserable everywhere, mankind will expect that, and be resigned to it. What you'd really want to do is make almost everyone sick and ugly and frightened and hungry. Then you'd have a few who didn't suffer at all—whom everything always went right for—who were young, rich, beautiful, healthy and happy. And you'd scatter them around the world to discourage the others; to remind them every day, every hour, of what they were missing." Sandy's voice was harsh. "That's what people like you and Brian are for."

"But things don't go right for us." Erica laughed uneasily, telling herself that Sandy was joking. "Not lately, anyhow."

"No. Your turn is over. You're being sent to join the majority." He did not laugh.

"You don't really believe all that."

"I don't know." He spoke more slowly now, in a fainter voice. "I believe it sometimes."

"I thought you believed in God, that God created the world, not the devil."

"I didn't say he created it. The devil can't create anything. You only have to go out into the country and look around to know who made it—look at the fields, the sky, the birds. But of course that was quite a while ago. You can tell by what's happening to the world that God doesn't care about it any more."

"And you think He doesn't care about us any more either, whether we're happy or not."

"Or that it's irrelevant to Him. A man I met at the monastery over in Elmira once said to me, 'God isn't interested in whether we're happy, only in whether we're good.' "

"And do you agree with that?"

"I don't know." Sandy shrugged and bent down to tie his boots. "Sometimes I think wanting to be good is just another form of vanity."

Of that whole sad scene, it is this last exchange which continues to press on Erica's mind; everything else she can dismiss as Sandy's fantasy, Sandy's superstitious self-doubt and self-induced failure.

She can sympathize with the fantasy, though, for she too—especially when reading the newspaper—has seen the world as a place of misery; she has often thought that if God existed, He would be the devil. But fortunately Erica has not believed in God for years. Her scorn of all religious faith is profound and long-standing. It dates from the age of ten, when her mother, in an uncharacteristic impulse of neighborly gregariousness and social piety after the departure of Erica's father, decided that it would be nice if her daughters attended Sunday school at the local Presbyterian church.

Erica was quite willing to go. Though raised almost as a heathen, she had observed the advantages of religious belief in her paternal grandmother. For Gran, life was orderly, serious and significant. Though she lived alone in a three-room apartment in Worcester, Massachusetts, she never complained of being bored like her daughter-in-law. Every day for her was important, presenting a constant series of problems in moral arithmetic. Every detail of behavior, down to setting a mousetrap or taking another slice of cake, was good or bad; every night there were complicated moral sums to add and subtract—even to multiply—in private dramatic consultation with God. Moreover, she explained, God does not make distinctions between persons; He was just as interested in the state of ten-year-old Erica's conscience as in Gran's own.

So they entered Sunday school. Little Marian went into the kindergarten, where she learned to sing simple hymns and make Easter decorations from pipe cleaners and lavender and yellow construction paper. But Erica was placed in the class of a fat elderly lady called Mrs. Winch, who wore a lace-bordered handkerchief pinned to her chest, with a gold watch dangling from it upside down so that only she knew what time it was. Mrs. Winch believed in old-fashioned discipline; she informed her class that they must always be clean and polite and good so that God would love them, and so that if they should die suddenly, He would wish to take them up to heaven to be with Him forever and ever Amen. If they were dirty and rude and disobedient—well, Mrs. Winch was not old-fashioned enough to go into what would happen then; but she hinted, and the other children filled Erica in.

Erica was not convinced by this doctrine, however, but morally shocked. She had been brought up to do the right thing for its own sake. Her father, who at that very moment was fighting for Freedom in a Canadian Army training camp, had taught her that she would be rewarded simply by a sense of self-respect, by the knowledge that she had done right and was a superior person. She was fastidiously revolted by the idea of a virtue which depended on bribes and threats—of a God whose opinion of people was so low that He only expected them to behave decently under the threat of being burned alive for ever. It was worse than the Christmas business, where little girls and boys were told that they'd better not pout and better not cry, because Santa Claus was coming. It was like her Aunt Ida saying "Give me a kiss, and I'll give you a candy"—what Gran referred to scornfully as "cupboard love."

Mrs. Winch's cosmology therefore struck Erica as greedy, cowardly, cruel and false. If God was really operating on that system, He was somebody Erica didn't want to know. She went home and told her mother that Mrs. Winch smelled of laundry soap and she didn't want to go to Sunday school any more. And Lena, whose enthusiasm for the social opportunities of the Presbyterian church was waning, acquiesced.

But Sandy's idea of a non–Santa Claus God who had no toys in his bag, but was watching Erica all the time to see whether she was still doing the right thing without thought of reward—that bothered her. Because if she were God, that is probably how she would have behaved.

And if there were this God, He might not like what she is about to do today. It is wrong by conventional standards, and also against the law. But that isn't what really troubles Erica, though she would dislike it to become known to most of her acquaintances or the police. What she is concerned about is the private purity of her motives. Has she agreed to go on this trip with Sandy for the sake of art and love—that is, to enlarge her creative vision and prove that she really cares about him and has forgiven his recent ineptness? Or is she just trying to escape from reality for a few hours?

But it is too late to back out now. Dumping the last pail of rinse water into the sink, she leaves the kitchen and goes upstairs to remove her damp jeans and sweater, and change into—what does one wear on a drug trip?

"I don't feel anything," Erica complains. She is sitting upright on the day bed in the room of one of Sandy's students who is away for the week. Half an hour ago she swallowed a white powder mixed with ginger ale; and ever since she has been watching all the furniture and the rain-streaked dormer window and the sloppily whitewashed walls hung with strips of batik and a poster of a many-armed dancing god, to see if they will begin to wriggle or change colors.

"It's pretty early yet. And we didn't take all that much," Zed replies for the third time.

"I think your friend cheated you. Nothing's going to happen, unless some policeman comes to arrest us for taking this stuff."

"They can't arrest you for having taken drugs; only for possession. It's the reverse of the laws on alcohol. We could walk into the police station stoned out of our minds and they couldn't touch us."

"I don't even feel drunk. A little sleepy, maybe. But everything looks just the same. I wanted the world to be transformed."

"Transformed?" Zed raises his pale eyebrows.

"Yes, so I could put it into my drawings, make them more interesting. Different, because I'm bored by them really. Or maybe I could have a vision, a religious experience."

"A religious experience," he repeats slowly, separating the words.

"I've heard that people have them. Of course I'm not religious, but you know how it is when your life goes wrong: there's a feeling you're probably being punished. But for what? That's what I'd like to find out."

"You mean God should appear to you now, in a long white bathrobe and a Canadian accent, and say 'Bad, naughty Erica.' "

*330*

Zed grins. "That's not religion. If you do have a vision, it won't be like that."

"What *will* it be like, then?" Erica asks, laughing rather sharply. "Tell me, since you're so far advanced on the Path."

"I'm not very advanced."

"Oh, come on." She is as annoyed by Sandy's perpetual, almost automatic self-denigration as she was by his joke about her father.

"It's true. I'm more like Brian and the rest of his friends up on the hill than you think. Those who can't, teach."

"You do all that astrology."

"Yes. It's a nice compromise for types like me who haven't been able to hack it spiritually."

Erica looks at Zed, unsure if he is joking or asking for sympathy. "But you know much more than astrology. The bookshop— Your lectures—"

"That depends what you mean by knowledge." Zed takes a heavy breath. "Essentially I haven't got to first base. I've tried, of course. I've read a lot of books, done a lot of exercises."

"But it takes time, you said that yourself. Years sometimes." She covers a yawn.

"I've been at it for years."

Erica registers the tremor in his voice; she sits forward and tries to attend. "Since you were in Japan."

"Longer than that. I began reading and studying before I went to California. By 1964 I thought I was really getting somewhere, only I needed more time to concentrate. So I quit my job, sold my car, gave away most of my possessions, and moved into one room in West Hollywood." Zed grins ironically. "I found out what most students find out: that it's not so easy to detach yourself from the material. You give up money and success—wanting to own a convertible and a good stereo system, and make tenure and win the American Philosophical Association award. Great. You feel very proud of yourself. Then you find you're consumed with desire for

*331*

something really petty, like a hot dog or a hot bath. You try to meditate, but you're pulled back down to earth by bodily needs—because you have hay fever, or your legs ache in the lotus position."

"Mm." Erica leans back against the batik pillows of the day bed, sleepier than ever.

"But I got past all that—or at least used to it—in Japan," Zed continues. "I worked hard all year there, and when I got back to America I wanted to take the next step. I wanted enlightenment; I felt entitled to it, even—I had a fairly good opinion of myself then. I decided I was going to go somewhere and meditate seriously: try to go into the Silence, to unite with the All—or however you want to put it.

"So first I went home to see my family, and then I hitched to Cambridge and shut myself up in an apartment some friends had lent me. It was a propitious time—a weekend in August; the phone was turned off, and everybody I knew was out of town.

"So I locked the door and sat down on the carpet and began meditating. I sat there for about two hours, first going through various exercises and then just waiting. Everything was really quiet. I'd lost consciousness of the street outside, of the room, my body; I was concentrating on a smooth blank field, a field of whiteness, expanding infinitely in time and space.

"Then something loud and violent crossed this field, very close to me. I opened my eyes without meaning to and saw it was a big housefly. It buzzed around the room four or five times while I tried to pay no attention to it, and then it flew straight for the window behind me.

"I was very glad of that, because I thought it would get out. But it was too stupid. If it had climbed up a few inches it would have been free; but instead it stayed between the glass and the screen, buzzing. I knew I had to forget about it. I thought of all I had read about enlightenment, all I had learned. I told myself that the fly represented everything I had to get clear of—that its pain and stupid confusion were unreal, part of the world of false appearances. I told myself it was a demon sent to test me. I regulated my breathing and began counting backward from three hundred, trying to turn all external sensory awareness off, to see nothing and hear nothing; I concentrated on whiteness, smoothness, extension, infinity . . . And finally—I don't know how soon, maybe it was only ten minutes, maybe half an hour—something began to happen. There was a kind of focusing, a closing in—

"But then I heard my fly again. It was still there, buzzing and bumping against the glass, and against the screen. Only a tiny sound now, but I felt it here in my stomach: thud, thud. Ow, ow, ow. I was licked. I had to unfold my legs and get up and let the fly out. I raised the screen, and it flew away unevenly into the sun, dizzy with fatigue and surprise and relief, and I said to myself, 'There go your spiritual ambitions, Sandy.'" He smiles wanly. "And I was right."

"Didn't you try again after the fly was gone?"

"Oh sure; I tried. For the next forty-eight hours, day and night. And for months afterward. But it wasn't any good. I couldn't get within five miles of where I was that afternoon."

"But you still meditate," Erica says, recalling past conversations.

"Yes." Zed has turned his head away and is speaking to a spot on the green tweed rug. "Only it doesn't work. I can detach myself from the world all right, but I can't get to God. I'm stuck in the middle. I'm like that fly, only there's nobody to open the screen."

"But Sandy, I don't see—" Erica frowns. "Why shouldn't you have let the fly out?" Zed does not answer. "It was kind of you, if it was suffering." She looks at the window, rises, then sits down again. "Oh. That's funny. I thought there was a fly here too, behind the glass. But it's only part of the tree outside."

"You're starting to get high."

"I don't feel high. The room looks just the same."

"That's because you haven't noticed. See that yellow ashtray there, that's like a flower?"

"I— Well, yes, sort of." Erica gazes at a shallow clay bowl

with round notches in the rim for cigarette butts, which at the same time, without ceasing for a moment to be a small ashtray, is a large golden flower. "You're right. That's nice: it's a primrose, I think. Or maybe a marigold, with those square petals." She puts out her hand and touches one petal of the ashtray; it feels warm and soft, cold and hard, simultaneously—or rather in rapid alternation.

"And look at Krishna dancing." Zed gestures at the poster above the day bed.

"Where? Yes, I see— No. He's not dancing; but he's waving his arms at us. The blue ones. Only they're not moving. Well, of course they're not moving; it's just a picture." With a sense of effort, Erica sits up. "I don't see it now . . . Yes, there, again, for a moment. Now it's stopped. What's happening? Why does he do that?"

"It's the gift of the drug. The world is what you say it is." Zed's voice seems to come from nearer than the other end of the day bed.

"I do feel sort of peculiar. When I move my head, the room goes all sideways. Do you feel strange, Sandy? Can you see the poster moving and things like that?"

"Not now. I might see them if I wanted to."

"Why not? Aren't you affected at all?"

"Yes. But I've had more experience with this kind of thing than you. And I'm not such a visual type." He shuts his eyes, opens them. "I'm more likely to hear things. I don't now; but last time I got high here, toward dawn, Ralph and I both heard the pigeons on the roof outside speaking in tongues." He laughs. "They were crying out to the Lord in artificial foreign languages, like a revival meeting."

"I don't hear anything outside at all," Erica says, glancing toward the window. "It's all muffled and far away . . . But the design of the curtains is weaving," she adds. "The plaid— Those green stripes like loose basketwork. They're weaving and woving over and under each other, very quietly and neatly. Do you see that? It's really lovely." She does not wait for or hear Zed's answer;

*344*

she is watching the rug now: all its different tweed greens. Moss, and grass, and lichen.

"It's growing together in jagsaw puzzles," she exclaims, laughing. She doesn't actually see "grass" or "puzzles"—only an ordinary rug; but one which is silently alive, motionlessly moving, constantly and gloriously renewing itself in existence. The world is alive, she thinks. I must remember that. Everything is alive, in every detail. And it comes to her that she is having the experience she wanted to give Sandy, of the goodness and truth of the real world.

"You must look at the rug, Sandy!" she cries. "It's so beautiful, because it's really there, and it's a rug."

"That's nice." But he doesn't even glance at the rug; he looks at her, with his usual abstract smile.

"You're not looking. But it's true. Everything in the room is real, and in the right place, and that's why it's beautiful. Everything in this room is beautiful."

"Everything?" Zed says finally, making a gesture that includes himself. Erica does not see it, but she hears him and unfixes her gaze from the contemplation of a very nice green lampshade which has perched on the lamp to her left and is holding the bulb neatly and politely with its circular wire claw.

"Yes." She looks around. "No. That's ugly, there." She points at the jelly glass from which they had drunk their ginger ale. "It's all lumpy and snotty, with loud smudges. Ugh. It's horrid. I'm going to hide it." She leans forward and takes the glass fastidiously by its extreme rim.

"Wait—watch out," he cautions.

The floor rises with Erica as she rises, and tilts slightly toward her; the walls flutter and circle. "Oh! It's okay. I just want to get rid of. This thing. Put it where it can't see us— Golly, the whole room's dizzy."

Slowly, holding the glass at arm's length (it grows uglier every second), Erica negotiates her way across the jigsaw carpet, which is

*335*

becoming semiliquid, and around a stuffed chair (it supports her in a kindly bearlike way). "Thank you. There." Reaching the bathroom, she sets the nasty object down, turns. A face is looking at her through a peeling yellow window frame only a foot away: an old woman's face, blank, white, creased— Recognizing it, she groans. She tries to turn her head away. Cannot. Groans louder.

"Erica?" Zed stands, with difficulty. "Are you all right in there?" He lurches across the room, catches her arm. "Come back and sit down. Christ, the floor's full of waves . . . Here. You all right?"

"Yes. No." She laughs shudderingly.

"Lean on me. Breathe slowly . . . That's better. You shouldn't get up so fast. Not good when you're high."

Erica breathes several times more. She looks around the room, but it has ceased to be alive or nice. Instead everything is flat and dead: the curtains, the pictures, the rug, the windows seem to have been badly painted onto the walls and floor, like cheap scenery.

"What I saw in the bathroom," she says abruptly. "In the mirror picture. It's not just the drug, I keep seeing her anyhow-where, this awful old woman. Only it's me. I'm turning into her. I'm forty already, isn't that horrible?"

"No," Zed says after a considerable pause. "You've lived forty years. If you didn't age, that would be horrible. Like those old film stars you see in L.A., made into plastic mummies of themselves."

"Yes— But—" Erica hears her voice; a thin disembodied wailing sound. "I'm not used to it," this voice continues. "You know I used to be very pretty, and wherever I went I looked well. A man came up to me when I was sitting in front of Emerson Hall and he said I added to the beauty of the scene, the yellow leaves. Like the sun, and the yellow leaves. And wherever. But now I don't any more. Pretty soon I'll be like that disgusting jelly glass, spoiling the landscape everywhere. I hate getting old and ugly, I hate it. I hate it!" The wailing turns to sobbing. "Somebody's crying," she remarks. "I think it's me."

*336*

"Right. All right." Zed is holding her, her face against his shirt, stroking her. The crying fades.

"That's weird," Erica says, swallowing a last sob. "I was crying, but not exactly."

"It's all right."

"Thank you." She hugs him and sits back. "But do you feel that too? Do you hate getting ugly and old?"

A pause. "It's different for me," Zed says finally. "I've always been ugly. Age doesn't change that much. What I don't like is the way time runs out. Knowing there are things I won't do in this life, places I won't see. People dying."

Erica looks around the room, which is no longer flat like scenery but insubstantially three-dimensional, full of colored shadows. "Dying, I'm not afraid of that," she says finally. "It's behaving badly at the end. Wearing out weak and whiny and disgusting. I'd like to escape in a car accident, so I won't have to go through the bad last part of my life. Sometimes I drive fast to help it along, especially when the icy roads last winter. But I might just be crippled for life, so I drive slower.

"I thought it would be nice for it to happen right after Christmas when I was going to fly to Boston," she adds, watching the shadows slide. "The plane could fall down, so quick and easy. But it snowed too hard, all the flights were folded." She laughs. "I was very disappointed. Not so much now . . . Did you ever feel that?"

A long silence. Erica watches the shadows ducking and sliding.

"Did you ask me something?" Zed says finally.

"It doesn't matter."

"No. I want to answer you. I was thinking about it, but then I forgot . . . What was the question?"

This time it is Erica who does not reply. She is absorbed in watching the shadows advance and retreat as the ceiling fixture sways on invisible streams of air. In the circle of brighter light

*337*

beneath the bird lampshade, skeins of dust swirl like pale silk and then slowly settle through air which is a thin lukewarm blue substance, with levels and currents. Behind it the figure of Zed seems to wobble and fluctuate.

"All the air is full of water," she says. "You're very far away . . . Why are you so far away in the water?"

"It's because I'm a double Pisces." Zed smiles. From a great distance he puts out his long arms to Erica, and around her, pulling her toward him. Oceans of air flow out from between them. "Is that better?"

"Yes." She leans against him, sighing. "I guess I'm really high now . . . How long will this last?"

"Not long. It's a short trip. The housewife's special. We should start coming down fairly soon."

"I like it. I feel all floaty, as if I were swimming. Diving, do you?"

Zed replies, or does not reply; she is not sure. She is watching the walls of the swimming pool standing up around them tall and white like three angels spreading out their wide white wings to one another. The fourth is sloping in to meet them, alighting; his face, the dormer window, is streaked with tears of rain from all the sorrow he has seen outside. Yet she isn't hallucinating in the conventional sense. She sees only walls; but she knows them to be angels. "The walls are white angels," she informs Zed.

"That's nice. What are they doing?"

"I don't know. I think they're protecting us, as long as we stay here." She relaxes against him, laughing gently. "I like it here. Let's stay forever."

"All right." Zed is absently stroking her left forearm with one finger. The fine hairs quiver like the antennae of a hundred moths, sending out tiny sparks.

"That's strange," she says. "It's pins and needles, but warmer. How does it feel to you?"

"Nice."

Erica raises her free hand and strokes his wrist, where the

338

freckles are shaded by red moth hairs. More sparks appear, explode outward; the room is no longer a swimming pool but an electrical field with concentric circles of tiny, bright plus signs pulsing out from the points where she and Sandy are in direct contact. "We're manufacturing electricity," she tells him. "The minus signs are in the corners of the room."

"Is that so." Zed looks sideways down. The pupils of his pale eyes are large and black. After a long time, or quite soon, he kisses her lightly. The effect is as of a blurred electric shock.

"It's very hot in here," she murmurs presently. "All this moth electricity makes it very very too hot. Should we open the window?"

"No." Zed's mouth is beside her ear; his voice comes from inside her head. "Let's take off our clothes."

"All right," Erica agrees, while a part of her mind which seems to be shut up in a small cage remarks in a weak whispering voice that this is something she had decided not to do.

"Careful, though. Don't sit up or move too fast, or you'll get dizzy. Pretty high now."

"I *am* dizzy." Erica begins to pull her sweater over her head in slow motion. "It's all right though . . . Only it takes so long, is all," she adds after several minutes inside the sweater, a hot mauve cave hung with moss. "I don't like it in here. Too much moss." She waves her arms.

"Wait. Let me help . . . There. Is that better?"

"Much better." She stretches. "That was a brilliant idea. You're really brilliant, do you know that, Sandy? You are, actually. That's funny." Naked, pleasantly dizzy, Erica flops back onto the cushions, laughing with delight at Zed, whose arms and torso shine with a watery Day-Glo light. "I never saw anything like that. How come I'm not brilliant like you?" she adds, holding up one leg. "My legs are extra long, but they're not shining."

"Sure they are." Zed drops his pants into the green tweed sea, where they float gently, and moves toward her. "You're shining all over, like the morning star."

She laughs, sways forward. Experimentally, she rubs his phosphorescent cheek with pursed lips. The effect is— Magnetic? Radioactive? "Or it's something to do with time," she adds. "Do you think it's time?"

"Yes," Zed says; or perhaps "No."

Erica looks down. Something amazing is happening: an exotic, pale, silky thing is growing, rising, reddening—

"What's that? Is that you?" She laughs. "It's like a big strawberry cone. Golly, fantastic." She bends over to lick the cone, which tastes faintly of strawberry ice cream. "It's good, you should have some," she says presently.

"No thanks. But help yourself."

"I never did this before," she adds a little later. "Something frowned me not to but she's got very small now in the cage and her hat is stupid so I don't hear her . . . Anyhow"—she raises her head again—"Brian is black raspberry, and I don't like black raspberry. It tastes too brownish purple." She begins giggling softly and falls back away on the day bed; she shuts her eyes again and watches the lights flowing behind her eyelids, mixed with colored ice cream. Zed lies down too, above her, around her—or is he inside her?

It doesn't matter. Because the lights—the colors—the strawberry electric current— She lets herself slide away, into it— Yes— Yes—

But then, from far off in her head, in a different, sharper voltage, something buzzes. An unpleasant flat doorbell vibration, dirty red. Danger—anxiety.

"Hey, wait! I didn't— We can't—" she cries. In very slow motion, slipping back into the current again and again, she begins to struggle, to kick and paddle. Finally, gasping, shuddering, she sits up, disengaged from Zed.

"No!" he calls out. There is an explosion, a fountain effect in the air, wet, silver. Erica watches it with blurred fear and regret from a safe distance. "Oh— Erica— God—" He falls back, shaking and sobbing.

*340*

Dizzy still, she bends over him. "I'm sorry," she says, patting his shoulder, averting her eyes from his face, which is squeezed into a knot: red, awful. "I was afraid— I didn't expect you to—"

"No," Zed replies finally, in a voice which seems to come from several miles off. He does not move.

"I'm sorry." Avoiding the place on the day bed where the fountain overflowed, and the fountain itself, she puts her arms around him; at last even looks him in the face. It is unknotted, human again, though the pale eyes are still damp, red-edged.

"Are you all right?" she asks anxiously, several times.

"All right," he answers eventually. "How are you?"

"All right, I guess. I'm not so high any more. The rug is slower."

"Yes."

Erica drops her arms. Silence.

"I see it now," he says finally.

Erica sits back, following his stare into the far corner of the room, noting that the sliding shadows are quieter now, their colors fading. "What do you see?"

"It was a kind of voice, actually. Out of the wastebasket." He smiles. "But it was right. It told me not to start the meditation center."

"Oh? Your students will be disappointed."

"They can go ahead on their own. If they want to. It'll be better for them that way, in the end."

"And much easier on you." She smiles. "And they can still come to you and get advice."

He shakes his head. "No. I've got to give up the bookshop, too."

"Give it up? Really? Why?"

"It's no good. It was all right at first; but now there's too many camp followers—kids who don't want to study seriously, just hang around and drink tea and gossip about each other's charts, and have me play the Great Guru . . . They're not all like that. But those that aren't, the serious ones, I've already taught them what I know. If I go on, I'll start telling them lies." He sighs, reaches over, and pulls his clothes toward him.

"It was the same in California," he continues. "For a while everything was fine; then people started taking me too seriously. Some of them wanted to put my lectures onto tape. I let them persuade me, and pretty soon I was involved with recording studios and sound experts and publicity hacks, really bad karma. And then this TV star, Mona Moon, tried to give me a house in Laurel Canyon. Her idea was I would live up there and do astrology and send out spiritual vibrations, and she and her friends would come and absorb them.

"I tried to tell her I was a spiritual fraud, but she thought that was just holy humility. We had this stupid scene where she flung herself on the floor and tried to kiss my sneakers." Zed laughs tiredly. "So I cut out. I decided then it was my own fault for picking a town like L.A. But it's the same everywhere. Eventually, every place goes bad. It only takes a little longer in a cold climate." He begins to drag his pants on.

"You're going to close the store," Erica says, trying to sort it out. She too has begun to dress, but slowly and cautiously, for her head still swims with light.

"I'm not sure. Maybe I'll leave it to Tim. He's got a good business sense; and he's a pretty fair astrologer."

"But what will you do, then?"

"I don't know."

"You could go back to teaching," she says, rather eagerly.

"I'm not so sure. I haven't taught in six years, not since I quit LA State in the middle of the term. I'm probably blackballed by the APA."

"I'm sure you could get a job somewhere. After all, you have a Ph.D. in philosophy from Harvard."

"I don't want a job," Zed says, pulling his gray sweater down, then reaching up to free his fringe of untidy, faded red hair from the turtleneck collar. "I don't believe in philosophy any more . . . All I know is, I'm going away."

"Going away?" As Erica echoes these words she sees an image: a man with a bundle and a stick going along a path, perhaps the Path Sandy speaks of. It is a painting somewhere, in a museum, or a book— Yes.

"You know, I just had a flash," she tells him. "A sort of vision, really, inside my head. You were in a painting. I mean, the painting was of you, all along, only I never realized it. It's by Bosch: a man in ragged clothes starting on a journey, and he looks like you."

"I think I know the picture you mean. Is there a dog in it, and a ruined house in the background?"

"Yes, I think so."

"It's his version of the last card of the Tarot. The Fool, it's called. The man in Bosch's painting has the same pose, and the dog at his heels, and the stick."

"Really? That's interesting. I didn't know that." She turns back to him. "I'm sorry you're going away."

"Are you."

"Of course I am. Very sorry. Without you, this town will be impossible."

"Come with me, then."

"I'd love to." Erica laughs. "I wish I really could."

"Why can't you?" Zed does not laugh.

"Well, because of the house— Because of Jeffrey and Matilda."

"I thought you were tired of Jeffrey and Matilda."

"I am," Erica says with feeling. "But that's why I have to stay with them. I mean, nobody else would do it. But it's my job to take care of my children, however tiresome they are, because I'm their mother."

"And Brian's their father. Why not give him a turn?" There is no doubt this time; he is at least partly serious.

Inside Erica's head, there is a sensation of expanding light.

The word "yes" forms in her mouth, but as she begins to voice it she looks at Zed, into his pale eyes with their enlarged dark pupils, and there she has a final, objective vision. It is double and achromatic, like a stereopticon slide. Reflected in the center of each eye she can see the tiny figure of Sandy going away on the Path; and she herself, just behind him, also dressed in dirty colorless rags. They are walking slightly uphill to the right, away from the house and the people, toward a dim cold misty blankness beyond the edge of the frame. In a moment they will both pass out of the picture into this void. She thinks that the picture is symbolically right; that it is the act of a Fool to set out for no known destination.

Zed blinks, and the vision disappears. Again Erica laughs briefly, but this time it is the laugh of fear, thin and hysterical, of someone who sees that she has almost stepped off the edge of a cliff.

"Oh, I couldn't possibly do that," she says. "Brian could never manage them." She laughs again. "Besides, it wouldn't be the right thing."

# 17

An ill-assorted company is mobilizing on the Corinth campus this May morning, in Norton Hall—at other times the scene of ROTC exercises, basketball games, religious services, indoor track meets, rock concerts and fall registration. On the broad glossy varnished floor and in the surrounding tiers of stands diverse groups are gathering, like fugitives from all the other crowds that have assembled there in the past, or might do so in the future.

Many are students; there is a large gang of long-haired, noisy undergraduates squatting and lounging on the floor in the center of the hall, and several smaller bands, each distinctive in appearance. Here is a bunch of pretty girls in flowered and pastel jeans, from Home Ec; there a group of solemn and rather formally dressed law students. There is a small contingent from the Africana Center, all dashikis and Afros, and another of Asians in turbans and saris. A flock of secretaries has taken over one of the tables set up along the south wall, and are unpacking sandwiches and cartons of coffee. Nearby, a squad of antiwar veterans, in complete or partial uniform, is milling about one of their number who is confined to a wheelchair.

Here and there, you can see representatives of the United Campus Ministry, in motley dress ranging from the loose white embroidered Indian shirt and dangling cross of Father Dave, the local radical priest, to the three-piece gray flannel of the Methodist chaplain; there are also several nun's habits, both traditional with starched white coif, and reformed. Over by the main entrance a party of graduate-student wives are pushing their giggling or complaining babies back and forth in strollers, or dashing away from their friends to chase toddlers down off the nearest grandstand, where a troupe of art students is encamped with paper streamers and gas balloons.

There is an air of determined holidaymaking; a clamor of talk punctuated by shouts as people try to attract the attention of newcomers; continual motion among the groups and between each group and the headquarters of the Peace March, which is located on a low platform (sometimes used for boxing matches) at one side of the hall. The crowd is thicker there, and persons with an important, occupied air are sitting behind a table piled with papers. These are mainly men, and mainly professors; Brian Tate is among them.

"Fine turnout," one of his colleagues remarks, coming up to help himself to two paper arm bands printed with blue peace symbols, and a bunch of handbills. "I'll take a couple more of these for Walt and Jimmie, if I may."

"Of course. No, it's not bad. Considering everything," Brian agrees modestly. He rises slightly in his chair to survey the hall. The march isn't due to start for twenty minutes, yet already there must be nearly a thousand people here. The handbills and arm bands have been printed on time and without serious typographical errors; the weather is good—mild and overcast, but not raining; and all academic business has been officially canceled for the afternoon.

Sitting down again, he congratulates himself—not only on the probable success of the event, but on his decision, two weeks ago, to help direct it. He knew from the start that most of the organizational work would fall upon him, for the other leaders— Archibald Matlack of the English department, and Father Dave—

are strong on commitment, but weak in practical knowhow. But he knew also that this was the opportunity he needed. If his reputation were ever to recover, it would have to be through something like this. Continued explanations of his real role in the Dibble affair would not suffice; like corrections to the newspaper story, they followed the original false account only limpingly and at a distance, in smaller type.

It was not enough that Brian should dissociate himself from the cause of antifeminism (refusing, for example, in spite of the generous fee offered, to contribute to an *Esquire* symposium on "Are Women Necessary?"). He must begin as soon as possible to attract public attention for other reasons; to associate himself with other, more appropriate—and more popular—causes.

But though he threw himself into the task with conscious energy, organizing the Peace March was much harder than Brian had anticipated. In part this was due to his success. Unexpectedly many groups responded to the initial canvas; his original plan had to be expanded, and expanded again, as pledges of support came in.

Beyond this, however, the job was complicated by the end-of-term press of work, and, most of all, by unexpected events in his own life: a series of awful revelations from which he is not yet recovered. Indeed, Brian thinks wearily, he may never fully recover.

The crisis began without warning a few days after he had agreed to work on the Peace March—at bedtime one evening when he mildly chided Wendy about her increasing weight. He was relating, as they undressed, a conversation he and Father Dave had had that afternoon with the editor of the local paper. The man was interested in their plans, and had promised to send a reporter and photographer to cover the story. If all went well, a photograph of the front-line marchers would appear on page one of the *Courier*. Since Wendy would presumably be in this picture, Brian suggested, she might try to take off a few pounds around her middle before May seventh.

He had spoken lightly; he was surprised therefore when she replied, in a voice full of choked feeling, that she couldn't take off any pounds. "Why not?" Brian asked, perhaps a little sharply, but still smiling. "It's only a matter of eating less—cutting out some of those late-night snacks, so you'll get a little smaller."

"I can't get smaller," Wendy insisted, laughing oddly. "All I can ever do now is get larger, and larger and larger and larger." With a hysterical sob, she collapsed upon the bed in her underwear.

Brian was used by now to Wendy's tears; he knew that the fastest way to dry them was to step forward and take her in his arms. But instead he stepped back. He looked at Wendy hard, and saw that she was thick in the waist, not from overeating, but because she was at least four months pregnant.

It was the first of a catastrophic series of mental detonations. As if the smooth white plaster walls and plush tan carpeting of his apartment were being strafed by an invisible fighter plane and exploding in a line of ugly holes, Brian realized: first, his own obtuseness—why hadn't he noticed sooner?—and second, Wendy's falsity. This simple, ingenuous girl, whom he had believed so candid, so devoted, had been systematically and sordidly deceiving him.

Questioning her, he dragged out the facts. Wendy had known that Brian did not trust her to remember to take her birth-control pills (quite naturally, after what had happened last fall); she had known that he occasionally counted them. Therefore, twenty-five days a month for the last four months she had flushed one pill down the toilet; and on the remaining five days she had inserted a series of unnecessary tampax into herself, removed them unused, wrapped them in paper, and placed them in the kitchen garbage can. Her only excuse was that she had been afraid to tell him the truth. Perhaps, Brian said furiously, she had imagined that if she did not tell him, it would go away?

Wendy, sobbing, admitted that she had had this thought; that she had hoped for a miscarriage. "But I don't now, you know," she added, half sitting up. "Not since last week, it was Thursday. On

Thursday I felt Life." She capitalized it with her voice as if speaking of the periodical, and laid her hand reverently on her thickened waist. A rapt, stubborn, stupid look came over her tear-streaked face; a look he had last seen in the Frick Museum on many painted female faces. "It zapped me like a bomb: there's a person growing in there. I mean, that's really outasight." She giggled weakly at her own pun.

Brian did not speak. The bomb had exploded; depression, thick and dirty and full of stones, rained down on him. A vision of his vain and foolish vigilance in the past made him laugh gratingly, then break off as he thought of what was to come in the future. Only two weeks ago a liberal abortion bill had been passed in the state, but by the time it took effect it would be too late for Wendy; it was too late even now.

He would have to marry Wendy. Also, he would have to do this right away, as soon as it became legally possible—before her pregnancy became so obvious as to make them a public joke. But if she had been as free with her confidences as last time, it was already a public joke. He would have to stand up with her in the county courthouse, while the witnesses sniggered behind their smiles. Then he would have to take her home, and live with her for the rest of his life. The depression rained on steadily; Brian could feel himself bruised, knocked down, choking in the heavy, muddy future.

Meanwhile Wendy, perhaps encouraged by his silence, went on chattering with increasing confidence. "It's a real freaky trip, you know, having somebody growing inside you—carrying them around everywhere you go. And knowing that everything you do affects them. Like if I smoke a joint or have a couple of beers, the baby gets high, did you know that? I mean, that's a big responsibility."

The responsibility was large not only generically but specifically, Wendy explained, because this child was destined for greatness. "It'll have the Sun conjunct Uranus, a powerful magnetic personality, very original; maybe a genius, Zed says," she confided, conveying to Brian the unwelcome news that her pregnancy was already known to that fool at the Krishna Bookshop. Indeed, as he soon discovered, it was an old story to most of her friends—who, in keeping the secret, had all also been deceiving him.

Though enthusiastic about the baby, Wendy received Brian's proposal of marriage with a composure which verged on lassitude. She also accepted his other proposals for their future (legal, economic, medical) without any great vivacity or gratitude. Brian assumed it was because all her attention was turned inward, upon her womb and its contents, that she took so little interest in planning when and how they would marry, or where they would live (Alpine Towers being forbidden to infants). Yet when he recalled the nest-building fervor that had overtaken Erica under similar circumstances, he felt puzzled.

He was furious, too, that additional responsibilities should be forced upon him now, when term papers were coming in and his phone, both at home and at the university, rang constantly about the Peace March. He had no time to call doctors or inspect apartments. Wendy, who did, apparently could not summon the energy. But when he complained of this one evening at supper, he received another severe, almost fatal shock.

"You don't hafta call up that real estate dude if you don't want to," Wendy told him, setting her elbows one on each side of a plate of overcooked chili (expectant motherhood had blurred her sense of time, never very acute). "You don't hafta do anything you don't want. I mean, shit." Her voice trembled. "You don't hafta marry me."

Controlling his own voice, Brian replied that she did not mean that.

"I do too," Wendy asserted. "I don't care if I'm an unwed mother. I mean, so what? I mean if people don't like it, screw them."

Brian gave a sigh of exasperation at these counterculture

histrionics. Wendy had managed to conceal her condition so far by wearing loose clothing, notably the garment she had on then: a huge, heavy, tentlike Indian poncho made out of an old red blanket with orange and black zigzag designs. But she was growing larger, and the weather warmer, every week. Soon she would have to take off her wigwam, and the coming papoose would be visible to everyone. And when it came to that, he explained to Wendy, she would care. She would suffer from embarrassment and from social censure, including that of her own family of origin.

Wendy denied this. "I can hack it," she insisted. "I may be a little uptight about what Ma will say, but I can hack it with her too, and the whole family if I hafta. I'm not freaked out over what your neighbors and the department will think."

"You say that now." Brian smiled, trying to lower the temperature of the discussion. "But even if it were true, it's not the only consideration. We can't be concerned only with you. Or me." He smiled even harder. "We have to think of the baby, of what it will mean for him or her to be illegitimate."

"Lots of kids in this country are bastards, and they don't always— I read this article—"

"No doubt," he said impatiently. "Lots of kids are also undernourished, and neglected, and ill-educated. I wish them all well. But I have no intention of placing that sort of handicap on any child of mine."

"Yeh, but—" Wendy had given up all pretense of eating; she shoved her plate aside and leaned over the table. "I mean, isn't that just going along with everything that's fucked up in this society? If you just do it because you're afraid of prejudice, isn't that sort of helping to perpetuate it?"

Brian groaned silently, and rebuked himself for having provoked a theoretical argument with someone who was constitutionally (in both senses, now) incapable of logical thought.

"Anyhow," she went on, "why should it be so important that it's your child? I mean, like Zed says: it's a karmic hangup to think of kids as *mine* or *yours,* as if they were private property. All children belong to God, really, and we're just appointed their guardians, the way it's written in *The Prophet.*

*"Lo, your children are not your children, but the sons and daughters of God"*

she recited in a trembly, emotional voice. "That's a really beautiful saying. And it's true, too."

Third-rate poetry, Brian thought to himself; mystical crap. Then another interpretation of Wendy's babbling, far-fetched but even less agreeable, occurred to him. "It is mine, though, I assume, this baby?" he said in a tone he tried to make pleasant. "Technically speaking, that is."

Wendy's reaction to this question—the mug-shot slump of her shoulders, the red, slapped expression on her face—should have been answer enough. But Brian, determined to know the worst, forced first an admission and then the sordid details out of her.

She wasn't really, absolutely sure, Wendy finally admitted. Because, you see, at the end of last year, when Brian was at those meetings in New York, and she came back to college early to finish a paper, "there was this guy Ahmed that Linda knows, this grad student in Engineering. He's really a nice dude, sort of shy and sensitive, you know? He writes prose poems." Ahmed was spending the holidays alone in his dormitory. "He couldn't go home for vacation because he's from Pakistan, and he had all this dumb work to make up, these crappy engineering problems. He was feeling really lonely and down, thinking how he was stupid and had no friends and would be a disgrace to his country and he might as well jump down the gorge . . . So I like gave myself to him for Christmas."

The night that followed this revelation was the worst Brian has ever had. Hour after hour he tossed and twitched, while Wendy, worn out by sobbing and self-justification, lay sleeping heavily beside him.

He could see no way out: it was like a multiple-choice test in which none of the answers were right. Marry Wendy? Abandon her? The odds were in favor of the child's being his, and certainly the moral responsibility, for he had lain with her a hundred times to the Pakistani's one. There was no chance of that character's assuming the burden, according to Wendy. ("Oh, Ahmed can't marry me; he's been betrothed to a girl back home since he was fourteen. He hasta marry a virgin anyhow, because of his religion.")

No escape. The pursuing forces of blind female error and blind female nature had finally caught up with and defeated him. Because of his own religion, duty, he would still have to wed Wendy, knowing that she had deceived him in every sense. There was also a good chance of his becoming the butt of a savage irony: that having paid over a thousand dollars to have his own child destroyed, he would have to bring up as his the child of a wog graduate student. Very likely it would be brownish in color and interested in machines.

But in that case, surely he would be justified in getting a divorce? A second divorce: more public scandal, more lawyers' fees, more alimony payments and child support. For legally the child would be his; economically he would be responsible for it until its twenty-first birthday. At which time, if he hadn't yet succumbed to these multiple pressures, Brian would be sixty-eight. How would he be able to afford it? Even if he were to teach summer school every year, move into an even smaller and nastier apartment, give up the idea of going abroad not only this summer but any summer, or on his next sabbatical, perhaps of even taking his sabbatical . . .

All night these thoughts ran though Brian's head. In the roar of trucks climbing the hill below Alpine Towers, the screech of planes overhead, the cackle of a radio next door, he heard the sound of laughter—the laughter of a monstrous regiment of women. He dozed briefly and was awakened by nightmares (mares, he noted with a crazy clarity, not stallions) in which the principal sound effect was a loud horselaugh.

When dawn, late and gray, bleached the window, he rose from beside Wendy and went to make himself a cup of tea, the solace of childhood illnesses and wakeful nights. In slippers and robe he stood before the stove waiting for the water to boil, feeling old for the first time in his life. He would be forty-eight at the end of this year, getting on for half a century. No age to play around with freaked-out college students, argue with abortionists, climb out of college buildings on a rope, wrestle with hysterical women, and become the father of a bastard.

Yet he had in a way chosen to do all these things, Brian thought as the electric coils reddened dully under the kettle. It was not only bad luck, but rash ambition, sensual greed and egotistic hubris which had led him onto these battlefields—finally into a labyrinth of trenches where he would wander for the rest of his life, mocked and harassed, clawed and bitten by female monsters. If only it were not too late to find a way out! He would ask nothing more; he was cured forever of wanting fame, power and the love of unbalanced schoolgirls.

Astonishingly, his prayer was heard. Two days later when he walked into his apartment at the end of a long day, Wendy stood up out of her chair by the window and announced that she was leaving him. It wasn't anything personal, she insisted. She loved Brian; but she just couldn't hack the idea of marriage, or of living in Corinth the rest of her life. Also, she didn't want her baby to be brought up here. "You see," she explained, "the stars can't do it all. I hafta figure out how the kid can have the best developmental experiences. If I stay here and get into this academic life style, he's bound to pick up some of its hangups and shitty mental sets."

Therefore, Wendy continued, while Brian stood stupefied by the door holding his briefcase and that evening's newspaper, she was planning to split after finals for a far-out commune she'd heard of in an unpopulated part of Northern California. Pressed, she admitted that she would be accompanied on this journey by an old friend named Ralph. And how did Ralph feel about her pregnancy? According to Wendy, he was tolerant, even enthusiastic. "Ralph wants to work out a total relationship. He really digs kids. He doesn't care whose kid it is; he hasn't got your thing about possessions. He lives completely in the Now."

Brian's reminiscences are interrupted by the sight of someone coming toward him, picking her way among groups of sitting and squatting peace marchers; someone he is, for the first time in over a year, very glad to see: Erica Tate.

"Oh, there you are," Erica says. She is looking well, though too thin; her hair is brushed back from her face, accentuating this. She is wearing a green sleeveless dress, and her paper arm band with its blue peace symbol is fixed high on a slim bare arm. "I left the station wagon down on Tioga Street, across from the orthodontist's. So I can drive you back here all right."

"That's fine," Brian replies; like his wife he speaks in a careful, almost formal manner. "Thank you." He smiles cordially, as if they were on opposite sides of a conference table, negotiating some important treaty. "I'll meet you there after all this is over."

"I'll probably be later than you are, though," Erica says. "I mean, if my group starts—"

"That's all right. I'll wait." Brian smiles again in the same manner. "I don't have anything to do this afternoon. Classes have been canceled, so I won't have to meet my seminar." He is conscious of deliberately elaborating his point, as if anticipating simultaneous translation. "If you'd like to walk with us, though, that would be fine." The Peace March is to be led by prominent representatives of the University, the Church and the Army (the wheelchair veteran, plus two of his buddies who will carry a banner).

"No, thank you," Erica says with careful good will. "I promised Danielle and the WHEN people I'd go with them."

"Ah." Attempting not to convey annoyance, Brian smiles some more—but briefly, for he also doesn't want to seem relieved at not having to march beside Erica. In fact, he feels neither relief nor annoyance—only a desire that she shouldn't be hurt or offended in any way.

Yet some emotion, some tension at least, must have shown on his face, for Erica frowns slightly, then smiles slightly, and finally offers:

"If you'd like to— I mean, would you like to come back to the house afterward for some lunch?"

"Thank you; that would be a help. The Faculty Club's sure to be jammed by then."

"Yes." She opens her mouth as if about to add something, then shuts it. "Well, I'll see you later," she says. "I'd better get back to the Hens."

Erica sets off in the direction of Danielle's party, but before she reaches it she consults her watch, and finding that the march will not start for fifteen minutes, turns toward the washroom—not because she needs to, but in order to think over what has just happened and organize her mind. In inviting her to walk with him, Brian was in effect proposing that they appear together in public for the first time in over six months. She had declined, not in order to reject all that this might imply, but merely out of surprise and confusion of feelings. Whenever something sudden happens, her first impulse is to withdraw, consider the situation, regroup her forces.

Of course in a way she isn't surprised, Erica thinks, shoving open the door of a long bare crowded room painted battleship-gray and smelling of pine antiseptic. There were signs of what might be coming when she spoke to Brian two days ago—even last Sunday evening, when after returning the children he came into the house, and upstairs to the study where Erica was working on drawings for the Art Festival. He shut the door behind him and told her, in a tight, strained, self-mocking voice, that Wendy was probably pregnant; not by him, but by a Pakistani engineering student, and that she had just left him for an unemployed Chicago film maker.

Erica's first reaction to this earth-shattering announcement was compassion for Wendy. The poor girl, she thought; the poor, silly, confused child. But during the next few days some of her sympathy began leaking out through the cracks. It was reasonable that Wendy should grow disillusioned with Brian. It was forgivable, though very careless of her to have got pregnant again, and understandable that she should try to conceal the fact for a while. But that she should have been so casually unfaithful; that she should have so calmly planned to present Brian with someone else's baby—that was hard to understand. Had she been lying to herself, then, or only to Brian and Erica, when she said last fall that she would "always belong to him completely"?

Erica found it all even harder to understand when, three days later, Wendy appeared in her campus office, on an afternoon when Erica was busy trying to get the files in order for her successor. She is moving next week to a better job at nearly twice the salary with the Department of Horticulture, working on their journal and—best of all—illustrating a book on ornamental grasses. Couldn't they meet later? she suggested.

"But I got to talk to you now," Wendy protested, clutching Erica's desk and knocking over a stack of three-by-five cards. "I hafta ask you—to explain— I mean, you know about the baby and everything?"

"Yes, I think so," Erica admitted, gathering the cards and starting to resort them.

"I guess you're feeling sort of negative toward me," Wendy remarked.

"Well, I—"

"Brian told me," Wendy interrupted, pushing back the pale wisps of hair which covered her face. "He said you thought I was irresponsible. I know there've been some bad vibes, but I've got my head together now, and everything's going to work out." She smiled eagerly and sat down on the corner of Erica's desk, knocking over the cards again with the fringe of her red wool poncho.

"Like I'm really happy I didn't marry Brian," she continued. "It would've been a big mistake: we don't actualize each other's potential at all. He's got this set against social psychology, for instance. Well, in some ways he's right, a lot of the professors in my department are off the wall, but I still hafta pass their courses." She drew her legs up and sat on the desk with them folded under her, forming, in her poncho, a pyramidal shape.

"What got to me most was I wasn't any help to him in his Work, which was the whole idea, you know? I really tried, but all I ever did was make him angry. Like when he read parts of his book to me he would get uptight because I never had any criticisms. It always sounded fine to me. Sometimes I tried to think up criticisms, but that just made him more angry on account of they were so stupid. He got so pissed once because I never heard of the Nazi-Soviet Pact he started throwing his books onto the floor. I guess I should have heard of it; I realize now it was a big deal, but I wasn't even born then." A complaining tone had entered Wendy's voice.

"Brian takes that sort of thing very seriously," Erica said noncommittally, feeling obscurely unwilling to join her ex-husband's ex-mistress in a discussion of his faults.

"Yeh." Wendy sighed exaggeratedly. "He really does. Ralph, this guy I'm going to California with, he says there's occupational diseases you get from being a professor, the way workers in asbestos plants get fibrous lungs. He says professors catch that kind of lecturing manner, you know, like Brian has, from talking in public too much. And they start organizing everything into outlines. Like one day he said to me, 'Could you bring me the newspaper? It's either a) on my desk, or b) in the bathroom.' I told him, 'Please don't talk to me in outlines, okay? I'm not a class.' Only he didn't hear me."

"No." Erica could not prevent herself from smiling.

"It was that way the whole time, really, you know. That's why I decided I've got to get out of this environment, before my kid catches the same disease."

Now Erica frowned. It was this plan which had made her call Wendy "irresponsible"; for surely any child would be better off brought up legitimate in Corinth than fatherless in some squalid mountain cabin, miles from the nearest doctor or school. As moderately as possible, she expressed this view, concluding with the suggestion that it was really not necessary to go to Northern California; that there must be some good commune nearby which would welcome a young married couple and their baby.

But Wendy shook her head, making wisps of pale hair fly. This place in California was special; and anyhow she wasn't planning to get married.

"The way I feel now, I don't ever want to be married to anyone," she explained. "I figure it's a bum trip. I mean if you've just got a relationship with a guy, that's cool; you can be really straight with him. Like Ralph says, you know either of you can split any time, so if you stick it out it's because you really dig each other. The world isn't telling you you hafta stay with that dude whether you feel like it or not; in fact it's probably making some hassles for you."

"But that's one reason why—" Erica interjected, while an unfavorable and suspicious opinion of Ralph began to form in her mind. "If you were to marry him, you'd have some security—"

Wendy shook her head even more vigorously. "That'd make me more insecure. Once you're married you can't ever tell if the guy comes home on account of he wants to, or on account of he has to. I mean, who wants to have somebody fuck you just because it's his job?"

"I see your point," Erica replied gently, but with some restraint, thinking that again—and probably not for the last time—Wendy was repeating as her own sincere opinion statements made to her by some man for selfish ulterior purposes. "But marriage isn't only sex: it's a social contract. If everyone thought like your friend, families would break up; parents would desert their children—"

"That's different," Wendy interrupted. "I couldn't ever desert a kid. Like this baby." She put a pink stubby hand, stained with ink, on the front of her poncho. "It's really heavy; not like some guy you're not even related to. I know already I'll never leave him; I'll always belong to him completely." And, brushing aside some shreds of hair, she looked at Erica with an expression of fervent sincerity.

Feet are visible below the door, indicating that someone is waiting to use the toilet; so Erica stands up, letting the two strips of perforated paper on which she has been sitting fall into the bowl. She rinses her hands, glancing once into the mirror over the row of basins, where a thin middle-aged woman is reflected between two smooth-faced girls.

Outside the washroom, Norton Hall is in noisy, churning motion; it is time for the march to begin. As quickly as possible, she makes her way through the crowd.

"Erica, here we are!" Danielle cries, waving from the grandstand. She is about halfway up, holding the stick of a large placard which rests on the bench below and bears, upside down, the astrological symbol for Venus and the motto WOMEN FIGHT FOR PEACE. Next to her stands Dr. Bernard Kotelchuk, in a loud red plaid shirt and bow tie.

"Oh, hello," Erica says to him with minimal enthusiasm, climbing up through a crowd of women. "Are you coming with us?"

"I'd like to. But Ellie's friends won't let me."

"Joanne wants us to make a unified appearance." Danielle shrugs. "She put it up to the meeting last night and they voted 'no men.' Silly, really."

"It doesn't matter; I can go with the vet-school contingent." Dr. Kotelchuk smiles broadly. "See you later, Ellie." He bends and kisses Danielle with a vulgar, smacking enthusiasm.

"He looks cheerful," Erica says, watching him descend into the crowd. "Resigned, even. Has he finally given up proposing to you?"

*360*

"Not exactly." Danielle leans on her placard. "He asked me again just last night. I'd been reading an article in *Sisterhood* about marriage contracts, so I told him I'd marry him on certain terms." She grins. "I said, first, I had to keep my job. I wanted separate bank accounts, and I'd pay half the housekeeping expenses and do the cooking, but I wouldn't touch any of the cleaning or laundry— he'd have to do it himself, or hire somebody. And I said I had to have three weeks' vacation by myself every year, with no questions asked afterward."

"And what did he say?" Erica is smiling now, almost laughing with relief and anticipation.

"He agreed to everything. He said it sounded like a good deal; after all, he's been doing all his own cooking and cleaning for two years. He said he was afraid I was going to ask for separate bedrooms."

"So what are you going to do?"

"I guess I'll have to marry him." Danielle shrugs, then suddenly smiles brilliantly. "It won't be so bad. He's a real help around the house, he can fix anything. Yesterday he put up that triangular screen in the attic that Leonard never could figure out, you know?"

Erica acknowledges that she knows.

"And he's great for my ego," Danielle continues. "He thinks everything I do is fantastic, and everything I say is brilliant. Well, you know, I'm sort of keen on him too. I guess I really love him." Unexpectedly, she flushes and looks down.

Below on the floor of the hall the crowd is beginning to thin; the other Women for Human Equality Now are getting to their feet. Danielle raises her sign and follows them, and Erica follows Danielle. She knows she ought to congratulate her friend, but cannot arrange the words in her mouth. "But why do you love him?" she wants to ask. "Nobody else loves him—none of all these hundreds of people here. I don't love him; I don't even like him."

"I can't figure out why I didn't say yes sooner," Danielle continues, descending the grandstand. "I think probably it was a kind of mind set. You get into the habit of being angry and hurt by life, and then when something good happens you can't accept it because it doesn't fit the pattern. You really have to make a big effort to stop brooding over the past and all your injustices."

"Mm." Erica thinks that this is what she had said to Danielle herself, a long time ago. But now—

"Another thing that probably stopped me was Lennie. Not my parents so much: Mama will cry because Bernie's not Jewish, and thank God that Grandpère didn't live to see it, but they'll come around eventually. But Lennie will make some lousy crack, and then he'll sneer at us for the rest of his life." Danielle's voice is harsh.

"But what the hell right has he to think he's so superior?" she adds, turning to Erica as they reach the floor of the hall. "Bernie makes a better salary than he does, and his work is a lot more use to the world than picking apart other people's books. Anyhow, he should be overjoyed. Now he can sell the house, like he's always wanted to, and buy himself a summer place on Martha's Vineyard or in Sag Harbor, or wherever all the fashionable intellectuals are going now."

"Mm." Danielle is going to leave town, Erica thinks as, jostled by feminists, she is propelled through the doors of Norton Hall into the cloudy spring noon outside. She's going to move to Brookdale, and I probably won't see her very often. Everyone is going away: Danielle and her children, and my boss, and Wendy; Sandy has already gone. He wouldn't even stay a few more days for the march.

"Leaving May fourth!" she had exclaimed as they sat having tea in the Krishna Bookshop for what turned out to be the last time. "But that's the day after tomorrow."

Sandy nodded slowly.

"But you'll miss the big peace demonstration. You must stay for that, at least."

"There's no point. I wouldn't go on it anyhow."

"You wouldn't go?" She lowered her mug of tea. "But aren't you against this war?"

"I'm against every war." He smiled in the faint, irritating way Erica associated with his religious fixation. Under further questioning it came out that he had never been in a peace march, or any political demonstration; had never written to his congressman, or signed a petition; and had not even voted since 1954. "I've been trying to detach myself from all that," he explained, resting his face in his bony hands and looking out at her from between them. "It doesn't matter, you know. It doesn't do any good."

"That's a defeatist attitude," Erica said, thinking that she had been right all along: Sandy *was* like an ostrich, hiding his head from the world in the sands of mysticism—just like the hero of her books, who had his own bucket marked SAND for use in emergencies. "If everyone thought like you—" She broke off, recalling that this was their last meeting. She didn't want to quarrel with Sandy; she was grateful to him. Not only for keeping her company all these months, but for something more important.

The trip he had taken her on had, as she hoped, been good for her work. It had inspired her—but not by supplying her with new and exotic images and patterns. The revelation instead had been that the most ordinary things are rare and strange; glorious, full of meaning. This unexpected vision had survived her trip. It was, whenever Erica chose, with her still; so that now, here on the bookshop counter, the thick white crockery cup with its dull-green stripe and chipped rim, the hexagonal wooden pencil, the piles of stacked change, the dagger-shaped brass letter opener—all were touched with this glory. All of them could, if she had time, be added to the collection of drawings of simple important objects she is now making.

The Peace March did matter, she told Sandy; it was part of what she had been trying to tell him all along, she said: that the real world and what you did in it mattered.

"You haven't had much luck with that effort, have you?" he remarked. "Just about as much as I've had trying to teach my students to detach themselves from the world." Sandy filled their mugs again. "They think they're free because they've quit school or got away from their parents. But usually it's right out of one bag into another: laws, duties, obligations. Did I show you the list of rules for membership in the bookshop that Tim and Danny have drawn up?" He sighed. "Well, it's one of the principles of astrology: you can't learn anyone else's lesson. What you have to do is keep learning your own, over and over again."

"But you worry about other people," Erica said. "You can't help that." She hesitated, remembering how chilly and silent Sandy had grown last week when she told him she was concerned about his future.

"For instance, Wendy," she said instead. "Of course she hasn't behaved very well. But now she's going off, pregnant, with someone who has no intention of marrying her. She doesn't know how they're going to get to that commune place, or even where it is, or what they're going to live on. Brian tried to give her some money, but she wouldn't take it—she said it had bad karma. It's all so vague and uncertain. It worries me awfully."

"A real Virgo. You've got to have everything neat."

"It's true." Erica laughed. "I keep wishing I knew somebody in California, so I could give her a few names and addresses. I really want to do something for her. I wondered if you—"

"Haven't you done enough?"

"I—what do you mean?" Something ambiguous and cold in his tone struck Erica. "I tried to help last fall. But you know that didn't work out."

"No." Sandy grinned. "God is good to us. He doesn't always grant our wishes."

"I suppose you're right. It would have been a mistake for her to marry Brian."

"It would have been a disaster. But maybe that's what you wanted."

"No, I didn't," Erica says, wounded. "I wanted them both to

be happy. It was very hard for me, but I thought I ought— That's a mean thing to say."

Sandy, provokingly, continued smiling. "You know, Erica, that's how you always manage it. When you want to do something, you convince yourself that it's a duty which demands great self-sacrifice. Like when you dropped Greek . . . Or in my case," he added, almost under his breath.

Erica heard this; she knew that something important and dangerous had been said, something she would have to think about— But not now, not yet! Frightened as well as hurt, she counterattacked. "If you thought it was such a mistake for Wendy to marry Brian, why didn't you say so? Why didn't you try to stop it?"

Sandy shrugged. "I don't believe in interfering in people's lives. What will be, will be."

That was mean too, Erica thinks as she and Danielle proceed past the squash courts under pink flowering trees. Almost deliberately, as if he had wanted to quarrel with her at their last meeting, so that they needn't meet again; so he could be completely detached, free of all human ties. But it was mean all the same. And also untrue—as she had discovered after he left town.

The truth had come out by accident in a conversation with Brian last Sunday. It was a mild evening, and they were standing outside talking after Jeffrey and Matilda had gone into the house.

"So Wendy came around and gave you her version of events," Brian said. "How long had you known she was pregnant, by the way?"

"I guess about two weeks," Erica replied, puzzled by this question. "Since you told me."

"I didn't mean—that is, I just wondered if you might have heard of it sooner. Everyone else in town seems to have known for months: Linda Sliski, and the rest of that female gang, and that fellow in the occult bookstore—all her pals."

"In the bookstore?" Erica said, her voice rising. "Do you mean Sandy Finkelstein? Do you mean Sandy knew Wendy was pregnant, the whole time?"

"So it seems."

"But he didn't tell . . . anybody," Erica exclaimed, substituting the last word for "me."

"Says who? For all I know, he told everyone who walked into the store."

"That's awful." Erica clenched her jaw; her head felt tight, like a bad headache coming on. "You know what?" she added after a pause. "Sandy never said anything to anyone, because he wanted you to marry Wendy. That's why he told her all that stuff about children belonging to God, so she wouldn't feel guilty about presenting you with someone else's baby."

"Oh, I don't think so," replied Brian, who now that Zed had left Corinth preferred to regard him as a harmless ninny. "Why would he want that?"

Erica, who could have told him why, remained silent. For the rest of her life, probably, she would remain silent. It would be hard enough for them without that, if they did eventually decide . . .

Already on Sunday, as they stood talking on the lawn in the mild, misty evening, she had thought that Brian might want to come back home. She is surer of it now. He hasn't mentioned the matter yet, but she knows he is going to mention it; probably today; perhaps within the next hour. He may say he wants it because of her, but that is only part of the truth. He is also embarrassed and worn out by the feminist crisis and the crises of Wendy, and tired of living alone. Also he thinks the children are getting better; and in a way he is right.

Of course they are older—Jeffrey is sixteen now, and Matilda fourteen—and therefore out of the house more. They are also marginally cleaner and more polite when in it. Erica really has very little to do with them; she maintains certain rules and schedules, but has more or less given up trying to control what they wear or eat or read or watch on TV. In return, they are minimally agreeable to her, like people forced by a war or flood or some other natural disaster to share living quarters. They have even made a few gratuitous gestures of good will: Jeffrey, without being asked, took down all the storm windows last month; and Matilda brought Erica's stereo back downstairs.

But the real change is that they have become strangers. Their names, their faces, their bodies, their voices, their gestures, their tastes and opinions—all are unfamiliar. They are no longer monstrous overgrown versions of her children, but two young people Erica hardly knows. In a way it is a relief that nothing now remains to remind her of her beloved, lost Jeffo and Muffy.

And it is not only Muffy and Jeffo who have disappeared, or are disappearing. Everything and everyone is in flux now, confused, disintegrating in time and space. The campus elms are dying and being cut down; they are demolishing the old courthouse; Jones Creek Road is turning into Glenview Homes, and Danielle Zimmern into Ellie Kotelchuk. Her serious, responsible, loving husband has changed into an unreliable adulterer and reputed antifeminist; and she herself has become the woman in the washroom mirror.

In this last respect, Brian has changed less than she. He is still the most handsome man Erica has ever met, though today he looked strained and worn. It can't be good for him to live in that stale sealed-in apartment, without even a balcony outside so he could get a little air and sun. He tans readily, and by this time of year is usually already brown from working in the garden; but now the garden looks unpruned and shabby, and Brian pale and unhealthy, like someone who is sleeping badly and eating frozen dinners. Probably he isn't taking proper care of himself because of self-hatred, a syndrome Erica knows very well. He is embarrassed and ashamed of his behavior over the past year, and he believes everyone is laughing and sneering at him because of Wendy's pregnancy and all those stupid newspaper articles. No doubt some of them are.

If she doesn't listen to him seriously today when he suggests moving back to the house on Jones Creek Road, it will be as if she wanted him to go on making himself ill in Alpine Towers; as if she were sneering at him too, and tramping on him when he is down, instead of magnanimously helping him up again.

On the other hand, if he does come home, she will have to be even more magnanimous afterward. She will have to make up her mind never to say anything that might remind Brian of how selfish and irresponsible and ridiculous he has been; of how much pain and embarrassment he has caused his family, not to mention Wendy Gahaghan and Donald Dibble and the Department of Political Science. That will be very difficult.

But she can do it, if she really tries. And Brian will be grateful—grateful enough, for instance, to agree that she should continue working. And perhaps there is something to be said for Danielle's marriage-contract idea. A separate bank account—A cleaning-lady once a week—A three-week vacation; and one for Brian too, that would be only right—

Erica has crossed campus now and turned downhill through Collegetown. The streets here have also been closed to traffic, and people stand watching the Peace March in the open doorways of shops, and on both sidewalks. Since most sympathizers are already marching, only a few of these people applaud or cheer. The majority look on silently, or whistle and call out wisecracks as the group from WHEN passes: "Burn your bras!" "Pussy power!" One makes an obscene gesture, another an obscene suggestion.

They wouldn't dare do that if Brian were here, Erica thinks; if Bernie Kotelchuk were here. It was wrong of the Hens to exclude men; we need them sometimes, if only to protect us from other men. Danielle's friends would say that was just another proof of our oppression—that when real equality is achieved, men won't be necessary. Are the sexes, then, to live apart forever in warring camps?

.　　.　　.

*368*

Downtown, the vanguard of the march has reached its objective, a small park near the courthouse. In the center by the fountain, the leaders are gathered under a ten-foot-banner bearing the inscription HOPKINS COUNTY MARCH FOR PEACE, watching the park fill with their followers. Brian is amazed and pleased by their number and enthusiasm, and the number and inventiveness of the signs they carry.

WOULD YOU BUY A USED WAR FROM THIS MAN?

WHAT HAS THIEU DONE FOR YOU?

He sees many faces he knows: friends, students, colleagues, neighbors; his ex-lawyer, Jack Lucas; Wendy's ex-roommate, Linda Sliski— And, yes, there is Wendy herself, accompanied by a tall red-bearded young man who is no doubt her present roommate, Ralph. She is wearing beaded moccasins and a long bunchy yellow dress made out of an East Indian bedspread, and is, to the informed eye, obviously pregnant.

Catching sight of Brian, whom she has not seen in nearly two weeks, Wendy waves and smiles—but not defiantly, or apologetically, or even consciously. It is, he thinks, exactly the smile and wave she would have given him if they had known each other only as professor and graduate student. The past is irrelevant, that smile announces; Wendy is living, as Ralph puts it, completely in the Now.

Up the street, still out of Brian's line of vision, more signs have appeared, which would please him less.

END THE WAR
EAT AT ELAINE'S COUNTRY COOKING

DON'T FIGHT IT
FANTASTIC DISCOUNT SALE
AT COLLEGETOWN RECORDS

NOEL LEE AND THE GNOMES
IN CONCERT
MAY 15     NORTON HALL

Several other local enterprises have seized this chance for free publicity, and there are also a number of political placards, some local and regional (GEORGE BRAMPTON FOR SCHOOL BOARD; VOTE NO ON SALES TAX), others national or international (BOYCOTT GRAPES; GIVE TO INDIAN RELIEF).

Farther uphill, in Collegetown, the Peace March is beginning to split into dissident and incongruous factions, physically suggesting to onlookers just the conclusion that Brian has worked so hard to avoid: that respectable liberal antiwar protest is dangerous because it brings in its train freakish, violent, and socially disruptive elements. Art students are popping and releasing balloons; the Footlight Players, a local drama group, is holding up the procession with impromptu guerrilla theater. Two young women in the WHEN contingent, just ahead of Erica, have raised signs reading NIXON IS A MALE CHAUVINIST WARHOG and STOP MEN KILLING WOMEN AND CHILDREN. Not far behind them, the Gay Liberation Center, which was not invited to join the march, has turned up anyhow with exceptionally colorful costumes and a large spangled banner:

MAKE LOVE, NOT WAR

GAY POWER FOR PEACE

Finally, at the rear of the procession, a large group of Maoists, also purposely uninvited by Brian, has appeared. Dressed in overalls, discarded army uniforms and assorted rags, wild-haired and wild-eyed, they carry homemade red flags of various shades from vermilion to dirty maroon. They are marching in unison, though not in rank, and chanting loudly as they pass through the campus gates into Collegetown:

*3 7 0*

"Ho, Ho, Ho Chi Minh!
NLF is going to win!"

In a few moments, as they pass a bar called the Old Bavaria, all hell is going to break loose. Empty beer bottles and other garbage will be thrown, fistfights will break out; there will be the sound of smashing plate glass, popping flashbulbs and police sirens.

Brian does not suspect any of this yet. He is imagining another event which lies ahead; his lunch with Erica. He recognizes her invitation as a favorable sign; if he puts it right, Erica will probably agree that he should move back home. After all, there are good reasons for this move: it will be much better for the children psychologically, and better for all of them economically and also socially. The Tates' marital conflicts and related events have caused a lot of gossip and unfavorable comment. Now that things are quieter, he and Erica can close ranks and present a united front.

Most important, it is what they both want and need. The conflict has damaged them morally as well as in reputation: they have both said cruel things and made bad errors in judgment. They will each have to admit this, without accusing the other. Brian, for instance, must be generous enough not to point out that all that has happened is in a way Erica's fault, since if she hadn't insisted he leave home and marry Wendy, the affair would have ended much sooner, and he wouldn't have become involved with hysterical feminists. Erica, in return, will be generous to him.

They will talk for a long while after lunch, Brian imagines. Moving into the sitting room—Erica curled on the blue sofa as usual, and he in his wing chair—they will relate and explain all that has passed. They will laugh, and possibly at some moments cry. They will encourage each other, console each other, and forgive each other. Finally, as the afternoon lengthens and the shadows of half-fledged trees reach toward the house, they will put their arms about each other and forget for a few moments that they were once exceptionally handsome, intelligent, righteous and successful young people; they will forget that they are ugly, foolish, guilty and dying.

More and more marchers are crowding into the park now. A group of mothers and small children has just come up to the fountain. One young woman leans over the basin beside Brian to wet a folded diaper and wipe the red-stained sticky face of a toddler in a stroller, while a boy just slightly older jerks the sleeve of her sweater to get her attention.

"Mommy?" he asks. "Mommy, will the war end now?"

ALISON LURIE lives in Ithaca, New York, where she teaches English at Cornell University. She is married and has three sons. *The War Between the Tates* is her fifth novel.